SILVER CITY

This Large Print Book carries the
Seal of Approval of N.A.V.H.

SILVER CITY

JEFF GUINN

THORNDIKE PRESS
A part of Gale, Cengage Learning

GALE
CENGAGE Learning·

Farmington Hills, Mich • San Francisco • New York • Waterville, Maine
Meriden, Conn • Mason, Ohio • Chicago

GALE
CENGAGE Learning

LIBRARY OF CONGRESS CATALOGING-IN-PUBLICATION DATA

Names: Guinn, Jeff, author.
Title: Silver city / by Jeff Guinn.
Description: Large print edition. | Waterville, Maine : Thorndike Press, a part of Gale, Cengage Learning, 2017. | Series: Thorndike Press large print western
Identifiers: LCCN 2017004764| ISBN 9781410498410 (hardcover) | ISBN 1410498417 (hardcover)
Subjects: LCSH: Large type books. | BISAC: FICTION / Westerns. | FICTION / Historical. | GSAFD: Western stories.
Classification: LCC PS3557.U375 S55 2017b | DDC 813/.54—dc23
LC record available at https://lccn.loc.gov/2017004764

Published in 2017 by arrangement with G. P. Putnam's Sons, an imprint of Penguin Publishing Group, a division of Penguin Random House LLC

Printed in Mexico
1 2 3 4 5 6 7 21 20 19 18 17

FOR HARRISON

GOYATHLAY (GERONIMO)

IKE CLANTON

PROLOGUE

ST. LOUIS
August 1, 1874

The fat man brought two armed guards with him to the midnight meeting along the Mississippi River docks in St. Louis. The bodyguards were rough-looking men who obviously relished a fight. There was a full moon, and its light revealed that both had pistols tucked into the waistbands of their trousers, with the handles angled for easy extraction. They stood close together behind their boss, shoulders almost touching. But Patrick Brautigan, unarmed and alone, was pleased rather than intimidated. He liked it when the opposition had guns. The weapons made them overconfident.

"Mr. Foley, my boss has raised his offer for your warehouse property another three hundred dollars," Brautigan said. His voice was low and void of inflection. At such a late hour, nothing else stirred along this stretch of docks. "You're getting somewhat above fair value, enough to move on and start over somewhere else. This is the final offer. Take it."

Foley glanced over his shoulder at his thugs, then smiled. "And if I don't?"

Brautigan looked impassively at Foley and the bodyguards, and said nothing.

"I know Rupert Douglass needs my warehouse lot for that foundry he wants to build," Foley said. "If I don't sell, he can't build in the best location. So I want more than just somewhat above fair value. I want double. Go back and tell him that. Double, and we have a deal. Otherwise, no."

Brautigan shifted his feet. The moonlight reflected off the steel-tipped toes of his boots. He was massive, and even this slight movement caused the two gunmen to reflexively twitch their hands toward their pistol butts. "You have the boss's offer," Brautigan said. "He's fair, but never foolish. Take it."

"I worked hard to build my business," Foley said. "It might not seem like much to a rich bastard like Douglass, but I'm a proud man, and if he won't meet my price, then to hell with him."

Brautigan asked, "Is that your final word?" His tone remained calm, but Foley still instinctively stepped back behind his body-guards.

"I know your reputation," the fat man said. "When Douglass's money won't get him what he wants, he sends you along to see what muscle can do. Killer Boots, they call you. This time it won't work." He nodded to the gunmen. "Show him, boys."

The two men reached for their pistols. They were very fast and Brautigan seemed to move in slow motion. But somehow before they could pull the guns from their belts he grasped each of their wrists in one of his huge hands and twisted. There were the sounds of bones breaking and screams of pain. These were short-lived. Brautigan yanked one gunman toward him with his left hand and delivered a crunching head butt that rendered the man unconscious. Then he shifted his right-hand grip from the wrist to the throat of the remaining bodyguard. With little effort he raised his writhing victim high in the air, then slammed him down hard against a wooden crate. The crate smashed; splinters flew. The second gunman lay still.

A few feet away, Foley stood paralyzed with fear. He opened his mouth to scream for help, but no sound emerged beyond a strangled croak.

"Now you," Brautigan said.

Foley tried to run, but the giant was already on him. He hammered a punch into the fat man's belly, driving the wind out of him. As Foley collapsed, struggling for breath, he twisted his face toward the sky. The last two things he saw were the bright moon and its reflection on the steel toe of Brautigan's right boot just before it caved in his skull.

Brautigan leaned down, grasped Foley's shirt collar, and dragged the fat man's corpse back to where the two bodyguards lay. Both were raggedly breathing but unconscious. Brautigan put an end to that with several more well-placed kicks.

The warehouse Rupert Douglass wanted to buy from Foley stood about fifty yards away. One at a time, Brautigan threw the corpses over his shoulder and carried them to its padlocked front door. He tossed them down and placed their arms at their sides. When all three bodies were properly positioned, he kicked them in the face repeatedly until their features were completely pulped. The only sounds were the sloshing of the river and the increasingly soggy thuds of metal toes against skulls and skin. Brautigan spent a quarter hour at this chore. When he was done, he used Foley's jacket

12

to wipe his steel toe tips clean. Then he straightened his own clothes and walked away, whistling tunelessly and appearing for all the world like a man returning home from a relaxing late-night stroll.

At precisely ten the next morning, Brautigan presented himself to Rupert Douglass in the upstairs study of his employer's mansion in central St. Louis. It was a grand house, filled with the finest furniture and rare antiques. Brautigan usually had time to study the exotic clocks, vases, and other items because his boss invariably kept him waiting. But on this occasion, a butler ushered him directly in.

As the door closed behind him, Brautigan sensed something else. Rupert Douglass, usually cool, was trying to keep his emotions under control.

"Last night's business was concluded satisfactorily?" Douglass rubbed a forefinger along his bristly mustache. "Foley is no longer an impediment?"

"I suspect it will be in the afternoon papers," Brautigan said. "Three bodies discovered outside Foley's warehouse on the dock."

"Three?"

"Foley brought along two gunmen. They

shared his fate."

"And no connection here?"

It was unlike Douglass to question the quality of Brautigan's work. The giant took pride in making clean kills that in no way implicated his employer. "None."

Douglass nodded. "Then tomorrow I'll call on the Widow Foley, ease her bereavement with some comforting words and ready cash from a property sale. All right, so the warehouse will be mine. We'll have it razed within a week, get that foundry built. Later on today I'll go over and visit with Chief Welsh, make sure his officers don't look too hard at last night's events. Never hurts to remind Welsh of his obligations."

Making payoffs to the St. Louis chief of police was one of Brautigan's responsibilities. "You don't want me doing that?"

"No, you'll be otherwise engaged." Douglass dropped into a high-backed, overstuffed chair and gestured for Brautigan to sit on a wide couch that offered sufficient space and support for his bulk. "How long have you worked for me?"

Brautigan sat. He was puzzled but didn't let it show on his face. "Four years, just about."

Douglass rubbed his mustache again, a telltale sign that he was agitated. "Four years. I brought you in from Boston when I faced those strike threats in some of my factories. And you handled them for me, handled them well, the strikes and other things."

Brautigan nodded. "Other things" meant bringing Douglass's property negotiations to successful conclusions when prospective sellers wouldn't accept what his boss considered fair offers. Usually, people quailed before Patrick Brautigan, and agreed to take Douglass's money. On the rare occasions when they didn't, Brautigan did what was necessary, and afterward Rupert Douglass negotiated, always successfully, with their survivors. The St. Louis mayor, police chief, and reporters from every significant city newspaper and magazine were in Douglass's pocket. These killings were never attributed to Douglass or even Brautigan himself, though kicked-in faces, the Killer Boots trademark, sent a clear message to anyone doing business with Douglass in the future. Counting the three last night, the kill total over four years was eight — Brautigan remembered, and did not in the slightest regret, each one. He did what he was paid to do, acting without remorse.

"Four years," Douglass said, "and in that time you've only failed me once."

15

Brautigan nodded again. Two and a half years earlier, Ellen, Rupert Douglass's only child, had been murdered in this very mansion by her husband, Cash McLendon, Douglass's trusted second-in-command. Actually, only Douglass thought his daughter was murdered. Everyone else at all familiar with the Douglass family knew that Ellen was crazy, her self-destructive violent tendencies held in check only by regular doses of laudanum. While Douglass and his wife were away, McLendon accidentally left a glass jar handy and a manic Ellen used its sharp shards to cut her wrists. McLendon fled to Arizona Territory, and Douglass sent Brautigan to fetch his son-in-law back and kill him before Douglass's own eyes. To Brautigan, it made no difference whether Ellen's death was self-inflicted or not. His boss had given an order, and he would carry it out. But in the small town of Glorious in Arizona, McLendon slipped away from him with the help of some raggedy frontier dwellers. After that, his quarry seemingly vanished. Brautigan stalked the major towns in California, where he and his boss suspected McLendon would eventually turn up, but he didn't. Finally, after six fruitless months, Douglass summoned him back to St. Louis, where Brautigan resumed his

16

enforcer role. But he never forgot McLendon, whose escape was the single blight on Brautigan's strong-arm history.

Now Brautigan said, "Do you mention this because there's word of McLendon? Has he finally shown somewhere?"

Douglass poured himself a cup of coffee from a steaming urn on a table beside his chair. He didn't offer any to Brautigan. "I've kept my lines out. I imagined myself inside McLendon's head, tried to understand what he'd be thinking. And it all came down to that Italian girl, the one he was with before my Ellen. After he murdered my girl he ran off to that Eye-tie out in Arizona, in that dirty little town. That's where you nabbed him, then let him get away."

"Yes." Brautigan didn't add that McLendon escaped only because of Douglass's ironclad rule that none of his employees should ever publicly break the law. A backwoods sheriff interceded for McLendon, leaving Brautigan no choice but to let him go.

Douglass sipped coffee. Agitation caused his hand to tremble as he raised the cup to his lips. "It took a while, but I figured it out. The Eye-tie. Wherever she ended up, sooner or later that's where McLendon would be too. Gabrielle Tirrito. Unusual name, easy for people to notice and remember. I learned that she went to work in a hotel in some other godforsaken town out in Arizona Territory. So I paid somebody there to keep a lookout for McLendon. Paid and waited. It's been hard. I want my girl avenged. And now, finally. Finally." He set down his coffee cup and pointed at Brautigan. "Pack a bag and get moving today, this morning. Take the train as far west as you can, then I suppose a stage from there. You'll have all the money you need. I'd prefer McLendon brought back alive. I want to watch you work on him. But this time if you can't get away with him clean, finish him there. One way or the other, I want him dead so my Ellen can rest in peace."

Brautigan said, "You've not told me where he is."

Douglass pulled a crumpled bit of paper from his pocket. It was a telegraph cable. "This came an hour ago, from my watcher out west. I'll give you that name, but make contact only if necessary. As much as possible, I want McLendon snatched discreetly."

He handed the paper to Brautigan, who smoothed it and read the simple message: "MOUNTAIN VIEW, ARIZ TERR. HE'S HERE."

■ ■ ■ ■

PART ONE

■ ■ ■ ■

PART ONE

1

The town of Mountain View, in Arizona Territory, was in every respect an impressive place. It bustled at all hours, since the two silver mines on its outskirts were in full operation around the clock. Changing shifts of miners were in constant need of meals in the town's half-dozen restaurants, none of which ever closed. They served quality, highly seasoned fare. After working underground in stifling conditions, when the miners emerged into the fresh air they craved sharp-tasting meals to revive their dulled senses. Freshly prepared Italian, French, and Chinese dishes especially satisfied them. No one on the frontier ate better.

The scenery was spectacular. The town nestled on the southeast edge of the Pinal Mountain range; the mountain slopes were dotted with saguaro cacti and their jagged peaks rose high in the sky. At first glance the mountains seemed entirely bloodred, but careful viewing revealed subtle ribbons of green, gold, and violet bisecting the rock. Eighteen months earlier beneath that rock, prospectors had first discovered wide seams of black-veined ore. Miners cut deep tunnels underground and extracted the ore, which was then passed through complex chemical washes to extract gleaming bits of silver. There seemed no end to this treasure trove; as strikes continued to be made, there was a constant influx of money into the community. As a result, Mountain View exploded almost overnight into a town of relatively fine houses and business structures, many built with stone and timber imported at considerable expense from California or Mexico. Dormitory-style housing provided shelter for the miners and other lower-class workers. Most mining towns on the Western frontier were hodge-podge collections of canvas tents, adobe hovels, and warped plank shacks. In contrast, Mountain View was a showplace.

It was also a town of burgeoning cultural sophistication. Large mining concerns headquartered in San Francisco and Denver quickly opened branch offices in Mountain View and staffed them with topnotch assayers, accountants, and engineers. Working mines meant the presence of supervisors to lead the workers and doctors to treat them. These higher-class individuals expected comfortable accommodations in upscale residences and hotels, plenty of fashionable clothing and other fancy goods available for convenient purchase in expansive shops, and quality entertainment in their leisure time. So Mountain View, its present population nearly two thousand and rising daily, had four hotels, each two-story, with all rooms including glass windows and soft mattresses with clean linens. Town saloons offered fine mixed drinks — sloe-gin fizzes were a popular choice. Traveling troupes of players passed through on a regular basis, presenting everything from Shakespeare to concerts of popular music to slapstick comedy. Saloons were currently used as makeshift theaters, but the Mountain View town council had plans to construct an honest-to-goodness performance venue soon.

Residents walked its streets in safety. A well-compensated police force stood constant guard against the thugs and grifters who plagued other thriving frontier towns. Word spread among territorial ne'er-do-wells: Be smart. Stay away from Mountain View. And, mostly, they did.

Mountain View's informal lending library,

conveniently located next door to a bank, comprised almost two hundred books. The town nine "baseball" team held regular practices; participants planned to test their skills at this newfangled sport under game conditions just as soon as an opponent in another community could be found. A bowling alley in the back of the Camp Feed Store provided additional opportunity for the recreation-minded. Proprietor Hope Camp was also the Mountain View mayor. In between resetting wooden pins by hand, he chatted with customers about the telegraph lines that had recently placed the town in instant communication with the outside world. With more silver strikes reported in the area on a regular basis and three more full-scale mining operations soon beginning operations, Mountain View's potential was unlimited, and its pleasures already plentiful.

Yet Cash McLendon hated being there. The woman he loved was the reason.

Years earlier in St. Louis, McLendon had courted and won the heart of Gabrielle Tirrito, who ran a small general store with her immigrant father, Salvatore, in a downscale factory district. But when McLendon's employer, rich industrialist Rupert Douglass, offered him the opportunity to marry his daughter, Ellen, and eventually take over the Douglass empire, McLendon accepted. He'd grown up as a poor orphan in the St. Louis slums, and the lure of wealth overcame him. Brokenhearted, Gabrielle moved with her father to the small prospecting community of Glorious in Arizona Territory. After Ellen's suicide, knowing her father would blame him, McLendon fled St. Louis with Patrick Brautigan on his heels. He made his way to Glorious, hoping to reconcile with Gabrielle, only to find her virtually engaged to Joe Saint, the softspoken town sheriff. Caught there by Brautigan, McLendon escaped with Saint's help. After many more months on the run, he ended up in Dodge City, Kansas, and was thrilled to learn that Gabrielle, now living with her father in Mountain View, had not yet married Saint. They exchanged letters and agreed that McLendon would come there; Gabrielle would allow him a final chance to change her mind. To pay for the trip, McLendon signed on to a buffalo hunt that ventured deep into Indian Territory. There, at an outpost called Adobe Walls, he fought in and miraculously survived an epic battle where thirty white men held off nearly a thousand Comanche, Cheyenne, and Kiowa. Chastened and matured by the bloody experience, McLendon used most of his money for train and stage passage to Mountain View, certain that he would win Gabrielle back from Joe Saint, who also lived there. But ten days after his arrival, it was obvious that he shouldn't have felt so sure. From the time Gabrielle greeted him with a hug and chaste kiss on the cheek more appropriate for an arriving cousin than a lover, things were awkward between them. They weren't meeting as equals — Gabrielle controlled their future, whatever it might be, and McLendon soon realized that she had no intention of making her decision quickly.

Gabrielle worked as the receptionist at the fashionable White Horse Hotel. It was managed by Major Mulkins, who had befriended McLendon back in Glorious. Mulkins generously offered McLendon a small room at no cost while he was in town and allowed McLendon to share the staff's free meals in the kitchen. Without any immediate financial concerns, McLendon could devote every waking minute to Gabrielle, but she had other ideas. Her work hours were long, from dawn to dusk on weekdays and half days on Saturday. Sunday mornings, she played piano during Catholic services held in the barn behind Tim Flanagan's Livery.

During the services, Flanagan's horses and mules were tethered outside. Gabrielle's father, Salvatore, now ill and bedridden in the room the Tirritos shared on the hotel's second floor, occupied much of her attention. And when she was free, Gabrielle insisted on spending just as much time with Joe Saint as she did with McLendon.

"All I promised you in my letters was a chance," she reminded McLendon when he complained. "Joe is a wonderful man, and I enjoy his company. If you're so dissatisfied with my behavior, you're of course free to be on your way."

"No, I wouldn't even think of that," McLendon said quickly. "It's just that I'm anxious. I've been here for two weeks —"

"Ten days. Don't exaggerate."

"Ten days. And not once have you let me talk about my plans for us, or tell you again how sorry I am for all I've done wrong. If you'd only let me do that, I'm sure you'd be persuaded."

"What you're saying is, you want to make a fine speech," Gabrielle said. "As we both know, I've heard them from you before. There's no need for another. I accept that you're sorry. I realize that you've changed."

Gabrielle was on a mid-afternoon work break. She and McLendon strolled down the wooden sidewalk past Camp's Feed Store. From the far side of the building came the rattle of tumbling bowling pins. The wind whipped Gabrielle's long, dark hair into wild tendrils, and she reached up to pat them back into place. Most women in town wore scarves or wide-brimmed bonnets when they ventured outside, but Gabrielle rarely did. Her lustrous hair was one of her most striking features, and, rather than cover it up, she liked to accentuate it with brightly colored ribbons. "For now I just want to talk about small things and get used to who you've become," she said. "Tell me more about your recent life in Dodge City. Collecting and selling buffalo bones sounds fascinating."

"It was tedious, and I always smelled bad from the stink on the bones," McLendon said. They reached the end of the sidewalk and paused in the shade of Flanagan's Livery. August was sweltering in northeast Arizona Territory. "This can't really be interesting to you. There have to be better things to talk about."

"But I am interested, and you should be pleased," Gabrielle said. "Much of a life together would involve relatively minor details. If either of us already finds casual conversation with the other to be tedious, then we won't match up well in the long term."

McLendon sighed. "Whatever you want, of course. But you have to understand — I constantly feel that I'm on trial with you. I'm never certain what to say or do."

"Don't overthink it. I know this is hard on you, but it's difficult for me, too, and also for Joe. Simply by asking for the opportunity to make this choice, I'm being unfair to him, after his years of love and loyalty. Look, there he is. School is letting out."

Two blocks down the hard-packed dirt street, a dozen children of varying ages ran gleefully from a one-room wooden shack that served as a schoolhouse during the week and a Protestant church on Sundays. Behind them, patting passing heads and calling out warnings to watch where they were going, was Joe Saint, thin to the point of emaciation, his thick-lensed spectacles and patchy beard adding to the overall impression of a human scarecrow. Saint had been named sheriff in Glorious because he was scrupulously honest and not at all capable of the casual brutality of many frontier lawmen. Prior to that, he'd been a schoolteacher back East, and always hoped to return to the profession. As a growing community with aspirations of greatness, Mountain View wanted a school and a teacher, even though, as yet, only a handful of youngsters lived in town. Saint gladly took the job, and, for four dollars a day, the same rate that miners in town were paid, presided over students ranging in age from five to fourteen. Now, looking down the street, he saw Gabrielle waving, and waved back. McLendon took note and said to her, "I guess I need to walk you back to the hotel."

"Yes, there's still so much to do today. Every room we have is spoken for, and Major Mulkins says we might need to set up tents behind the building for the overflow. The other hotels are full up too. The town council is never happy to see tents because they think these detract from the town's image, but it's either that or turn away visitors who'd spend money with local businesses. It's a good problem to have."

"I suppose I'll move into the Major's room with him. He said I could, if you needed my room for a paying customer." Moving wouldn't require much effort on McLendon's part. He'd lost all of his possessions at Adobe Walls and arrived in Mountain View with only his Colt Peacemaker and the clothes he was wearing. He used most of the few dollars that remained to him after travel costs to purchase another shirt, a pair of pants, socks, and drawers. Having no income bothered him; so did taking ongoing advantage of Mulkins's generosity. If Gabrielle took much longer deciding between him and Joe Saint, McLendon knew he would have to find work in town.

Outside the White Horse, McLendon asked Gabrielle, "Will I see you tonight?"

"Well, perhaps at dinner in the kitchen, if I can get away from the front desk. But afterward, Joe is escorting me to a poetry reading in the meeting room of the Eagle Hotel." She nodded toward a building across the street. "You could join us, but that might be uncomfortable."

"It would be," McLendon admitted. During his ten days in town, he and Saint had deliberately avoided each other. In all but one instance, their encounters were formal and polite, since Gabrielle was present and neither wanted to upset her. The single time they'd passed on the street and Gabrielle wasn't around, McLendon nodded perfunctorily while Saint glared and didn't nod or speak at all.

Gabrielle started toward the door, then stepped back and put her hand on McLendon's forearm. "I know this is wearing on

31

you. I'm sorry. I have to be certain."

"I understand," McLendon said. "Just decide when you can."

Gabrielle smiled. "Well, I'm sure you'll find ways to amuse yourself tonight. Bowling? Reading a book from the library?"

"I think I'll stand the Major to a drink at one of the finer local establishments. I still have a few dollars in my pocket, not many, but enough for that. He's being so kind to me."

"That's because he's glad to see you again," Gabrielle said. "But I'm gladder still." She took a quick look around, and then, assured no one was watching, leaned forward and kissed McLendon lightly on the lips. It was the first time she'd kissed him since the cheek peck upon his arrival, and he was momentarily thrilled. But as Gabrielle disappeared inside, McLendon couldn't help wondering if she had already decided and was drawing out the suspense to make him suffer. It was, after all, human nature to savor revenge.

Major Mulkins sipped bourbon and sighed appreciatively. "A good brand, this," he told McLendon. "Jim Beam is what they call it. There was no such quality liquor back in Glorious, just raw red-eye."

"Tonight there's fine whiskey and surroundings to match," McLendon agreed. He was glad to see the Major lingering over his bourbon, since the Jim Beam cost an appalling two bits a glass. Though McLendon had deliberately brought Mulkins to Mountain View's finest saloon to treat his friend to the best, he couldn't afford many fifty-cent drinks. "There was never an establishment like this in Glorious either."

They were in the Ritz saloon. Businesses in the frontier frequently boasted names far more glamorous than the establishments themselves, but in this case it was apt. The Ritz was well lighted with oil lamps, allowing patrons to enjoy views of flocked wallpaper, mounted hunting trophies — a ferocious grizzly raged in a particularly lifelike manner just inside the ornate swinging entrance doors — and reasonably tasteful paintings depicting attractive women with minimal clothing. Well-dressed businessmen seated in low-backed captain's chairs conversed at cloth-covered tables or else stood comfortably bent over their drinks at the long wooden bar, propping their well-shod feet on a footrail. Card games, poker and faro, were played in an adjacent room. Dice was forbidden at the Ritz — it smacked of lower-class wagering. There were plenty of ashtrays and spittoons, all regularly emptied by bow-tied staff. Hostesses in low-cut gowns circulated, accepting drink orders and, discreetly, assignations in upstairs rooms. Only high-class, pox-free whores were permitted to ply their trade in the Ritz, and each paid a monthly tax to the town for the privilege.

"I hope things are progressing to your satisfaction," Mulkins said, holding up his glass to admire its amber contents. His comment offered McLendon the opportunity to talk about his wooing of Gabrielle without openly asking. Frontier etiquette discouraged direct questions.

"I'm trying," McLendon said, and took a small sip of the much cheaper beer that he'd ordered. "I won't take advantage of your generosity much longer, I hope."

Mulkins shrugged. "Gabrielle's a fine woman. If she leaves with you, it will be hard to replace her at the hotel. But as long as she's happy — well, look who's here! Cash McLendon, this is McGehee Fielding, better known as Mac. He's editor of our newspaper, and he's been wanting to meet you."

A tall man with near shoulder-length hair extended his hand. "A pleasure, Mr. McLendon. It's exciting to have a celebrity

34

in our midst."

The remark made McLendon uncomfortable. Since fleeing St. Louis, he'd done his best to remain inconspicuous. "I'm nothing of the sort, Mr. Fielding."

"Of course you are. May I sit down? And stand another round of drinks?"

McLendon wasn't sure he wanted further conversation with the man, but any drink Fielding bought Mulkins was one less that McLendon had to pay for. Fielding sat down, fresh drinks were ordered, and the journalist immediately got to the point.

"We're trying to get *The Mountain View Herald* solidly established, and for that we need colorful stories. It makes the mayor happy when we write about businesses opening here and additional stage routes from Florence, but what keeps our circulation growing is stories with some snap to them, some excitement. There just aren't enough of those to suit my purposes — the Apache are mostly tamed now, Sheriff Hove and his men won't allow even the occasional gunfight, and the Witch of the West doesn't claim victims frequently enough."

"I thought the Witch was mythological, like St. Nicholas at Christmas or Robin Hood," McLendon said.

"If my readers wish to believe in her, then

she's real enough for me," Fielding said. "People want entertainment as well as actual news, you see. We publish once a week on Saturdays, when folks want to put aside for a while the cares of work."

"Of course, but I don't understand what that has to do with me," McLendon said. "I'm simply visiting old friends. There's no entertainment for your readers in that."

Fielding took a notebook and pencil from his coat pocket. "But they'd relish a first-hand account of the epic battle barely six weeks ago at Adobe Walls in Texas, the one where you and a handful of other heroes obliterated thousands of bloodthirsty savages. Indian stories always sell newspapers, especially when the white men humiliate them like that."

McLendon looked hopefully at Mulkins; maybe the Major would politely ask Fielding to desist. But the Major smiled and nodded encouragingly.

"Tell Mac about it," he urged.

"Well, we weren't really heroes, and the Indians certainly weren't obliterated," McLendon said. "We were fortunate to survive. Wait — why are you writing that down?"

Fielding said to Mulkins, "Your friend is not only a hero, but modest. Mr. McLendon, how many savages did you personally kill? All with a gun? Any hand to hand? That would be a nice touch."

"I don't wish to discuss it," McLendon said.

"Pardon me," Fielding said. He turned to Mulkins. "Major, you assured me he'd co-operate. That's why I wrote about the amenities at your hotel being the finest in town, and put that story smack on the front page. I'm going to the outhouse, and when I come back, I expect this to be fixed." He stalked away.

Mulkins said, "C.M., I'm sorry. I didn't think you'd mind talking to Mac."

McLendon drank beer and tried to keep his composure. "The last thing I want is to have my name in the newspapers. I think the people chasing me have given up, but there's no way to be certain. Jesus, Major, you were with me in Glorious. Remember what happened there? You of all people should understand."

"The White Horse needed the publicity," Mulkins said. "We're full up now, but we've got to stay that way if I'm ever to convince the owner to add a third floor. Then I'd make some real money running the place, maybe get the chance to build another for myself. I want to own a fine hotel again, not just manage one for somebody else."

"You helped save my life back in Glorious, and I haven't forgotten that," McLendon said, as much to remind himself as to reassure Mulkins. "And now when I need it, you're giving me free room and board. I'm grateful for all of this."

"It was mostly Joe Saint who stepped up for you that night in Glorious," Mulkins said. "And now here in Mountain View, I'm glad to lend a hand when you need it. Don't worry — even if you refuse to talk to Fielding, that won't change. I overstepped and I apologize. But here's the thing — Fielding's paper only gets read right around here. The people who were after you are never going to run across a copy of *The Mountain View Herald.* So if you could see your way clear to talk to him, I don't think you'd be putting yourself in any danger. I wouldn't ask if I believed there was the slightest chance of it."

McLendon thought about it. "All right, but I'm not doing it tonight. I need to get my story straight, figure out what to tell him. I mean, he didn't seem real interested in the truth."

Mulkins laughed. "Hell, he runs a newspaper. Truth's the last thing Mac Fielding wants."

When the journalist returned, McLendon offered to be interviewed at the newspaper office one day the following week. Fielding suggested Monday, first thing, and McLendon countered with Wednesday afternoon. That satisfied Fielding, who ordered more drinks for McLendon and Mulkins and went on his way. The two men sat in the Ritz for another hour, reminiscing about Glorious and the people they'd known there — Crazy George Mitchell and his common-law wife, Mary Somebody; Bob Pugh the livery owner who'd died so tragically; and rascally Ike Clanton.

"Any idea whatever happened to Ike?" McLendon asked. "Now, there was a total bastard, a man hardly fit to live."

Mulkins sipped bourbon. "Ike and the rest of the Clantons are trying to get their own town started somewhere south of here. It may be that you get reacquainted. He shows up here from time to time, trying to peddle individual property lots. To date he's had no success. People in this town know better than to throw away their money with fly-by-nighters like Ike."

"Somehow, the Ikes of this world always survive," McLendon said. "Well, let's figure out what I can tell your newspaper friend that'll be at least somewhat true, yet still satisfy him." McLendon shared some stories about Adobe Walls: how he'd panicked during the first attack by the Indians, the terror of subsequent onslaughts, and how, finally, the Indians essentially defeated themselves by wasting ammunition.

"I believe Mac Fielding is going to want something more colorful than that," Mulkins said, so McLendon told him about how buffalo hunter Billy Dixon shot an Indian off the top of a bluff at the distance of nearly a mile. "That one'll please Fielding considerably," the Major assured McLendon, and insisted on buying the next round. To get even for the newspaper interview, McLendon ordered Jim Beam instead of beer.

The atmosphere in the elegant saloon was congenial until ten p.m., when a rat-faced man in trail-stained buckskins elbowed his way into a prime spot at the bar and shouted for whiskey. He had a pistol stuck in his belt; as he drank, he made coarse remarks to the Ritz's hostesses.

"That fellow acts like one of the Silver City bunch," Mulkins said. "Though we generally discourage it, sometimes they drift up this way. Silver City's a week's ride southeast of here in New Mexico, where they've had some pretty good strikes. In every other way it's the opposite of Mountain View — lots of rough types, and mostly tents and whorehouses. Thing about mining towns is they either turn out fine or nasty. Silver City's one of the nasty ones. I passed through there some months ago on business and the town was a sty, and dangerous in every way. They don't care about laws and decency in Silver City, just money."

The newcomer at the bar finished his initial drink and called for another. When a second, then a third, were consumed just as quickly, the bartender said politely, "Friend, you might want to slow down."

"You might shut your goddamned mouth," the drinker snarled. "My name's Will Antrim, and I'm no friend of yours. Now get me another — be quick about it."

The bartender nodded to a guard seated in the corner of the saloon. The guard stood, flexed his shoulders, folded back his shirt cuffs, and walked up to the bar. He put his hand on the belligerent's back and said, "Time to be leaving." Antrim whirled, grabbed the guard by the shirtfront, and punched him in the face. Stunned, the guard fell to the floor and his assailant leaped on top of him, still swinging while the guard tried to block the blows with his arms.

"We've got to stop this," McLendon said to Mulkins, but the Major gestured for him to remain seated.

"No need," he said. "Someone's gone for the sheriff."

Moments later, a rangy man perhaps forty years old walked briskly through the swinging doors. The gleaming badge pinned to his coat identified him as the Mountain View sheriff. He didn't draw the Colt holstered on his hip. He stood over the men struggling on the floor, reached down to grasp Antrim's shoulder, and jerked him to his feet.

"You're under arrest, mister," the sheriff said.

"The hell I am," Antrim growled. He pulled back his fist to throw another punch, this time at the lawman. Now the sheriff drew his gun, but instead of firing, he spun the weapon so he grasped the barrel like the handle of a hammer. Then he coolly cracked the gun butt against Antrim's temple; the man dropped back onto the saloon floor, holding his hands to his head.

The sheriff leaned over the fallen guard and helped him to his feet. "You all right, Paul? Go get cleaned up. He only marked you a little, I'd guess twenty dollars' worth when the fine's assessed." The bartender helped the guard away and the sheriff hauled Antrim to his feet. "Don't even think about running," he warned. "If I have to cold-cock you again, your skull might split."

McLendon was impressed by the sheriff's efficiency. "Nicely done," he said as the lawman pulled Antrim along.

"Appreciate it," the sheriff said. "Don't believe I've met you. Jack Hove — welcome to town."

"We've got the best lawman anywhere in the territory right here in Mountain View," Mulkins told McLendon as the sheriffled his groaning prisoner through the swinging doors. "Jack Hove's a hell of a man, honest and tough besides. Never seen him have to fire a shot. When force becomes necessary, he smacks 'em alongside the head with a gun instead. Jack calls it buffaloing. Says he learned it from some lawman in the Dakotas, I believe it was."

"He seems to be a good man," McLendon agreed. "The town's lucky to have him."

"Jack's got four deputies, and they're all top-notch, too," Mulkins said, tipping his glass for the last dregs of Jim Beam bourbon. "I'll tell you this, you couldn't be safer anywhere else in the territories. Long as Jack and his boys are on the job, nobody's going to get you in Mountain View."

2

When stalking hometown targets specified by his boss, Patrick Brautigan never needed to plan in advance. It was a simple process: corner the quarry, make appropriate threats, and, if the target didn't submit, kill him. With the St. Louis police chief complicit in Rupert Douglass's violent schemes, there was no danger of legal repercussion. Douglass once ordered Brautigan to perform a chore in Albany, New York, and on another occasion sent him to Washington, D.C. In these cases somewhat more discretion was required, but still intimidation (and, in Washington, a kill) came easily. Brautigan was comfortable in big cities. He operated instinctively in their alleys and shadows.

But that instinct was less effective on the frontier. There, practically everyone lived with so much daily menace — Indians, outlaws, dust storms, flash floods, and other dangers unique to their still mostly untamed region — that they were constantly on their guard. Two years earlier in Glorious, Brautigan had employed the same basic approach he always used back East. He caught McLendon by surprise, overpowered him, and prepared to haul his quarry home to die according to the boss's wishes. The small town's sheriff intervened, so Brautigan claimed he'd been deputized to arrest McLendon for murder and return him there for trial. With anyone but this most amateurish lawman, the bluff almost certainly would have worked. Lawmen everywhere routinely deputized civilians to undertake out-of-town arrests. But that custom apparently was unfamiliar to the sheriff of primitive Glorious. He'd insisted on wiring St. Louis chief Kelly Welsh for confirmation. Brautigan could, of course, have killed the local lawman on the spot, but it was Douglass's rule that his enforcer should never openly break the law. So Brautigan, arrested on suspicion of impersonating an officer, cooled his heels in a cell for days while Cash McLendon escaped. Though Chief Welsh eventually wired that Brautigan was indeed a deputy and charges against him were subsequently dropped, it was too late. Brautigan swore that if he ever again tracked McLendon down to some isolated hellhole on the frontier, he'd first learn more about the location and have a plan in place before making his move.

And so he found himself in Silver City.

The obvious route to Mountain View from St. Louis was by train to Denver, then stagecoach to Tucson, Florence, and finally Mountain View itself. But Tucson was where Brautigan was held following his arrest in Glorious; if he returned, he might be recognized by someone who would wire ahead and warn McLendon that he was coming. This was unlikely, but he couldn't risk it. Rupert Douglass would never tolerate a second failure. So Brautigan took an even more circuitous route, leaving the train in Wichita and taking the stage from there to Santa Fe, then Albuquerque and finally to Silver City.

As he stepped down from the stage carriage into a dirt street fouled with horse shit, Brautigan felt as though he had reached the end of the world. To begin with, it was ugly — rickety buildings of wooden planks without paint or varnish, some cabins of crookedly nailed logs, vast expanses of patched canvas tents in assorted sun-faded colors. The cabins apparently had mud roofs, which would surely melt when it rained. But the swirling dust indicated that it didn't rain that often, in itself a shame, because a cloudburst might have washed a bit of stink off the grimy people teeming everywhere. Above all, there was the noise, an eardrum-rending cacophony of clanking mine equipment, barking dogs, human shouts and screams and, most painfully, shrieking steam whistles that Brautigan guessed signaled the end of some work shift or other. Yet this ongoing chaos pleased him. Silver City was a bustling Western mining town. If Mountain View was similar, then it might be a simple thing to get in unnoticed and take McLendon away without anyone the wiser. Brautigan knew Mountain View lay somewhere to the north — he wasn't certain how far, or the best way to reach it. These were only a few of the things he needed to learn. For that, he'd have to rely on some of these disreputable locals. Time to get started.

A sign over one of the sagging buildings advertised ESTES HOTEL. There were other equally unattractive structures whose signage proclaimed them hotels, but this was the closest. Brautigan walked there, carrying his valise and sweating hard. Even in mid-morning, the sun was scorching. He went inside, noting cobwebs everywhere, well positioned to trap at least some of the

47

ubiquitous buzzing flies.

He asked the thickset woman behind the counter, "Have you a room available?"

Her eyes widened. A first sight of Brautigan was inevitably startling. He knew this and often used it to his advantage, but now was a time for information rather than intimidation, and so he smiled, though the effect was almost as disconcerting. Brautigan had large, square teeth. No matter how he stretched his lips, if the teeth behind them were exposed Brautigan gave the impression of a great beast about to bite.

"A room to let?" he said. "I'm here from the East to do some business. A fine, bustling town, this seems to me." Brautigan had grown up poor in Irish Boston. Now he let creep into his voice the accent that he muted in St. Louis.

The woman's face twitched as she tried not to stare. After a moment she said, "We have a few. How long will you be staying?"

"It's hard to say. Perhaps I'll take one for a week to start."

"There's no refund if you leave earlier." From her tone, it was clear that many guests at the Estes Hotel left sooner than originally planned.

"If my business concludes sooner, I'll undoubtedly stay on to enjoy your town's

48

amenities. Now, what might be your rates?"

"Fifteen dollars for the week. Fresh linens and towels on the first and fourth day only. You empty your own chamber pot in the buckets out back."

Brautigan reached into his pocket and extracted a twenty-dollar gold piece. "Well, then, take this."

The woman brightened. "Let me get your change."

"No need. In return, perhaps you'll give me the best room you can. I like a good view of the street."

"We have oilcloth over the windows, but no glass. You can pull the curtain aside and have a street view if you don't mind the additional dust."

"That's fine," Brautigan said. He didn't expect to spend much time in the room, so dust be damned. He extended a hand. "Mr. Brautigan, from Boston." There was no reason not to use his real name. If things went awry, they would look for him in Massachusetts.

The woman's hand barely fit around a few of Brautigan's fingers, let alone his palm. "Emily Estes. This is my place. I guessed Boston from your accent, Mr. Brautigan. Are you possibly acquainted with my dear friend Lisa Bohrer? She hails from there,

49

and perhaps recommended us."

"Pleased to meet you, and sorry to say I don't know your friend. Boston is a sizable place. Now, as soon as I've visited my room and cleaned myself a bit, I'll be off to find a meal and perhaps a sociable drink. Is there any spot of particular merit?"

The bar was named the Gilded Cage, but there was nothing gilded about the place. A long board anchored on either side by packing crates served as a bar. Drinkers leaned over shot glasses or mugs there or else perched on tottery chairs beside splintered tables. There were shabby cloths on the tables, but the material was thin and wood splinters poked through. Still, the Italian food on offer wasn't bad, though the sauce and meatballs accompanying the pasta Brautigan ordered were spicier than he expected. He sat by himself as he ate, sipping beer from a chipped mug and observing the bar's patrons. They were a rowdy bunch, speculating in loud voices which son of a bitch was going to offer one too many insults and get his balls blown off, or haranguing the whores working in four cubicles behind oilcloth curtains to get done with their current limp-peckered customers so real men could get serviced. A stoic middle-aged man cradling a shotgun sat at a table near the cubicles. The whores' customers dropped money into a tin box on the table before they went behind the oilcloth for their fun. It always seemed to take only a matter of minutes, after which the men would emerge buttoning their pants and looking not a bit abashed at the ribald comments they attracted. The whores never came out at all. Every minute of rest for them was a minute of profit lost.

Shortly after noon, the saloon's doors swung open and the din lessened. Brautigan sized up the newcomer, taking in his relatively clean clothes, Peacemakers holstered on both hips, and the badge pinned to his vest. Though he was just under middle height, he stood straight enough to seem taller, and he kept his hands close to his gun butts. The crowd parted as he walked to the table by the whores' cribs and spoke quietly to the guard there. Then the lawman nodded, reached into the tin box, and took some of the money. As he put the coins in his pocket, he looked carefully around the room. When his eyes met Brautigan's, he studied the larger man carefully for a few moments without attempting to disguise his interest. Brautigan sat calmly. He realized that he was being scrutinized by another professional. That this Silver City constable, police chief, whatever the right title, was someone Brautigan could possibly work with was evident; helping himself so openly to a portion of the whores' earnings was characteristic of an entrenched lawman on the take.

The man walked over and said, "What's your name?"

"Brautigan. Will you sit?"

"I'm Wolfe, the town sheriff. If you want to talk, the back office will do better. It's loud out here."

Brautigan tossed back the last of his beer. "Won't the owners be inconvenienced if we impose?"

Wolfe's mouth smiled and his eyes didn't. "I'm sheriff, and also one of the owners. Fact is, I own a piece of quite a few places in town."

"Lead on," Brautigan said. Now he was even more certain that Sheriff Wolfe was a man willing to do business without asking too many questions.

When they were seated — Wolfe in a chair behind a desk, Brautigan on a sofa — the sheriff dispensed with small talk. "What's on your mind?"

"I'm deputized by the chief of police in a

52

city back East, and in pursuit of a killer who needs to be returned there."

"And this killer's in Silver City?"

"I've reason to believe he can be found in a place called Mountain View."

Wolfe grimaced. "Then you're still a far piece from where you need to be. Mountain View's near two hundred miles, and the country's hard going in between. We've got no stage service that direction. Best thing you can do, take the stage from here to Tucson, then again by stage north to Florence and finally east to Mountain View."

Brautigan shook his head. "Tucson won't do. I might receive undue attention there."

"You consider attention unwelcome?" There was a new hint of avarice in Wolfe's voice.

"I have funds for discreet arrangements."

Wolfe took a whiskey bottle and two glasses from a desk drawer. He poured drinks, then asked, "You got some kind of badge to show me, or a letter from this police chief back East?"

Brautigan sipped his drink. It was decent liquor, undoubtedly better than the Gilded Cage bar brands. "I'm traveling without credentials."

"What can you offer instead? Make it your best price. I find bargaining to be tedious. If your pockets aren't deep enough, you can get the hell out of my town."

Brautigan leaned back on the couch. "There are different amounts for different methods of assistance. Would you go to Mountain View, make the arrest yourself, and deliver the man back here to me?"

"On a warrantless request from some nameless lawman back East? Not in Mountain View. They got a sheriff named Jack Hove who's one of those strictly-by-the-rules types. His deputies are the same."

"No persuading them? With money or otherwise?"

Wolfe took a thin cheroot from an inner coat pocket and lit it. He blew some smoke toward the ceiling and said, "It's plain that you're a hard man. But that bunch, you'd have to kill them, and you've already made it clear you don't want to make noise. My advice, figure a way to get your man out of Mountain View and down here to Silver City. I'll make sure you get him on a stage heading east with the documents needed to get past the law all the way back to wherever you want to take him."

"How about providing paperwork before I go to Mountain View? Something I could wave at this sheriff?"

"Hell, no. Jack Hove's the sort who'd wire

54

every judge in Arizona Territory wanting to know if the warrant was valid. That'd cause problems I don't need. If you get your man from Mountain View to Silver City with a minimum of fuss, I can provide what you need to finish the job from here."

"This is less than I'd hoped for."

"It's all you'll get. Now make me an offer."

It was Brautigan's turn to ponder. "All right, five hundred. Two-fifty now. Two-fifty when I bring my man back here, you deliver me the documents I'll need, and you put us on the stage back East."

"I make nearly that much each month from the whores alone. I'd appreciate sweetening."

Brautigan stood. This was the critical moment. He'd been taught by his boss that every deal, legitimate or otherwise, was never an equal partnership. One party was always in control. Once on his feet, Brautigan didn't lean in toward the sheriff or demonstrate any other sign of aggression. Yet he knew that Wolfe, a dangerous man in his own right, felt the threat. Brautigan observed the sheriff's elbows jerk back a fraction of an inch on the arms of his chair. That flinch tilted the balance between them.

"Like you, I don't care for bargaining," he

told the sheriff. "There's no risk involved on your end, unless you play me false." Brautigan counted greenbacks onto the desktop. "Put the money in your pocket, Sheriff. We're partners now."

Wolfe took the bills. "You still got to get up to Mountain View, apprehend your man without undue commotion, and return here with him. It won't be easy."

Brautigan flashed his square-toothed smile. "I'll manage."

3

On Wednesday afternoon, McLendon went to the office of *The Mountain View Herald* to be interviewed by Mac Fielding. It was a typical print shop filled with the sharp, somewhat pleasant smell of ink. Until his ears adjusted to the constant clamor, McLendon had trouble hearing Fielding's questions above the rattles and thuds of small handpresses operated by a man and two women in the next room.

"Sorry about the noise," Fielding said, his voice raised above the din. "Until newspaper circulation is sufficient, we pay the rent by printing posters, public notices, and so forth. Still, I'm sure it's an improvement over war whoops. It must be a great relief to find yourself back in civilization."

"It's certainly a change," McLendon said. He then spent the next forty-five minutes trying to answer the newspaperman's questions colorfully enough to please him without completely sacrificing fact. Yes, at Adobe Walls there was a great horde of attacking Indians; no one afterward was certain how many. The fight lasted all day, with the Indians trying to get at the vastly outnumbered white defenders in three small sod-and-log structures.

"Satanta the great Kiowa chief, I've heard he was there," Fielding said. "Did you personally see him, shoot at him, maybe?"

"I'm not sure I know that name," McLendon said. "I was told that there were Kiowa, and Cheyenne and Comanche as well. Most of the men fighting beside me were buffalo hunters and their crews. They'd been in lots of Indian fights and knew the differences in the way the warriors of those tribes look. But to me they all seemed the same — frightening."

"But you overcame any fear and fought courageously," Fielding said.

"If you say so."

"Be certain that I will."

When Fielding finally ran out of leading questions about the battle at Adobe Walls, he wanted to know more about McLendon's arrival in Mountain View. He'd mentioned visiting old friends — who were they?

"Major Mulkins of the White Horse Hotel, an exceptional establishment. You'll quote me on that?"

Fielding cleared his throat. "I've heard it's really someone other than the Major. A lady, perhaps?"

"Miss Gabrielle Tirrito is an acquaintance of long standing. As is her father, Mr. Salvatore Tirrito. Both fine people, and it's a privilege to once again be in their company." Gabrielle might be pleased if that comment made it into print.

"Your relationship with Miss Tirrito — is it of a courtship nature? I'm informed that she already has someone who might be termed a beau."

"I agreed to discuss my battle experience," McLendon said. "My personal life is private."

"Major Mulkins promised me —"

"Even so."

"I'll see if Miss Tirrito would perhaps care to comment."

McLendon said, "She would not. And you won't approach her."

There was sufficient steel in McLendon's tone to give Fielding pause. "Well," he said, drumming his pencil on his notebook and taking a moment to regain composure. "Then let's talk about your visit here in Mountain View. An extended stay? What's the possibility of permanence?"

"I have no idea how long I'll remain. My intention is to move on to California. I've already stayed longer than intended, but for now I suppose my time here is open-ended. In fact, I'm thinking of seeking employment, though of transitory rather than long-term nature."

Fielding scribbled in his notebook. "I think that'll do for the moment. I'm going to ask a few people for comments — no, not Miss Tirrito, you've made your wishes quite clear in that regard. I'll write the story, and we'll go to print day after tomorrow, with distribution beginning Saturday and copies available during the next week in all our town's finest establishments. It's been a pleasure. I hope you'll enjoy what I write."

Beyond hoping the finished story wouldn't be too florid, McLendon thought that was the end of it. But that evening, Hope Camp sought him out in the White Horse lobby.

"Have you a moment, Mr. McLendon?" he asked.

McLendon hesitated. He was on his way to join Gabrielle for dinner at the staff table in the hotel kitchen. But it seemed impolite to refuse the town mayor.

"I spoke earlier with Mac Fielding," said Camp, an older man with wispy white hair and kind eyes. "It was in regard to the story about you for Saturday's newspaper."

"I hope it won't exaggerate my role at Adobe Walls," McLendon said. "That would be embarrassing."

Camp led McLendon off to a corner. "I'm sure your heroism in that fight can't be exaggerated. But my interest is in your comment that you'd like to find work here in Mountain View."

"In fact, I would. My stay has become extended, and I don't wish to impose any longer on the generosity of friends."

"Certainly you don't. As it happens, I have need of some assistance with an aspect of my store business. I understand from Major Mulkins that you have some management experience."

McLendon chuckled. "In a sense. Back East, mostly, and a little a few years ago at a livery here in Arizona Territory. If you require details —"

Camp shook his head. "No further explanation needed. The fact is, I'm almost ashamed to suggest this employment to a hero such as yourself. Though the income would, I think, be more than adequate, it's possible you might find the job itself to be beneath your dignity."

"I doubt my dignity will be an issue. What's the job?"

61

"As more men come to town to work in the mines and get their pay, they look for recreation beyond ladies and whiskey," Camp said. "You know of the bowling alley in the back of my feed store? I had it built there some months ago on a whim. Bowling has become popular in the big, established cities, and I suspected that it might catch on here if enough of our residents had sufficient income and inclination. Now it's surpassed my expectations. My employees and I have all we can do to serve regular customers and keep these so-called bowlers happy at the same time. What I'd like is, you come in and run the bowling games for me. There's always a long line awaiting turns. Many of them come after quaffing a drink or two and so are impatient. Having a man of your reputation for, shall we say, a certain readiness for action if required, would be helpful in maintaining order."

"I have that reputation?"

"You already do, and it will only increase after Saturday's story in the *Herald*. Oh, don't worry. You would never have to dirty your own hands if someone becomes too obstreperous. Sheriff Hove and his deputies would be called."

"I do like keeping my hands clean," McLendon said. "The job sounds fine.

Now, as to pay?"

They came to a quick bargain. Bowlers were charged two bits a game. McLendon would keep a dime, with another two cents a game going to the boy who picked up and reset the wooden pins between rolls of the bowling ball. Since most of the bowlers played quickly, McLendon could likely earn at least a dollar every two hours. On any days that he failed to make at least four dollars, Camp would make up the difference. They shook hands and agreed McLendon would start the next morning at nine a.m. and work until six in the evening. Sundays off, since the feed store was closed.

After his first few hours on the job, McLendon felt bored. Little thought was required. He took players' money, explained the rules of bowling if they didn't know them, and let them play. With some, he had to deliver constant reminders to *roll* rather than *throw* the ball. The miners had the most aggressive approaches. They were less interested in proper form than in knocking things down. The pin boy was sometimes as much of a target as the pins themselves. But a word from McLendon was always sufficient to rein in such tomfoolery. The constant rumble of wooden ball on wooden lane and then the clatter of the ball scattering wooden pins sometimes irritated him, but it felt good to have a job and be generating income. He earned nearly five dollars on Thursday, and five-fifty on Friday. That was more than Joe Saint made teaching; McLendon didn't share with Gabrielle the satisfaction that this gave him. She, in turn, was pleased to see him gainfully employed: "It demonstrates a welcome work ethic." McLendon insisted on paying Major Mulkins two dollars daily for room and board at the White Horse. Gabrielle still hadn't made up her mind, but at least he was no longer subsisting on charity while he waited. Things in Mountain View were looking up.

Then, on Saturday, the latest edition of the *Herald* was published.

The headline read *"Hero of Adobe Walls Battle Shares Tales of Exploits, Exclusive for Herald Readers."* According to the article, "Mr. Cash McLendon's dead-eye shooting" took down "a minimum of two dozen red assailants, including three war chiefs, and several at distances up to a mile." Following the battle, McLendon, frequently referred to throughout as "Our Hero," turned down pleas from the Army and the governors of

Kansas, Oklahoma, and Texas to personally lead combined military and civilian troops in "teaching the red savages a firm and final lesson." The *Herald*'s front page also featured a sketch, no doubt copied from a magazine, of a stern-visaged frontiersman shooting a spear-brandishing Indian from the saddle. The marksman looked nothing like Cash McLendon, but the caption still bore his name. The Indian was identified as "Kiowa war chief Satanta."

Inside the same issue, readers learned that Mr. McLendon was currently visiting friends in Mountain View and residing at the White Horse Hotel, which was acknowledged to offer the finest luxury lodging in central Arizona Territory. Mr. McLendon, known to intimates as "C.M.," had no idea how long he might remain in town, though he was enjoying himself immensely and felt in no hurry to leave. "Though Mr. McLendon has mentioned plans to travel on to California, everyone here who has encountered this champion prays that he will settle among us in Mountain View," Mac Fielding wrote. "There is reason for hope to flutter in our breasts: Mr. McLendon has entered into at least temporary partnership with Mayor Hope Camp, and can be found daily at Camp Feed Store in a managerial capacity." Mayor Camp, asked to comment, said that great men like Cash McLendon were always welcome in Mountain View.

McLendon was awakened at five a.m. by Major Mulkins, who lit the lamp in their room at the White Horse and handed him the *Herald.*

"Just a few minutes ago they placed some of these in the display box in the lobby," Mulkins said. "I've read your story. It's possibly not as bad as you feared."

Eyes blinking as they adjusted to the light, McLendon began reading. His groans gradually increased in volume until, finally, he crumpled the paper and threw it on the floor.

"Jesus, Major, this is too much," he said. "I might as well leave town today. After this I'll be a laughingstock. Who could take such swill seriously?"

"It's not a bad thing to be so highly praised," Mulkins said. "Readers are more likely to respect than mock you."

"The hell they'll respect me. All I can hope is that nobody reads this tripe."

An hour later at the table in the White Horse kitchen, everyone waited for McLendon to help himself from the platters of eggs and bacon. When he finished his first cup of coffee, a second was poured without him having to ask. Conversation was muted. It was as if they all felt obligated to let McLendon speak first about whatever he liked. When he ventured that it seemed like a pleasant morning, there was immediate agreement that a finer day might never have dawned. His remark that he'd better leave for work resulted in everyone pushing back from the table. Gabrielle didn't help; she reveled in his discomfort. As McLendon left the hotel she clasped his hand, whispered, "My hero," in his ear, fluttered her eyelids dramatically, and laughed.

A crowd was gathered at the door of the feed store. As soon as McLendon walked up, it became obvious people had come to see him rather than shop. A young girl asked him to sign a copy of the paper "right over your picture." Several men requested handshakes. McLendon signed and shook, trying all the while to keep moving toward the door. He went inside and was greeted by a beaming Mayor Camp.

"Now, isn't this a fine thing?" the mayor asked. "Let's get these folks inside so they can demonstrate their respect for you by spending some money." And they did. As soon as it became clear McLendon was running the bowling alley, a long line formed beside the wooden lane. Almost everyone was more interested in getting close to McLendon than in bowling. Mayor Camp assured a considerable day's profits by having a clerk walk down the line collecting two bits a person before they reached McLendon where he stood beside the alley. Some paid and never bothered rolling a single ball. All they wanted was some words with the hero. McLendon did his best to keep the line moving, but it was hard. An extremely stout woman crushed him in a tight embrace and gushed, "I'd take you home, but my husband wouldn't let me keep you. I've never met such a gallant gentleman before."

"I promise there's nothing gallant about me," McLendon wheezed, trying to regain his breath. "Don't believe that story."

"If it's in the newspaper, it must be true," the woman said. "Will you take dinner with my family some night soon? I make an exquisite quince cobbler."

Camp overheard the exchange. When the woman departed — she was one of those who declined to bowl — the mayor sidled over to McLendon and said, "You need to let people believe what they want. What does it hurt? When they praise you, just say 'Thanks.' "

"I can't thank them for embarrassing me."

"Well, then, thank them for a rise in salary. You're bringing in so much business, I'm upping you from a dime to fifteen cents a game."

After that, McLendon was more patient. After a while, he began enjoying the compliments. The mayor was right — what did it hurt? The fact was, he'd nearly died at Adobe Walls, and now that he thought about it, he'd fought pretty damned bravely. He'd left the scene of battle with just the clothes on his back. It was only right that he received some recognition, and some money, from it afterward.

When his shift was over at six p.m., McLendon's pay totaled twelve dollars. He nodded to well-wishers on his walk back to the White Horse. After washing up and rereading the story in the *Herald* — perhaps Mac Fielding wasn't such a bad writer, after all — McLendon insisted on taking Gabrielle to dinner at Erin's House, by reputation the finest restaurant in Mountain View. Gabrielle wore a dark green dress accented with hair ribbons of the same shade; McLendon told her she was the most beautiful woman in the place and meant it. Then he and Gabrielle studied the menus — they weren't sure what *poulet au vinaigre* or

69

tournedos were. They laughed at their mutual confusion. It was a happy moment to share, one untainted by old memories.

The proprietor, a slender woman in an exquisite silk gown, came over to greet them. "Mr. McLendon, I'm Erin Rich. We're honored to have you here tonight. I only hope that our fare meets the approval of you and your lady."

"Let me introduce Miss Gabrielle Tirrito," McLendon said. Gabrielle asked what their hostess would recommend, and they accepted Miss Rich's suggestion of *poulet au vinaigre,* which turned out to be a very tasty dish of chicken and onions. Dessert was *torte,* which McLendon was pleased to learn meant cake. He insisted they have wine with dinner. Gabrielle drank two glasses and her cheeks flushed in a very fetching way. While they ate they chatted about inconsequential things, and for the first time since he'd arrived McLendon felt that Gabrielle was simply enjoying his company instead of judging him. For his part, he was careful to stick to inconsequential subjects rather than pressing her about the future. It was a memorable meal, capped by Miss Rich's refusal to present McLendon with a check.

"This is my small acknowledgment of your heroism," she said. "To me, you're

Washington at Valley Forge, or Davy Crockett at the Alamo."

Afterward they stopped at the Ritz. McLendon had brandy. Gabrielle, claiming some dizziness from the wine, drank coffee. A number of Mountain View's leading citizens came by their table to introduce themselves — livery operator Tim Flanagan, a member of the town council; Arthur and Amanda Scarcello, who owned a large dry-goods store; and Sheriff Jack Hove, who was enjoying an off-duty evening with his wife, Mamie.

"I'm glad to see that you're thinking of staying on," Hove said to McLendon. "We need your type of man to keep this town growing right."

"You seem to be doing fine without me," McLendon said. "But I thank you for the kind words."

After the sheriff moved along, Gabrielle said, "That was nicely done. You accepted the compliment with grace."

"This is strange for me," McLendon said. "I've spent these last years trying to avoid notice. Being the object of so much attention is somehow making me feel, I suppose, free, like a bad time is ending."

Gabrielle put down her coffee cup, reached across the small table, and took

McLendon's hand. She leaned forward and, quite daringly in such a public place, rested her forehead against his. He felt his pulse quicken. Was this the moment when she decided?

"Tell me again," Gabrielle murmured. "At Adobe Walls, how many hundreds of Indians did you shoot?" Then she laughed and told him, "It's been a wonderful evening, but my father needs his medicine. Please escort me back to the White Horse." On the way, she walked close enough to McLendon so that their shoulders brushed.

4

The next day, Brautigan prowled the streets and in the bars of Silver City. From a garrulous old man outside a seedy general store, he learned it would certainly take an experienced rider on a good horse perhaps six days to travel the one hundred eighty miles from there to Mountain View, or as many as ten if a dust storm blew over. Some of the terrain was rugged, but there was nothing impassible to a man who sat a good saddle. Brautigan knew himself to be only an adequate horseman. Maybe a week for him, then. Returning with McLendon in tow, the whiny shite howling and complaining every mile of the way, might take ten days. That length of time would require more supplies than saddlebags could handle. A wagon would provide needed cargo space, but wagons were so much slower — two weeks to Mountain View, perhaps as many as three on the way back to Silver

73

City. That was too long to be out in the open with a captive. He needed a base of operations in between, a place to resupply. But where?

The sun still blazed even though it was low in the sky. Brautigan felt parched. He went into a saloon called Painted Lady, which took its name from the crude portrait of a naked, splay-legged woman prominently displayed above its plank-and-crate bar. Painted Lady was crowded, but Brautigan easily made a place for himself at the bar. Even on the frontier, most other men automatically stepped aside for him. He ordered a beer and, as he took his first sip, became aware of a man on his right who loudly harangued listeners about some property he wanted to sell them.

"I speak of a garden in the desert, a veritable Eden," the fellow proclaimed. He had longish hair and an elegant mustache and Vandyke beard. "It's only a fool who won't jump in now while the best lots are still available. Plenty of water, fine soil, grass for grazing."

"Bullshit," someone said. "I been by there and seen for myself. You and your daddy and your brothers dug a trench or two off the Gila River and did some planting. Nothing much took. Now you want to sell lots sight unseen so you can make some money and get the hell away."

"How long ago was this? Six months? Well, then. We were just getting started. Now the land's transformed — my word as a gentleman on it. And besides its new abundance, I urge you to consider the location, just a few days' ride from Mountain View on a direct line between here and Silver City. A year from now, no more than two, there'll surely be a stage line passing through. That means more business opportunities. A lunch stand, perhaps. A blacksmith shop. There's simply no limit."

The described location caught Brautigan's attention. He looked at the salesman and realized there was something familiar about him. Brautigan had an excellent memory for faces and knew he'd seen the man somewhere before, perhaps only fleetingly. Where and when?

"Clantonville is the future," the fellow insisted. "It's not someplace that appears in the territory one day and disappears the next, like Beacon to Tucson's south or Glorious just west of Mountain View," and with those words Brautigan had it, he knew him. In Glorious on the night when he'd caught and lost Cash McLendon, this man with the Vandyke had jumped astride a mule and fled from the firefight. In his panic, he surely would not have noticed Brautigan. Here was opportunity.

Brautigan drank beer and waited. The man raved on about Clantonville for another ten minutes. His listeners gradually lost interest and turned away. Finally he was left standing alone, eyes glancing about for other potential customers. No one would look directly at him. "It's your loss," he said loudly. "You'll never have another chance like this." There was no response. He walked out into the street. Brautigan set his beer mug on the bar and followed.

"Hold on there," he said. The man stopped, turned, and flinched. His hands instinctively came up in front of his face. Brautigan always elicited defensive reactions, though not to this extent. "I heard you back in the saloon."

The man relaxed. "Fools is what they are. Are you looking for property? Ready to invest in the future?"

"In a way. I'm Brautigan."

"Ike Clanton."

"Pleased to make your acquaintance, Ike. Let me buy you a drink somewhere better than where we just were. A gentleman like yourself must prefer good whiskey."

Clanton shaped the point of his beard

with his fingers. "That's my fondness."

Brautigan took him to the Gilded Cage, and ordered them both Jim Beam bourbon. He occasionally wet his lips with his drink while Ike tossed down two before slowing on the third. In between gulps he prattled about Clantonville. A year earlier, just about the time that silver strikes resulted in Mountain View's first explosive growth, Ike, his brothers, and their father, Newman, acquired land some fifty miles to the southeast near the Gila River. Their intention was to establish a town where they could sell off lots to investors and still retain overall economic control.

"We've seen it done in other places, though of course we'll do it better," Clanton said. "We combine both wisdom and experience."

"You mentioned Glorious?" Brautigan asked, mostly to ascertain whether Clanton might remember him too.

"If me and my family had been running Glorious, it'd still be around," Clanton said. "Thing is, the big man there hired on a bunch of Meskins and so it all went to hell. Only white men in Clantonville, that's going to be my family's rule."

"Tell me more about Clantonville," Brautigan urged. "Not what you think it will be, but how it is right now."

Clantonville was already a little bit of paradise, Clanton claimed. There were just a handful of houses so far, put up by him and his daddy and his brothers, adobe and wood for now.

"When the money starts coming in we'll replace what we currently live in with fine stone mansions, bring the stone up from Mexico," he bragged. "The territorial governor himself won't enjoy such a fine abode."

Because of the river, water was no problem. They'd done some irrigation and planted experimental patches of cotton and tobacco. These had grown in well. Next they'd try corn. Even a fool could make a fine living as a Clantonville farmer.

"Do you get many people coming through?" Brautigan asked. "It would seem to me that passersby would be charmed by your place and you'd be overwhelmed with arrivals."

"Now, that's the ass end of it," Clanton said. "The location's pretty much perfect except for the damned reservation."

"Reservation?"

"The San Carlos agency. It's where they put Geronimo and most of the other Apache. It's somewhat between Clantonville and Mountain View, not directly, but the southern part sort of pushes down betwixt. So from Mountain View to us, you got to make a detour, adds I guess ten miles, half a day." Brautigan looked into Clanton's eyes, and Ike blinked. "Well, maybe twenty miles, a full day. Depends on your horse and the weather."

If there was pursuit, Brautigan knew, delays could be critical. "If the Indians are at peace, can't a man just ride through part of the agency? Save time that way?"

Clanton swallowed the last dregs of whiskey in his glass and looked hopefully at Brautigan. He was slightly drunk already and some of his words were slurred. Brautigan nodded at the bartender and decided this was Clanton's last drink. He wanted him talkative, but not incoherent.

"Two reasons," Clanton said. " 'Paches, for one. Once in a while, some of the braves get frisky. But the main thing is, they got a new agent at San Carlos. Name's John Clum. Damned stickler for rules, puts me in mind of the hard-ass sheriff in Mountain View. Treaty says no white man crosses agency land without special permission from the agent himself, and Clum's not generally tolerant of violators. Sics the damn Indians on them, is what I've heard. 'Cause of that, we don't get the people we should

79

coming our way from Mountain View. Clum wasn't such a sumbitch, Clantonville'd already be full of people. What will happen is, like all the other agents Clum won't last there long. We'll get someone more sensible in his place. Then anyone can just ride through San Carlos as they please and things will improve for us."

"Just now, though. If someone was careful, maybe riding through the agency after dark, are the odds good he'd escape detection?"

Clanton's throat convulsed; he emitted a loud, wet belch and grinned slyly. "Might could, if he knew his way or had a guide who did."

"Someone such as you?"

Clanton belched again, softer this time. "I been there enough. You thinking of giving it a try?"

Brautigan slapped his palm on the table, noting Clanton wince at the explosive thump. Good. He wanted to keep this fool off balance. "Tell me, Ike. Are you a man to be trusted?"

"I am indeed. No man's word is more solid."

"I see. And now I have some thinking to do. Will you perhaps join me for dinner and further conversation, then? At, say, eight?

I'm staying at the Estes Hotel. Where may I call for you?"

"Oh, I'm a man requiring little in the way of comforts. I'm bunking at the livery beside my horse."

Better and better. Clanton had no money for a room. "Come by the Estes at eight, then. I'll stand you to a fine repast."

Brautigan spent the next few hours in his dingy hotel room, brushing away flies and thinking. The problem wasn't subduing McLendon. The fellow was a talker, not a fighter. Capture and extraction were the initial issues. The Mountain View sheriff sounded like a sharp sort of man. The longer Brautigan had to spend in town spotting McLendon, then finding just the right place and time to lay hands on him with a minimum of notice, the more likely it was he'd come to the lawman's attention, and that would make the job much harder. Brautigan was confident he could fight his way out of any situation, but that would bring the kind of attention he didn't want. But if he knew exactly where to come in and quietly nab his man, then slip away . . . and now he might have met just the right man to help him do it. And if, afterward, Ike Clanton proved troublesome, he could be easily eliminated.

Clanton appeared at the Estes Hotel a good ten minutes before eight. Some hay was stuck to the seat of his pants and the back of his hair — he'd been napping in his horse's stall, sleeping off the effects of afternoon whiskey. Brautigan took him to a place offering thick beefsteaks. Ike ordered the biggest one on the menu and tore into it, chewing loudly with his mouth open. He talked while he chewed. Bits of beef spewed on the table and down the front of his shirt. Brautigan ate his own steak quietly. He let Ike yammer. Clanton bragged about personal prowess on many levels — as a gunman, hand-to-hand fighter, businessman, and lover. He and his family had suffered some bad financial luck, but Clantonville was going to make their fortunes, he was sure.

"I'm a man of some destiny," Clanton declared. "A hundred years from now, more, ever'body'll recall Ike Clanton's name."

Brautigan nodded. "Perhaps, Ike. Your steak is almost gone. Will you have another?"

"No, though it's tempting. What I would like, that cherry pie on the counter looks tasty. A slice of it, if you please, and perhaps a brandy to follow. You're treating me to a

82

slap-up meal. My ma has passed, but should you come see us in Clantonville, my sister Hettie'll serve you one to rival it."

"I believe I may do that. I'd like to see Clantonville."

Ike finished his steak and dug into pie, piling crust and gummy filling high on his fork. "Clantonville, and then across the San Carlos agency? To Mountain View or somewhere near, and in secret? What's your game, Brautigan?"

"After you've finished your pie, let's get a brandy bottle and go back to my room to talk. There are too many ears out in public."

Clanton winked. "I understand you. We're men of mystery, you and me. Clever fellows. Make it good brandy."

Brautigan called the waitress over. She balked at selling him a bottle and two glasses, but was persuaded with a greenback that left plenty of change as a gratuity. She brought his purchases to him in a cloth sack. The bottle and glasses rattled together and made tinkling sounds as Brautigan carried them out of the restaurant.

The hotel was a few blocks down the street. Brautigan and Clanton had walked only a few yards when three men stepped into their path. They were hard-looking and carried ax handles. Though their intentions were obviously malevolent, no one else on the street paid attention. Such goings-on were routine in Silver City.

"Hold there, Ike Clanton," the trio's leader snarled. "We'll have a word."

Clanton drew back. He was about to run, but one of the accosters moved behind him.

Brautigan took a step forward, but the toughs didn't quail. They were clearly experienced brawlers and confident in their prowess and superior numbers.

"Whoever you are, fellow, step aside," the leader said. "This business is between us and Clanton."

Brautigan said, "Oh?" in a reasonably cordial tone that would have panicked anyone who had previous dealings with him.

"Our money, Ike Clanton. You lost seventy dollars in last night's poker game and swore you'd go to the bank and get us our money today. Sun's set, and we've not been paid what we're due. So now seventy dollars on the spot, or we take it out of your hide."

"I promise I'll pay," Clanton said. His voice quavered. "I had business dealings today, long discussions, and the matter slipped my mind. I'll go to the bank and pay you tomorrow without fail."

"The money, Clanton."

Ike whined to Brautigan, "The cards were

marked." Behind them, the third assailant stepped closer.

"Marked cards cancel any debt," Brautigan said conversationally. "So that's the end of this."

"Then you'll get it, too," the lead tough declared. He raised his ax handle.

Brautigan gently set down the cloth bag with the brandy bottle and glasses. Then he leaned back past Ike Clanton. His huge hand gripped the shoulder of the man behind them and in one motion yanked him forward and threw him into the other two. All three toughs staggered back off balance. Brautigan moved forward and delivered quick punches to two of their heads, sending them sprawling and unconscious. The third man, the ringleader, regained his composure, smashed his ax handle against Brautigan's back, and stood back to watch the much bigger man fall. But Brautigan didn't budge. It was as though he hadn't felt the blow. Almost delicately, he grasped the remaining attacker by the collar, raising him up on his toes. He drew back his fist and hammered it into the man's abdomen, targeting the area near the liver. The fellow gasped rather than screamed, his body paralyzed by the blow. Brautigan dropped him onto the street. Some passersby had stopped to watch. He said to them, "They're only hurt a little. Give them air." He stooped to pick up his bag of bottle and glasses, then took Clanton by the arm and led him on to the Estes Hotel.

Ike Clanton shook for several minutes after Brautigan seated him on one end of the bed. He poured him some brandy, but Ike's hand trembled and he spilled as much as he got in his mouth. Brautigan sat on the other side of the bed and waited. Though he himself never felt fear — caution was a far different thing — he knew it took some time to subside in others.

Finally Clanton stopped shaking. He looked wonderingly at Brautigan and asked, "Don't your back hurt?"

It did, a little, but Brautigan simply ignored pain. It was an annoyance, but nothing of real concern, like too much cold or heat. "I'm all right," he said.

"What you did —"

"Was nothing much."

Clanton held out his glass for a refill of brandy. He drank most of it down in long, loud gulps. Color returned to his face. "I could have taken those three myself, and was about to," he said. "You beat me to it, is all. Though you did some fine work with your fists."

"Obliged."

"That one behind us, you didn't even look when you snatched him."

Brautigan nodded.

Clanton said, "I wish you'd killed them."

"There was no need," Brautigan said. He drank a little brandy from his own glass and watched Clanton, waiting.

After moments of awkward silence, Ike asked, "So what's your game? With your questions about the San Carlos agency and all."

"If we speak of this, you'll need to stay mum about it, Ike. I'm not a man who warns twice."

Clanton gulped air, then brandy. "My word as a gentleman."

"Then I'll tell you straight. There's someone in Mountain View I need to collect and take elsewhere, with no fuss as I do it. Discretion is the thing."

"There's a grudge involved? Getting even?"

"That need not concern you. More brandy?"

Clanton held out his glass and Brautigan poured. Ike asked, "How do I play in this?"

"Are you well known in Mountain View? Do you go there often to tout your Clantonville lots?"

Clanton looked sour. "Very little. They think themselves high rollers there, that their shit don't stink. A man goes in to talk a little business and the damned sheriff runs him right out."

"But you've been there?" Brautigan asked. "You know your way around at least a little?"

"I'd say so."

"And no one would be surprised if you came again, talking up Clantonville, seeking investors, making your way about town?"

"Not a bit."

Brautigan smiled, square teeth gleaming in the smoky light of an oil lamp by the bedside. "What would your family say if you brought a new acquaintance to Clantonville for a visit, just for a while? Not to stay permanent, but willing to pay what we'll call rent for the temporary privilege of a roof and meals?"

"You'd be welcome."

"And if this person had someone with him, someone reluctant to be there?"

"That'd be no concern if the money was sufficient."

"Would they ask many questions, your family? Will they let a man tend to business without interference? Perhaps even lend a hand if needed, for additional recompense, of course."

"If you're a friend of the Clantons, we can be trusted in all things. We're businesspeople and stick to our agreements."

Brautigan took a small pouch from his pocket and spilled some gold coins onto the bedspread. They glittered in the lamplight. He picked them up and let them trickle through his thick fingers. Ike licked his lips as he stared at the gold.

"And you, Ike. If I paid you well, would you undertake a task for me? Work of a nature that must remain discreet, never to be discussed then or afterward?"

"Yes," Ike said. "I'm a man of considerable discretion."

"All right, then. We'll start with this — here's seventy dollars. Tomorrow, seek out those bruised debtors of yours and pay them in full. After all, we don't want you having to watch over your shoulder for them the next time you're in Silver City. The seventy's just a down payment to you. There should be much more to come."

"Much more for doing what?"

"Helping me nab a man, and then get him from Mountain View back here to Silver City with a minimum of notice. I'll do the heavy work. Your task is to make some arrangements, do some guiding through the agency land and some seeking out in Mountain View. After that, perhaps another day of guide work. Nothing beyond your abilities and intellect."

"Sounds promising."

Brautigan gestured for Clanton to lean forward. He said, "Tell me, Ike. Have you any knowledge of a man named Cash McLendon?"

Ike stiffened. "You say Cash McLendon? Who used to be in Glorious? He's the one you're after?"

"That's right."

Clanton grinned so wide it seemed his face might split. "If you have bad intentions toward Cash McLendon, then I'm surely your man."

5

Ten days after the *Herald* published its story about McLendon and the battle of Adobe Walls, he could walk the streets of Mountain View and not be constantly accosted by admirers. But the effect of the publicity still lingered. Business at the feed store bowling alley remained brisk, with some patrons clearly there not for sport but the opportunity to spend time near a hero. When McLendon visited the barber for a haircut and beard trim, he was ushered to the front of the line. Now that he had money, there was often no need of it. In saloons, people vied to buy his drinks; in restaurants, at least coffee, and sometimes full meals, were on the house. In return, McLendon favored those treating him with a colorful tale or two about the battle. He was always careful to praise the heroism of his fellow fighters and not exaggerate his own exploits.

Several community leaders took McLendon aside to question him about future plans. If he did stay in Mountain View, he surely didn't want to keep on working at the feed store bowling alley. That was beneath a man of his stature. The president of the town bank offered twenty dollars a month just for the privilege of listing McLendon on its board of directors — "That will surely attract significant new accounts." Mayor Camp, clearly unwilling to lose his prominent employee, described potential partnerships — "Stay with me a year or two, and who knows? Maybe there'll be Camp and McLendon Feed Stores Inc. locations all over the territory. We can work out the details as we move forward." Two members of the town council strongly suggested that McLendon settle in Mountain View, stand for council election himself, and then, after a term or two, run for territorial office.

McLendon thanked them all. He said, and meant, that it was gratifying to be held in such high esteem. But he still intended to go on to California. Everyone said that they hoped he'd change his mind, and McLendon let them think this was possible. It was intoxicating to feel *wanted,* especially since Gabrielle still had not chosen between him and Joe Saint. Still, he thought her decision would come soon, and McLendon was becoming increasingly certain what that decision would be. Despite her mocking response to the story in the *Herald,* public reaction to the story — the admiration, the fine job offers — demonstrated to Gabrielle the potential Cash McLendon had to become someone of position and respect in a community. There were immediate rewards for her too. A few nights after the *Herald* article, he and Gabrielle dined in the home of Orville and Pauline Hancock, the unquestioned social leaders among Mountain View citizenry. Orville Hancock managed the largest area silver mine for the San Francisco conglomerate that owned it. He controlled hundreds of local jobs and thus a significant share of the Mountain View economy. His wife, Pauline, oversaw the town's most prestigious social functions — she organized every cotillion, fund-raising extravaganza, and holiday gala, and kept ironclad control over who was permitted to attend.

The Hancocks' dinner invitation came in the form of a card delivered to the White Horse Hotel on Wednesday afternoon. Its envelope was addressed to "Mr. C. McLendon, late of Adobe Walls." The card itself was embossed at the top with a simple "H."

The impeccably handwritten message read:

Dear Mr. McLendon:
Please forgive the presumption of an invitation from strangers. My husband Orville and I wonder if you might be free for dinner in our home tomorrow night at eight p.m. It would be our pleasure to host an American hero. Please bring the lovely young woman we saw you with the other evening at Erin's House restaurant. No need for special dress, this will be an informal occasion. Do come. We would so love to make your acquaintance.

Yours sincerely,
Pauline Hancock (Mrs. O. Hancock).

When McLendon showed the invitation to Gabrielle, she panicked.

"I can't go to Pauline Hancock's house," she said. "I don't have anything to wear. I wouldn't know what to say to her. Go by yourself."

"She specifically invited you," McLendon said. "See? Right here. 'The lovely young woman we saw you with.' What's the problem? You're the one who's always told me that everybody's the same."

"I believe it, but that doesn't mean they

94

do. I'm Italian. I work at a hotel. People like them call that 'being in service.' Once she finds out, she'll probably ask me to leave."

"Then I'll leave with you. But it won't happen. The Hancocks are going to love you. Everyone who meets you feels that way."

Gabrielle chewed her lower lip. McLendon was shocked. In all the time he'd known her, he'd never seen Gabrielle act unsure of herself. His immediate inclination was to decline the Hancocks' invitation — he'd had more than enough dinners with wealthy people in the past — but her reaction signaled a chance to demonstrate to Gabrielle just how much he loved her in a particularly meaningful way. McLendon walked over, put his hands on her shoulders, and kissed her cheek. "You're an amazing woman, the most wonderful one in the world. Come with me. I'll be proud to be seen with you, just as I always am. These people think they're having dinner with somebody special, and they're right. But the special one is you, not me."

"You mean it?" Gabrielle asked. "I'll try. But if it's uncomfortable we'll leave as soon as we politely can, do you promise?"

"I promise. Just keep a straight face if they start telling me what a hero I am."

McLendon knew enough about society customs to send a return note to the Hancocks:

Mr. Cash McLendon and Miss Gabrielle Tirrito accept your generous invitation with pleazure, and will call tomorrow night at eight p.m. promptly. Your servant, C. McLendon.

He wrote the note on White Horse stationery, and asked Gabrielle to check the spelling. She pointed out that *pleasure* was spelled with an *s* rather than a *z,* so he had to rewrite it.

"You never could spell," she said. He thought he discerned a new, fonder tone to her voice.

Thursday afternoon McLendon left the bowling alley early. He went to Scarcello Dry Goods and bought a suit, a dress shirt, and a tie. His purchases totaled almost thirty dollars, but he reasoned that the nice clothes were worth it. He'd need them in California.

McLendon returned to the White Horse, bathed and shaved in a tub of steaming water, put on his new clothes, and went to the lobby to wait for Gabrielle. He caught his breath as she came down the stairs. Ga-

96

brielle wore a simple gray dress that accentuated her dark eyes. Tonight her hair was pulled back behind her head, and there were no ribbons woven in it. She looked lovely, just different.

"I thought you'd wear your special green dress," he said.

"Mrs. Hancock saw me in it at the restaurant. I won't want her thinking I have only the one. This is my church dress. She'll never have seen it because she'd never set foot in a Catholic service. You look handsome in your suit."

They walked a few blocks to the Hancocks' home, which was two-story brick. Orville Hancock himself opened the door and ushered them in. Pauline Hancock exclaimed over Gabrielle's dress and said drinks would be served in the sitting room. There they sipped sherry, nibbled bits of cheese and fruit served by a Mexican woman in black dress and white apron, and engaged in the kind of icebreaking conversation McLendon remembered from soirees in St. Louis. Orville Hancock observed that the usual heavy rains of late summer had never arrived, so workdays hadn't been lost at the mine. Pauline said she wished the wind and blowing dust would stay away, too, and commiserated with Gabrielle about the difficulty of keeping hair and dresses clean under such conditions. By the time dinner was served — poached chicken with rice and vegetables — Gabrielle was at ease and McLendon felt proud as she suggested some books she hoped would soon be added to the town library.

"Longfellow of course, and Fenimore Cooper although he portrays women so badly," she said. "Cooper was perhaps the first American author of widespread note. And I don't think any library deserves the name if it lacks novels by Charles Dickens."

"You're fond of Dickens? So am I," Pauline Hancock exclaimed. "*Martin Chuzzlewit* — now, there's my favorite!"

"The Pecksniffs and the Spottletoes," Gabrielle agreed. "And Dickens's vision of America. Priceless."

Orville Hancock suggested to McLendon that they leave the women to talk literature. "I've some reasonable port you might enjoy," he said. "We'll have that and burn a few cigars in my study."

Once seated and served by the same Mexican woman, Hancock asked McLendon, "Are you certain you want to move on to California, which is what I've heard? There's opportunity here."

"I'm sure there is. But I believe California's the right place for me. San Francisco, probably, or perhaps San Diego. Despite my misadventures at Adobe Walls, I'm more a man of the city than the frontier. So that's where I mean to go."

Hancock puffed his cigar and exuded a cloud of pleasant-smelling smoke. "With Miss Tirrito, I presume?"

"If she'll have me."

"Intelligent young woman, I can tell. She's made quite the impression on my wife. Well, if you can't be persuaded to stay here, let me say this: my mining operation here is under the auspices of the Smead Company out of San Francisco. Smead's always on the lookout for men of experience and talent. If you don't object, I'll contact some people there, make them aware of you. Company's involved in lots of things besides mining. I think you'd find employment there rewarding."

"I'd be grateful, Mr. Hancock."

"Call me Orville. Consider it done, and when you take your leave of town I'll send a letter of introduction along with you. Now, I must know — what did old Satanta look like as he and his savages charged you at Adobe Walls?"

When McLendon and Gabrielle left an hour later, she and Pauline Hancock exchanged warm farewells. On the walk back to the White Horse, Gabrielle said, "Mrs. Hancock is forming a committee to raise funds for a permanent library building. She asked if, should they be successful, I might consider serving as librarian."

"What was your response?"

Gabrielle stopped and turned to McLendon, looking hard into his eyes. He was medium height and she was tall, so she didn't have to peer up. "Don't take this to be any form of commitment."

McLendon's pulse galloped. "I won't, but what?"

"A move to California — for three, not two, with my father included. In your current position, and with what I could contribute from my salary, how long would you estimate it would take to accumulate the necessary funds?"

"Stage and train fares would total a few hundred dollars. A place to live in the city, costs of setting up a household. Let's say five or six hundred. So if I continue to earn what I currently do with Mayor Camp, maybe four months, possibly three if we economize."

"Once there, you'll have to find employment. That could take some time."

McLendon told her of Orville Hancock's

offer to recommend him to the Smead Company in San Francisco. "I think San Francisco would be an exciting place. But if you didn't like living there, Smead has branch offices all over the state. San Diego, San Bernardino. We could find somewhere suitable."

"Well," Gabrielle said. She thought a moment. "I'm sure San Francisco would appeal."

They resumed walking. McLendon said, "You never told me your response to Mrs. Hancock regarding the librarian position."

"Oh, yes. I told her I was flattered, but that I was uncertain how much longer I'd remain in Mountain View. I'll say good night now and go upstairs. I have a great deal to think about — stop smiling! I told you, don't assume anything."

He tried not to, but his belief Gabrielle was about to decide in his favor was reinforced a few days later when a furious Joe Saint confronted him outside Camp's Feed Store. It was just after six p.m. and McLendon had finished work for the day. He was anxious to see Gabrielle at the hotel staff supper in the kitchen. She'd been to dinner with Saint the night before. Now the scrawny schoolteacher with the thick glasses and thinning hair quivered with fury as he

101

hissed at McLendon, "You're a bastard. Despicable, low-life scum."

"Hold on," McLendon said. "Don't do this here in the street."

"I don't care. Everybody else thinks you're such a hero, but I know what you really are."

"You're a schoolteacher, Joe. You don't want any of your students to see you like this."

Saint made a visible effort to control himself. "All right. Behind the building, then."

McLendon wondered if Saint meant to physically assault him. It seemed unthinkable; in the past the former sheriff of Glorious had always avoided violence, even seemed terrified of it. "Calm down, Joe. Let's go and talk over a drink, like gentlemen."

Saint glared; the thick lenses of his glasses magnified his eyes. "You're no gentleman. Behind the building. Don't worry, I won't hit you. She'd hate me if I did that. But I'm going to speak my mind."

Because the building itself was so long, with extensions for the bowling alley and grain bins, the area behind Camp Feed Store was largely out of sight to anyone passing on the street. There was a raised dock where shipments from Tucson and

Florence were unloaded, and rising from the dock a narrow stairway leading to a small second-story office where Hope Camp kept documents and cash in a safe. In recent days, Camp had asked McLendon to count receipts after the store closed, and lock them in the second-floor safe. That let the Mountain View mayor get home a little sooner. McLendon obliged, even though it extended his own workday. Now Saint walked up to the dock; McLendon followed.

"Twice," Saint said. "First Glorious, now here. She and I could have been happy, would have been. You had your chance in St. Louis and threw it away. Why didn't you let her alone after that?"

"I couldn't," McLendon said. "It's that simple."

"All you bring is trouble. In Glorious, that killer came after you. I saved you that night."

"You did."

"I wish I hadn't. I should have let him have you. Gotten you away from her for good. Now you're coming between us again. What a fool I was."

"Look, Joe," McLendon said. "I'm not claiming any of this has been fair to you. I'm sorry for that."

Saint hawked and spit. The glob of saliva splattered between McLendon's feet. "I don't believe for a minute you're sorry. You show up here claiming you're a hero —"

"I never claimed that. A fool wrote it that way in his newspaper."

"Were you even there at that place, Adobe Walls? Or are you making it all up?"

"I was there. I wish I hadn't been."

"The Indians should have killed you." Tears began to well in Saint's eyes. "Somewhere, sometime, you're coming to a bad end. And you'll drag her down with you, I know it. Don't do it, McLendon, she deserves better. If you really care about her, go away and leave her be. That'd be the best thing."

"If Gabrielle tells me to go, I will."

Saint pulled a handkerchief from his pocket, took off his glasses, and wiped his eyes. He put the glasses back on and said in a sad voice, "She won't. I know what she's going to do."

McLendon said eagerly, "Has she said something to you?"

Saint sighed. "No, she hasn't. Not yet. But she's getting ready to. I know her and I can tell. You got her head filled with dreams about life in California and you being a changed man, which I know you're not. I wish I was different. If I was, I'd kill you myself just to save her from what's coming.

6

The day before he headed out with Ike Clanton, Brautigan shopped in Silver City. With Ike in tow, he started at a dry-goods store, where he purchased trail clothes — denim pants, a broadcloth shirt, and a hat with a wide brim. When he worked in cities, Brautigan always wore dark suits. He felt comfortable wearing them. But out on the trail, such attire might attract notice. The shopkeeper made several bustling trips to his storeroom. It wasn't easy finding items large enough to fit his towering customer.

Brautigan also purchased a good length of rope, several canteens, and a Winchester rifle. The Winchester was Clanton's suggestion. On previous assignments for Rupert Douglass, Brautigan never armed himself. It wasn't necessary. His boots and fists were enough. He believed they would be all he needed to take Cash McLendon, who couldn't fight worth a damn. But Ike argued that not openly carrying a gun might attract trouble.

"We pass any bad fellows on our way north, why, if they see you aren't heeled, even at your size they might take you for an easy mark," Clanton said. "I don't doubt you'd prevail, but you've also emphasized the need for stealth. So as a precaution, arm yourself."

"A fair point," Brautigan conceded. He thought that perhaps Clanton wasn't a complete fool. He purchased the Winchester and some ammunition. Ike wanted him to buy a handgun and holster, too, but Brautigan demurred.

Brautigan and Clanton moved on to the same livery where Ike stabled his horse. There Brautigan bought two horses and a mule. For his own mount, Brautigan chose a rawboned sorrel that seemed capable of accommodating his heft. The second horse was smaller and more docile. Clanton complained, "That one appears slow-footed to me."

"Slow-footed suits my needs exactly," Brautigan replied. "It's for my companion on the return trip."

Ike thought about it a moment, then said, "Oh, yes. Now I see."

The mule was needed as a pack animal.

Clanton explained that they had to take along a cask of water in addition to full canteens — "There'll be waterless stretches, and we'll not want to go thirsty" — as well as sacks of feed for the animals, since much of the area they'd be crossing had little to offer in the way of forage.

Then, with Clanton's help, Brautigan bought riding tack for the horses and extra saddlebags for the mule. After that, it was back to the dry-goods store to purchase canned fruit and tomatoes, which would provide both solid food and liquids. Clanton asked why he didn't acquire a coffeepot, frying pan, and bacon.

"We don't need such fripperies," Brautigan said. "Water and canned food will do us fine."

"I like my coffee and bacon," Ike groused. "Well, I've got a pot and pan in my own saddlebag. Being a gentleman of considerable generosity, I'll share with you at mealtime if you go ahead and purchase the fixings."

Brautigan also bought a blanket, and Clanton reminded him to buy some packets of matches — Lucifers, he called them.

"Even in late August it can get frosty at night in the open," Ike said. "At least a small campfire is a necessity."

They carried their purchases back to the livery and loaded the saddlebags. "Now we're almost outfitted," Clanton said. "A stop by the saloon and the task will be complete."

"Saloon?" Brautigan asked.

"Yes, for a bottle or two. Something to take the edge off after a hard day along the trail."

"No more whiskey for you, Ike, once we head out."

"I believe I must insist."

"Must you?" Brautigan looked calmly at Clanton, who tried and failed to stare back.

"All right," Ike grumbled. "But it's a hard thing not to allow a man a drink when he's proving to be a loyal friend."

"When it's over you can drink all you please."

"I'll hold you to that, especially if it's at your expense."

Brautigan rummaged in his pocket and extracted a few coins. He handed them to Clanton and said, "Here's two dollars. Go have yourself some final refreshment, but not so much that you're muzzy in the morning. I mean to depart early, get in some distance before the worst heat. Are you certain it's no more than five days to your family's outpost?"

"Most likely. Might be four if we ride especially hard."

"We'll see. Go have your libations, Ike. I'll meet you at the livery tomorrow morning, six o'clock prompt."

After Clanton scuttled off to the Painted Lady, Brautigan went to the telegraph office. He sent a terse message to his boss: "MOVING ON TARGET NOW. YOU WILL HEAR FROM ME APPROX TWO WEEKS." He thought a moment and added, "GOOD RESULT ANTICIPATED."

Then Brautigan searched for Sheriff Wolfe. He found him in the Gilded Cage, counting receipts outside the whores' workrooms.

"I leave tomorrow and expect to return in about two weeks," Brautigan told him. "I'll need you to have the papers ready. It's my intention to get clear of this region as quickly as possible."

"I'll have what you need," Wolfe said. "Just you be certain to hand over the remainder of my fee in return for the documents. If you attempt to cheat me, then big as you are, I've got some boys to lay you low."

Brautigan shrugged. "I keep my bargains. Be certain that you do the same. Two weeks, or a day or so either side of that."

After a good dinner, Brautigan returned to the Estes Hotel, where he informed Emily Estes that he'd be leaving in the morning.

"It will be quite early," he said. "Before six, I'm sure. Shall I leave my key here at the desk for you?"

"I rise much earlier, Mr. Brautigan. If you like, I'll prepare some breakfast for you before you depart."

"Don't trouble yourself. I'll leave the key."

Estes said hopefully, "Will you be returning to town? Perhaps I should keep a room available?"

"No, if I return to Silver City, it will be of a very brief nature. I have a short journey ahead, and then business calls me home."

"To Boston, you mean?"

"Certainly. Boston."

Up in his room, Brautigan sat on the edge of his bed and thought through his plan, trying to discern any omissions or inconsistencies. After an hour, he turned in and fell asleep immediately.

Ike Clanton was badly hungover in the morning. Brautigan had expected it, and didn't mind. It would keep the voluble fellow quiet during the first few hours of their ride. They headed north out of town at first light. Brautigan led the extra horse and Ike tied the mule's reins to his saddle horn.

112

They made steady progress. Brautigan had occasionally ridden horses in St. Louis, but never for an extended period. His current lanky mount had a somewhat uneven stride and it took him some time to become accustomed to it. He soon felt discomfort in his seat and crotch, but, as always, Brautigan simply ignored the pain. He carefully studied the terrain. There were low mountains looming ahead, but Clanton promised there were passes through them. Of greater concern were the crevices, eight- or ten-foot drop-offs seemingly out of nowhere, apparently level ground that abruptly dropped precipitously down. There weren't many of these, but the two riders had to be constantly on the lookout for them, Brautigan more than Clanton until Ike's hangover finally receded. By the time they stopped to rest the animals and share some tinned peaches, Clanton was recovered enough to start conversing, and his chosen topic was Cash McLendon. To Brautigan's surprise, Ike showed no interest in why Brautigan was pursuing the man. Instead, Clanton launched into a litany of McLendon's sins against him. Apparently, back in Glorious, McLendon tried to cheat Ike out of some livery business, and also grossly insulted Ike's honor as a gentleman in front of the whole town.

"For some time I've been hoping to square accounts with the sumbitch," Clanton said. "He's a lowlife for certain."

"But he'll remember you, Ike?"

"To be sure. My fear is he'll run at the sight of me and so be lost to you."

"Then we'll hope he won't run."

"Never fear. If he does, I'll prevent him. My word on that."

It grew terribly hot during the afternoon. Both men were soaked in sweat. It was necessary to make occasional stops so the horses and mule could briefly rest. When they rode they had to pick their way through clumps of cacti and other prickly plants. Occasional crevices forced detours, sometimes of as much as half a mile. They spooked a few rabbits, spotted some snakes, and once, in the distance, spied what appeared to be elk, but did not encounter any human beings.

"Not much traveling between here and Mountain View," Clanton observed. "Of course, that'll change as Clantonville grows and somebody reasonable gets put in charge of the 'Pache reservation. A year from now, maybe two, and there'll be a good trail from Silver City, with stages passing up and down 'round the clock."

"Perhaps. For now, I'm glad of scant company."

As dusk approached, they stopped and made camp. It was too dangerous to try to continue after dark. A fall into a crevice could cripple a mount or rider. They ground-tethered the horses and mule. There was some patchy grass where they'd stopped, so the animals could graze. The men gave the livestock sparing drinks from the cask, using their upside-down hats as buckets.

"We'll cross a small crick tomorrow and the beasts can drink their fill then," Clanton said. For a moment Brautigan didn't understand; then he translated "crick" as "creek."

Clanton built a fire. Brautigan watched him stack larger sticks around a small pile of twigs. Ike crumbled some cigarette papers around the twigs and lit the paper with a match. Flames curled up from the papers, then the twigs. Clanton blew softly on the twigs, and soon the sticks blazed.

"Coffee and bacon for supper," Ike announced. Afterward he scoured the frying pan with sand — "We don't want to be wasting water" — and stored it back in his saddlebag. After gathering more sticks to feed the fire through the night, the two men wrapped themselves in their blankets. Clan-

115

ton wanted to talk, something about the near-magical growth of crops along the river in Clantonville, but Brautigan said he wanted to sleep. Soon Ike was snoring. It took Brautigan longer than usual to drop off; his lower body ached from the long day in the saddle. He woke twice, once when Clanton rose to put more sticks on the fire and again when there was rustling a few dozen yards away in the dark.

"Night varmint," Clanton called from his blankets. " 'Pache or bad man, we'd never have heard anything."

On the second day's ride, the land flattened. There were no more crevices, so they made better time. It was still very hot, and Brautigan's discomfort in the saddle increased. Clanton chattered constantly. In early afternoon they found the narrow creek. The shallow water looked dirty to Brautigan, but the horses and mule drank thirstily. So did Ike. Brautigan looked around, memorizing landmarks. Most of the area looked identical — a bluff here and there, scattered patches of sharp-tipped vegetation, low-slung cacti. But there were some variations — a lone towering saguaro, an oddly shaped boulder. With these committed to memory, Brautigan bent down and filled canteens.

Late in the day they spied riders well to the north, four of them. "Whites and not 'Paches," Clanton assured Brautigan. "Likely prospectors. Still, you might pull out that Winchester, have it obvious and handy, should they drift over for a word." But the other riders kept going and were soon lost to sight. "Out in the open like this, long as it's light, alert men are seldom taken by surprise," Ike added. "It's just a matter of keeping our eyes open."

On the third day they eased through the mountain pass. Clanton said the mountains were called the Pinalenos. High cliffs towered over them; for a while, there were blessed shafts of shade. The air was cooler, and though the incline was gradual, Brautigan eventually felt his ears pop a little from the pressure. They didn't encounter anyone else. Toward dark a rabbit rushed in front of their horses. Clanton yanked out his pistol, aimed, fired, and missed. The loud *crack* echoed off the stone walls to either side. That night they ate canned tomatoes along with the few bites of bacon that were left.

"You want, tomorrow you could practice with that Winchester," Clanton suggested. "Just to get your shooting eye in, and all. There'll be plenty of room, no danger from ricochet."

"I see no need," Brautigan said. "If all goes well, there'll be no gunplay."

"You ought to take a few shots," Clanton insisted. "I'm handy with a rifle myself, and could offer some valuable instruction."

"No need," Brautigan repeated. In any fight, he trusted his steel-tipped boots more than a firearm.

On the fourth day the land completely flattened, though a few peaks rose ahead. Ike predicted they'd reach Clantonville by noon the next day. He spent several hours rhapsodizing about the beauty of the settlement.

"We got the Gila River bubbling right past, and me and Pa and my brothers have dug a good deep ditch for irrigation," Clanton said. "When I call it paradise, that's the correct term. When you see it, you might not want to leave." When Brautigan didn't reply, Ike went on. "When we arrive, how do you want me to describe your business? What manner of arrangement have you in mind?"

Brautigan was hurting. The insides of his thighs were rubbed raw after days of riding. Some cactus needles were stuck deep in his left hand. They were too small to cut in after; he'd have to let them work their own way out. Wind blew dust into his eyes, nose, and mouth. He was very thirsty, but tired of the warm, brackish fluid left in their canteens and water cask. Still, he gave no outward appearance of discomfort. He never did.

"We'll keep things simple," he told Clanton. "In exchange for a fee, your family will put me up for a night or two, and perhaps let me use a building to hold someone on a temporary basis."

"Cash McLendon, you mean. I can't wait to spit in that bastard's face."

"None of that. And after I'm gone with him, you and yours will forget we were ever among you. That's no matter who comes asking — not that Mountain View sheriff, not other lawmen, not anyone. Your father, brothers, other family, they'll all give their word on that and keep silent if needed?"

"Here, now," Ike said indignantly. "I've already assured you that all the Clantons are the soul of discretion."

Brautigan pulled off his hat and wiped a forearm across his sweaty brow. The gesture emphasized the enormity of his fist. "That had better be the case. If any of your family abuse my trust, it'll go badly for all of you without exception. Should you and I negotiate further payment now?"

119

Clanton looked abashed. "Pa speaks for the family. You need to work out Clantonville doings with him. No matter what, though, I'm your daisy for dealings in Mountain View, whatever you're of a mind to be doing there. But in Clantonville it's Pa."

The next morning dawned somewhat dimmer; there were gray clouds overhead.

"Hope the rain holds off," Clanton said as they rode. "This part of the country, floods are a problem. There's some dirt right underfoot, but beneath that's rock and water can't soak in. We get a bad storm, we might have to swim, though that's been true ever since we left Silver City."

"Are you exaggerating?" Brautigan asked. "I've no time for delays, weather-induced or otherwise."

"Hand to my heart," Clanton said. He studied the sky for a few more moments. "We'll likely stay dry since we're no more than ten miles or so out from home. Two hours at the most, and then some comfort after these days in the saddle. I can't wait."

Not much later, Clanton raised up in his stirrups and pointed. "There it is. Clantonville."

Brautigan looked. He had especially keen

eyesight. Six or seven miles ahead there were specks on the land, roughly built houses, and between them were patches of green, a startling contrast to the dull tan of the desert. He could see the Gila River curling into the natural basin where the town lay. *Almost,* he thought. *I'm almost within reach of him. Not long now.* He reflexively twitched the toes inside his steel-tipped boots.

7

Gabrielle Tirrito prided herself on clarity of mind. Throughout her twenty-four years, decisions came easily. She was not coldly calculating, weighing options with a view to always choose those to her own best advantage. Rather, she trusted her instincts. Only once had they utterly failed her, in St. Louis, when she'd allowed her heart to be stolen by a glib, ambitious young man named Cash McLendon. Though McLendon served an unscrupulous businessman named Rupert Douglass, Gabrielle sensed an inner decency in him, a yearning to move beyond his questionable employment and live decently. In time her feelings for McLendon deepened from skeptical affection to love. She taught her unschooled beau to read; drew him into a warm family circle that included her widowed father, uncles, aunts, and cousins; and encouraged him to adopt a more generous attitude toward others. Gabrielle and her father, Salvatore, ran a small dry-goods store. She suggested that McLendon consider the life of an honest shopkeeper, and felt he was receptive. Marriage and long, happy lives together seemed inevitable. Then one day she read in her morning paper that Mr. Cash McLendon was betrothed to Miss Ellen Douglass, daughter of the well-known business magnate. Their wedding was planned in three months. He never contacted her to explain and Gabrielle concluded, correctly, that McLendon chose money over love. Her immediate reaction was to wonder what she would do if, somehow, she ever passed McLendon and his wife on a St. Louis street. Should she leave town to avoid that horrific possibility? At least initially, her pride would not allow it.

Besides feeling deeply hurt and humiliated, Gabrielle also found herself overwhelmed by shame. During their courtship, she and McLendon had what she privately termed "relations." He pressed, and she found it increasingly difficult to deny him. As a devout Catholic, Gabrielle was forbidden by her faith to have sex outside of marriage. But she eventually reasoned that she and McLendon would soon be married anyway, so in a certain sense relations might be morally permissible. She never mentioned any of this to Father Daniel, her priest, during confession; she kept sex a sweet secret among herself, Cash McLendon, and an understanding God. But after her lover's betrayal, seeking consolation, Gabrielle went to the priest and confessed everything. She hoped for some compassion. But Father Daniel responded angrily. He completely ignored her emotional pain and made no reference to McLendon's unconscionable treatment of her. Instead, he told Gabrielle that she was a base sinner whose whoring had turned the Lord's face from her. No amount of Hail Marys could cleanse her. Father Daniel recommended that Gabrielle seek out a convent and take the veil, after which she should spend the remainder of her life repenting and praying for God's forgiveness. That might spare her from damnation, though the priest had his doubts.

"But if you don't do this, you'll no longer be welcome in my church," Father Daniel said emphatically. "Harlots are abominations in the eyes of the Lord."

Gabrielle stood straight and said, "I was a fool, not a harlot. And you need not fear that I'll ever enter your church again." Having lost first her man and now her church, she went home and told her father that they must leave St. Louis as soon as possible. He loved her enough to agree without any argument. Within a month they'd sold off the stock in their small dry-goods shop and used the limited proceeds to move west. They knew nothing of the frontier other than it was supposed to be a place where hardworking men and women could succeed free of the social and economic strictures that framed the more civilized sections of America. In Tucson they met people intending to build a town in a region reportedly flush with silver. The Tirritos joined in founding Glorious, a tiny settlement with big dreams. Soon there arrived a slender, quiet man named Joe Saint, a former schoolteacher from Philadelphia. After his wife and infant daughter died of a sudden illness, he drifted west and, like Gabrielle, nursed a broken heart. After Saint was named sheriff of Glorious — because of his decency rather than even the remotest ability as a gunman — he and Gabrielle began spending time together. Saint was caring, thoughtful, and, above all, loyal — Gabrielle considered him the antithesis of McLendon. Once again, marriage seemed imminent, though this time she was determined to abstain from relations until after the ceremony. She also discovered that she retained her Catholic faith — Father Daniel had failed her, not the church. Then, just as she'd made her peace with the past, Cash McLendon appeared in Glorious. His wife had died a tragic suicide, and he was on the run — his powerful father-in-law blamed him for his daughter's death. Rupert Douglass assigned Patrick Brautigan to find and bring McLendon back to St. Louis to die in his own turn. So far, McLendon had eluded his pursuer.

In Glorious, McLendon told Gabrielle he'd realized his mistake. He swore that he was a changed man who still loved her; he asked her to go to California with him. When she demurred, he stayed in town. Gradually, grudgingly, she began to think McLendon might really have changed for the better. To her surprise, she found herself considering taking McLendon back, but the temptation was countered by her new commitment to Joe Saint and memories of what happened in St. Louis. She was determined never to be a fool again. Then, on a terrible, violent, night, Brautigan came to Glorious. Only Joe Saint's quick thinking prevented Brautigan from capturing McLendon and taking him back East to his death. McLendon fled again, Gabrielle had no idea where.

When prospectors found silver on the other side of the mountains from Glorious, the little settlement died and the new boomtown of Mountain View sprang up. Both the Tirritos and Saint moved there. With her father now too ill to work, Gabrielle joined the staff at the White Horse Hotel. Saint became the town schoolteacher. With his rival gone, he assumed that he and Gabrielle would now marry and she did not disagree, but somehow Gabrielle could not take that final step. Then, a year later, McLendon sent a letter from Dodge City, Kansas, saying he'd learned she and Saint had not yet married and begging her again to choose him instead. Gabrielle determined to make a choice once and for all. She invited McLendon to come to Mountain View, emphasizing that she promised nothing beyond hearing what he had to say in person. Saint was understandably unhappy when she informed him.

"Haven't I proven myself to you?" he asked.

"You have. This in no way reflects upon you."

"McLendon's a lying poltroon. You know it."

"Don't blame him for this. Blame me."

When McLendon arrived, Gabrielle was

unsettled by her own joyful reaction at the sight of him. This time he came to her not as a fugitive, but as a hero of a great Indian battle in Texas. His modesty regarding his part in that fight impressed her most. The old Cash McLendon would have preened and exaggerated his exploits in hopes of benefiting himself further. In Mountain View, he modestly explained his limited role and accepted compliments with a grace she'd never seen him previously display. He appreciated her concern regarding Joe Saint's feelings, and accepted the very limited physical contact she allowed. McLendon was even respectful of her need for time to decide. Gabrielle's heart and head were soon in conflict. She knew what she wanted to do, and also the reasons why she shouldn't.

She had made two close female friends in Mountain View, and asked their advice. Rebecca Moore, who operated a laundry, urged her to act decisively as soon as she could: "Anything else would be unfair to all three of you." Marie Silva, who did bookkeeping for the White Horse and another hotel, urged the opposite. "Take your time, all you need and more. This affects the rest of your life. Besides, the longer you delay, the more anxious they'll both be to win you.

Make them sweat awhile." When Gabrielle said, "That would be cruel," Marie replied, "It's what men deserve." Gabrielle decided Marie must have suffered her own traumatic mistreatment by a man sometime in life.

Dinner with the Hancocks tipped the balance. Gabrielle carefully observed McLendon's behavior toward rich, influential Orville Hancock. He was respectful of the older man, but never obsequious. After McLendon turned down permanent employment in Mountain View, Hancock offered to help him find a suitable job in California. That meant he had discerned quality and potential in McLendon, and Hancock was a pragmatic businessman who surely would not waste a recommendation on anyone insufficient. Too, Pauline Hancock's suggestion that Gabrielle assume the post of town librarian was thrilling — it indicated that, should she go to California with McLendon, Gabrielle might also have possibilities for fulfilling work. Surely there were libraries there.

As they walked back to the White Horse after taking their leave of the Hancocks, Gabrielle was certain, though she stopped short of telling McLendon so. First, she felt, it was necessary to break the news to Joe Saint, and to do all she could to make him understand how her regard for him remained undiminished. Besides her father, Gabrielle considered Saint to be the finest man she'd ever known. He deserved a wife who loved him unconditionally, and that would not, could not, be her. Life with Joe Saint would be secure and — she couldn't help thinking — somewhat dull. Frontier routine and blowing dust were things Gabrielle had learned to endure, but the lure of a major city with libraries and symphonies and public gardens was far more attractive. And frankly, so, too, was Cash McLendon. After all he'd done wrong, after all the pain he'd caused her, she still felt better, more alive, when she was with him.

A few nights later, Joe Saint cooked Gabrielle supper in the small house he rented on the edge of town. One of his students had brought him a ham hock that day — parents sometimes indicated their appreciation of his teaching by sending along such tokens. Saint roasted it with carrots and wild celery, and served the food with glasses of red wine from an inexpensive bottle he'd bought at the Scarcellos' general store. His crockery was battered, and the dining table where they sat listed slightly to the side. Even a schoolteacher should have afforded better, but Saint spent much of his salary on paper and pens that many of his students could not afford, and also on clothes and shoes for some of the very poorest children. Not every Mountain View family was prosperous.

They both picked at the meal. Saint never ate much, and because of what she was about to tell him, Gabrielle had no appetite. As they pushed the food around on their plates, they chatted awkwardly about inconsequential things. Tension mounted until Saint finally said, "All right. I know what you're going to say."

Gabrielle felt a lurching sensation in her chest and struggled to think of the right words. All she could manage was "I'm sorry."

Saint gulped down his glass of wine and poured another, slopping some on the table. "Well, thank you for that."

"I mean it."

"I know."

They sat silently for a while. Then Saint said, "What I can't understand is, you're an intelligent woman. You remember what he did to you before. People don't change that much. Why can't you see it?"

"I know this isn't fair."

Saint set his glass carefully on the table. The knuckles of the hand gripping the glass were white and Gabrielle realized that it took all of Joe's self-control not to slam it down. "I'm not concerned about what's fair. I'm worried about what's going to happen to you."

Gabrielle reached across the table and touched his hand. "I'll be all right. Will you?"

"I should have let that big man have him back in Glorious," Saint said, more to himself than to Gabrielle. "If I'd known this was going to happen, I'd have found some way to bring that bastard McLendon down."

"No, you wouldn't have," Gabrielle said. "You're too good a person for that."

"I'd do anything to keep you safe." Saint took several deep breaths. "You can't be talked out of this?" he asked.

"No," Gabrielle said. "I'm determined."

"All right," Saint said. "Then let's finish our dinner." For the next half hour he told stories about his students, mostly funny tales about amusing misbehavior. Then, after the table was cleared, Saint told Gabrielle that he was sure she had things to do. He kissed her on the cheek and opened the door.

"Joe, I don't want things to end badly between us," Gabrielle said. "I need to assure you of how grateful I am —"

"Not now," Saint said, struggling to maintain his composure. "Good night, Gabrielle."

She stepped into the street and heard the door close firmly behind her, just short of a slam. Gabrielle stood there for a long moment, then walked back to the White Horse. Because of the location of Saint's house, it took some time. The route involved smaller backstreets. When Gabrielle reached the hotel, she nodded to the night clerk at the lobby desk and walked upstairs to the room McLendon shared with Major Mulkins. Gabrielle rapped on the door and the Major opened it. His collar was undone and he had an unlit cigar clenched in his teeth. Gabrielle looked past him to where McLendon sat on a chair reading the latest edition of *The Mountain View Herald*.

"I need to speak with you," she said to McLendon. "Now, if you please."

McLendon followed her downstairs. The lobby was mostly empty; they took chairs in the farthest corner.

"All right," Gabrielle said firmly. "There are things to discuss. I require complete candor. Is that understood?"

"Of course," McLendon said. "Are you upset? What's wrong?"

"Just be honest. First, there's my father.

133

He's ill and will require ongoing attention and care. But I go nowhere without him. He is my responsibility and will be yours too. Are we agreed?"

"So you're finally saying it?" McLendon asked eagerly. "You've decided?"

"Answer my question."

"Of course I agree. Your father comes with us, and we'll both care for him."

"He still dislikes you for your actions in St. Louis," Gabrielle warned. "He's likely to treat you in an unpleasant manner."

"I don't blame him. I think with time I can win him over."

"We'll see. Now, as to our personal arrangement. There must be a wedding. I'll not be a mistress."

McLendon couldn't stop smiling. "I'll marry you right here and now."

"No, that would hurt and humiliate Joe. We can have some simple ceremony in California. But there must be one."

"There will." McLendon reached for her, but Gabrielle pulled away.

"And there will be no . . . *relations,* until after marriage," she said. "I won't compromise on this."

"I accept that," McLendon said, though he looked disappointed.

Gabrielle pondered a moment. "Regarding St. Louis."

"What of it?"

"Your former father-in-law, and the man he sent to pursue you. Are you satisfied it's no longer of concern?"

McLendon shrugged. "That's a difficult question."

"Respond as best you can."

"I'll try. It's been almost three years since Ellen died. I've seen and heard nothing of Patrick Brautigan, Killer Boots, since that night more than two years ago in Glorious. With the exception of the article in the *Herald*, I've done my best to lay low. In California it's my intention to find gainful employment and provide well for us, including your father, but in some manner that doesn't attract undue attention. It's my belief we can live safely in anonymity. There's no way to be entirely certain." McLendon added defensively, "You asked for honesty. All I can say is, I wouldn't knowingly place you or your father in danger."

"And there's really been no trace of this man Brautigan? To your knowledge, nothing at all?"

"Rupert Douglass must have all manner of urgent business concerns requiring Brautigan's special sort of skill. It's been a long time. At some point, he surely called him off my trail."

Gabrielle once again lost herself in thought. McLendon tried not to squirm as he waited.

"All right," she finally said. "There's a last thing. I want us to leave as soon as we reasonably can. The longer we remain here in Mountain View, the more Joe will suffer. We need to move along and let him get on with his own life. There's money to save for the journey and resettling, I know, and so we'll economize. All meals from now on at the staff table. If you want the occasional evening drink, limit yourself. We'll remain discreet about our plans to discourage local gossip."

"Certainly we have some friends who should know."

"Only a very few." Finally, Gabrielle smiled and said, "I must go upstairs to see to my father." She held out her arms. "One kiss only. Oh, well, perhaps two."

8

Given Ike's penchant for exaggeration, Brautigan expected very little of Clantonville. But the settlement in the shallow Pueblo Viejo Valley wasn't the eyesore he'd anticipated. Green crops grew in neat patches — Brautigan didn't know enough about plants to recognize what they were, only that they seemed to be thriving. Some women and children worked in the gaps between the plant rows, squatting down to pull weeds. The town buildings, a dozen in all, were small but well built from split logs sealed tight with chinked clay. A few of the structures apparently served as barns and storage facilities. A corral held a dozen horses and several mules. Chickens clucked in a pen. Though small, it was an attractive community.

"Told you," Ike crowed. "Paradise on earth. It's good to be home." He and Brautigan rode up to what apparently was the main house, a somewhat wider structure than the others. "Hey, Billy," Ike called, and a towheaded twelve-year-old appeared in the doorway. "Take our horses and mule, get them fed and watered. We've had a long, hot ride." Ike got down from his horse; he and the boy hugged. "Billy, meet Mr. Brautigan," Ike said.

"Howdy," Billy said politely. Brautigan responded with a curt nod. He had no interest in children.

"Where's your father?" he asked Ike. "Let's get this business conducted."

"Pa's likely taking his ease inside," Ike said. "Why don't you stop here a moment, take a dipper of water from the barrel there on the porch. I'll go in first, provide Pa with the facts, and then you can join us."

"Be quick," Brautigan said. "I've no time to waste." As soon as Ike entered the building, Brautigan did several knee bends. His entire body was stiff from days of riding. Saddle rash on the insides of his thighs made even short steps uncomfortable. He drank several dippersful of water, then soaked a handkerchief and used the dripping cloth to clean trail dust from his face and hands. After perhaps ten minutes Ike emerged and said, "Come on in. Pa's ready to see you."

It was warm and dark inside the house. Most of the window openings were covered with oilcloth. Two were open to allow the circulation of a faint breeze, and also to supply minimal light. In one corner, slouched on a patched davenport, was an enormous man, wide rather than tall, whose bulging belly extended far in front of the rest of his body. As Brautigan's eyes adjusted to the dim light, he saw more: a bald pate, bushy gray chin whiskers, and thick brows over deep-set, glittering eyes.

"Newman Clanton," the man said in a rumbling voice. "Founder of Clantonville. My boy says you're named Brautigan, and you want something. What?"

"Discretion above all, from this moment forward."

Newman Clanton studied his guest, taking in Brautigan's own bulk and looking directly into his eyes. After a moment, satisfied with what he saw, Clanton said, "Ike, you go on. Brautigan and I will converse."

"I should take part, Pa," Ike protested. "It's me who brought him here."

"I said go," Clanton said, and Ike did. Clanton told Brautigan to sit — there was a hardwood chair opposite the sofa. Then the Clantonville patriarch said, "So talk to me, and be as plain as you please. There's no

139

one else to hear."

Brautigan sat, enjoying the relative comfort of the chair after so many excruciating hours in the saddle. "What did your boy tell you so far?"

"Only that you're on your way to Mountain View with the plan of nabbing someone we Clantons don't remember fondly. Ike figures you want to first get him to Silver City and then back East wherever you've come from. You're not the law, so it's a private matter."

"That's correct. I need a base to work from. Clantonville would do."

"What specifically is required?"

"I may need a place to keep someone, just for a night or so. An unwilling guest, you might say."

Clanton nodded. "I've got a shed that would do. Use it to shelter sick animals sometimes. Door bolts from the outside. Enough air to breathe, some room to stand and move."

"What if there are shouts from within, pleas for assistance?"

"All in Clantonville hear only what I tell them that they should."

"I'll need trail supplies for two. First from here to Mountain View and back, then the necessaries for travel from here to Silver

City. Water, bread, canned provisions. Also some feed for my two horses and a mule."

"We'll have what you require. I doubt further information is necessary. The less I know of your business, the better. One question remains — what further play will my boy Ike have in this?"

"We came to an agreement in Silver City. He's obligated to gather information for me in Mountain View."

Clanton sat straighter on the sofa, which creaked as he shifted his bulk. "You'll have noticed Ike lacks common sense, and he talks too much. I'd not want him placed in any situation where his lack of discretion leads him into direct conflict with the law."

"I plan to completely avoid any contact with the law."

"The two you mention traveling from here to Silver City — that's you and your prisoner? Ike's not included?"

"No. Once I have my man and return with him here, your boy is clear."

"Glad to hear it. Let's come to a financial arrangement." They did, quickly. Newman Clanton would receive two hundred dollars for his assistance and an additional hundred and fifty for discretion. In return, Brautigan could have the use of the shed as needed with no questions asked, and all the food and other supplies he might require.

"We'll seal the bargain with a drink," Clanton said. With some difficulty, he hauled himself up from the couch. Despite the heat, he wore a vest with a pocket watch and chain. The thick links of the chain clinked together as he walked toward a table where a bottle and glasses rested. He reached for the bottle, but before he could pour, Brautigan said, "I'll decline. There's still plenty of daylight, and I'd like to be well on the way to Mountain View before dark."

"Are you certain? For a fellow from the East, you've ridden a fair distance already. I believe I discerned a slight hitch in your step as you entered my home. Perhaps an overnight respite would relieve some discomfort."

"I'm fine," Brautigan said. "If that boy Billy has the animals watered and you'll oblige me in the matter of resupply, Ike and I will be moving on. It's another day to Mountain View from here?"

"If you cut across the San Carlos agency instead of circling around it. Is this your intent?"

"It is. When there's business to be done, I dislike delay."

Clanton poured himself a drink and

downed it in a single gulp. "Remember that discretion works both ways. You run afoul of Clum, the agent, leave Clantonville out of it."

Ike Clanton was particularly garrulous as they rode out, and Brautigan understood why. He'd felt humiliated when his father ordered him out of the house. Brautigan needed Ike to feel confident when they reached Mountain View, so he let the other man prattle about women he'd seduced and fistfights he'd won.

"Pa acts like a lord, but it's really me who handles most of the Clantonville business," Ike bragged, forgetting he'd told Brautigan the opposite as they'd ridden in to the family settlement. "All the details and such. It's fortunate I'm a man of the world."

Brautigan kept quiet, trying to think about what had to be done in Mountain View and not about the aching at the base of his spine as his ass jostled constantly against the saddle. The ground was breaking up again, and the horses' gaits were ragged. Ike pointed out the Mescal Mountains on their left, and ahead Brautigan could see arching, sharp-angled slopes that stopped just short of being mountains themselves.

"There's some decent bottomland on the

other side," Clanton said. "White men should have it, but the guvmint gave it to the Indians. Makes no sense. They don't want to be farmers and never will."

"Should we be on the lookout for Apache?" Brautigan asked.

"Another few miles, we're on agency land," Clanton said. "Even if we see any or they glimpse us, there ought to be room to maneuver away. Their big chief died not long ago. Name was Cochise and he was sheer hell. But without him, they got no real leader. Any of the young bucks start feeling froggy to fight, they don't stick around the agency. They ride south down into Mexico and the Army's got to go after them. It's the agent who's the danger. John Clum, if he finds the likes of us doing what he considers trespassing —"

"Would he attempt to take us into custody?"

"Prob'ly not, but at the least he'd be displeased."

"His displeasure won't concern me," Brautigan said, and lapsed back into silence.

By dark they were well onto the agency. Though they'd seen no one, Indian or white, they kept a cold camp that night without a fire. They drank canteen water and slurped canned peas. After the meager

144

meal, Brautigan gave Clanton instructions.

"Just outside Mountain View, you'll go on without me. I'll camp outside town. You go in, find McLendon, and quick as you can figure out where he goes, what he does. He's a man of routine. I need to know where and when he'll be someplace isolated, where I can snatch him free of observers. That's what you'll scout out and report back to me. You do your job right, you'll be well paid and that's the end of your obligation."

"You've never specified the amount," Clanton said. "I'd like to know."

"If I get McLendon out clean, two hundred dollars. Any trouble, any untruths or omissions in the information you provide me, and there's nothing but a bad end for you. One or the other, Ike."

"That's a hard way to speak to a fellow who's been nothing but helpful."

Brautigan didn't reply. He soon slept. Ike couldn't.

They broke camp when the sun was still a thin red speck on the horizon. By full daylight, Clanton said they were almost through San Carlos. "From here, another twenty miles and we're outside Mountain View. Not long now."

Then as they splashed across the San

Carlos River there suddenly were Apache in front of them, a half-dozen copper-skinned men in dun-colored shirts. They were mounted on unshod ponies. Though the two intruders had been keeping constant watch, the Indians seemed to spring up from nowhere. Brautigan was startled but didn't show it. He sat stoically on his horse and gestured for Clanton to do the same. Ike twitched nervously. His right hand dropped toward his holster.

"Leave the gun be," Brautigan hissed. He thought the Indians were unarmed except for some knives he saw at their waists. The odds weren't great, but Brautigan made himself ready, easing his boots from the saddle stirrups, preparing to spring. His back ached and the insides of his thighs burned, but he ignored it. Then another rider appeared from a wash to the right, a wide-shouldered white man whose height was accentuated even more by his upright posture in the saddle.

"Ike Clanton," the newcomer said. "Ike and a companion."

"Clum," Ike said, sounding petulant rather than defiant. "You and your red men, delaying two innocent travelers."

"Somehow Ike Clanton and the word 'innocent' don't match up right together,"

Clum said. "Just stay on your horse as you are." He turned to Brautigan. "I'm John Clum, the agent here at San Carlos. I'd appreciate your name and your purpose for trespassing."

"I'm Brautigan, and we're riding through with no intention of causing trouble. Mr. Clanton here has just given me a look at his family's property, the town they've founded. I'm thinking of investing."

"Yet you're riding away from Clantonville," Clum observed. "On your way to Mountain View, I suppose. If you're seeking Tucson, you're headed in the exact opposite direction. Even Ike, here, should know that."

"Why does our destination interest you, Mr. Clum?" Brautigan asked. "And why are these Apache necessary to the conversation?"

Clum pulled a pipe from his pocket, tamped down tobacco, and lit it. All the while, his eyes never left Brautigan. "Perhaps Ike didn't inform you that it's illegal to cross an Indian agency without permission of the designated government agent. These Apache here would be within their rights to pull you off your horses and do what they wished to you. I hope you appreciate their forbearance."

"I'd like to see 'em try," Ike spluttered,

147

but his voice shook a little. The Apache noticed. One, a bandy-legged fellow, hopped off his horse and muttered something to the others, who laughed.

Clum snapped, "Back on your horse, Goyathlay," and added something else in Apache.

"You speak their filthy tongue?" Clanton asked.

"Some, and you ought to learn it too. It's a beautiful language," Clum said. "Well, Ike and Mr. Brautigan. Of my two choices, the first is to escort you to the agency office, then turn you over to the authorities for trespass. There would be fines, substantial ones. The other is to warn you never to trespass again and send you on your way. There's some risk to you in that. These men are offended by your presence. They intend to trail you until they see you entirely off the agency, and unless I'm present they might attempt physical chastisement."

"We'll accept the warning and move on," Brautigan said. "Tell these Apache there's no reason to follow us."

Clum spoke to the Indian men in their language. Goyathlay barked something back and hopped on his horse. "It seems they're going to ride behind you whether you wish it or not," Clum said. "Goyathlay promises

148

that you won't be harmed as long as you head right off their land."

Brautigan said curtly, "We will." Clanton, reassured that any immediate danger was past, snapped, "Clum, you warn them that we're considerably ferocious and armed besides. We're leaving, but if they raise a hand to us, they'll regret such action."

Clum chuckled. "Ike, I already know you're a fool. You don't have to prove it so often. Have you any idea who Goyathlay is?"

Clanton studied the Apache, who sat hunched forward on his horse. Goyathlay's brow was furrowed as he glared at the two intruders. "All I see is a flea-ridden red runt."

"Look again," Clum said. "Goyathlay's one of the worst hotheads on the agency, the hardest to hold in check. Before we got him in here, he raised so much hell below the border that the Mexes called him Geronimo, though I personally don't know the significance of that name. He and his pards there could have you down and dead before you so much as blinked, Ike. Be clever for once and ride off nice and meek. And you, Mr. Brautigan. Never cross this agency again without permission. We straight on that?"

"I'll make certain our paths don't cross in the future," Brautigan said. "We're on our way. Come on, Clanton."

"Good afternoon to you," Clum said cordially. "Keep that mule you're leading close, Ike. These Apache have a powerful taste for mule meat. They might want to take it from you as a kind of toll."

"Better not try," Ike grumbled, careful to keep his voice so low that no one but Brautigan could hear. They rode northwest, Goyathlay and the other Apache trailing a few hundred yards behind. Clum sat astride his horse at the top of a rise and watched awhile.

Brautigan and Clanton rode for almost an hour without speaking. Then, as they splashed across a narrow creek, Ike said, "This is the agency boundary." They stopped to let the horses and mule drink. Looking back, they saw the Apache riding away.

"Goddamned Indian-loving John Clum," Ike said. "Day's coming when he'll get his. I don't forget an insult."

"Put it aside for at least the present," Brautigan said. "I need you giving all your attention to the task at hand."

Because of the delay at the agency, it was

almost dusk before they neared Mountain View. Brautigan found a small wash about two miles south of town; its embankment provided cover from easy detection. He told Ike to tether the animals and give them feed and water. Brautigan sat with his back against a rock and thought while Clanton did these chores. When Ike was done, Brautigan had him sit down too.

"The task is simple but important," he told Clanton. "I must know where I can lay hands on McLendon with no one to notice. No guessing. You have to be certain. Let him see you, speak to you. It's all right if he's antagonistic."

"If McLendon spies me, won't that put him on his guard?"

"McLendon's a weak man, but always watchful and suspicious. It's better he first sees you out in the open. Then he'll likely consider your presence to be coincidence rather than dangerous. Just get the full sense of him. And no threats. I don't want him spooked."

"I'll be as smooth as you please," Clanton said. "No man surpasses me at easy charm."

"Make it a natural thing, your showing up there. Talk up Clantonville like you did in Silver City."

"I need no such instruction," Ike protested. "What would aid me is a handful of coins. When I tout my town, I like to treat prospective investors to drinks. It's my custom, and some observing me might think it strange if I didn't."

Brautigan gave him several dollars. "Be certain that almost all the drinks go down throats other than your own. Keep in control of your faculties. I want no faulty information. Watch him tonight, observe him tomorrow, and then tomorrow night return here with what I need to know."

"I shall," Clanton said. "Rest easy until then."

"Ike," Brautigan said quietly. He grasped Clanton's shoulder in his huge hand and squeezed just enough to hurt. "You'll not want to fail me. I found McLendon. If need be, I could always find you."

"Then let me be on my way," Clanton said. Brautigan loosened his grip and watched as Ike rode off toward Mountain View.

9

The next few days were happy ones for Cash McLendon and Gabrielle Tirrito. They shared their news with a few select friends — Major Mulkins, Sheriff Jack and Mamie Hove, Mayor Camp, Rebecca Moore, Marie Silva — and everyone seemed glad for them. Gabrielle's father, Salvatore, was the exception. He still despised McLendon for abandoning Gabrielle in St. Louis.

"I believe he'll come around," Gabrielle said. "For now, let him get used to the idea that we're back together. Reconciliation between the two of you will take longer."

"In his place, I'd probably feel the same," McLendon admitted.

Despite Gabrielle's determination to economize, each evening the newly announced couple celebrated at the Ritz. They could do this because their friends insisted on paying for drinks. For the first time since fleeing St. Louis, McLendon contemplated

153

a joyous future. That was more intoxicating than the Jim Beam bourbon Mayor Camp insisted on buying everyone. Major Mulkins stood several nightly rounds too.

"It will be impossible to replace Gabrielle on the hotel staff," he said. "But love trumps business. I'm happy for you both."

Hope Camp was equally sorry to lose McLendon's services.

"Bowling income will be reduced by half in your absence," he predicted. "It was quite profitable to employ a person of such renown."

There was considerable discussion about when Gabrielle and McLendon would be on their way to California. Doc Vance, Mountain View's Harvard-trained physician, thought Salvatore Tirrito could endure the journey if he was allowed to rest as needed.

"Common sense is the best medicine for your father," Doc Vance told Gabrielle. "Whenever he seems especially tired, stop for a while. You say you're aiming for San Francisco? That's fine — I think the ocean breezes will do him good."

When she and McLendon mentioned their intent to leave within a few months, both Marie and Major Mulkins objected.

"That's just too soon," Marie said. "With

all you have to do, the planning and everything else. Six months at least are required, probably more."

"Oh, it won't be that long," Gabrielle said. "As soon as we've saved sufficient funds, we hope to be on our way."

"But you must be practical. Build up your father's strength —"

"Doc Vance assures me he'll be fine."

"I want to give you a formal engagement dinner, and those arrangements will take time."

"For heaven's sake, Marie. Don't go to any such trouble. I love you for the thought, but truly Cash and I are just anxious to begin our lives together."

Major Mulkins, on the other hand, urged them to leave at once.

"After all you've been through, all the time you've lost, you don't want to put this off. Get your tickets on the stage, pack your bags, and get going west," he said as everyone crowded around a table at the Ritz. It was Saturday night and the room was packed.

"We'd like to, Major, but it's impossible," McLendon explained, raising his voice slightly to be heard above the general commotion. "Even with Gabrielle's and my current savings combined, we're still several hundred dollars short of what we need for fares plus expenses while I look for work in San Francisco."

Mulkins exchanged quick grins with Mayor Camp. "Hope and I want to speak to that." He leaned forward and motioned for the others to do the same. "We think a lot of the two of you. So we propose this — we'll front you the money you need to leave just as soon as the arrangements can be made. You can repay us at your leisure."

Gabrielle gasped, and McLendon had to catch his breath. "Major, Mayor Camp — that's too generous. We couldn't possibly —"

"You could, and will," Mayor Camp said. "McLendon, in the past weeks I've made considerable money thanks to you. I'm thinking of christening my store's game area the Cash McLendon Memorial Bowling Emporium so I can keep profiting from your reputation, if not your actual presence. So you and your lady work out the amount you need and inform the Major and me. Why, you can be on your way by midweek, and honeymooning in California by month's end."

"You're too generous. Thank you," McLendon said, and Gabrielle leaped up from her chair to give the mayor and

Mulkins huge hugs. Rebecca Moore proposed a toast to the happy couple, and everyone raised their glasses.

It seemed to Gabrielle that Marie Silva was downcast. *For some people, it's especially hard to say good-bye to friends,* she thought. *I'll make extra time for Marie before we leave.*

The original plan had been for everyone to linger for just one or two drinks, but no one seemed to want the night to end. There was so much to talk about, including the clothes Gabrielle needed for the trip, and also for a wedding trousseau, as well as McLendon's California job prospects. Sheriff Hove felt that Orville Hancock's letter of recommendation was all he'd need. The Smead Company would surely hire him in a well-compensated capacity. Major Mulkins and Mayor Camp advised McLendon to expand any employment search beyond Smead. He had too much talent, they assured him, to confine himself to exploring jobs with only one company, no matter how established it might be.

Sheriff Hove eventually excused himself to make his regular ten p.m. rounds. "You stay and keep visiting with our friends, Mamie," he told his wife. "I'll be home in an hour's time." Just as Hove pushed his chair back from the table, a loud voice rose over the rest in the saloon.

"I don't give a damn what you say about the charms of this place. It's stinkweed, it's horse shit, compared to the wonders of Clantonville. Climb on your horse and come see for yourself. You'll never return to this shantytown."

"He's back again," Hove said, and groaned. "How many times do I have to run him off before he finally stays gone?"

To McLendon, the voice was all too familiar, though it had been more than two years since he'd heard it. He stood along with Sheriff Hove and saw Ike Clanton not a dozen yards away, holding court with his back to the Ritz's black walnut bar. Ike looked exactly the same, from the pointy Vandyke beard to his wide, insincere smile.

"You'll find it difficult to believe, but prime lots are available for one dollar," Clanton assured his audience, which seemed less interested in his sales pitch than in calling drink orders to the bartender behind him. "Prime farming, grazing, plenty of water, in the best location in the territory. Who'll be the first tonight to avail himself of this opportunity?"

Sheriff Hove wove his way to the bar. McLendon was right behind him.

"Ike Clanton, cease your bellowing," the sheriff commanded. "You want to tout your place, do it outside in the street."

"Jack Hove, we're well met," Clanton said. "How about I buy you a drink and tell you in some detail why you need to be moving out Clantonville way?"

Ike extended his hand in friendly fashion and Hove brushed it aside. "Outside, Clanton. Don't make me tell you again."

Clanton drew back, assuming a look of mock hurt. "Sheriff, I just want to enjoy some refreshment and talk a little business to anyone interested."

"Look around you. No one's interested. Out."

"Of course they're interested. They just want to get their drinks first, is all. Your discourtesy pains me, Sheriff, and — wait! Right there behind you — can it be Cash McLendon, late of Glorious?"

"It is," McLendon said. The sight of Ike Clanton angered him so much that his head ached. "I ought to shoot you. I swear I'm considering it."

Ike said beseechingly to Hove, "There, now, Sheriff. I'm being threatened for no reason. Do your job. Step in and protect me."

Hove glanced at McLendon. "Even with

Ike Clanton, that's a hard reaction, C.M. What's your quarrel with him?"

McLendon glared at Clanton. "Two years ago in Glorious, Clanton threw in with a rich man named MacPherson who was willing to kill to have his way. Some good people died because of it. Do everyone a favor, Jack, and run him right out of town."

Ike said to Hove, "Don't let's be precipitous. Tell you what — I'll suspend further talk of Clantonville for the present. I'll just have myself a quiet drink or two like any other patron of this fine establishment. You can't expel me from the premises for that, now, can you?"

Hove frowned. "Just one word or gesture out of place, Ike. Provide any excuse and you'll sleep in a cell tonight. C.M., step away. Go on back to the table and resume celebrating."

"A celebration?" Clanton said. "McLendon, what's the occasion? Why, looka-there. I believe it's Major Mulkins, and Miss Gabrielle Tirrito. A reunion from our days together in Glorious! Might I join you?"

"Hell no," McLendon said. "Jack, can't you at least throw the bastard out of this saloon?"

"Not if he abides by my warning," Hove said. "Ike, cease further conversation with

Mr. McLendon. He clearly disdains your company."

"I'll regretfully do so," Clanton said. "McLendon? May I at least buy you and your party drinks? No? Well, then, I'll treat myself." He waved over the bartender and called for whiskey. McLendon glared at Ike's back until Sheriff Hove said firmly, "Go back to the table. I'll not tolerate trouble made by anyone, including a friend."

After that, conversation at the table was subdued. McLendon, Gabrielle, and Major Mulkins were all distracted by Clanton's presence in the saloon, though he stayed at the bar drinking and did not make any further approach. Mayor Camp, Mamie Hove, Rebecca Moore, and Marie Silva all picked up on the new mood and spoke quietly of inconsequential things until McLendon glanced at a wall clock and said, "It's well after ten. I'd best go collect the day's receipts at the store and move them to the upstairs safe."

"I can do that," Mayor Camp said. "You stay and enjoy the company of Miss Gabrielle and these other lovely ladies."

"No," McLendon said. "It's part of my job, and thanks to your generosity, it's a chore you'll have to resume soon enough. Major, will you see Gabrielle back to the

161

White Horse? I'll return there as soon as I'm done."

The party broke up in friendly fashion. Mayor Camp offered to escort Rebecca Moore to her home and Mamie Hove to hers, where she would wait for her husband to complete his rounds. Marie Silva said she could walk home herself — she had a room in a hotel on the opposite side of town from the White Horse. McLendon gave Gabrielle a brief, warm kiss. She now permitted modest public displays of affection. Then he left the saloon and walked across the street to the Camp Feed Store, where he visited briefly with the late-night staff, bid them good night, and, after counting the day's receipts, put the coins and greenbacks in a cloth sack and carried the money behind the building and then upstairs to the store office. He unlocked the door, went inside, lit an oil lantern, and opened the boxy safe, using the combination that Mayor Camp had shared with him. McLendon locked the sack in the safe. The store would be closed Sunday, and on Monday morning Mayor Camp would collect the money sack from the safe and take it to the bank for deposit. After closing the safe, McLendon blew out the oil lamp, locked the office door, and walked back to the

White Horse.

On Sunday mornings, Gabrielle went to Catholic church services in the barn behind Flanagan's Livery. Mountain View had no official priest, but a traveling *padre* who spent weekdays in the area ministering to tame Indians was always there to preside. He heard no confessions and did not offer Communion, but did lead prayers and hymns. That was enough for Gabrielle — Father Daniel in St. Louis had cured her of any need for ostentatious church ceremony. She was pleased that on this Sunday, McLendon accompanied her without being asked.

"In California, we can be married as Catholics," he said as they walked from the hotel to the livery barn. "And I'll take instruction from a priest beforehand, or whatever else I'm needed to do."

Gabrielle was touched, and told him so. "We'll see once we get there," she said.

McLendon found the Sunday service in the barn to be tolerable, though not interesting. He himself had no particular belief in God — a hard childhood scrambling for food and shelter had taught him to depend on himself rather than on anything spiritual. But he sat patiently beside Gabrielle while she recited incomprehensible Latin phrases and sang in her lilting voice. Afterward he shook the *padre*'s callused hand. As he and Gabrielle walked out of the barn into the bright noon sunlight, McLendon noticed Ike Clanton leaning against Scarcello Dry Goods Store down the street.

"He's still in town," McLendon muttered to Gabrielle.

"Ignore him," she said. "He'll be gone soon, or at least we will."

They went back to the White Horse and brought lunch up to share with Salvatore Tirrito in his room. The old man felt well enough to sit in a chair as he spooned soup and ate crackers. He talked easily to Gabrielle in Italian, and in grudging, halting English to McLendon on the few occasions he bothered responding to something he said. Afterward Gabrielle settled her father back in bed for a nap.

"How much English does your father really understand?" McLendon asked Gabrielle. "I'd like to think at least some of his hesitation is because he's trying to think of the right words, and not because he hates me."

"It's mostly hate, I'm afraid," she said. "He understands much more English than he lets on. I promise, he'll come around in time."

Gabrielle had to spend some of her afternoon teaching another hotel staffer how to run the front desk. She felt obligated to train a replacement before giving up her job at the White Horse. Major Mulkins suggested to McLendon that they join Mayor Camp while Gabrielle was otherwise occupied: "We need to be figuring out the necessary finances for your California trip," he explained.

McLendon and Mulkins walked across town to the mayor's home and spent a few hours there. Afterward they returned to the hotel. After Sunday dinner at the staff table, McLendon and Gabrielle sat in the lobby and made plans for the trip. She thought she'd wait to buy any new clothes until they were in California: "Styles there will certainly be different than here in the territory." McLendon said that Major Mulkins and Mayor Camp suggested loaning them $1,000. It was a great deal of money to repay, but he expected to find a well-compensated job, and Gabrielle said she would work too. They decided that in the morning, they'd buy tickets to leave Mountain View for California on the Friday stage. Thanks to the generous loan from their friends, they could afford four seats instead of three, so, if necessary, Salvatore Tirrito could have more room to stretch out and sleep on the way.

"Can you believe it?" Gabrielle asked McLendon. He admitted that he couldn't.

They went outside for a quick breath of evening air, and once again McLendon spotted Ike Clanton. This time he was walking slowly down the street in front of the White Horse. He didn't appear to notice them. This second sighting of the day bothered McLendon. He wondered if Ike was spying on them, and almost immediately decided he wasn't. If Clanton had any bad intentions, he wouldn't have shown himself so openly at the Ritz.

Still, all day on Monday McLendon made periodic checks for Clanton lurking about, but didn't see him anywhere. Then, preoccupied with preparations for leaving town, he forgot all about Ike.

10

Brautigan was unhappy with Clanton's report after Ike returned to their camp Sunday night from Mountain View.

"All you can say for certain is that he's in town. But nothing useful beyond that, no information that makes it easy for me to lay hands on him."

"It's not my fault," Ike whined. "I handled McLendon just fine. It was the damned sheriff. After he run me off from the saloon, every time I turned around he was right there watching. He hates me for no good reason. You ought to see to him first, hurt him good, get him out of our way. Then McLendon'd be easy pickings."

"Don't blame your failure on the sheriff."

"I did what you told me. McLendon saw me in the saloon and spoke hatefully. And like I said, this morning he and the girl came out of the White Horse Hotel to go to church. I told you, it seemed like they was

167

living in the hotel. But there's no back way in, so if you went for him there you'd need to go through the lobby."

Brautigan shook his head. "I can't do that. People congregate in hotel lobbies at all hours. Too many possible witnesses. And beyond that, you're sure he stayed only in open places?"

"Just like I said. He stuck to the main streets, always in sight of many others. Even when he went calling in the afternoon, the house was right there in town."

"All right. Tonight you're going back to town again, Ike."

"Don't make me play the spy again," Ike said. "Even if McLendon don't sight me, the sheriff will for sure, and he'll throw me in a cell."

Brautigan flashed what passed as his grin. "No, this time you're going to contact someone, fetch this person out here to me. I need another source of information. It'll be easy work, Ike. Soon you'll be on your way home with money weighing down your pockets. Now, soon as it's dark, here's what you'll do."

The rest of the day passed slowly for them. The heat was blistering, and the only shade available in the dry wash camp was a few thready patches behind scattered scrub brush. Flies were a bother too. Clanton wanted to move somewhere else, but Brautigan insisted that they stay put. "So far, no one's ridden out of town this way. If we change location, we might be spotted." So despite the heat, they covered themselves as best they could, blankets over their heads to discourage the flies.

When darkness blessedly arrived, Ike rode back to town, leading the small, slow extra mount by its reins. Brautigan rarely demonstrated any emotion, but while he waited for Ike's return he paced restlessly. McLendon was so close. He couldn't be allowed to escape this time. The boss's wrath if that happened would be unimaginable.

Hours passed. Finally, near midnight, Bautigan detected the faint *thud* of hooves. Ike trotted into camp. Behind him, barely discernable in the pitch darkness, another figure straddled the spare horse.

"May I help you down?" Brautigan asked.

"I can dismount a horse myself," said Marie Silva. "I thought my part in this business was concluded when I wired St. Louis that McLendon was in town. Why have I been brought all the way out here by this buffoon?"

"Hold, now," Ike protested.

"This won't take long, and there'll be additional compensation," Brautigan said. "There are things I need to know."

At first, Marie said little that helped. Yes, she confirmed, McLendon was living in the White Horse Hotel. No, she didn't think there was any way Brautigan could get up to his room without attracting notice: "Besides, he shares quarters with his friend Major Mulkins, who is always there." During the day, McLendon worked at a bowling alley in a constantly crowded store. He was never alone, never isolated. When he wasn't back in the hotel at night, McLendon and Gabrielle Tirrito, his *intended* — Marie enunciated the word in a particularly scornful manner — were joined by friends at the Ritz saloon, also crowded at all hours. Their circle of friends included the mayor and the sheriff.

"It gets even worse," Marie said. She was a woman who relished sharing unwelcome news. "They're leaving soon for California. I've been doing all I could to delay them, so it's not my fault. You should have come sooner."

Clanton expected Brautigan to make some intimidating response, but the big man's reply was surprisingly conciliatory. "I regret that I didn't. Still, we've a little time yet. What else can you tell me?"

"They're taking her father with them to California. He's quite ill."

"Any idea where they're going in California?"

"They've said San Francisco is most likely. Will you pursue them there?"

Though it would be harder finding McLendon in a major city than in a frontier town, Brautigan was certain he could. But the delay would anger Rupert Douglass, who was expecting immediate results.

"I want to take him here," Brautigan said. "Think on this — has McLendon a daily routine, things he always does at the same time? Besides the job during the day, and the socializing at night?"

"Just what I've told you."

"Anything. The smallest detail may help."

"I don't know. Give me a moment. I'm trying to think. Well, there's the task about ten o'clock each night but Sunday."

Sitting in the bottom of the wash next to Brautigan, Clanton felt the big man's body tense.

"What task?" Brautigan asked.

"Hope Camp, Mayor Camp, who owns the store where McLendon works, has him return there after close of business, collect the money they've taken in that day, and put it in a safe on the second floor of the building. Every night at the Ritz, McLendon excuses himself to perform that chore."

"Always at the same time?"

"Well, around ten. Perhaps a few minutes after."

"Now tell me about the building itself."

Marie explained how Camp Feed Store was an extended structure with the bowling alley to the rear of the first floor. The only entrance to the small second-floor office was an outside stairway around back. You couldn't see it from the front of the building.

"You're certain it's not visible from that direction?"

"Of course not," Marie said crossly. "It's even hard to see when you go 'round back, since it's in an alleyway that's perpetually dim. The stairs are hardly more than a ladder. Mayor Camp's up in years and would break a hip if he fell, but he's too cheap to put in anything sturdier. I'm certain that's why he's had McLendon assume the nightly chore for him."

"When he does this, is McLendon alone? Is anyone else ever involved?"

"No, just him."

"This happens every night but Sunday? You're certain?"

"It's as I've said. I've been there when he

talked about it, when he left by himself to go do it. Are we concluded? I have work in the morning, and thanks to you will have very little sleep to refresh me."

"We're almost done. I'd like to hear a bit more about the Tirrito girl."

After initially feigning reluctance Marie had several things to say, beginning with the opinion that Gabrielle was a spoiled little witch. She took shameless advantage of friends, sometimes asking them to help tend her sick father, Salvatore, when a busy woman like Marie had her own responsibilities. But Gabrielle never considered that. All she really cared about was herself. Well, Marie almost always put her off with excuses, though that simpleton Rebecca Moore, the one who owned the laundry, always did whatever Gabrielle wanted. Marie thought there was something a little strange about Rebecca's friendship with Gabrielle. And there was the matter of Gabrielle and Joe Saint, the Mountain View schoolteacher who'd once been sheriff back in Glorious.

"Do you know about Joe Saint?" Marie asked.

"We've met," Brautigan said. "What of him?"

"He and Gabrielle were together back in

Glorious and afterward everyone in Mountain View expected them to marry, Joe himself above all. And she led him on and then broke his heart when she resumed with McLendon. Though, of course, she claims to me that she still cares for Joe deeply and hates to see him hurt in any way." Marie heaved an exaggerated sigh. "As I've said, she's a witch. Is that sufficient? I'm quite tired."

Brautigan nodded. "Yes, we're finished. Here's an additional fifty dollars for your trouble tonight. Ike, here, will escort you back to town." Brautigan's tone shifted from courteous to the threatening timbre Clanton was used to hearing. "You'll never speak of this meeting, or anything else involving McLendon. If you do, I'll find you. All right, Ike. Get going, and make a prompt return."

After sunrise, Brautigan surprised Clanton by suggesting they take their horses and mule out of the wash in search of water.

"We'll need them rested and ready tonight," he said. Ike told him that Queen Creek ran just to their west and south.

"The same one that bordered Glorious," Clanton said, but Brautigan was clearly uninterested.

They watered the animals and filled their

174

wooden cask. On the way back some riders passed and waved, but didn't stop.

"Any idea where they're heading?" Brautigan asked.

Ike guessed they were on their way to Florence. "There, or maybe Phoenix are all there is directly west of here, and there's not that much to Phoenix."

"Just so long as they won't remember us."

"Two men and their animals. Nothing to remember."

Back at the wash camp, Ike sweated and swatted flies. Brautigan ignored the insects and heat. Flies buzzed around him unnoticed as he explained what was about to take place.

"I know we're perhaps a half hour's ride from town in daylight. Will it take twice that in the dark?" Clanton nodded. "All right. We'll leave here at eight, give ourselves time. When we get there, I want to be seen as little as possible, if at all. You know where this feed store is located?"

"It's on Main Street, about the middle of a block."

"To reach it, must I walk in the open?"

Ike thought a little. "Perhaps not. The town's laid out long but narrow, on account of all the mountains to the side. You ground-hitch your mount just to the east, work in that way, you could stick to a couple alleys and come up behind the store."

"And that's where the only stairs to the second-floor office are."

"So that woman said. Say, did you hear her revile me? There was no call for that."

"And it's dark in the alley. Well, there'll be time to take a look, find the best place to wait." Brautigan looked at Clanton. "Tonight it's especially important that you do just what I tell you. There'll be consequences if you fail me in the smallest way."

"I won't."

"There'll be no tethering. You'll wait just outside town with the horses and mule. I'll go in alone. When I return, I'll have McLendon. We'll put him on the small horse and ride for Clantonville."

Clanton said, "I've some experience with McLendon, and he'll be howling his head off. I don't expect he'll mount up and ride out quietly."

"He'll be quiet," Brautigan said. "His behavior is my concern and none of yours. Just have the animals ready."

"You thinking of crossing the San Carlos agency at night? Those Apache sleep light."

"We'll divert around the agency to the south. Do you know the way?"

"I do, but it's harder in the dark."

Brautigan looked at Clanton. "Ike, can you guide us or not? Because if you can't, then you're of no further use to me."

Clanton recoiled; Brautigan's stare was almost as hard as a blow. "I can do it. I can. South around the agency, and then on to Clantonville. It'll take longer, though, with the added distance as well as the dark. I can't be blamed for that."

"Just get us where we're going as efficiently as possible. And understand this — if we're spotted and it appears we're to be apprehended, I'll kill McLendon on the spot and then you. Do you doubt that I will?"

"No," Ike muttered.

"But if we reach Clantonville safely and your father is as good as his word, after perhaps one night I'll ride on south with McLendon and your part in this is over. Not much longer."

"What's to become of McLendon?"

"It's none of your concern."

"If you're just going to kill him anyway, I want to watch."

"No. Now get some rest. Tonight I'll need you at your best."

That night they lit a fire and cooked — bacon and canned beans. Clanton said they had only a few cans of peaches and peas left. Brautigan said that would last them until they were back in Clantonville.

Just before eight they saddled the horses and loaded up the mule. Ike made a show of checking his Peacemaker, twirling the cylinder and repositioning the gun in his holster for easy extraction.

"Might be we'll have to shoot our way clear," he said. "Best check your rifle."

"Gunplay won't be required," Brautigan said.

They picked their way across the valley floor in pitch darkness. The half-moon was obscured by clouds. Brautigan asked Clanton if there was any possibility of rain, but Ike assured him it was probably too late in the season. Brautigan's saddle sores had healed somewhat, but soon after he was mounted the scabs covering the rash on the inside of his thighs broke open. He hardly noticed; his thoughts were elsewhere.

Even on Tuesday night, the streets of Mountain View were bustling. Some mining shifts ended at six p.m., and once workers had cleaned up, they stepped out for dinner and carousing. Just outside town, Brautigan and Clanton heard hoots and, from the saloons, the sounds of a rinky-tink piano.

"Some boys having fun," Clanton said enviously. "I wouldn't mind being among them."

"Not tonight," Brautigan said. "All right, Ike. I'll leave you here. Be certain I'll find you on this spot when I return." He dismounted, handed his reins to Clanton, and walked through ankle-deep brush toward the backs of some buildings perhaps two hundred yards ahead. Clanton, watching, was reminded of a mountain lion he'd once seen stalking a deer. Like the big cat, Brautigan moved swiftly without seeming to hurry. After a few steps, he disappeared into the darkness.

"Wonder if I could quick hustle in and get a beer?" Clanton asked the night. But then he remembered Brautigan's glare, and, even more, his threats, and decided his thirst could be slaked another time.

Brautigan kept to the shadows. Mountain View's alleys were narrow and mostly uncluttered compared to those of big cities. As he worked his way through the areas between streets he passed one vomiting drunk and three entangled couples. The drunk was too sick to notice him and the couples were too preoccupied.

He recognized the back of the feed store from Marie Silva's description. It was longer than the other buildings on the block. Lights flickered from first-story windows —

the store was still open. Brautigan took a watch from his pocket, snapped open the case, and studied its face in the dim light from the windows: just after nine-thirty. They'd undoubtedly close at ten. There was no other movement in the area behind the store. He studied the structure. There was a loading dock, and then to the left the staircase to the second-story office that the woman had told him about. He examined the staircase, which was no more than a rickety ramp with plank steps. A man starting to climb the steps, holding a container of some sort filled with money, would have to move slowly and carefully. That perfectly suited Brautigan's purpose. All he needed was a moment's hesitation. The noise on the street around the front of the store was helpful too. Nothing short of a full-lunged scream from the alley would be audible there, and McLendon wouldn't have time to scream.

Brautigan imagined, for a moment, how this would ultimately end. He'd get McLendon to St. Louis, he felt sure, and then the boss would pick just the right spot. A place down by the docks, probably, one of the boss's own factories, where they wouldn't be disturbed. Then Brautigan would be given a sign and start to work. Too often, he had to kill quickly. With McLendon, he'd have all the time needed to truly demonstrate his art. A man could suffer almost innumerable injuries and unimaginable pain before he died, if the one meting out the punishment knew his business, which Patrick Brautigan did. McLendon had embarrassed Brautigan by his previous escape. In St. Louis he'd pay, and how satisfying that would be.

But these were idle thoughts when it was time now to focus on the task at hand. Brautigan checked his watch again. The store would close in minutes. There were some barrels on the loading dock a few yards from the bottom of the staircase. Brautigan eyed them, calculating distance and cover. Satisfied with his assessment, he rearranged a few barrels and stepped behind them, allowing room to move to either side if necessary. McLendon, walking around to the alley and the stairs behind the store, would never see him there. As McLendon paused at the base of the stairs and prepared to take his first step, Brautigan would take him instead, muffling any sound by clapping one huge hand over McLendon's mouth and rendering his prey unconscious with a blow to the head from his other fist. Then he'd boost McLendon's limp body over his shoulder, carry him out to where Clanton waited with the horses, and ride away. By the time McLendon came back to himself, they'd be far from town.

"Ready, then," Brautigan murmured to himself. He settled back to wait. It wouldn't be long now.

11

Mountain View mayor Hope Camp spent much of Tuesday thinking gloomily about failure and mortality. At age sixty-eight, he'd outlived three wives — the frontier was hard on women. Both his daughters were married and living back East, having fled the territories as soon as they'd found prospective husbands willing to take them away. He heard from them only at Christmas, when they sent cards but no gifts. Camp knew he had some grandchildren but was uncertain of how many, or of their ages and genders. His life centered on his political career and his business, and now both seemed to be in jeopardy. Lately, some of Mountain View's other civic leaders had begun dropping hints about the desirability of a younger man to head town government. Camp resented it but couldn't really blame them. He'd missed several council meetings in the last months because of aching joints and all-around weariness. Much of that exhaustion came from overwork at his feed store. As Mountain View's growth exploded, so did Camp's business. That was fine in terms of profit, but the additional demands took their toll on the elderly man. There was always more stock to order, more shipments to monitor. The bowling alley was a particular drain on him. On a whim, he'd installed the wooden lane in the back of his shop, thinking it might amuse youngsters while their parents shopped. Instead, it seemed every adult in Mountain View wanted to roll heavy wooden balls at pins. The resulting constant clatter gave the mayor headaches. He wished bowling had never been invented, but the alley was too popular with customers for him to remove.

Cash McLendon's arrival in town, and the heroic Indian fighter's willingness to run the alley for Camp, seemed like a gift from God. The mayor hadn't been in church for decades, but he offered up a silent prayer of thanks anyway. It occurred to Camp that McLendon might, in fact, be a prospective partner in the feed store business. All the Mountain View profits could finance branch stores in other territorial towns — Florence, surely, and perhaps Phoenix. Even though McLendon initially declined Camp's offer, insisting he planned to move on to California soon, the mayor had hope. McLendon seemed to be a young man of considerable energy and salesmanship. A chain of Camp and McLendon feed stores throughout the Southwest — that would be a considerable legacy.

But McLendon's news that he had won the heart of Gabrielle Tirrito, and that they would depart for the West Coast as soon as possible, dashed the mayor's plan. It wasn't only the loss of his prospective business partner that stung. McLendon took the girl away from Joe Saint, the town schoolteacher who Camp had personally recruited. It was hard for territorial towns to find qualified educators; Saint was a daisy, a smart, kind man beloved by pupils and parents alike. Camp feared that Saint's broken heart might cause him to pull up stakes and leave town, too — what would Mountain View do for a teacher then? As soon as McLendon and the girl were gone, the mayor planned to sit down with Joe and reaffirm his importance to the community.

Camp knew that Orville Hancock, the most influential man in Mountain View, was helping McLendon find employment in California. He and Mrs. Hancock had even had McLendon and the girl — what *was* her name? The mayor kept forgetting — over to their home for dinner. They'd never asked Camp to share a meal at their table. But if the mayor exhibited any animosity toward McLendon for leaving, Hancock might respond by supporting someone else for the town's leading office.

So Mayor Camp publicly celebrated the happy couple. He decided that the sooner they were gone, the better the chances that he could convince Joe Saint to stay. Every day McLendon and — Gabrielle, yes, *that* was her name — walked about arm in arm, the more Joe's suffering must increase. So when Major Mulkins approached Camp and suggested they lend McLendon enough money to leave town immediately, the mayor agreed.

On Tuesday, when McLendon arrived at work, he took Camp aside and said that Wednesday would be his last day supervising the bowling alley.

"Gabrielle and I want to leave Friday morning on the Florence stage with her father," McLendon said. "I'll need Thursday to pack and make last-minute preparations."

"Well, we'll miss you," the mayor said. "You've made yourself a good reputation in this town. Are you certain you can't be

186

persuaded to stay? My partnership offer still stands."

"No, we're determined to go. But I'll never forget your generosity."

That afternoon, the mayor and Major Mulkins took McLendon to the bank, where they withdrew the $1,000 they'd agreed to loan him. Mulkins's share of the loan was $300. Camp contributed $700. McLendon tucked the wad of greenbacks in his front pants pocket.

"I'll begin repaying this as soon as I'm employed in California," he promised.

"Just do so as you find convenient," Camp said, forcing himself to sound cheerful. "We know you're good for the money."

McLendon and the mayor left the feed store just before six that evening. An employee named Lauer would supervise until ten p.m. closing. McLendon went off to dinner with his girl at the White Horse, and Camp returned to his modest home, where he warmed some soup. At about eight, he walked to the Ritz, where, as he'd expected, he found McLendon, Gabrielle, and others already at a table, drinking lightly and chattering about San Francisco and weddings. The mayor joined them; he ordered a fresh round of drinks and studied the faces around him. McLendon, beaming; Gabrielle, glowing the way only young women in love seemed to do; Major Mulkins, bearded and ruddy-cheeked. Rebecca Moore the laundry owner was there, too, but not Marie Silva. Camp didn't mind that. Silva was a gloomy sort who reminded him of his second wife. The mayor hadn't been especially saddened when that one died.

"C.M. just bought the stage tickets," Mulkins said. "Here to Florence, Florence to Tucson, Tucson to Arizona City, and west from there. Two weeks, maybe as little as ten days, given good roads and weather, he and Gabrielle will be in San Francisco. A toast to their safe passage!"

"Friday morning," Gabrielle mused. "This is happening so quickly."

"Is your father excited?" Rebecca asked.

Gabrielle pursed her lips. "Not entirely. The journey will be difficult for him, given his health. But once Papa is in California, Doc Vance believes the sea air will prove revivifying."

The group laughed and chatted until just before ten, when McLendon said, "Time for me to attend to my nightly chore. Will one of you gentlemen please see Gabrielle back to the White Horse?"

Mayor Camp felt compelled to make a

188

gesture. Surely McLendon would speak to Orville Hancock before departing on Friday, and perhaps he would mention it.

"Sit, sit," Camp said to McLendon. "I'll go to the shop, count and store the daily receipts."

"That's still my responsibility, at least for the next few nights," McLendon said. "You stay here, have a nightcap."

Camp pushed back his chair and stood. "No, I can tell that every second you and Miss Gabrielle spend apart is painful for you both. I may as well get back in my old routine. See you in the morning."

It was a cloudy night, and the flickering streetlamps provided scanty illumination. The mayor had some difficulty making his way down the street. Of late he'd become concerned about his eyesight. He wasn't sure what cataracts were but thought he might have them. He'd have to ask Doc Vance about that soon.

When Camp entered his store, he saw that his staff had cleared the premises of customers and were closing bins and putting away shelf displays. Lauer, the evening manager, asked, "Where's C.M.?"

"Back at the Ritz, celebrating his imminent departure from town," Camp said, unable to keep a sour undertone from his

189

voice. "You're back to seeing me at this time each night."

"I could take over from C.M. in the matter of storing receipts upstairs," Lauer offered. He'd been employed by Camp for almost a year, and had hopes of promotion. "Then you wouldn't need to trouble yourself."

"Perhaps," Camp said. Though he knew Lauer to be honest, he doubted his brainpower. "Right now I'll carry on. What's the daily total?"

"Near nine hundred dollars," Lauer said. "Also, some customers you've approved for credit did another three hundred. So there's that additional money to come."

Camp took the sack of greenbacks and a few jingling coins. "All right, you and the others go on. I'll finish closing." When he was the only one remaining in the shop, Camp blew out the oil lamps one by one. He left the lamp by the door for last. Then he stepped out into the street and locked the door behind him. Camp walked around behind the building thinking of how, soon, he ought to either reinforce the outside stairs or else build an indoor staircase. But that was additional expense, and why spend the money if the business had no future beyond his own limited life span? Camp hadn't a doubt in hell that the minute he was in the ground, his daughters would sell the feed store and everything in it. It would be like Hope Camp never lived.

"Damn it," the old man grumbled. Guided as much by memory as failing eyesight, he gingerly walked past the loading dock to the staircase, where he paused momentarily, feeling with his foot for the first step up.

Patrick Brautigan prepared as the lights inside the shop went out. His legs were stiff from riding and stinging from his rash. He bent down and did a few quick knee bends. Then he hid himself again behind the barrels on the loading dock.

Noise from the street on the opposite side of the building prevented him from hearing McLendon lock the front door, but he knew that must be about to happen when the last light was extinguished. A quiver ran through Brautigan's body. He always found last-moment anticipation to be gladsome. *Any minute, any minute.*

And now here came McLendon around the corner, moving slower than Brautigan expected. But on he came. It was too dark to distinguish features, so Brautigan sensed rather than saw the man come past the barrels and approach the stairs. He paused at the base of the stairway, just as Brautigan had thought he would.

Time!

Brautigan stepped smoothly from behind the barrels. He reached out his heavy hand and grasped McLendon's collar, yanking his quarry around, and as he did he realized something was wrong, this man was smaller, slighter than Cash McLendon. Then the wind picked up, the clouds blocking the moonlight cleared, and there was sufficient illumination for Patrick Brautigan and Mayor Hope Camp to look at each other full on. The mayor's eyes bulged in terror. He opened his mouth to scream and Brautigan couldn't have that. He swung his right leg in a hard, vicious arc. The steel toe caught the old man flush on the jaw, snapping his head back so violently that his neck broke. Camp died instantly.

Brautigan stood over his victim. He automatically looked in all directions. *Good, no witnesses.* Then he was nearly overcome by a combined sense of fury and frustration — what happened to Cash McLendon? Who was dead in his place?

But Brautigan was too savvy a killer to let emotion more than momentarily rule him. There were things to be done. He dragged the limp corpse halfway up the stairs, which swayed and creaked under their combined weight. Then Brautigan pushed the body back down; it bounced off some steps on the way before coming to rest on the ground at the foot of the stairway. *Good.* It would seem as though the old man, whoever he was, tripped going up and fell, breaking his neck in the process. An accident, not murder.

Brautigan thought hard as he went back through the alleys toward the edge of town. What would the boss say if Brautigan had to admit McLendon had eluded him again? The search could resume in San Francisco; that was where the bastard would be going next. But the boss had no tolerance for failure. He might well dismiss Brautigan and hire someone else in his place. The possibility of unemployment didn't concern Brautigan — he well knew there would always be rich men in need of his violent skills. But the thought of a second failure pursuing the same puny man was intolerable. No, he would take McLendon here. There had to be a way. He'd surely think of it.

"Where's McLendon?" Ike Clanton asked as Brautigan emerged from the darkness. "What happened back there?"

"Shut up and get mounted," Brautigan

said. "We're going back to our camp."

Mayor Hope Camp's body was discovered at six a.m. on Wednesday by employees coming to open the feed store. Sheriff Hove and Doc Vance were summoned. Word reached the White Horse Hotel soon afterward. McLendon hurried over. The blanket-covered corpse still lay at the foot of the staircase.

"Seems to have been an accident," the sheriff told McLendon. "I found the sack of money lying not a foot away from where he landed, so it couldn't have been a robbery."

"Old Hope slipped going up the steps and broke his neck during the fall," Doc Vance concurred. "Terrible thing. Everybody told him those steps were rickety and he needed to fix 'em. Too late now."

"I feel responsible," McLendon said. "I was going to put the daily receipts in the safe, same as always, but the mayor insisted on doing it."

"No sense blaming yourself," Doc Vance said. "Hope had a good run. Sheriff, don't I recall he had daughters back East? I guess they need to be notified by wire."

"I'll see if I can come up with addresses," Hove said. "All right, Doc, let's get poor Hope over to your office so you can write up the proper death notice. Then he can be taken on to the undertaker's."

McLendon watched as Doc Vance directed a couple of helpers to pick up the body. As they did, the blanket fell back from Camp's face and upper body. His head was bent at an odd angle from the broken neck, but what caught McLendon's eye was a massive contusion on the dead man's jaw.

"What happened there?" McLendon asked, pointing to the abrasion.

Doc Vance shrugged. "Must have hit his chin during the fall. That might have been when his neck broke."

"Probably so," McLendon said.

By mid-afternoon one of the mayor's daughters was informed by telegram of her father's death. She lived in New York, and responded by return telegram that she and her sister would be unable to come to Mountain View to claim their father's body.

"Telegram said that we are to bury him here, box up all his possessions, and send them east," Sheriff Hove told McLendon, Gabrielle, Major Mulkins, and Rebecca Moore at the Ritz that evening. "She also said her lawyer'd be in touch to sort out bank accounts, property like the feed store, and so on. I didn't detect any love or sense of loss in the message."

"Well, we'll give him a proper burial here," Rebecca Moore said. "Gabrielle, do you think I should talk to the *padre,* or else that lay minister who does the Protestant services in the schoolhouse on Sundays?"

"Either one, I suppose," Gabrielle said. "Mayor Camp didn't seem a man of specific faith."

"The *padre,* then," Rebecca said. "I hear his prayers are the more impressive. Gabrielle, you folks are departing Friday morning. If we set the mayor's service for Thursday, you could attend."

"We'd like to," McLendon said. "The mayor was more than good to me. I owe someone seven hundred dollars on his behalf. Do you suppose I should send my repayments to his daughter?"

"I'll ask her lawyer about that," Hove promised. "If Hope himself could speak, I suspect he'd tell you the loan was forgiven. With his daughter, I'm not so sure. But it's commendable you're concerned about it, C.M. Most men would keep quiet and hope the matter was forgotten."

"He isn't like that," Gabrielle said proudly. "I'm just sorry the mayor's funeral on Thursday will be our last memory of Mountain View."

■ ■ ■ ■

On Wednesday morning, Patrick Brautigan sent Ike Clanton into Mountain View to reconnoiter. He made his instructions simple and clear: "Don't let McLendon see you. Listen to what people in town are saying about what happened to the old man. As soon as you have the sense of it, ride back here and report."

Ike returned soon. "Everybody's talking about their mayor falling down some stairs and breaking his neck."

"They suspect nothing beyond that?"

"Not from what I heard. What did happen?"

"You've no need to know."

Ike wanted coffee, but Brautigan hadn't allowed a fire since their return. "Is at least my part in this over? Can I go home now?"

Brautigan shook his head. "Wait awhile. We'll discuss the next steps directly."

So Clanton waited. He rolled and smoked cigarettes, tried to doze despite the sweltering heat, and occasionally heaved histrionic sighs. But it was mid-afternoon before Brautigan spoke to him again.

"Tell me, Ike. Somewhere near Clantonville, far enough away to be out of sight and

197

sound of your family, but close enough to reach from Clantonville with ease, is there a flat area with good sight lines? A place where a man could glimpse others lurking, say, a half mile away or even farther?"

Clanton thought for a moment. "Well, there's Devil's Valley, maybe two hours' ride west of our place. Gila Peak's some to the north. Nearest hills are near a mile away. Anyone down in the middle of the valley can see a long way in all directions. Nobody could creep up there."

"How long a ride from Clantonville?"

"Two or three hours, maybe."

"You're certain about this Devil's Valley?"

Clanton snorted. "I oughta be. It's one of the places Pa looked at for settling. But there's no water, no shade, just a terrible place. What's it to do with us?"

"I'll explain in a moment. Now, keeping south to avoid entering the agency, is it two days' ride from here to Clantonville?"

"I'd say so."

"Without you to guide me, could I find Clantonville on my own?"

"So long as you kept going southeast at all times. Pueblo Viejo Valley's considerably extended, and the green of our crops should catch your eye from quite some distance. Say, are you done with me after all?"

"No, I continue to need your services. There's some action coming, Ike. Can you handle that?"

Clanton grinned. "I can handle anything if the money's right."

"It will be. Now, here's what's required."

12

Gabrielle regretted that her last few days in Mountain View were to be painful ones. Though she was thrilled to be back with McLendon and eager to begin their life together in California, her joy was considerably tempered in two ways. The tragic death of Mayor Hope Camp saddened her — though Gabrielle had hardly known the mayor, he'd been extremely kind to McLendon, and his part in the loan allowing them to leave sooner for California was generosity almost beyond imagining. His funeral on Thursday would be a sorrowful occasion.

The second damper on her happiness involved Joe Saint. It was now Wednesday, and already twice during the week, on Monday afternoon and Tuesday morning, Joe had essentially rebuffed her when she'd tried speaking with him. He hadn't been rude — Joe, she thought, was incapable of that — but he'd used obvious excuses to get away. Gabrielle knew it was too much to expect or even hope that Joe would accept her decision with aplomb. She had invited him to love her, and he had, sweetly and completely. Through no fault of his own, she was leaving him for someone else, the very person whose earlier betrayal had subsequently sent her into Joe's arms. Gabrielle understood how he felt — it had to be much like the nearly unedurable pain McLendon had caused her back in St. Louis — yet she couldn't keep herself from trying to make things as right with him as possible. On Monday Joe said he had papers to grade. Tuesday morning he claimed that a pupil was waiting for pre-school tutoring.

"But we need to talk, Joe," she pleaded as he walked away toward the schoolhouse.

He looked back over his shoulder and said, "Another time."

But after Friday morning when she, her father, and McLendon departed on the Florence stage, there might not be another time. Gabrielle understood very well the vagaries of the frontier. It was possible to continue encountering the same person over and over in a variety of locales, or else to lose contact with someone forever. The latter was the likely case for her and Joe. He was settled in Mountain View, and, once in

San Francisco, Gabrielle couldn't imagine any reason she'd return to the territorial boomtown. That made her determined to have a private talk with Joe, to explain better, and, she had to admit to herself, to ease her own guilty conscience. All Wednesday morning and afternoon, while she continued training Melinda, her replacement at the front desk of the White Horse, Gabrielle racked her brain for the right words to say to Joe. Her frustration in thinking of anything suitable made her all the more determined. Even if he refused to forgive her, she wanted him to *understand.*

During an afternoon break, she went out to the hotel porch where McLendon sat talking with Major Mulkins. Because of the mayor's death, his feed store was locked and shuttered, so McLendon's job there was over and he had no immediate demands on his time.

"Major, would you excuse Cash and myself for just a moment?" Gabrielle asked. She refused to call him "C.M." as everyone else now addressed him. The Major smiled, nodded, and went inside. Gabrielle seated herself next to McLendon and said, "You won't like this, but I'm doing it anyway."

"Those are hardly the words to secure my approval."

Gabrielle bristled. "I repeat — your approval isn't required."

"Don't get riled. What is it you're going to do?"

"After supper tonight, I'm going to see Joe. We haven't spoken properly since I informed him of my decision."

"I believe you've already made attempts. If he doesn't want further conversation on the subject, you ought to let him be. In his place, I know I couldn't stand it. Leave the man alone. We'll be gone on Friday. He'll feel better when we're out of sight."

"I owe it to Joe to explain myself. I need to thank him for his years of devotion. I want us to part as friends."

McLendon sighed. "I don't think that's possible, at least for the present. Maybe in time he'll feel different, but for now, the wound's too fresh. Let him be."

"I won't be dissuaded."

"I know. I'll say this on Joe's behalf — don't hold against him any hard words he might offer. They'll come from his hurt, not his heart."

Though the hotel cook prepared succulent venison steaks for dinner at the staff table in the kitchen, Gabrielle only picked at her food. When Mulkins asked if she and

203

McLendon would join him for postprandial drinks at the Ritz, she replied that only Cash would, at least initially.

"I have some other business, but may appear after a while," Gabrielle said. She excused herself and left the kitchen.

"More packing, shopping, or perhaps pre-bridal nerves?" Mulkins asked McLendon.

"Worse than that. She's going to try and make things right with Joe Saint."

"That's a mistake. And you're letting her?"

"Nobody stops Gabrielle when she's determined."

Mulkins speared a last bite of venison with his fork. "Well, then, I'd best get you fortified with good bourbon. She's not likely to be in the best of moods when she returns."

Before leaving, Gabrielle went upstairs to check on her father. Salvatore Tirrito was already asleep, snoring softly. One corner of his open mouth was wet; Gabrielle gently wiped the saliva away with a small towel. Then she changed into her gray church dress, something more formal than a workday frock. It seemed important to look her best.

When she stepped into the street, Gabrielle discovered that the wind was blowing hard. There were clouds overhead, thick rather than the usual thready tufts dotting the late-summer night sky. Rain seemed possible. She considered returning to her room for a bonnet, but didn't. She was very nervous — if she delayed any longer she might not go at all. As she walked, her hair whipped into tangles, very unbecoming. Well, Joe had seen her disheveled many times before.

The street leading to Saint's home was particularly narrow, and behind it was open land. Though it was too dark to see more than a few feet ahead, Gabrielle knew tumbleweeds were flying across the outlying sand. She could hear faint crunches as they ricocheted off rocks and cacti. There were occasional howls from coyotes, and some owl hoots in near harmony. In spite of the blowing dust, the scent of sage hung in the air. Nighttime in the desert — it would be quite different in San Francisco.

There was light behind Saint's curtained windows. At least he was home. Gabrielle took a breath and knocked on the door. There was no response. She knocked again, harder. A crash came from inside, the sound of a chair falling over. Then Saint yanked the door open and Gabrielle smelled the whiskey on his breath.

"You're drunk, Joe," she blurted.

Saint's eyes widened as they struggled to focus. "What of it?" he slurred. "None of your damned business anymore."

"You shouldn't be like this. Let me come in. I'll make you coffee."

Saint shook his head so hard that his glasses nearly flew off. "You're not coming in. I don't want you here."

Gabrielle was dismayed. She'd never seen Saint in this condition. "Let me in," she said again. "We can talk. Drinking won't help, Joe."

Saint emitted a loud, guttural belch, a transgression he would never have committed in any woman's presence if sober.

"It's helping a lot. Go away. Go to San Fra—" His tongue couldn't handle the next sibilant syllables. "All right, go to California. Anywhere. Jus' go."

"I'm not leaving until you listen to me."

Saint straightened in the doorway. With great effort, he said, "No need t'say anything. Once y'tole him to come on here, I never had a chance. Y'knew what you'd do."

"I didn't, I swear —"

"You always loved him, not me. Ever'thin' you said in Glorious, love me f'ever, none of it true."

Gabrielle reached for his arm, but Saint knocked her hand away. "That's not true,

Joe. It's just that everything changed and I —"

"Enough!" Saint bellowed. "Go away. Go t'California. Go t'hell." He slammed the door in her face.

Gabrielle wept. She stood in front of the door for several moments, hoping Saint would come back and open it. But he didn't, and behind the door she heard things being thrown, guessing from the thumps that books, Joe Saint's beloved books, were being tossed against walls. In his drunken rage, might he injure himself? Should she summon Sheriff Hove? No, that would only humiliate Joe more.

Wiping away tears, Gabrielle turned and began walking back down the narrow street. The wind blew dust in her eyes, further diminishing her vision. Gabrielle found herself wishing it would pour rain; maybe a deluge would wash away all the guilt she felt. Mountain View's main streets loomed fifty yards ahead. She had to stop crying before she reached them. Otherwise people would see, and Gabrielle's pride could never permit that. No, she'd stop crying now, enough of this, and then a huge arm wrapped around her from behind, a massive hand clapped over her mouth, and a deep voice hissed in her ear, "Not a sound, miss, or you die."

McLendon and Major Mulkins had several drinks at the Ritz. Mac Fielding came by their table and asked McLendon for permission to print "the happy news of your betrothal." McLendon didn't think that it could hurt. Perhaps Gabrielle would be pleased. But then he realized she'd hate the idea because reading about them in the paper might hurt Joe Saint. Always this terrible concern for Joe Saint's feelings. McLendon understood and felt resentful at the same time.

"Sorry, Mr. Fielding. I believe we'll pass on that," McLendon said.

The newspaperman was aggrieved. "You misunderstand a free press," he said. "I don't need your go-ahead. I just might write the story anyway."

"Do what you need to," McLendon said. If Fielding did and Saint was bothered, at least Gabrielle couldn't blame him.

Sheriff Hove came in to the saloon just after ten p.m. as part of his evening rounds. "Just the two of you tonight?" he asked Mulkins and McLendon. "I hope Miss Gabrielle's not under the weather?"

"Just occupied with last-minute things before our Friday departure," McLendon said. "Are all the arrangements made for Mayor Camp's interment?"

"Orville Hancock himself will deliver the eulogy," the sheriff said. "He and Mrs. Hancock will host a gathering in their home afterward, since the late mayor had no family in town. You'll attend, of course?"

After the sheriff departed, McLendon and Mulkins drank a little more. Because they'd each downed three bourbons, they switched to beer.

"Getting late," Mulkins said. "Do you think Gabrielle might still be joining us?"

McLendon checked his pocket watch: twenty after ten. "Probably not. Her intention was to talk things out with Joe Saint, and you know Gabrielle. She'll take as long as necessary. If Joe agreed to the conversation, as he must have done since she's been absent so long, I suspect they'll be at it for hours yet."

"He might forgive her, but never you," Mulkins said.

"I can't blame him. Well, one more beer, and then let's head back to the White Horse. If Gabrielle's not there, I may as well go to bed myself. You and I both need some rest for the funeral tomorrow, seeing as we're pallbearers."

When they returned to the hotel, the night

desk clerk told McLendon that Gabrielle hadn't yet returned.

"Yep, talking all night," McLendon said to the Major, who nodded. The two men went up to the room they shared and went to sleep.

13

Besides panic, Gabrielle's first sensation was that she was floating. Her abductor used the arm wrapped around her waist to carry rather than drag her; her feet dangled inches off the ground. She was not a small woman, but the arm lifting her never trembled from fatigue.

Gabrielle was borne to the desert side of the narrow street, back beyond the row of houses. Because she was gripped so tightly, she couldn't twist to look at the man who had captured her. The dark night sky made it impossible to see much else. Then, ahead of them, there was a tiny flicker of light, and in a moment of clarity she knew it was a match, struck to provide a small guiding flame for an instant before a wind gust blew it out. Immediately, Gabrielle was set down.

"Walk," said the man behind her. He twined his fingers in her curls, using the hair as a halter. She did her best to walk in the direction that the flame had been, ten yards, twenty, and then she first sensed, then saw, the shapes of animals, three horses and a mule. Another man was with them. He was careful to keep his back turned.

"Go on," the man behind her said to him, and the one who'd been waiting went to one of the horses, mounted, and trotted off. Gabrielle's hair was released. She stood stock-still and trembling; she'd never been so afraid.

"Turn around and look at me," the man ordered, but Gabrielle was too terrified to move. A blow to the back of her head knocked her sprawling in the dirt. She lay there stunned, and then was yanked to her feet and turned so she had no choice but to see her captor. Gabrielle's first impression frightened her even more. The clouds had blown away, but the person manhandling her was so massive that he blocked out the moon.

"That was merely a tap. Always do what I tell you, or there's worse to follow." The monster's voice was pitched low. She could see now, looking just around him, the faint outline of the houses on Joe's street perhaps a quarter mile away. The distance could have been a hundred miles. Her legs felt rubbery and she knew she could never reach them.

The man hit her again, high on her cheek this time, and she was knocked to her knees. He pulled her up and said, "Attend to me. The first rule is, you never speak, never utter a sound. Nod if you understand."

Gabrielle's head ached terribly, from shock as well as pain. In all her life, she'd never been struck before tonight. Her captor pulled back his arm for another blow, but before it was delivered she managed to nod.

"That's better. I'll have more to tell you later. For now, this is what you'll do. You'll mount the smaller of the two horses over there. You will ride directly at my side and make no attempt to escape. Your horse is small and slow, and you can't outrun me on foot. Scream or otherwise try to call attention to us and you'll die on the spot. Do you understand?"

She nodded.

"Do as I tell you, obey me at all times, and you'll live. Now get on that horse." He grasped Gabrielle tightly above her left elbow and propelled her toward the animal. When she reached the horse's side he released her arm and she paused. The horse was saddled conventionally, stirrups dangling down. But Gabrielle wore a dress; she couldn't mount without pulling the skirts up to her waist. Despite the peril in which she now found herself, lifelong modesty prevented her. The huge man understood and didn't care. "Yank up your garment or I'll rip it off," he said. Gabrielle reached down with shaking hands and hoisted her dress. She wore a chemise and pantaloons underneath. The chemise had to come up too. The pantaloons were knee-length. Gabrielle reflected briefly that they might prevent her legs from chafing as she rode, and then thought that potential chafing was the least of her concerns. She put her foot in the stirrup and threw her right leg over the horse. Her dress billowed out in front and behind her. She pulled the material bunched in the front off to the side.

The big man mounted quickly; he reached over and took her horse's reins. "We ride now," he said. "Remember, not a sound. Don't try to get away. There's no escape." Gabrielle swallowed hard because she knew that it was true.

They rode away from Mountain View. It was hard to tell in the dark, but Gabrielle thought they were headed south. What was that way? The Apache agency — surely they weren't riding there. But what else? The mule was tethered to the big man's saddle horn and following docilely along. It must be carrying supplies. A long ride, then? To what purpose?

Gabrielle was smart, but headache and panic made it hard for her to concentrate. She thought of Cash. When would he realize that she was gone? Would he come to save her? How would he know where to look? And then it came to her who her captor was — Brautigan, the killer from St. Louis. Her abduction must be part of a plan to get Cash. But then why were they riding away? Brautigan said that if she obeyed, she'd live — so there was hope. But what if she was to be used as bait to lure Cash?

They rode slowly, letting the horses sense and pick their way around occasional patches of cacti and rock piles. Gabrielle was exhausted from the tension. In spite of herself, she fell into a light doze and almost toppled off her horse. Brautigan caught her shoulder and said sharply, "Stay awake." She did her best. After another hour it was easier because of pressure from her bladder. She needed badly to stop and relieve herself, but couldn't ask because she'd been commanded not to speak. Gabrielle wondered whether it was better to risk another blow or to wet herself. She gritted her teeth and did her best to avoid either, thinking hard instead on ways she might escape. Her horse was a plodder, and Brautigan was right — she could never outrun her captor on foot. She didn't doubt that he could kill her with a single blow if he chose to. She thought she remembered something else, and tried to peek from the corner of her eye without turning her still-hurting head — didn't he have a Winchester in a scabbard dangling from his saddle, on the side of his horse away from her? Yes, she could hear the faint flapping of the scabbard on the horse's flank. She couldn't reach across Brautigan's body to get at the weapon. He was too quick for that. But perhaps if they stopped . . .

The first faint pink streaks of dawn had just appeared to their left when Gabrielle carefully reached out with her left hand and tapped Brautigan's arm. He asked, "You need relief?" She nodded emphatically. "All right." He pulled the animals to a halt. They were crossing a valley. Brautigan dismounted. To Gabrielle's disappointment, he immediately moved between their horses, placing the Winchester well out of reach. "Jump down," he said.

Gabrielle clambered off her horse, hampered by falling skirts. She automatically reached up to touch her hair and felt a rat's nest of knotted curls.

"Go on," Brautigan said. "I'll allow only a short delay."

Gabrielle looked around for some bushes, or perhaps a large rock. But there was nothing — the ground was empty and flat in every direction.

"Do it here," Brautigan commanded. She shook her head.

"Then you'll hold it until you explode or you'll piss all over the horse," he said. Gabrielle knew he meant it. She walked a step away from him. "No farther," Brautigan said. "Right there."

Crimson with humiliation, Gabrielle gathered her skirts, pulled down her pantaloons, and squatted. She turned her face away from Brautigan, then couldn't help looking over at him. He watched her impassively; she might have been a pet dog pausing on a walk. She stood and rearranged her clothes.

"Stop there a moment," Brautigan said. He unbuttoned his pants and urinated, the stream splashing on the ground. It seemed to Gabrielle that he took a very long time. When he was done he said, "All right. Let's be going. You can have some water first."

Two canteens angled on straps from the packs on the mule. Brautigan went to get one. As he did, Gabrielle made her move. She darted to the big man's horse and yanked the Winchester from its scabbard. She expected him to try to stop her, but he didn't, watching her as incuriously as he had while she relieved herself.

"Stand back," Gabrielle said. She hadn't spoken since she'd first been taken and her voice cracked. "Get back away from me."

"Put it down," Brautigan said.

Gabrielle kept the rifle pointed at him. The barrel shook a little because her hands felt fluttery, but she knew she could pull the trigger and get a bullet in him before he could possibly reach her. There were at least ten yards between them. "I'll kill you. I mean it."

Brautigan walked toward her, not hurrying. She'd never physically hurt anyone, certainly had never shot a man, but now she raised the rifle to her shoulder, and since he didn't stop coming she pulled the trigger. There was a sharp *click* as the hammer fell on an empty chamber.

"It was never loaded," Brautigan said. He reached out and yanked the rifle away from her. "I've no use for guns," he added as he replaced the Winchester in its scabbard. Then he turned back to Gabrielle. "You spoke, and you tried to escape," he said.

"You were warned against both."

Gabrielle shrieked. Her cry was lost in the vastness around them.

"You're still of use, so I won't kill you," Brautigan said matter-of-factly. "But you need to be hurt somewhat, so that the lesson will take this time." Then he beat Gabrielle, administering blows not to her head but to her body, pounding her kidneys and stomach and ribs. She fell often. Once she found herself prone and staring at Brautigan's boots. The toes were tipped with steel, just as McLendon had described. She wondered if he'd kick her with them, but he didn't. He used only his fists, and those were sufficient.

It seemed that the beating would never end, but finally Brautigan stood back. It took Gabrielle long moments to sit up. She hurt all over, but there was particularly sharp pain in her ribs. She guessed some were broken. Even in such agony, Gabrielle realized that the giant had only used a fraction of his strength. He'd pummeled her with the practiced control of a veteran torturer.

"Next time, worse," Brautigan promised. "Get up. There's still a long way to go. It's light now, and we might see others. Should that happen, you stay in your saddle and behave normally, like a woman out riding with a friend. The slightest sign otherwise and I'll kill whoever and also you. Then I'll just get McLendon some other way. Now up on your horse."

Mounting was hard; it was excruciating just lifting one foot up into the stirrup. Brautigan could have helped but didn't; she understood that he wanted her to suffer without assistance. When she was up in the saddle he remounted too. Before they continued riding he pushed a canteen toward her face.

"Drink," he said.

She shook her head. It made her very afraid to have his hand so near her.

"I said, drink. I don't want you dropping from dehydration."

Gabrielle gulped some of the water. It was warm and not at all refreshing.

"Indicate to me when you want to stop and piss again," Brautigan said. He gathered her horse's reins and they rode on, still going south.

When the sun was about midway across the sky Brautigan halted again. Gabrielle saw a mountain range to her right. She didn't know its name; she'd never gone this way before and was completely lost. Where could they possibly be going?

"Pee if you need," Brautigan said, and Gabrielle did there in front of him. She no longer concerned herself with modesty. Her body hurt too much from the beating to squat. She relieved herself standing up, trying to keep her skirts and underthings dry and only partially succeeding.

Brautigan fished a can out of a pack and used a knife to open it. He handed it to Gabrielle.

"Peaches," he said. "Eat what you can and drink the juice."

She tried; the sweetness of the fruit and juice was cloying, especially in the heat. After a few mouthfuls she handed the can back to him. He tipped the can to his mouth and emptied it.

"Wait there while I attend to the animals," Brautigan said. He got water from a cask, using his hat as a pail, and gave both horses and the mule some water. One at a time, he undid their bridles and let them eat some grain that he also offered them in his hat. That done, he wiped bits of grain from the hat and put it back on his head. On another man it might have seemed ludicrous, but nothing was ever humorous about Brautigan.

Gabrielle didn't dare move while he

performed these chores. She stood still until he said, "Back on the horse," and she obeyed. Now she rode in a mental daze. It seemed too hard to think of anything beyond not being struck again. In late afternoon they crossed a creek — the animals drank, and Brautigan refilled canteens. They rode on, and the ground broke up somewhat, so they had to go slower. Gabrielle wondered if they would stop when it turned dark, and they did.

"No fire," Brautigan said. "We don't want company." They ate canned peas and drank canteen water. The horses and mule were tethered nearby; Brautigan gave them more grain because they had no grass or plants to feed on.

"Tomorrow you may see some people you know," he told Gabrielle. "Afterward, you'll never name them to another soul. Do you agree?" She nodded. "Sleep on this," he told her, and handed her a blanket. "No, don't lay down yet. Hands out in front of you." He bound her wrists with a length of rope. "Now down on the blanket."

For a terrible moment, she thought he meant to rape her. But instead he said, "Legs straight out. Keep them together." He used more rope to bind her ankles. "Don't try to undo the knots and sneak away in the night. I'll catch you, and you know what will happen." She soon fell into a fitful sleep because she was so emotionally and physically exhausted. She woke several times during the night. Each time, Brautigan was seated nearby, watching her. Did he not need to sleep? How could he not be tired after the long, hot ride? She thought of Cash and wondered how this terrible man intended to use her to catch him. Then she remembered her father — who was caring for him? Events were entirely out of her control. She was at Brautigan's mercy, and he had none.

Stu Vincent was a happy young man as he rode through the early morning, heading for a small camp he and some pards had going a few more miles east. Plenty of ore had been found up in Mountain View near the Pinals and down New Mexico way around Silver City. Stu and his friends, hearing about it while working their parents' spreads out near Tucson, decided to turn their own hands to prospecting. There had to be more silver somewhere in that great middle distance between Mountain View and Silver City, just had to be. A family named Clanton staked out a town right about where the Tucson boys wanted to prospect, so Stu told the others he'd scout out other possible places to the north and west. He'd ridden hard for two days and finally paused near Table Mountain. The creeks along its base had some promising float, bits of eroded rock that Stu believed bore the faint black lines indicating silver. He had some in his saddlebag. Another three, four hours and he'd be back in camp. If the other boys saw what he did, they'd all head back to the mountain and stake a claim. Riches all around, and sweet little Patty Pressley back in Tucson would pay Stu a considerable amount more attention. Stu's life was about to change in precipitous ways — he felt certain of it.

The terrain was alternately flat and lumpy with rock formations. Stu mostly concentrated on guiding his horse through when he saw movement ahead and to his left. Maybe a half mile away, two riders headed south, one of them leading a pack mule. Stu's first inclination was to leave them alone. He wanted to get back to camp fast so he and the boys could get their claim staked. But another look at the riders baffled him. One was a big man, maybe the biggest Stu had ever seen, and the other was a woman. She was wearing a dress, not at all suited for this rough country, and even less so for riding. Stu had sisters and he knew they'd never venture out in such unsuitable garb. Maybe there'd been some accident, and these two were needing help. Stu had been raised right; he prodded his horse with a light nudge of his heels and galloped over to intercept the pair.

The closer Stu got, the odder things seemed. He expected these people to wave when they saw him, greet him in some way — it wasn't a usual thing to encounter other riders in this portion of the territory. Maybe they feared he was a bandit. Stu made sure to keep his right hand well away from the butt of his Peacemaker.

"Hello," he called out as he neared them. "Are you folks all right? Is there any assistance I can provide?"

The big man pulled his mount to a halt; Stu saw that he also had the reins of the woman's horse, and wondered why. "We're fine," the man said. "Just riding through. No need for you to stop."

That was fine with Stu. This man looked scary. Stu was about to nod and ride on when he took a closer look at the woman. Her dress was dirty; surely she hadn't intended to ride out dressed like that. And though she didn't look directly at Stu, he sensed that she was afraid — of the big man,

225

obviously. Something here was wrong.

"Are you all right, miss?" he asked.

She didn't answer, still didn't look at him. The big man said again, "We're fine. You go on."

Stu maneuvered his mount in front of them. He dismounted and walked toward the woman, reaching down slightly with his right hand so it was close to his gun.

"Stay on that horse, mister," he said. "Miss, it appears to me —"

Something happened, a blurry motion from the direction of the big man. How had he gotten off that horse so fast? Then Stu's world turned black.

Brautigan stood over the body, its face caved in from the force of his kick. Gabrielle sat trembling on her horse. She uttered a thin, horrified wail.

"None of that," Brautigan said. He looked at Gabrielle, then down at the corpse. "Off your horse. Get over here."

Gabrielle had trouble dismounting. Her foot shook so much she couldn't use the stirrup and had to slide down. Because her horse was so small it wasn't much of a drop, but even the slight jarring elicited a knife-like pain in her ribs.

Brautigan knelt and stripped the body of

its shirt and trousers. He tossed his victim's gun into a patch of cacti. "Get out of that dress. He wasn't very big. His clothes ought to fit you, at least well enough not to fall off." Gabrielle looked at him. "You heard me. Put on his clothes. If you don't do it yourself, I'll do it for you. It was you riding in a dress that attracted his attention. That won't happen again."

Silently, she stripped, leaving on only her pantaloons, and dressed in the dead man's clothing. The trousers fit reasonably well, but the shirt was much too large and flapped around her body. Brautigan watched without any indication of carnal interest.

"Don't forget the boots. You can stuff some grass in the toes if they're too big." They were too big, but Gabrielle put them on anyway without grass padding. Her feet slid about inside, but what did it matter?

When she had the shoes on, Brautigan handed her Stu's hat. It was stained with blood; she shuddered as she touched it, and let it drop to the ground.

"Your choice, but you'll regret this squeamishness," Brautigan warned. "It'll be the sun that makes you pay, not I."

They rode away, leaving Gabrielle's gray dress and chemise on the ground by Stu Vincent's naked corpse. Overhead, buzzards croaked and circled.

For the first time since he'd taken her in the street by Joe Saint's house, Gabrielle sensed that Brautigan was worried. He looked intently ahead of them now, scanning the horizon, clearly looking for something.

"Maybe some to the west," he said aloud to himself. "We've drifted too far south." They rode a while longer. Soon, Gabrielle knew, she'd need to stop and relieve herself again. Just when she was about to tap Brautigan's arm, he said, "There, that tall cactus. That's the one," and kicked his horse into a trot. Gabrielle's creaky mount and the mule labored to keep up. In a while they came to the rim of a valley. Looking ahead, Gabrielle saw some scattered buildings and squares of green.

"Found it," Brautigan said, and they rode down into the valley.

14

Just before seven on Thursday, McLendon came downstairs for breakfast in the hotel kitchen. Gabrielle was always there ahead of him, but not today.

"Perhaps her father's doing poorly and it's taking extra time to get him shaved and dressed," he said to Major Mulkins. "I'll go inquire."

"More likely she's just moving a little slower than usual, worn out from her talk last night with Joe Saint," Mulkins said. "I'd let her come down in her own time, were I you."

"That's likely it," McLendon agreed. He helped himself to oatmeal and eggs, and lingered over a second cup of coffee while he waited for Gabrielle. By eight, he wondered again if there was something wrong with her father. He decided to wait until eight-thirty. If Gabrielle wasn't downstairs by then, he would go up.

229

Eight-thirty, and no Gabrielle. McLendon went upstairs and knocked on the door of the room she shared with her father.

"Gabrielle?" he called. There was no response. He knocked again and pressed his ear against the door. He thought he heard a faint groan on the other side. McLendon tried to open the door, but it was locked. He rushed downstairs and found Major Mulkins.

"Something's wrong with Gabrielle, and her door's locked. Bring the master key."

They raced back up and Mulkins unlocked the door. Inside, they found Salvatore Tirrito struggling to sit up in his bed.

"Chamber pot," the old man croaked. Mulkins fetched it from a corner and held Tirrito steady as he stood and relieved himself.

"She wasn't here at all last night," McLendon said, gesturing toward Gabrielle's bed.

"You don't know that," Mulkins said. "She might have risen extra early, made her bed, and gone out for a walk or on some errand."

McLendon shook his head. "She'd never have left her father like this. His care is always her first concern. No, she never got back from seeing Saint last night. I've got to get over there — the bastard may have done something to her." He helped the old man

230

button the fly on his long johns and asked, "Mr. Tirrito, where is Gabrielle?" But Tirrito seemed too confused to reply.

Mulkins eased Tirrito back on his bed and caught McLendon's arm. "Don't go jumping to conclusions. You know Joe'd never do anything untoward, especially where Gabrielle's concerned. Let me fetch one of the staff to stay with her daddy here, and I'll go with you. Chances are we'll encounter Gabrielle on her way back, and won't you feel foolish then?"

The main streets of Mountain View were crowded with people on the way to mine shifts or jobs in shops or breakfast in a town restaurant. McLendon and Mulkins tried to hurry without pushing others aside. Just before they left Main Street, they saw youngsters crowded around the front door of the schoolhouse.

"Why aren't you in class?" Mulkins asked.

One of the older girls said, "Mr. Saint ain't here yet. We don't know whether to go in or go home."

McLendon panicked. "He's done something, I know it," he blurted out, and ran for Saint's street.

"You all go ahead on home," Mulkins told the girl, and tore after his friend.

They dashed to Saint's house. McLendon pounded on the door until it finally creaked open. Joe Saint, bleary-eyed and unshaven, peered out and croaked, "What?"

"Where's Gabrielle, you bastard?" McLendon shouted.

"What? Gabrielle?" Saint mumbled. "What about her?"

Mulkins placed a restraining hand against McLendon's chest and said gently, "Joe, it looks like Gabrielle didn't get back to the White Horse last night, and we're concerned. She told C.M. before she left that she was coming here to see you. Did she?"

Saint squinted in the morning glare. "I guess. Jesus, what's the time?"

"Where is she?" McLendon demanded.

"That won't do, C.M.," Mulkins said. "I believe Joe here has a morning-after head. Joe, may we come in?"

"Is it already school time?" Saint asked.

"Don't fret on that, Joe," Mulkins said. "I told the youngsters to go on home. Guess even a teacher's allowed the occasional sick day. Now, with your permission we'll just enter your home." They did, and gasped. It was a wreck, with chairs overturned and books thrown everywhere. The sour stench of vomit clogged the air.

"A struggle," McLendon exclaimed. He

grabbed the scrawny schoolteacher and began shaking him. "What did you do to her? Where is she?"

Mulkins dragged Saint from McLendon's grasp. "This gets us nowhere, C.M. Joe, look at me. What happened here?"

Saint pulled a chair upright and slumped down on it. "I guess I got drunk."

"While Gabrielle was here?" Mulkins suggested in a coaxing tone. McLendon hovered behind Saint's chair.

"No, I opened the door and I think we talked a minute, but she never came in. Hard to remember. My head really hurts."

"No doubt," Mulkins said, gesturing toward an empty liquor bottle on the floor. "Are you sure she never came inside, Joe?"

Saint nodded gingerly. "She wanted to talk and I told her no. Told her to go away. Then I shut the door."

McLendon leaned down and pushed his face directly in front of Saint's. "If that's true, then where is she now?"

"I've got no idea. I just kept drinking and I guess I passed out."

"I think you hurt her. She fought you — I know she did. That's when things got strewn around in here."

Saint exhaled. His breath was a vile combination of whiskey fumes and vomit. "No,

I did that myself. You're the one who hurts Gabrielle, not me. She never came inside." He hung his head for a moment, trying to concentrate. Then he said, "So she's missing? You say she never got back? Hell — have you told the sheriff?"

"Not yet, Joe," Mulkins said. "We wanted to look around ourselves, first. When you and she talked last night — briefly, by your account, and she never came inside — did she say anything else, mention any other place she might go, someone else she might see?"

Saint rubbed his face hard with both hands. "No, I'm sure she didn't. She wanted to talk about what she was doing, why she was doing it" — he raised his head to glare at McLendon — "and I wouldn't. And I closed the door and that was all."

Mulkins said to McLendon, "C.M., I believe it's time to visit Sheriff Hove."

"Give me just a minute to wash and change clothes," Saint said. "I'll come along."

"Don't bother," McLendon said. "Stay here and nurse your hangover."

Saint stood up. "I'm coming, and I don't care if you like it."

Jack Hove was concerned but not alarmed

234

by the news of Gabrielle's disappearance.

"In times of stress, people often go off, do some odd things," he told the men in his office. "You three need to settle down a bit." McLendon frantically paced back and forth, Saint visibly quivered with hangover, and only Major Mulkins seemed even slightly composed. "Gabrielle's fixing to pack up, get on a stage with her sick daddy and soon-to-be husband; that's a lot to handle even for a woman as sensible as she ordinarily is. You tell me that she had some unpleasantness last night with Joe, here. Possibly she needed some time afterward to gather herself."

"She would never have left her father to wake up alone and confused," McLendon snapped. "She's not like that, she takes her responsibilities seriously."

"C.M., there's a lot of good people at the hotel and in town who've lent Gabrielle an occasional hand with Mr. Tirrito," Hove said. "For all you know, she asked someone to look in on him during her absence, and that person got delayed this morning or else forgot. Such things happen all the time. It seems unlikely she came to any kind of grief. None of my night deputies reported disturbances beyond a few drunks in the lower-end saloons. Anyone assaulting a lady, well, it surely would have been noticed."

"Gabrielle didn't just disappear," McLendon insisted. "You need to get all your men, get them out looking for her — *now*."

"Most of them are off duty," Hove said. "Every officer I've got will be needed at the mayor's funeral in a few hours. There'll be a considerable crowd. And it's still only a bit past ten in the morning. Tell you what — Major, you and C.M. go on back to the White Horse. You might just find Gabrielle right there waiting for you. Joe, go take a bath. You frankly smell like a cesspool. Even a schoolmaster deserves occasional indulgence, but you hold a place of considerable regard in this town and your current state is an embarrassment. I'll go look about for Gabrielle myself. If there's no sign of her by the time the funeral's over, I'll put some of my men on it. I'm fairly certain that won't be necessary. No, don't any of you argue. It's the best I can do."

Gabrielle wasn't at the White Horse. McLendon fumed, and Mulkins tried to calm him.

"Jack Hove's right, C.M. No use in us losing control."

"Come on, Major. This isn't like Gabrielle. You know something's wrong."

"I admit my concern. What do you want to do about the mayor's funeral?"

"What about it?"

"You and I are to be pallbearers."

McLendon's gaze fixed on the hotel's front door. He was willing Gabrielle to appear. "I can't think about the funeral. They'll have to use someone else in my place."

"I'll remain with you," Mulkins said. "Let me send word to the Hancocks, who are organizing the proceedings, and inform them that they'll need two additional volunteers to carry the casket."

"We can't just sit here waiting," McLendon said. "I'm going out to search this town from one end to the other."

"That's fine. Give me a moment to write a note to the Hancocks and have it carried to them. Then we'll go."

For two hours, McLendon and Mulkins walked the Mountain View streets, stopping in shops and asking proprietors if they'd seen Gabrielle. None had. Livery operators reported no horses or wagons rented by anyone that morning or the previous night. The Florence stage had just departed, but the depot manager knew Gabrielle and was certain that she wasn't a passenger.

Mayor Camp's funeral began promptly at one in the afternoon. Though the streets and stores were now virtually deserted, McLendon and Mulkins didn't give up their search. The more they looked without result, the more convinced they became that something terrible had happened. McLendon was on the brink of completely losing control, and his near hysteria wasn't helped when a freshly shaven and clothed Joe Saint reappeared and insisted on helping hunt for some clue regarding Gabrielle's disappearance.

"Get him away from me," McLendon insisted, but Major Mulkins refused.

"Three sets of eyes are better than two, C.M.," he said. "You need to firm up. Being overwrought's a hindrance in situations of this sort. And Joe, both you and C.M. be civil to each other. No time now for any foolishness."

As the sound of off-key singing came from the barn behind Flanagan's Livery — the mayor's mourners were attempting "Bringing in the Sheaves" — the three men heard another voice. This one was hailing them.

"McLendon, Saint, Major Mulkins!" Ike Clanton strolled down Main Street toward them. "I urgently need a word."

"Not now, Clanton," McLendon snapped.

"We're too busy to waste time with you."

"You'll want to hear me," Clanton said. "It concerns Miss Gabrielle."

Rage flooded through McLendon. It was as though red mist had fallen over his eyes. He leaped at Clanton, knocked him down, and straddled him.

"What is it? What have you done with her?" he shouted, grasping Ike by the front of his shirt and shaking him. Clanton fought back, pulling his arms free and punching. A blow glanced off McLendon's ear, and then Mulkins and Saint pulled the two apart.

"You bastard! What have you done?" McLendon shouted.

Ike made a show of brushing dirt off his pants. "I've a mind not to share what I know," he complained to Mulkins and Saint. "This man had no cause to treat me so, especially when I have helpful information."

"Then offer it quick, Ike," Mulkins said. "Otherwise, Joe and I may well join C.M. in thrashing you."

"I'm wounded by your words," Clanton said. "I'll expect an apology once you've heard me out."

"Talk," Joe Saint commanded in a stern voice completely unlike his usual soft-spoken tone.

239

Clanton did.

"I've been camped south of town, venturing in now and again to talk of my family's fine settlement down on the Gila River," Ike began.

"Hell with your settlement — what do you know about Gabrielle?" McLendon asked. His ear was swollen and slightly torn at the lobe from Clanton's blow.

"I'm coming to that. I was having early-morning coffee by my campfire, just enjoying the fine fresh air, when up rides this man leading Miss Gabrielle on another horse behind him. A big man, a giant, I'd term him, like none I'd ever seen before."

Cash McLendon long believed that he had experienced the worst heart-stopping, stomach-wrenching dread. Now he realized he hadn't.

"A giant," he said.

"Precisely. And this giant, he says this: 'You, there, I need you to go into town and give a message to Cash McLendon. Do you know him?' 'I do,' says I. 'Well, then,' says he, 'you tell McLendon we're going to make a swap. He'll understand my meaning. In two days' time' — that's Saturday," Clanton added helpfully — "'McLendon's to meet me in Devil's Valley, where after our exchange this lady returns home safe and

240

sound. Saturday noon, straight up. He's not to be in contact with the law, and must come unarmed. He knows the consequences to the lady should he fail to follow my instructions in any regard. You go tell McLendon all this, and he'll give you twenty dollars for your trouble.' Then he and Miss Gabrielle rode on."

"Gabrielle — was she all right?" McLendon asked.

"She seemed fine, though she said not a word."

"And you didn't try to save her?" Saint asked.

"From a man the size of a mountain? And there was no evidence she was a prisoner. I saw no gun held on her. I'd have to testify that way, should it come to court."

"Brautigan," McLendon said to Saint and Mulkins. They nodded. McLendon felt light-headed with fear.

"Did the big man say anything else, Ike?" Mulkins asked.

"He just said the exchange, whatever it is, would be Saturday in Devil's Valley, at exact noon. Also, while no one was to talk with the law, McLendon could bring someone to get Miss Gabrielle home safe afterward."

"Where is this Devil's Valley?" McLendon asked.

241

"I've heard the name. I think it's maybe a day and a half ride from here," Mulkins said. "I'm not certain exactly where. Ike, have you forgotten to mention anything more this man said?"

"I don't believe so. I especially remember the mention of me getting twenty dollars."

"You bastard," McLendon said with a snarl. He lunged at Clanton again, but Mulkins stopped him.

"Settle down, C.M." Mulkins dug in his pocket and extracted a greenback. "Here's your money, Ike. Now, can you tell us how to get to Devil's Valley from here?"

"I can do better than that," Clanton said. "Out of concern for a lady's safety, I'll escort you there myself. It already being well past noon on Thursday, we'll need to be leaving soon to reach there by the appointed time on Saturday. How long will it take you gentlemen to provision yourselves and secure mounts?"

The other three exchanged glances.

"Let us talk a moment among ourselves, Ike," Mulkins said. Clanton agreeably walked a short distance away, humming to himself.

"Ike's in on it with Brautigan, he has to be," McLendon said.

"Oh, it's a ruse, all right," Mulkins agreed.

"But how do we respond? The proper thing would be to pull Jack Hove out of that funeral service and tell him what we've learned. He'd soon have the whole story out of Ike."

"Stay away from the sheriff," Saint said. "You heard what Clanton said. That man Brautigan will kill Gabrielle if we don't do exactly what he says. We've got to get her back safely. Nothing else matters."

"The exchange, Joe," Mulkins said. "You know what that means. C.M. has to trade himself to Brautigan for Gabrielle, a sure death sentence. It can't be permitted."

"That's not your decision, Major," McLendon said. He looked over to where Clanton now stood, idly fingering his twenty-dollar greenback. "Here's what we're going to do: You and I will rent horses and ride out with Ike to this Devil's Valley. Afterward, you'll bring Gabrielle back here. No — don't argue. My mind's made up. If you don't agree, if you won't come along to see her safely home, I'll go by myself, and then who knows if Gabrielle can find her way. Do this for her, if not for me."

"All right," Mulkins said. "Maybe on the way we'll think of something."

"No," Saint said, so vehemently that Ike Clanton, two dozen yards away, was startled.

243

"We'll do exactly what Brautigan wants. McLendon hands himself over, we get Gabrielle safe and sound. Yes, Major, I said *we.'* I'm coming, too, just to be certain McLendon doesn't attempt some foolish trick that further endangers Gabrielle. So let's get provisioned, rent horses, and get riding with Clanton." He glared at McLendon. "This is all because of you. I feel like killing you myself."

McLendon shrugged. "Don't bother, Joe. Soon enough, someone else is going to do it for you."

■ ■ ■ ■

PART TWO

■ ■ ■ ■

Part Two

15

At age fifty-eight, Newman Clanton believed he was finally about to make his fortune, one he damned well deserved. For more than forty years he'd failed as a farmer and cattleman in Tennessee, Missouri, Texas, and California, always working hard, always falling short. These failures were never his fault. Sometimes the weather foiled him — floods at planting and harvest times, droughts in between. In Texas, it was the Comanche, marauding at will. And always — *always* — the government did its best to keep a poor man down, using taxes and land titles and lawmen bought by rich men. Even in wide-open Arizona Territory, Newman's initial try went bust. The little town of Glorious was supposed to be surrounded by mountains rich with silver ore, but there was none, and once again the Clantons had to move on.

This time, they hit it square. Pueblo Viejo

Valley had everything a man needed to succeed provided he really tried, and, like always, Newman did. Though his wife passed from some wasting disease or other, he and his four sons and two sons-in-law put their sweat into building paradise in the middle of the desert. First, they cleaned out an old irrigation ditch initially dug by Army engineers. The ditch supplied river water to the nearly six hundred acres they planted with assorted grain and vegetable crops. There was plenty of well-watered land left, twenty thousand acres or more, to sell off in segmented town lots in a new settlement called Clantonville. When the silver boom around Mountain View played out some, prospectors would move on and would-be farmers would need land. Newman held some of the choicest. The nearby San Carlos agency was bothersome, but the Apache on it were mostly tamed. Also, Newman was close to buying a good-sized herd of cattle. There was great need for beef throughout the territory. Soon as he had his cattle business established, he'd go down to Silver City and take a new wife. A man needed company at night. He had a couple possibilities in mind. The one named Elena was younger and likely would live longer than Ada. Newman didn't know Ada's last name yet, but had heard she was a widow with some money of her own. Well, either would be proud to marry a man of his substance, fine land and fat cattle, the best combination. Finally, Newman was in the right damned place at the right damned time. Barring catastrophe — and Newman had already experienced more than his share — he and his family were going to be fine.

Which was why he was truly provoked when Patrick Brautigan showed up with the Tirrito girl Newman remembered from back in Glorious. It was one thing when the big bastard wanted to snatch Cash McLendon and hide him in a Clantonville shed for a night or two. The way Newman saw it, a couple men had a private dispute that was about to be settled — it was really no concern of his. Sure, the law wouldn't approve, but the law would never find out. McLendon was going to die and his captor was clearly tight-lipped. All of the Clantons knew how to keep quiet. Bottom line, Newman made some risk-free money.

But bringing the girl instead of McLendon changed everything. After locking her in the shed, Brautigan said he intended to swap her out the next day for McLendon.

"What do you mean 'swap her'?" Newman bellowed. "She knows us from back in

Glorious. You release her alive, she'll run right home to Mountain View and tell all to the sheriff. You'll be long gone with McLendon, and the law will descend here. I won't have it — me and mine have worked too hard. You kill her now, or I will!"

"Don't touch her, you or any of your brood," Brautigan said. They were in Clanton's long, low house. It was stuffy, though not as bad as it was in the mid-afternoon heat outside. Brautigan sat on a low-backed wooden chair, Clanton on the cushion-strewn davenport. "When she gets back, all she'll say is she went on a short trip. There'll be no mention of you or this place, now or ever."

Clanton scowled. "You can't be certain."

"I can."

"And Ike? Have you got him in deeper?"

"He's doing me one last service, but nothing that the law can pin on him. You need have no concern in that regard."

Clanton shook his head. "Even so, that's not enough for me. You try to make this swap, it's not just the girl we need to worry about. You tell me somebody's coming with McLendon to see she gets home afterward. Well, what about that one? Even if she doesn't talk, he might."

Brautigan shut his eyes for a moment. He

was tired. The insides of his saddle-chafed thighs burned, and his head ached from riding so long in the daylight glare. "No one will talk. I'll explain things to the girl. That will be enough."

"So you say. But after tomorrow you'll be on your way, and we Clantons'll be here waiting to see what may befall us. No, I can't have it. Kill the girl, or I will, and we'll bury her miles away where she'll never be found. Then you go, and don't come back. We're done with this."

It was Brautigan's turn to shake his head. "No. I need you to do all you've promised, all I've paid for. And keep your hand away from that gun behind the cushion. I can strike you dead before you touch the trigger."

Newman Clanton knew himself to be a hard man, a capable fighter, but still he flinched.

"Touch me, and my boys —"

"Will die, too, if they test me. You're in this to stay, Mr. Clanton. Best thing you can do is cooperate and do what I ask. If so, all will be well. And, of course, there will be additional payment for this unexpected change in plans."

Clanton carefully moved his right hand away from the gun. "How much extra?"

Brautigan calculated. What amount would cause Clanton's greed to overcome his trepidation? "A thousand, to be paid tomorrow morning when the girl and I ride out."

Added to what Clanton had saved, it was enough to buy the cattle. "All right. But you better make certain that nobody talks."

Brautigan stood. "I'll remind the girl of that now."

The shed was built of logs, with river clay chinked into the spaces between them. High on the walls, these gaps were unchinked. That allowed in enough air for Gabrielle to breathe, though not for enough breeze to cool the sweat running down her face and body. The sweat was caused by fear as well as heat. When they rode into this little settlement, whatever it was, Brautigan pulled her off her horse, grasped her firmly by the arm, and led her to this small structure. Gabrielle thought it was about ten feet square. He unbolted the door, pulled it open, and pushed her inside.

"Not a word now, not even a sound," he warned. "I'll be listening." The door closed beyond him, and there was a metallic *clank* as the bolt slammed home.

As her eyes adjusted to the interior gloom, Gabrielle saw that there wasn't much inside.

The floor was hard-packed dirt. A few sacks of some kind of grain were stacked haphazardly in one corner. Outside, she heard muted voices, none of them deep enough to be Brautigan's. As they rode in, she'd seen some people who looked familiar. Did she know them from Mountain View or from somewhere else? If somehow she signaled to them, would anyone respond?

There were other immediate concerns. Her ribs hurt terribly. If any were broken, Gabrielle feared that the jagged ends might pierce internal organs. She also needed to relieve herself. There didn't seem to be any container in the shed that could be used to catch the urine. But she had to go. Gingerly, Gabrielle pulled down the dead man's pants that she was wearing and squatted in a corner. At least she had some privacy. When she was done, Gabrielle moved to the farthest point opposite, sat down, and leaned against the log wall, trying to think of what to do. She knew she'd been taken as a hostage to be traded for Cash McLendon. Brautigan said that she would live if she did as she was told. Gabrielle wanted badly to survive — but at the expense of Cash's life? A noble thought occurred. She would do something to let him get away, sacrifice her life for his. Then a less noble one. Cash McLendon's greed, his selfishness back in St. Louis, was the cause of Gabrielle's terrible plight. Maybe he deserved to die. She certainly didn't. And what if McLendon, who'd previously acted the coward, reverted now to form and didn't agree to exchange himself for her? What would Brautigan do then? Gabrielle believed she would suffer his wrath. All at once, she realized she hadn't thought about her father. What if he hadn't had the strength to get out of bed? How long might he have been all alone, wondering where she was, why she had deserted him? Tears came. She couldn't help it.

Gabrielle hadn't sobbed long when heavy footsteps approached and the door bolt shot open. Brautigan came inside. He had to duck because of the low roof. The immensity of his body emphasized the cramped dimensions of the shed's interior. Gabrielle shrank as best she could against the wall.

Brautigan sniffed. "I forgot to get you a slop jar. I'll do that presently." He stood over her, still slightly crouched. "First thing, the same rules apply. You are not to speak. Nod or shake your head. Understood?"

She nodded.

"You're going to be here for a time. The

rest of today and tonight. We leave not much after sunup tomorrow. Again, understood?"

Another nod.

"If someone other than me comes in here, you are not to speak to that person. You are not to attempt communication with anyone else but me. If you do, you will be hurt more than you already are." He nudged her with the steel-tipped toe of a boot, and she flinched. "But you needn't suffer any further injury. It's your choice. Will you in any way disobey my instructions?"

Gabrielle shook her head. Her entire body trembled.

"Good. Tomorrow, if he does as I tell him — and he will — McLendon will exchange himself for you. You may be tempted to warn him off, or even attempt something so foolish as trying to save him. You can't. Any such attempt, even the slightest, and I'll kill you both on the spot. He can't be saved. He's dying, no matter what. But you can live. Do you want to?"

A nod.

"After McLendon hands himself over, I'll let you ride away. Someone's coming with him to bring you back home — I don't know who."

Major Mulkins, Gabrielle thought.

"Now I'll explain something. Listen carefully. Once I'm out of sight, you may think you can tell it all, go back to Mountain View and set the sheriff on me," Brautigan continued. "And you could, you or whoever is escorting you. But what you'll say instead to anyone who asks is you took a short trip and now you've returned. Anything else, even a hint about me or anyone you see here in this place, and there will be consequences. No matter what you tell, I'll end up in the clear. Maybe the law will catch up to me before I get McLendon back where we're going. But I'll kill him before anyone takes me, and I'll still walk free after because the man I work for knows ways to buy any court. Then I'd find you in your turn, and you would die. But that would only be the beginning. Your father, Salvatore. I'd kill him too. Maybe you think he's sick and soon to die anyway, so that wouldn't matter. Don't look shocked — I know all about you, your father and much more. Your father would only be the beginning. One by one I'd get your friends — the man you're working for, that Mulkins, and also the woman who runs the laundry, Rebecca." Brautigan sounded matter-of-fact. "I'd turn my attention to that schoolteacher who used to be sheriff in Glorious. Joe Saint annoyed me that night. I'd take my time with him. You can imagine his agony. Yes, cry. Cry hard. Believe that I mean every word, for I do. None of you could run anywhere that I couldn't find you. And when I finished with that, I'd go back to St. Louis, and your aunt Lidia, uncle Mario. And soon they would be dead, all because Gabrielle tried to peach on me. You don't want that, do you? Do you? *Respond!*" He kicked her shin.

Gabrielle frantically shook her head. She thought her shinbone might be broken, but that agony was nothing compared to her fear for her friends and loved ones.

Brautigan bent down. He took her chin in his massive hand and pulled her face close to his own.

"There are times in life when no one can save you, when you're beyond help. This is one. Accept it. You have my word on what I'll do if you disobey in the slightest. I keep my word in all things. Don't forget you also have my promise that if you do exactly as I say, you'll live, you and everyone else. Except, of course, McLendon. But he's a dead man anyway. So be a smart girl. I think you will." He let go and Gabrielle sprawled on the dirt floor. "You'll have your slop jar, and also some dinner directly. It might be that they're fetched to you by someone other than myself. In that case, have no conversation. I'll know if you do."

It was many minutes after he left, bolting the door behind him, before Gabrielle summoned the nerve to try to stand. He'd kicked her left shin. Though it hurt badly, the bone apparently wasn't broken, because the leg supported her weight. But now she could walk only in an awkward lurch. Not that it mattered — there was little room to move in the shed. So Gabrielle slumped back down on the floor. Most of what she'd just heard was so overwhelmingly horrible that she focused on small things. Brautigan had promised a slop jar and dinner, and he always kept his word.

Brautigan was also in pain as he walked from the shed back toward Clantonville's main house. The chafing damage to his inner thighs was considerable, and there were at least another half-dozen days of saddle time over rough terrain to come. But at present there were also things to attend to, starting with finding out what was going on past the main house, over by the corral. Brautigan suspected they were plotting how to get rid of him — he'd expected something of the sort. Newman Clanton considered himself the master of a considerable kingdom and wouldn't take kindly to orders from any interloper. Now the old man had gathered four other men, probably the sons and sons-in-law he'd referred to. They watched Brautigan as he approached the corral.

"I'll just join your discussion," Brautigan said.

The four men with Old Man Clanton sized him up. One said, "We don't tolerate disrespect for Pa."

Brautigan liked that. Direct challenge was always best. Things got understood quicker.

"And you are?" he asked.

"John Wesley Clanton. I guess you scare most people. It won't work here."

Brautigan sized John Wesley up. He had Ike's wide facial features but not his shifty expression. This one was action rather than bluff. Since he'd spoken first, he was the leader among the younger men. Brautigan dropped his gaze to John Wesley's waist — no gunbelt. He checked young Clanton's boots, but there were no bulges, no sign of a knife or pistol tucked there. A quick glance around confirmed that none of the other Clantons were armed. They hadn't had time yet to fetch their guns.

John Wesley knew what Brautigan was doing. "We're not heeled. Don't need to be. How about you get this girl you brought and clear out?"

Brautigan shifted his feet slightly, distributing body weight evenly so he could move quickly in any direction. "I can't take that suggestion."

John Wesley moved, too, leaning straight ahead, looking to establish primacy, making the typical barroom brawler mistake of getting all his weight in front, which meant he could only lunge forward. "It's not a suggestion."

"Easy, Wes," his father cautioned. "Let's give Brautigan a moment to think."

"All I'll give him is some help on his way," John Wesley said, and made his move. Brautigan nimbly stepped aside and John Wesley stumbled past, flailing his arms and trying not to fall on his face. Brautigan reached out as he lurched by, catching John Wesley by the belt. He swung him around and effortlessly tossed John Wesley into the rails of the corral. He bounced off the thick, unforgiving wood as horses whinnied in alarm. Then Brautigan took John Wesley by the throat and lifted and dangled him in front of his shocked family.

"I could kill him before you blinked," he said. "I could lay out all of you. But I want to be a good guest."

"Don't hurt my boy," Old Man Clanton

said, not quite pleading but close.

Brautigan dropped John Wesley, who fell to his knees, coughing hard.

"All I want is for you to hold up our bargain," Brautigan said. One of the other younger men moved and he snapped, "Stop where you are!"

"Phin means no harm," his father said. "He just wants to help Wes up. Brautigan, we'll do as promised. You were the one who altered the arrangement. Are you sure the girl will keep quiet?"

Brautigan rubbed his forehead. He still had a terrible headache. "I've seen to it. Now I'd like some rest. Is there a place I can lay down?"

Clanton gestured toward a building to the left. "There's a corner of the barn where blankets can be spread. Smell of horses is a little strong, but it's out of the sun and blowing dust."

"That'll do." Brautigan remembered what Gabrielle needed. To be entirely safe, he should bring her a slop jar and food himself, but he was weary. The Clantons were suitably intimidated, Brautigan felt certain. "There are some things that should be taken to the girl. Food, and also something to piss in. Don't worry, she'll mind her manners. She's not to speak to anyone. Keep her

locked up. I can be summoned if needed."
He looked at each of the Clantons in turn
and added, "I'm an exceptionally light
sleeper."

Gabrielle lay on the floor of the shed for
some time. She had no idea how long.
Gradually the light between the gaps in the
logs faded into dusk. She'd just begun
wondering if Brautigan had forgotten her
food and the slop jar when the outer bolt
shifted and the door opened. A young
woman came inside. In one hand she held
the handle of a small pot covered by a cloth;
in the other, a jug. Tucked under an arm
was a wide-mouthed jar. She put the things
down on the dirt floor and said, "Here's
some supper." Gabrielle sat up, wincing
from the pain in her ribs and shin. "Are you
all right?" the woman asked.

Gabrielle started to reply, then thought
better of it. This might be a test; Brautigan
could be just outside, listening. So she
shrugged instead.

"What? Oh, I forgot. You're not to speak.
Well, I'm Hettie, and I've brought you water
and some stew. You'll have to drink straight
from the jug. There's no plate for the stew,
but I've got a spoon in my apron pocket.
And here's a jar for you-know-what."

Gabrielle nodded. She didn't think she'd met Hettie before, but found it comforting to be in the presence of anyone other than Brautigan. It seemed as if she'd been his prisoner forever, and it was less than two days. The dimming light made it hard to see the girl's features clearly, but she seemed kind, even friendly. Gabrielle thought that if she really did survive, if she ever was back among people again, safe and allowed to speak, she'd savor every moment. For now, she reached out and took the jug from Hettie. She drank in several long gulps, then put down the jug and picked up the pot of stew and spoon. The food was very hot and burned her mouth, but she gobbled it anyway.

Hettie watched Gabrielle eat. When the spoon scraped the bottom of the empty pot, Hettie said, "I've got to take that pot in, but I'll leave the jug so you'll have more water if you want it. And the other jar, of course."

Gabrielle did her best to look thankful. A nod didn't seem sufficient for the gift of food and brief, nonthreatening companionship, so she waved, a shaky motion of her hand that she hoped would convey gratitude.

Hettie picked up the pot and moved to the door, then hesitated. "I don't know anything of your situation," she said. "We've been told not to inquire or tell anyone afterward that you were ever here. But I hope you come out of this all right." She went out and bolted the door shut. It was only after Gabrielle heard the bolt slide home that she realized the door had been unlocked the whole time Hettie was with her. Should she have pushed past the woman, tried to escape? No, Brautigan was undoubtedly lurking. He would have caught and punished her. Maybe there was still some way she might get away, some way to save her own life and maybe Cash McLendon's, too, but her brain felt muddled with fear and she couldn't imagine any. Full dark came on. Small as the shed was, she couldn't see the wall opposite. Gabrielle decided that she'd sleep a little, see if rest might revive her mind and spirits. It was a shameful thing, that she hadn't even considered making a break through the unlocked door.

16

It took longer than anticipated for McLendon and the others to get out of Mountain View on Thursday afternoon. Packing took very little time. Mulkins and Saint each took an extra shirt. McLendon left his few possessions in the room he shared with Mulkins — he could foresee no future need of anything. He did jam the greenbacks he had on hand — almost $800 was left of the loan from Major Mulkins and Mayor Camp — into a pants pocket. There might be unexpected expenses before the exchange, or even during it.

They had no difficulty getting provisions — canned goods were readily available in town shops, and Major Mulkins added biscuits, bacon, and coffee from the White Horse's kitchen. But renting horses proved a problem. All four owners of the Mountain View liveries were attending Mayor Camp's funeral, and only Tim Flanagan's operation was big enough that he had assistants keeping the place open in the interim. But the available horses at Flanagan's were wanting. The good ones were just returned after days of hard use and weren't up to immediate rental for more of the same. Those left were clearly unsuited for the ride ahead. That left no option other than waiting for Camp's service to conclude, which it did just after three. When Garth Gould's livery reopened shortly afterward, McLendon, Mulkins, and Saint all picked suitable mounts. McLendon paid the rental fees, six dollars a day for each horse and saddle tack, four days' expected rental before their return, seventy-two dollars total. They loaded provisions in saddlebags and, for the first time, addressed ordnance.

"I've got a shotgun I sometimes use for hunting," Mulkins said. "What about you, Joe?"

"I gave up my guns when I quit being sheriff," Saint said. "With luck, we'll have no need of weapons. McLendon's going to hand himself over, and you and I will bring Gabrielle home. If we arrive armed, Brautigan might suspect we mean to fight. It's better for Gabrielle if we don't."

"Once we've got her, we still have to see her safely back," Mulkins said. "There could be Apache about, or some bad men besides Brautigan. Don't you agree, C.M.?"

McLendon did. "I've got my Peacemaker, and now that I think of it, a Winchester might prove useful." Seeing Saint's face contort, he hastily added, "Not to use against Brautigan, Joe. But if Gabrielle needs protection afterward, you and the Major might need more than a shotgun and Colt to fight long-range."

Saint admitted that he saw sense in that, so Mulkins bought a Winchester and shells. With that purchase, they felt they were finally ready to leave. Saint went to fetch Ike Clanton from a saloon; when they returned, Clanton was slightly tipsy, but not drunk to the point of impairment.

"Let's sally forth," Ike said gaily. "We're off on our adventure."

"Enough of that," Major Mulkins said. "This is no joyful excursion."

They began riding around four. Clanton led them east. He set a brisk pace. Major Mulkins was a good rider and had no trouble keeping up, but Saint was adequate at best and McLendon was always challenged just to stay in the saddle. This time, he was less concerned about his tailbone jouncing up and slamming down with pistonlike concussion. That discomfort,

McLendon knew, was nothing compared to his suffering to come.

Just before seven, with darkness setting in, Clanton called a halt.

"We'll eat supper, let the horses rest, and get some sleep ourselves," Ike said. "We get an early start tomorrow, we still ought to make Devil's Valley by noon on Saturday."

Saint disagreed. "We could ride another hour at least."

"It's all right, Joe," McLendon said. "All that matters is, we're there at the time appointed. Brautigan's exact that way. He won't do business even a minute earlier than planned."

"You would know," Saint said bitterly. "Being as familiar with him as you are."

"And he's going to be more so," Clanton cracked, and despite the scowls from the others, he laughed at his own joke. "You people hitch the horses, and I'll get a fire going. Coffee and bacon, coming right up."

Ike ate heartily. Mulkins and Saint picked at their food. McLendon only drank coffee. Panic threatened to overcome him; he knew what a terrible death awaited. Would it come right there in Devil's Valley? Probably not. Rupert Douglass would want to witness his vengeance. A trip back to St. Louis, then? That might provide some opportunity for escape. But after losing McLendon once in Glorious, Brautigan would be particularly vigilant. No, the odds greatly favored eventual death at the giant's hands, or, rather, his boots.

McLendon tried thinking of something else: Gabrielle's return to safety. It was always possible Brautigan would kill her, might already have, figuring McLendon would show up in Devil's Valley anyway. But it was an odd truth about Killer Boots and his employer that they kept their sides of unequal bargains, so long as the other side did exactly as instructed. Brautigan must have a plan in place, one that would allow Gabrielle to survive if McLendon willingly handed himself over. *All right,* McLendon silently commanded himself, *for now think of that, and only that. Getting her back alive.*

After the pans and tin coffee cups were scoured clean with sand, Mulkins said, "Isn't there a decision to be made? We're close to the border of the San Carlos agency. Trespassing's forbidden, but I believe that if we ask to see John Clum, the agent, he'd grant permission to cross. The distance involved isn't that great, but it might save an hour."

Clanton said quickly, "It's not to be risked. Clum's a harsh one. If we so much

269

as venture over an inch of agency land, he'll likely clap us in irons and call the Army to take us to the stockade. Then we'll miss the appointed hour in Devil's Valley, and who knows what harm might come to the lady?"

"Surely Agent Clum would be more reasonable," Mulkins said. "We could just explain ourselves as businessmen in a hurry to a meeting, and that we offer no trouble to anyone."

"No, we can't deal with Clum," Clanton insisted. "He's too liable to detain us. Then we'd lose days instead of saving a single hour."

"For once, Clanton's making sense," Saint said. "We can't take the chance of not being on time where Brautigan wants us. We have to skirt south around the agency."

"What do you think, C.M.?" Mulkins asked.

"I'm with Joe and Clanton, so long as we can still make Devil's Valley by noon on Saturday with this longer ride," McLendon said.

"We will, we will," Clanton said, sounding enthusiastic. "You boys just listen to Ike, and all will be well."

As they prepared to sleep, Saint ostentatiously placed his bedroll between McLendon and the tethered horses.

"Just in case you feel the urge for a night ride in a different direction," he said. "Don't even think of running."

Mulkins started to protest, but McLendon hushed him.

"Good night, Joe," he said mildly, and lay down on his blanket.

After a pre-dawn breakfast of coffee and biscuits, they started out again, swinging south on a route that briefly took them through a forest. There was no permanent trail. They had to thread their horses through the trees. The only conversation concerned when to rest the horses. They stopped soon after reaching open ground again, and fed the animals a few handfuls of oats from a saddlebag. As they did, two riders approached from the east. One was a white man, the other an Apache. When they pulled up, the Apache stayed mounted. The white man jumped down from his horse and said, "I'm Fred Nolan, the assistant agent at San Carlos."

"I believe we're significantly south of the agency," Mulkins said. "We took special care not to trespass."

"I make no such accusation," Nolan said. "Yesterday a few renegades broke away, we think on a ride down toward Mexico.

They're unlikely to bother travelers in this vicinity, but Agent Clum's got some of us out patrolling the area, just in case."

"How many?" Mulkins asked.

"We think a half-dozen. Mostly they're youngsters, but the leader's Goyathlay, who the Mexes call Geronimo. He's a bad one. I see you're armed, and that's good. Keep a sharp eye out, and you ought to be fine. Say — is that Ike Clanton?"

"What of it?" Ike said, ducking his face away from Nolan.

Nolan frowned. "Clum mentioned you'd been caught recently on agency land without permission. You were with someone."

"My pa," Clanton said quickly.

"Agent Clum said this man was sizable — clearly not one of your present companions."

"Daddy's taken to fat in recent years. Is it all right if we move on?"

"Just as you please," Nolan said. "Safe travels. And Ike, were I you I'd not come on the agency uninvited again. John Clum will show no pity, and the Army will take you off in irons."

As they continued their journey, McLendon said to Clanton, "A big man? Ike, if you're leading us into a trap, you'll be the first to die."

"It was my pa," Clanton insisted. "You three knew him back in Glorious. He's wide as a wagon."

"We're watching your every move," Mulkins warned.

"My word as a gentleman. My only wish is to help you recover the lady."

The ride had already been tense. Now they watched nervously in all directions. Apache were adept at seeming to appear out of nowhere.

"We can't allow Indians to kill you," Saint said to McLendon.

"Yes, that would be tragic," McLendon said. "We wouldn't want me dying at the wrong hands."

They crossed a creek and stopped to water the horses and gulp down a lunch of canned fruit. McLendon ate this time, though only a few bites. The food seemed tasteless to him. Clanton emptied one full can and asked for another. After a short break they remounted; Clanton steered them slightly to the southeast.

"Devil's Valley's maybe nine, ten hours farther on," he said. "Of course, that's barring Apache attack, or downpour." He gestured at scattered gray clouds. "Late in the season for floods, but you never know."

"Get us where we're going, Ike," Mulkins said.

After another hour, Mulkins pointed at the sky ahead to their left. "What's that?" he asked. "Buzzards?"

"Whatever they're circling, it's none of our concern," Clanton said. "Could be a dead elk, or even a rabbit."

Saint turned pale. "What if it's Gabrielle?" He yanked his reins, kicked his horse in the ribs, and rode madly off. The others followed, McLendon trying hard not to fall off his mount. The birds were farther away than they initially seemed. After almost a mile, Mulkins begged Saint to stop riding all-out.

"You'll run your horse to death, Joe," he called. "We can't be down a mount."

Reluctantly, Saint slowed to a trot. As they approached the circling buzzards, the riding turned hard. There were large patches of boulders to circle around. Saint wanted to rush ahead, but Mulkins advised caution.

"We don't know what's ahead," he said. "Let's prepare." He pulled his shotgun from a scabbard by his saddle and gestured for McLendon to hand the Winchester to Saint. "You draw your Colt, C.M.," Mulkins whispered. "Those renegade Apache might be in front of us."

"I'll just stay to the rear in case you run

into difficulty and need cover fire," Clanton said.

"All right, Ike," Mulkins said. "You can hold our horses too. We'll advance on foot."

Mulkins and McLendon worked their way around the rock pile, keeping Saint behind them so he couldn't impetuously dash into the open. The schoolteacher was breathing hard. McLendon thought that if the renegades were just ahead, they'd be alerted by Saint's gasping.

But there were no renegades, just a naked body. Saint couldn't be held back. He rushed forward and bent over the corpse. "A man," he said. "Not Gabrielle. Thank God."

"The buzzards have already done considerable work," Mulkins said. Much of the man's face and body were pecked away. "I think he was young. And look, the side of his face — could birds do this?"

McLendon looked, and knew. The exposed skull and cheekbone were crushed.

"Brautigan's work," he said, swallowing to hold back vomit. "His style. Unmistakable."

"What's this over here?" Saint asked. He walked a few yards away, reached down, and then held up an item of clothing in each hand. "Her dress," he said, extending torn gray material to McLendon and Mulkins.

"And *this*" — Gabrielle's chemise. "You know what this means."

McLendon's mind worked even as he struggled to control his gag reflex. "No, Joe," he gurgled.

"Go on and puke, C.M.," Mulkins advised, and McLendon did. He wiped strings of vomit from his chin and turned back to Saint.

"The corpse is naked, Joe. I think we're the first ones on the scene. So Brautigan stripped him after he killed him. Gabrielle's clothes there — he probably thought she could move faster in shirt and pants."

"He made her undress?" Saint hissed. "What else did he do?"

"I don't think anything. Rape's never been Brautigan's way. Take comfort from this. It proves he's keeping her alive."

Mulkins suggested they give the corpse a decent burial to save what was left from the buzzards. Ike Clanton was summoned — he emerged from the rocks only after they swore there were no Indians — and complained when he was tasked with scraping out a shallow grave.

"This is slave work," Clanton groused. Since they had no shovel, Ike had to use a flat, sharp-edged piece of rock. "The birds have pretty much picked the bastard clean, anyway. Why go to this trouble?"

"Dignity for the dead," Mulkins said.

Ike nodded toward McLendon. "Well, it's more than he'll likely get."

When the body was buried and a rudimentary stick cross placed over the grave, they rode on.

"Now we need to direct ourselves more south than southeast," Clanton said. "This interruption took us off our proper route."

"Say, Ike, isn't your family's settlement almost directly east of here?" Mulkins asked. "Are we close to Clantonville?"

"You haven't traveled much in these regions, have you?" Clanton asked. When Mulkins said he hadn't, Ike said, "As it happens, Clantonville's not at all nearby. You'd have to ride almost two days or more to reach it from where we are."

"That's nearly across the border to New Mexico," Mulkins said. "I feel certain that the Gila River is considerably closer."

"Clantonville's my home, and I suppose I'd know its location," Clanton said. "We're wasting time with this idle talk. Devil's Valley's that way to the south, and we need to be moving."

They fell into a makeshift column, with Clanton in front, Mulkins and McLendon riding side by side, and Saint bringing up the rear. Except for the constantly jabbering Clanton, no one had much to say. The horrible sight of the buzzard-mangled corpse and the thought of Gabrielle being forced into the dead man's clothes completely occupied the minds of the other three. All of them forgot about renegade Apache.

They stopped for the night at the northern foot of a mountain range that extended south. Clanton called it the Gilas. "Tomorrow morning we'll cut through a notch not far from here, ride down an hour or two more, and then we'll come to Devil's Valley."

"Tell us what we'll see there, Ike," Mulkins said.

Clanton smacked his lips over a bite of canned peaches. "It's not necessarily a fearsome place; it gets its name because of a lack of water. Mostly it's a deep valley surrounded by hills. But the valley itself is going on a mile across. Somebody sets up in the middle of it, there's no way he can be taken by surprise. I expect this man you call Brautigan will be waiting there with the lady. McLendon'll have to ride down into the valley by himself, leaving you others behind. Anything else, Brautigan will spot you right off. He picked the perfect place."

"I wonder how he did that, Ike," McLendon said. "Seeing how he'd be a stranger in this area and all. Funny that he'd know about Devil's Valley, how it sets up perfectly for this kind of exchange."

"I have no clue," Clanton said defensively. "All I know is you wanted me to take you there and I am."

This time it was Joe Saint who ate no supper. McLendon ate bacon and biscuits and some canned pears, thinking he might as well. Should Brautigan plan to take him back to Rupert Douglass in St. Louis, rations might prove short along the way. When McLendon was through with his meal, he walked over to Saint, who was huddled miserably a dozen yards away from the campfire. He sat down beside the schoolteacher and said, "Stay strong, Joe. Tomorrow night, Gabrielle will be with you and the Major. You can take her home."

"Maybe," Saint said. "If she comes out of this all right, it's no thanks to you."

"That's true. If I'd known Brautigan was still on my trail, I would never have come to Mountain View. I'd have stayed away from Gabrielle forever if that's what it took to keep her safe. But I made a mistake, that's obvious, and now I'll pay for it."

"She's been taken. She's paying too."

McLendon sighed. The next words came hard. "After all this, she'll need healing. Her life has to go on. Do what you can about that. I want you to." Saint didn't respond. He stared into the night until McLendon got up and walked away.

As Clanton snored, Mulkins said quietly to McLendon, "Have you any thoughts about tomorrow, what we might do?"

"Beyond trading myself for Gabrielle, nothing. Brautigan's got us boxed."

"I'm willing to try him, C.M.," Mulkins said. "Maybe get Gabrielle clear, send her off with Joe, and come back for you. Between us, who knows? We might prevail."

McLendon reached out and grasped Mulkins's shoulder. "It's a fine offer. But that night in Glorious, you saw Brautigan in a fight. He'd kill us both with no trouble, and then he could set out after Gabrielle and Joe. My best chance is go off with him and hope he doesn't mean to do me in right away. If I'm to be brought back to St. Louis, maybe along the way I'll see a chance to get free."

"I feel myself a coward, letting a friend be taken like this."

"You've proven the best of friends, one of the few I've known in my life. Get Gabrielle safely home. That's what matters."

McLendon couldn't sleep. After a while he got up and walked off a way to piss. He thought he'd better make sure to have an empty bladder at noon the next day. It wouldn't do for Gabrielle's last memory of him to be wetting himself with fear at the sight of Brautigan.

17

Brautigan knew that it was dangerous to take even a short nap in the barn. There were enough Clantons to swarm him, if that's what they chose. His opinion of Newman Clanton, though, was that the old man was practical. Yes, if all his boys and sons-in-law came at Brautigan together they'd win out, but the cost would be fearsome, leaving at least several Clantons dead and others badly hurt. Newman needed every one of them to keep Clantonville blooming. Far better for him to let Brautigan go on and make his swap tomorrow, trusting that somehow Gabrielle and whoever came with McLendon would keep quiet afterward as Brautigan promised.

Still, Brautigan wouldn't have risked sleep except for being so worn out. Aches and rashes from riding were the least of it. In his usual role back in St. Louis, there was no pressure to speak of. The boss pointed him at targets. He intimidated or killed them. Little thinking was required, and the job was over in a few days, if not hours. But this McLendon pursuit had dragged on for better than two years, and this last part of it was the worst. Brautigan was so close to cleaning up after his only failure ever, getting hands on McLendon and delivering him back to the boss. The run-up, though, was wearying. He'd never dealt with a hostage before, and a woman at that. Brautigan could tell from the moment he snatched her that Gabrielle Tirrito was a spitfire, someone who'd cause him no end of difficulty if he didn't cow her quick. So he did some things to break her down, not allowing her to talk and putting her through the humiliation of relieving herself in front of him. He'd deliberately let her think she had a chance to get at the Winchester so he could demonstrate punishment for any escape attempt. Brautigan's beatings of Gabrielle were judicious — first to the ribs so that every movement would hurt some, and later to the shin so running would be impossible. The girl probably thought her ribs and shinbone were broken, but there'd been no chance of that. Brautigan was a master of assault; each blow he delivered inflicted exactly the desired amount of damage.

Now, for the rest of the night, the girl needed to be isolated in the shed, left alone with her thoughts. She'd be afraid for herself and McLendon and her daddy, letting those fears occupy her imagination to the exclusion of further attempts to escape. Brautigan sensed that, scared as she was, the girl still had spunk. So far his intimidation held. After all, she'd never been in any prior fix like this. That kept her off balance — this kind of terror was new to her. But any more threats, even another beating, and she'd start feeling like maybe the worst that could happen already had, and then she'd be troublesome. Not that Brautigan couldn't handle it, but now he needed to turn as much attention as possible to McLendon himself. It wasn't going to be easy, maybe five days crossing wild, strange land from Clantonville to Silver City. Brautigan felt certain that once he got McLendon on the stage and then the train back to St. Louis, all would go smoothly. But getting to Silver City, finding his way there without a guide, having all the while to keep McLendon subdued — that would be the hard part. Well, better get started on it now. It was dark outside; he'd probably slept three or four hours. Brautigan rose from the blanket he'd spread on some hay in a corner of the smelly barn, brushed bits of straw from his clothes, and made his way to the main house.

Newman Clanton, too, was reflecting. Earlier, he'd had to come down hard on his boys. When the big man went off to the barn to nap, Wes and Phin and the rest wanted to fall on him in his sleep, avenge the slights and eliminate the risks he'd brought on the family. Newman told them no, a man like Brautigan was never taken completely by surprise, so leave him alone. Phin and Andy Slinkard, who was married to Newman's daughter Mary Elise, argued hard, and finally he had to mete out some cuffs to heads. Now they were all off in their cabins, and Newman was alone in his, except for young Billy asleep in the loft. This would have been a good time to have a wife, pleasure from between her thighs, and afterward words of comfort and encouragement. Even when Brautigan left with the girl tomorrow, Newman would be on edge long after, wondering if any minute the law would come thundering in because somebody blabbed despite Brautigan's promise.

Eight o'clock came and went on Newton's pocket watch, then eight-thirty. It was full dark. Out beyond the settlement, coyotes howled as they always did. Newman heaved himself up off the davenport with some difficulty; taking two or three suppers a night with various Clantonville daughters and daughters-in-law meant he kept gaining weight, but he liked the company and so had multiple meals. Being together, that was what family was for.

Just before nine, Brautigan knocked on the door. Newman had been expecting him.

"Get some rest?" he asked pleasantly.

"Enough. I want to go ahead and get provisioned now, have everything ready so there's nothing more to do in the morning."

"Easy to do." Newman gestured toward a table and chair. "Hungry? There's some stew still warm by the fire. I'll get you some, and whiskey to wash it down."

Brautigan looked at Newman carefully, calculating motive. "All right. But water rather than whiskey."

"Of course, water. You've got things to do tomorrow. No, I'm not asking about them. Less I know, the better." Newman used a dented ladle to scoop stew into a bowl. He poured well water into a mug and took the bowl and mug over to the table. "Eat hearty. I won't join, I had my dinner earlier. But I believe I'll indulge in a toddy."

Clanton drank while Brautigan ate. The

big man accepted a second bowl of stew and declined a third. He pushed back his chair and said, "Now, about the provisions."

"I've already got things put aside," Clanton said. "Food for two, enough for five days. Canned peas and peaches. Biscuits. Bacon too?"

"No, I won't be having fires."

"Well, then, no bacon, or coffee either. But surely some dried beef? Two saddlebags of feed for the animals. I'll have four canteens filled from the well, also the cask to be carried by your mule. Enough, I think, for three days of drink if you're modest in use. After that, you'll be within striking distance of the San Simon River, and there are also occasional creeks sufficient for water replenishment. Thirst should not prove a problem."

"If you'll lead me to these supplies, I'll pack the saddlebags."

"No need. My daughters will see to it. Don't worry, you'll have every scrap and drop promised. Clantons keep their word. As, I'm sure, will you. Prompt and full payment tomorrow morning?"

"Yes." Brautigan pushed away from the table.

"What now?" Clanton asked. "Will you look in on the girl? I assure you she's safely locked in the shed."

"I want her left alone until morning. Don't let any of your women bring her breakfast. She'll mind better if she's hungry."

"I admire your thinking," Clanton said, and meant it. In Brautigan's place, he wouldn't have given the girl breakfast either. "Let me speak of one other matter. Ike — will I see him tomorrow? You're certain he'll be free of any . . . *consequences*?"

Brautigan paused by the door. "As long as Ike does as I've told him, he'll be fine. I'm going back to the barn and sleep a little more."

"What time should we wake you?"

"When I need to, I'll be awake."

A scraping sound just outside the shed woke Gabrielle. Then there was the metallic clink of the bolt, and the door creaked open. Gabrielle thought, for a moment, that Hettie might have returned. The young woman was clearly sympathetic. But instead a man's voice said, "Let me close the door and get this candle lit." There was the scratch of a match, a tiny flame, and then more illumination as a wick flared. The man holding the candle had lank hair and a drooping mustache.

"I'm Phin," the man said. "Remember me?"

Phin Clanton, Gabrielle remembered. *From Glorious. If he's here, this must be Clanton-ville.* But she didn't reply. Brautigan might be outside.

"If you're worried about the big man, don't be," Phin said. "He's off sleeping in the barn. Nobody to bother us."

The candle was wedged in some kind of small tin holder. Phin set the holder down on the dirt floor. The flame provided enough light for Gabrielle to see Phin's expression, and she didn't like it.

"Now, you're in a fix," he said.

She decided to risk conversation. Anything to delay what he obviously planned. "I can scream," Gabrielle said, but the threat was tempered by the croakiness of her voice. She hadn't spoken in forty-eight hours and her throat felt thick.

"You don't want to do that," Phin said. He grinned conspiratorially and sat down just a few inches from her. "I'm here to help."

"How?" Again, her voice cracked.

"That big man, maybe you think he'll be letting you go sometime. But I'm here to tell you he's not. He's been boasting to my pa and the rest of us. He's going to kill you

289

tomorrow."

Gabrielle couldn't suppress a gasp. It made Phin smile.

"Yep, kill you dead. Maybe he's promised you otherwise, but he means to. Whatever it is he's doing, he won't want to leave witnesses. No, you're a dead woman for certain unless I help you."

"How?" At least her voice sounded a little stronger.

"Oh, so you want to know? All right. I've got some brothers here, also some brothers-in-law. We're all tough and capable. I'm the leader. I give them the word and we put that big man down. He can't fight all of us. Easy as that, you're rid of him."

"You'd do that?"

Phin leaned toward Gabrielle. He extended a hand and tugged lightly at the collar of the dead man's shirt she wore. "I might if you're nice to me. No screams, no struggling."

She pulled back. Even that movement brought agony from her ribs and shin. Her shoulders brushed the shed wall. There was very little room. "Go away."

"Go away?" Phin sounded incredulous. "I'm your only chance to get out of this alive and you're denying me? And you'll enjoy it too. Every woman who's been had by me never wants to be with any other man again." He moved forward; she tried to elude him but almost immediately found herself in a corner. "All right," Phin said, sounding mean. He pulled a knife from behind his back. It must have been tucked in his belt — she hadn't seen it. "Should you even open that pretty mouth to scream, I'll have your throat slit before a sound comes out." He reached for her, and Gabrielle had no way to elude him.

Brautigan lay on his blanket in the barn, thinking about the next day. McLendon was so slippery. What trick might he try? The surest thing would be to kill the bastard on the spot. Brautigan had the boss's permission if — *What exactly had Mr. Douglass said? Oh, yes* — if he couldn't get McLendon away clean. So once the exchange was made tomorrow and he had McLendon by himself in the middle of nowhere, Brautigan could snap his neck and later tell the boss sorry, there was unexpected pursuit and this was the best way. Maybe Brautigan could cut off a finger or an ear to bring back as proof of death. Then he could make his way home unencumbered, back to the city where he belonged instead of this hell on earth they called the frontier. Tempting, tempting.

But this easier option seemed incomplete. The job was designed to let the boss watch McLendon die. If it didn't happen that way, Mr. Douglass might wonder if Brautigan couldn't really have gotten McLendon all the way back to St. Louis. And with that doubt fixed in his mind, the boss would no longer trust Brautigan completely. He might begin thinking Brautigan knew too many of his secrets, and that for safety's sake it was Brautigan's turn to be eliminated. Brautigan knew himself to be a hard man, but Mr. Douglass was even more so. He was the only man Patrick Brautigan feared. If at all possible, McLendon had to be brought to Mr. Douglass in St. Louis.

Brautigan tossed on his blanket for a while. There were still hours before dawn. He decided that since he couldn't sleep, he'd check on the girl in the shed. Just a quick look, to make certain the door was still bolted.

It was very dark in Clantonville. But as Brautigan neared the shed he thought he discerned a faint flicker of light from gaps in the upper, unchinked portion of the log wall. He hurried up; the door was closed but not bolted. There was movement inside.

Brautigan pulled the door open and saw by dim candlelight two figures struggling on the dirt floor. A man was on top of the girl. His head jerked around as Brautigan entered — it was a Clanton son, the one called Phin. Brautigan wound his thick fingers in Phin's long hair and yanked him off and up. He struck a single punch to his temple, enough to stun but not kill. Phin went limp and Brautigan dropped him. Then he turned to the girl. She was curled on the floor, trying to hold the front of her shirt together with one hand and pull up her trousers with the other. Brautigan looked down at Phin, whose own trousers were unbuttoned halfway but no more.

"Sit up," Brautigan told Gabrielle. "The bastard didn't get the job done? This once, you can speak."

"No. He didn't."

"All right. I'll deal with him. I'll return in the morning." Brautigan blew out the candle, then dragged Phin outside. He closed the door behind them and shot the bolt.

Gabrielle sat in the darkness and tried to adjust her clothes. All but two buttons were torn from her shirt. She fastened those. There were gaps, but at least she was somewhat covered. The trousers had been loose anyway. She pulled them up over her hips and they seemed secure enough. Phin had bitten her a few times on her neck and shoulders. She gently prodded the sore spots but didn't think there was blood; he hadn't broken the skin. Phin had gotten her pants completely down but not his own when Brautigan interrupted. So assault but not complete rape.

There was a noise outside and then another, curious thuds. Gabrielle scuttled across the small shed on hands and knees because her shin and ribs hurt badly and she didn't want to stand. More thuds; Gabrielle poked at the chinking between the logs and managed to dislodge enough clay to provide a peephole. It was dark outside, but she'd been sitting mostly in the dark already that night and could see fairly well that Brautigan stood over Phin, kicking him in the most brutally methodical way. Even one of the kicks could have killed Phin if it had been to his face, but Brautigan seemed to be starting on the legs and moving gradually higher. Phin must have regained at least partial consciousness from the head blow he'd suffered in the shed, because he began first to moan, then emitted a high-pitched scream. Brautigan kicked him in the ribs next, breaking some — she heard the *crack*

— and then Phin was mostly quiet again. But a moment later lights appeared; people, other Clantons, she presumed, rushed out with lanterns; and first among them was a fat old man clad only in underdrawers, his thick white beard tumbling down his bare, flabby chest. Newman Clanton, whom she recognized instantly, had a shotgun, and he pointed it at Brautigan.

"Back off," the Clanton man said. "Leave my boy be."

The gun didn't seem to intimidate Brautigan. He said almost conversationally, "I found him in the shed, raping the girl."

"Get away from him a bit," the old man said, gesturing with the shotgun. There were others gathered around now. Some of them were men with guns, too, mostly pistols drawn and aimed at Brautigan. He paid them no notice. He took a few steps back from where Phin lay moaning, far enough so the old man had room to bend over Phin, but close enough to kick either of them if he chose.

The old man lifted Phin's head, not gently, and said, "Is that the truth? Did you go and rape her?" Phin whimpered. "You ain't hurt so bad that you can't talk. Tell me."

Phin hawked and spit what Gabrielle

hoped was blood. He replied in a pleading whine, "Daddy, he's gone kill her in the morning anyhow."

Clanton sighed. "No, he isn't," he said. Then he looked at Brautigan and said, "You'd do considerable damage prior, but we can still put you down right here. There are enough of us, most armed."

Brautigan nodded. He looked around at the people and lanterns and guns, and said, "So?"

"You've got my word. Short of killing or crippling Phin because he's my son, whatever you were going to do to him, I'm going to take him now and do as much or worse. Can you be satisfied with that?"

Brautigan thought for a moment. "All right."

"The rest of you, *git,*" Clanton commanded. They obeyed. The area in front of the shed was left illuminated only by the lantern brought by the old man. "I need more room," he said to Brautigan. "Get back some farther, if you please. I got to fetch something and I'll be right back. Phin ain't moving from where he is."

The giant stepped back to the shed. He was directly in front of Gabrielle's peephole, so she could only hear what came next. After a few moments there came a series of sharp smacks, the sounds of leather lashing flesh. Clanton must have gone for a belt or something similar. Phin screeched at first, but as the smacks continued Phin's shrieks diminished in volume, until finally there were only the smacks and then they stopped. After a few moments more, Brautigan moved from outside the shed wall to its door. Gabrielle scrambled back. The giant said to her, "For the rest of the night, I'll remain right outside." He left, bolting the door behind him. Then the wall by the door creaked; Brautigan had sat down and leaned back against it.

Gabrielle made herself as comfortable as possible, given her physical discomfort and the near-rape she'd just endured. No one had given her blankets to lie on; the hard-packed dirt floor offered little cushion. In the hours until dawn, she found herself remembering over and over the old man's reply when Phin whined that Brautigan was going to kill her in the morning anyway: *"No, he isn't."*

Gabrielle was still very much afraid for Cash. She couldn't imagine any way he could escape once Brautigan had him. But her immediate concern was her own survival. The old man seemed quite certain that Brautigan meant to spare her. If Brautigan didn't, why not let Phin rape her? So, apparently, she was going to live — but at awful cost to someone she loved. Brautigan had no right to do this. No one did.

In the past forty-eight hours, Gabrielle had experienced abject terror and hopelessness. Now a new emotion took hold of her.

Anger.

18

On Saturday morning, Ike Clanton smiled as he rode toward Devil's Valley, and why not? As far back as Ike could recall, his daddy pounded into his head, his and his brothers', that it was always Clantons against the rest of the world. The Clantons seldom won, but today was an exception. Cash McLendon was going to be handed over to Brautigan. Ike didn't know exactly what would befall McLendon afterward, but he was certain it was going to be nasty. No son of a bitch deserved it more. McLendon had held himself above the Clantons back in Glorious, had mocked Ike himself openly. Finally he was getting his, and Ike played a key part. "Cream rises," Ike's poor dead ma liked to say, and now Ike had finally proven himself to be cream. *Vengeful* cream.

Much of the time it seemed to Ike that Pa didn't quite respect him as he should. Ike was a grown man, smart and shrewd, someone with lots of possibilities if only he caught a break here and there. Clantonville looked like a near sure thing — Ike knew enough about his family's history of bad luck not to think any success was certain — and instead of letting Ike help him run the spread, Pa sent him out selling lots in it. Ike didn't mind the selling, he figured he was good at spreading charm, but once again he was taking orders from Pa instead of giving them out to other people.

Maybe this McLendon business would change Pa's opinion. When Ike thought about it, it was him who'd done all the important parts of it. He'd found Brautigan wandering the Silver City streets, all confused and not knowing what to do. So Ike set him straight, got him first to Clantonville and then Mountain View, and once in Mountain View saved the day by finding the Silva woman and getting Brautigan the information he needed to snatch the girl. And now Ike, clever as usual, was leading McLendon right to his doom without anyone knowing it was Ike himself who'd arranged it!

Money had been made from all this, for Ike himself and also the Clanton family. Pa had a fondness for money, often liked to say that if a man got rich enough, it made him bulletproof. Ike thought Pa was wrong about that — bullets could kill anybody, regardless of wealth. Anyway, Ike had put together and carried out a winning plan. Pa couldn't deny that. Now maybe Wes and Phin would get sent out to peddle lots, while Ike stayed home and gave orders for a change.

The only bug in Ike's beer was that he guessed he personally wouldn't see McLendon die. Brautigan planned to drag him back to Silver City and, after that, Ike assumed, somewhere east with a view toward killing him there. Ike didn't know the details. No doubt if Brautigan had chosen to confide them, Ike could have sharpened them up a bit, helped the big man do the job better. Oh, well. It would have been a fine thing to hear McLendon beg for mercy, then get his head kicked in or whatever was going to happen. Instead Ike would imagine it in all sorts of wonderfully bloody variations.

McLendon was silent as they rode this morning, which would only be expected, since he was handing himself over to his killer soon. Maybe he'd try to run off at the last minute. Ike figured that was why Joe Saint rode behind McLendon all the time, to discourage escape attempts. There'd been bad blood between the two back in Glorious, Ike recalled. Was it because of the girl? Probably. The third man, the Major, whispered to McLendon a lot. Comforting him? It didn't seem to Ike that there was any way to truly ease a friend on his way to death.

The morning was hot, befitting the season. In another month the winds would change from south to north and it would gradually turn cool, but for now sweating was the order of the day. Ike drank some canteen water, being sure to leave a few gulps. It was only a few hours' ride from Devil's Valley to Clantonville, but he might get thirsty again and there was no creek in between. He wondered how much Saint and Mulkins had left in their canteens, and considered warning them to reserve some for their ride back to Mountain View with the girl. Then Ike thought better of it. He didn't care if they went thirsty.

They moved down slopes, some steep enough that it was necessary to climb from their saddles and lead the horses. Then the land turned flat again, and there was cacti instead of trees. There were no clouds today. Ike pulled his hat brim low against the glare.

"How much farther, Ike?" Mulkins asked.

"Three, four miles," Ike estimated. "Might take two hours. Devil's Valley is surrounded by hills, so we'll have some climbing to do."

"Just so long as you get us there by noon," Mulkins said. "You're sure you know where you're going?"

That annoyed Ike. "Of course," he snapped, and lost himself for a while in daydreams of killing Mulkins and Saint once McLendon was handed over to Brautigan. Just draw his pistol and shoot them down. He could bury them under some rocks. No one would ever likely find them. There would be no witnesses — wait, there was going to be the girl. Kill her too? No, Ike remembered her as a pretty one. She might very well be impressed by his skills as a gunman. Women were like that. Sure, kill the two, take the girl back to Clantonville as a prize, make Pa proud, and have a wife besides. So nice to think about . . .

A ring of hills loomed. They were still two miles or more ahead, but because the land in between was so flat and bare, they seemed closer. Ike pointed and said, "Right there." He noticed McLendon swallowed hard. Mulkins looked sad. Saint glared at the back of McLendon's head.

Another mile, and Ike felt compelled to offer reminders. "The big man, he said to come at noon and not before. We'll have a half hour or so in hand. Might find some shade in the rocks on a hilltop. You other two stay back with me, McLendon rides down into the valley. The lady will ride up to join us."

The hills were long and only gradually became steep. They were able to stay mounted. The horses had no difficulty with the ascent. Near the top of one hill, several large boulders nestled close together and offered a broad patch of shade.

"Let's light here," Ike suggested, and they did, first looking carefully for any rattlesnakes curled under the rocks. They tethered the horses, trying to keep them at least partially in the shade too. As Ike had predicted, they had almost thirty minutes to wait. So they sat in the shade by the horses. Ike rummaged in his saddlebag and withdrew a can of peaches. "Share, anyone?" he asked. Mulkins said no, and Saint shook his head. McLendon didn't respond, didn't acknowledge Ike's generous offer with so much as a nod. He just sat with his back against a rock, staring off into the distance. Under other circumstances Ike might have thrashed him for his discourtesy, but, things being as they were, he chose not to take offense.

Ike ate his peaches with considerable slurping and smacking of lips. The fruit and juice were delicious. He thought idly again about killing Mulkins and Saint once McLendon had been swapped, but burying them afterward seemed like a terrible bother. Maybe he'd just leave them for the buzzards, like that poor bastard they'd found naked and bird-pecked the day before.

This happy rumination was interrupted by Mulkins, who leaned over and whispered, "Time, Ike?"

Ike made a show of extracting his watch from a pocket and carefully studying its face. "Let's see," he said. "Just about . . . looks like . . . yes, five minutes from straight-up noon. There's still a little bit of hill to climb, so we'd best get going. We can leave the horses here, except for McLendon's. He'll need to ride down into the valley to keep his appointment."

19

At dawn on Saturday, Patrick Brautigan walked away from his guard position by the shed, heading, Gabrielle guessed, to an outhouse or to breakfast. With him gone, she resumed a position at the peephole and watched the rest of Clantonville come to life. Those people she could see seemed subdued. Phin's beating probably weighed heavily on all who'd witnessed it or even just heard his screams.

Gabrielle waited for someone to bring her breakfast, but no food arrived. There was some water left in the jug Hettie had brought the previous night. Gabrielle drank it all. Then, more to keep busy than out of any sense of modesty, she tried adjusting her shirt. Its remaining two buttons seemed firmly in place, but the front still gaped. She experimented and found there was less bosom exposed if the shirt remained un-tucked, so she left it that way. There was no improving the rats' nest that was her hair. The knots in it offered painful resistance when she tried untangling them with her fingers. The combing motion made her ribs hurt. So Gabrielle studied her fingernails instead. She'd never decorated them with polish or paint, and kept them relatively short. Now several were broken in places, and all ten nails had packed crescents of dirt underneath. She scraped at these with her teeth, to little avail.

This very basic toilet concluded, there was nothing left to do but wait. Gabrielle tried not to imagine the exchange, how it would feel to see Cash McLendon arriving to save her life by surrendering his own. Such thoughts would lead to further despair, which in turn could sap her resolve to do something, she wasn't sure what. The main thing, she decided, was not to let Brautigan sense her new resolve. In some way, perhaps he could be taken off guard.

Gabrielle waited several more hours in the shed, until at least nine or so by her estimate. Then footsteps approached, the door opened, and Brautigan gestured for her to come outside.

"No talking," he reminded her. "Do precisely as I tell you."

Gabrielle nodded and blinked in the

bright morning sunlight as she emerged. A few feet away were the two horses and the mule. There was one more horse, a big one. Newman Clanton held its bridle.

"Mount up," Brautigan ordered, gesturing toward the small horse she'd ridden since her abduction. Before she could, Hettie approached, looking at the old man for permission.

When Clanton nodded, Hettie said to Gabrielle, "Here. For your shirt," and handed her two crudely carved clothespins. "I hope they'll help. I was told you didn't have time for me to properly mend it."

Gabrielle took the clothespins and squeezed Hettie's hand. She was tempted to defy Brautigan by speaking her thanks, but didn't want to alert him to her new, braver attitude. She used the pins to close her shirtfront on top and toward the bottom.

"On the horse," Brautigan said, and Gabrielle obeyed. Once she was in the saddle Brautigan told her, "For now I won't bind you. You can guess what will happen if you try to get away." Brautigan extracted the Winchester from its scabbard on his saddle and thumbed cartridges into the rifle. "Every precaution," he said to Clanton. "Now let's be going."

It seemed impossible to Gabrielle that the fat old man could possibly swing his thick leg up and over the back of a horse, but he did, and in quite a spry manner. "We ride west," Clanton told Brautigan. "Soon as we sight the hills around the valley, you're on your own."

"After what your boy did last night, you owe me additional service," Brautigan said. "Make sure we get close, and accounts will be squared. For now, lead the mule. I'm keeping my eye on the girl."

They kept a steady pace. Gabrielle listened to the creak of their saddles, and to water sloshing in canteens. Brautigan rode to her left and slightly behind. He was well positioned should she kick her horse in the ribs and attempt to bolt, not that any such attempt would be successful. Her horse was so very small and slow. Why had Brautigan brought such an undistinguished mount?

Because they were riding west, the morning sun was behind them. This lessened glare but burned the backs of their necks. As Brautigan had predicted, Gabrielle regretted not taking the hat of the young man he'd killed. Blood-soaked as it was, it still would have afforded protection from the sun. At one point, Brautigan produced kerchiefs from his pocket and dampened them with canteen water. He handed one to Gabrielle and said, "Wear this." She wrapped it around her neck and felt immediate relief, but not gratitude. Brautigan didn't give a damn about her discomfort. He just wanted her upright for the exchange, not collapsed in the saddle from heatstroke.

After some two hours, Clanton reined his horse and pointed. A ring of hills was ahead. Because the morning was so hot, the air between the riders and the hills shimmered, so that the hills seemed to dance in place.

"Devil's Valley's in there," the old man said. "The hills circle right around it. I'd appreciate you approaching from a different direction, maybe from the south instead of east. Don't want a straight trail back to my place."

"A reasonable precaution," Brautigan said.

Clanton said, "Now pay me." Brautigan produced a roll of bills and peeled most of them off. He handed the money to the old man, who jammed the bills in his pocket. He wheeled his horse alongside Gabrielle's and said, "My boy shouldn't have done it. I apologize sincerely. Forget the Clantons." He handed the reins of the mule to Brautigan, said, "Make sure nobody talks, now," and rode east.

Brautigan tied the mule's reins to his saddle horn. Then he told Gabrielle, "Stay as you are." He produced some rope and bound her hands in front of her. The knots were tight. Her fingers tingled with immediate loss of circulation. "If you behave, this'll be only for an hour," Brautigan said. "After the exchange, whoever's bringing you home can get you untied."

They rode along the hills. When they had reached the southernmost, they began riding up. Brautigan led Gabrielle's horse by the reins because by now her hands were too numb to guide the mount herself. A few isolated saguaro cacti dotted the upslope. There were boulders at the top. Brautigan halted behind them. Gabrielle welcomed the shade.

"We're about to get to it," he told her. "This is how it will go. You'll follow my instructions exactly. If you don't, I'll kill McLendon before your eyes, and then it will be your turn. Do you understand?"

Gabrielle nodded.

"In a minute we're going to go over the rim and down into the valley. We'll ride to the center and wait there. McLendon and some other will be on the hill across. He'll ride down. You will stay at my side as he comes. You'll not say a word at any time. When McLendon reaches us, when I've satisfied myself that he's unarmed and cooperating, you'll be allowed to ride across the valley and join whoever it is that's taking you home. When you reach him, he may untie your hands. Then ride north. Do not look back. And do not tell this person, don't tell anyone, anything about what's happened. They can guess all they want, but you're never to so much as hint about me or any of it. If you do, you die, and your father dies, and also the sheriff turned schoolteacher and your relations back in St. Louis. I have your promise?"

She nodded and wondered how she could do something with her hands so numb. In the same moment, she felt hungry, practically starving. Odd how the body expressed its basic needs even in the most suspenseful moments.

"You'd best keep your word," Brautigan said. He pulled out the Winchester and brandished it in front of her. "Don't think about trying to thwart me at the last moment. I expect I'd kill you both with my hands or boots, but failing that, I'd shoot you. Dead is dead." He stowed the rifle back in its scabbard.

Brautigan drank from a canteen. He

didn't offer water to Gabrielle. Then he leaned down and took each foot in turn from the stirrups. Using the kerchief he'd previously soaked with water and tied around his neck, Brautigan lovingly polished the steel tips on the toes of his boots. When they glistened in the noon sun, Brautigan took his horse's reins in his left hand, the reins of Gabrielle's horse and the mule in his right, and led the way to the top of the hill. There was a little wind, not much, but enough to swirl loose dirt. Looking down, squinting against the dust, Gabrielle saw a vast flat valley completely unpunctuated by plants or rocks or water. The hills opposite were fully a half mile away, perhaps more.

"We'll ride down now," Brautigan said.

The slope into the valley was slightly steeper than it had been going up. The horses and mules had to pick their way. Gabrielle, watching Brautigan, was reminded of some animal predator sniffing the wind, looking suspiciously in all directions, all senses alert. For the first time that day, she felt a wave of helplessness. She couldn't stop him. No one could. *Don't think that way,* she told herself. *It doesn't help. There has to be something. I can't let Cash die like this.* But as they made their gradual way down, she didn't seem able to think of anything besides her numb hands and the futility of fighting Patrick Brautigan.

When they reached the valley floor, Gabrielle gasped for breath. It was torturously hot. The sun overhead cast down roasting rays, and the surrounding hills blocked any wind. There were no clouds.

"Devil's Valley deserves the name," Brautigan muttered. He raised his hand to shade his eyes, looking up at the northern hills ahead. "Nothing yet." He fiddled with the reins, arched his shoulders to loosen his back. "He'd better show," Brautigan said to Gabrielle. "If he doesn't, and this has all been effort wasted, it'll be you who pays."

All morning, she hadn't considered that possibility. Maybe Cash had thought better of it; perhaps he'd chosen to run. Now that she had her own experience with Brautigan, in some sense she couldn't blame him if he'd made that decision. Brautigan was a monster without conscience. If Cash even now was in flight, leaving her to die instead, she wished she had some way of telling him that she understood. And if she was about to be murdered, she hoped she'd at least be able to kick at Brautigan, strike at him with her numb, bound hands, anything to demonstrate that yes, he could kill her, but no, she disdained him to her last breath.

Gabrielle was thinking of what she would do, what final gesture she might make, when Brautigan, still staring at the northern hills, grunted.

"There they are," he said. "McLendon's here."

20

When Ike Clanton announced that it was time, McLendon stood up and walked a few yards away from the others. He unbuttoned his trousers and relieved himself against a rock. His hands trembled, though not much. He hoped that no one would notice.

"All right," he said when he was finished. "Ike, I guess you can stay here, or go on, whichever you choose."

"Oh, I believe I'll stay around to see things through," Clanton said. He sounded excited, like a child being treated to the circus.

"Makes no difference," McLendon said. He mounted his horse and rode up the remainder of the slope. Clanton, Saint, and the Major followed on foot. They didn't have to rush to keep up. McLendon rode slowly.

They reached the top and looked down into the wide bowl of the valley. Saint blurted, "Yes, there she is!" and pointed.

Perhaps a half mile away, blurred by the shimmering air in between, a figure on a small horse was dwarfed by the hulking man on horseback beside her. Details were difficult to discern. "Get down there, McLendon. We need Gabrielle back safe."

"I'm going, Joe," McLendon said. He stared down at the two figures, fixing his gaze in spite of himself on Brautigan's unmistakable bulk. Death on horseback.

"I could ride down with you, C.M., at least for a ways," Mulkins offered. "Just to provide company."

"None of that, Major!" Saint snapped. "He's to go alone. We stick completely to the instructions. What matters is Gabrielle."

"And McLendon's to be unarmed," Clanton added. "That gunbelt's got to go."

"Shut up, Ike," Mulkins said. "If you're going to stay here, keep your damned mouth closed."

"They're both correct," McLendon said. "We have to think of Gabrielle." He unbuckled his gunbelt and handed the holstered Peacemaker to Mulkins. "I guess you can have this, Major."

Mulkins gazed into the valley. "A half mile shot's not unheard of. We've got the Winchester. I could try to take Brautigan down. You've told of that mile-long shot by someone at Adobe Walls."

"That was Billy Dixon, maybe the best shot on the frontier, and he had a Sharps. At this distance with a Winchester, you'd be as likely to hit Gabrielle, if your bullet came close at all. No, I'm going down." McLendon fumbled in his pocket and extracted the bills he'd brought from Mountain View. "Here's at least a portion of your generous loan back, Major, and also part of the money from Mayor Camp. If possible, could you return some of it to his family? Perhaps you might keep a hundred or so for Gabrielle, in case she might need it."

"All right," Mulkins said, swallowing hard.

McLendon turned to Saint. "Joe, I'm sorry for the pain I've caused you. Will you shake my hand?"

Saint kept his hand at his side. "Just go."

"As you wish." McLendon said to Mulkins, "You've been my true friend. You and Joe get Gabrielle home safely."

There were tears in Mulkins's eyes. "We will." He and McLendon clasped hands.

"So." McLendon wheeled his horse.

"You've not bid farewell to me," Clanton complained. "I demand that courtesy."

"Good-bye, Ike Clanton," McLendon said, and rode down the slope toward the valley.

■ ■ ■ ■

It took Gabrielle several moments to make out the men atop the hill. At first they were wavering dots, three, no, four of them. That many? Her heart leaped; Cash had brought a posse to rescue her. Then she saw that three were on foot. Only one was mounted, and he began riding down the slope into the valley while the others waited. Cash was going to do it, then, trade himself for her.

Beside Gabrielle, Brautigan began breathing harder, just a little, more air pulled deeper into his lungs and then exhaled swiftly, with a slight snorting sound emanating from his nostrils. The change would have been undetectable to almost anyone else, but Gabrielle had been with Brautigan for some time now, and she could tell. His victim was arriving, and the monster was exhilarated. There were only moments left. If she was to do something, it had to be now. Even if the binding around her wrists was cut, Gabrielle doubted she could inflict much damage to Brautigan with her numbed hands. Feet, then? Could she kick him, knock him off balance? But her horse was much shorter than Brautigan's. The angle was impossible. Maybe kick her horse's ribs, startle the animal into bolting forward? The other men on the hill might storm down then — wait, they were dismounted, and there were no horses beside them. They must have tethered their mounts on the other side of the crest. The distance was too great for them to cover on foot before Brautigan could spur his own horse and overtake Gabrielle.

As she pondered these things, Cash came ever closer, not galloping but keeping his horse in a brisk trot. He got completely down the slope to the flat valley floor — dust kicked up around the horse's hooves, the dirt was very loose there. He'd covered half the distance, she could see him clearly now, the thin dark beard, the wiry frame, the man she loved. So much time together had been lost, and now she had to think of something, do something, she had to try, and so because she couldn't think of anything else she flexed her feet to drive her heels into her horse's ribs, and that was the moment when Brautigan's massive hand gripped her arm hard and he hissed, "Be still, missy, or I'll kill him right now. Then it's your turn, and after that I'll get those on the hill." His grasp was viselike. Brautigan held on to Gabrielle as Cash rode up. "Still no talking," the giant warned Gabrielle. Then he called to Cash, who was a half-dozen yards away, "Stop there, McLendon. Just for the moment."

"I'm here like you wanted, Brautigan," Cash said. He looked at Gabrielle, his expression one of concern for her, not fear for himself, and asked, "Are you all right?"

Before she could even nod, Brautigan said, "She's fine, just not allowed to talk."

"I want to hear her say it."

"You can take my word. You know I keep my bargains, if others hold up their end."

Cash kept looking at her, not at Brautigan. Gabrielle saw him wince as he took in her disheveled state. "If you've hurt her, Brautigan . . ."

"If I have, there's not a damned thing you can do about it. But aside from some small thumps, the girl is whole, and will remain so if you continue to follow instructions."

Cash finally looked at Brautigan. "All right."

"You're going to get down off that horse and turn around for me slowly. Pull your shirt out of your pants and raise those shirttails up."

Cash did as he was told. "I've got no weapon, Brautigan."

"I'll see for myself. Pant legs rolled up. Boots off. Turn them upside down and shake them." All the while, Brautigan maintained his grip on Gabrielle's arm. "Next, the hat. Remove it, run your hand around inside the band."

"There are no blades concealed there. I'm completely unarmed."

Brautigan was satisfied. "Step away from your horse, McLendon. Two paces, three. Stop there." He let go of Gabrielle and said to her, "Now you get down. Stand just between your horse and mine."

She did, though with some difficulty. It was hard to dismount with her hands bound in front of her and numb besides.

"Remember I can kill you both in an eyeblink. Without touching each other, you, girl, go get up on McLendon's horse. McLendon, come over and mount hers."

"Why this?" Cash asked.

"No questions. Do it." For emphasis, Brautigan jabbed a massive knuckle into Gabrielle's collarbone. She gasped with pain; her knees buckled. "You want the girl hurt, keep talking instead of moving."

"Yes," Cash said. He began walking toward Gabrielle's horse. She came in the other direction, limping because of her injured shin.

"Don't touch," Brautigan barked. "Keep considerable space between you."

When they were opposite, they paused. It was instinctive. Oblivious to Brautigan for a moment, Gabrielle and Cash looked at each other. He summoned the courage to smile. It simultaneously thrilled her and broke her heart.

"Can I tell Gabrielle something, Brautigan?" he asked. "Even if you won't let her talk?"

"Since you asked permission. Make it quick. Remember, no touching. You're both dead if you do."

Cash said, "Joe and the Major are waiting for you on top of the hill. They'll take you back home."

Gabrielle nodded. She had to blink tears from her eyes because her bound hands were too numb to brush them away.

"Your father is all right. The Major has hotel staff tending him during the day, and Rebecca Moore stays with him at night. He's fine."

"That's enough," Brautigan said.

Cash looked up at him, then back at her. "I'm sorry for my mistakes, Gabrielle. I love you."

"Get on the horses," Brautigan ordered. Gabrielle pulled herself up on Cash's with some difficulty. He mounted hers.

"I love you," Cash said again, and Brautigan swatted him across the face with the back of his hand. Cash swayed in the saddle. He almost fell but didn't. Blood trickled from his nose.

"Ride, girl," Brautigan said. "Hurry before I change my mind. And remember to keep quiet. You know the penalty if you don't."

Gabrielle looked at Cash. He motioned with his head in the direction of the hill behind her: *Go.* Her last impression was that the blood dripping from his nose to his shirt was forming the pattern of a heart on the front of his shirt. Awkwardly fumbling at the reins with her bound hands, she turned her new horse and rode slowly away. Fifty yards, a hundred. She fought the urge to look back. What good would it do? Another hundred yards, and grief began giving way to calculation.

Joe and the Major met her halfway up the hill. They helped her down off the horse. She was glad because she thought she would have fallen if she tried on her own. "Thank God you're all right," Joe said. He pulled her down from the horse and swept her into a bear hug. She moaned with pain. Joe pulled away and gasped, "What? Are you hurt?"

"Give her room, Joe," the Major said. "Gabrielle, let's get those hands untied."

He produced a knife and cut the ropes. Her hands burned with immediate agony as circulation returned.

"There's shade behind some rocks just over the crest," Joe said. "Let's get you there, get you cleaned up. Walk easy. Lean on me."

"Water," Gabrielle croaked.

"Plenty in canteens where we left the horses by those rocks," the Major said. "Let us help you there." He took one of her arms and Joe took the other. Before she let them lead her away, she twisted to look back down into the valley. There, still in approximately the center, Cash sat on horseback beside Brautigan. Why hadn't they moved?

"They haven't left," Gabrielle said, her voice remaining scratchy from thirst and strain.

Joe said firmly, "Forget about them. It's done and we've got you back. You'll have some water and we'll be going."

It was hard for her to climb the rest of the hill. Joe and the Major did their best to assist, the Major supporting her with one hand and leading the horse with his other. But Gabrielle's limp was pronounced.

"Is your leg broken? Should I carry you?"

Joe asked, and she was touched by his concern.

"I can walk," Gabrielle said. It was a relief to get to the top. She could see the downslope ahead, hear the whickering of tethered horses. There was someone at the crest. Ike Clanton hurried over, holding his hat in his hands.

"At your service, Miss Gabrielle," he said. "Shall I help escort you down?"

Bile rose in her dry throat, an awful sensation. Ike Clanton was vile enough on his own. But his brother had attempted to rape her, his family had held her prisoner. She hated him and all the Clantons. "Stay away," she rasped.

Ike looked offended. "Why so harsh? Like these other two, I rejoice at your rescue. I led the way here. Without me, you'd still be captive."

Gabrielle glared at him. Then she said, "Some water?" to Joe and the Major, who helped her down the slope and into the blessed shade behind the rocks. The Major fetched a canteen. She drank it dry with great heaving gulps. Thirst slaked, her next priority was her empty belly. "Is there anything to eat?"

"We could cook something," Joe said, but the temperature was very hot for a fire, and

326

besides, Gabrielle was too hungry to wait. She ate stale biscuits, gobbling the first one, savoring the second and third. No food ever tasted better. As she ate, the Major watched anxiously, and Joe absolutely hovered. Ike Clanton stood to one side, nervously popping his knuckles.

She wiped biscuit crumbs from her mouth. "That's better."

Joe said, "That clothing exposes too much. Why did you change clothes, and how did that shirt get torn? We need to cover you properly. Even in this heat, perhaps a blanket —"

Gabrielle waved impatiently. "My clothes don't matter. Will one of you go back up the hill, look into the valley, and see if they're still there?"

"There's no need," Joe grumbled, but Major Mulkins said, "Of course." When he returned he reported, "No sign. They're gone."

"We need to be going too," Joe said. "Gabrielle needs Doc Vance. She's hurt, I can tell. What happened to you?"

"I'm all right for the moment," Gabrielle said.

"You're in pain, and besides, your father needs you," Joe said. "Even if you won't think of yourself, think of him. Let's be riding."

Gabrielle said, "Wait." She looked over at the tethered horses. "I see a Winchester in one scabbard and a shotgun in another. Whose guns?"

"The shotgun's mine," Mulkins said. "Joe's been minding the Winchester."

"Could you get them?" Gabrielle asked. "And that gunbelt on the ground by your feet, Major?"

"It was C.M.'s. He left it with me."

"Why don't you put it on, Major?" Gabrielle suggested. The Major looked quizzical, but buckled the gunbelt around his waist.

Now comes the risk, Gabrielle thought. She knew the lives of everyone she cared for were at stake. But evil had to be fought, not surrendered to. "Ike Clanton, aren't you armed as well?" she inquired.

"I am," Clanton said eagerly. "My trusty gun, holstered snugly at my side."

"May I see it for a moment?" Gabrielle asked. "After my captivity, I feel safer with the weapons of friends to protect me."

"What's this?" Joe said. "Ike, leave your gun be."

Clanton ignored Joe. He pulled the gun from its holster and held it out to Gabrielle.

"Handle it all you like," he said suggestively. "I'm at your service in every way."

"Could you bring it directly to me?" Gabrielle said. "My leg and body are bruised, and it hurts to move."

"My pleasure," Ike said. "Now, be tender with the trigger. We wouldn't want it discharging." He took another step toward Gabrielle, turned the gun in his hand and, holding it by the barrel, extended it to her handle first.

Gabrielle took the gun from Ike and turned it in her hand, admiring it. Ike noticed that her shirt had tantalizing gaps, and he leered, giving her bosom his full attention. Then Gabrielle had the barrel of the gun in her hand and, in one swift motion she cracked the butt against Clanton's temple. He collapsed, moaning, at her feet.

"I believe Sheriff Hove describes this as buffaloing," Gabrielle said. She leaned over Ike and slammed the butt into the back of his skull. The swinging movement hurt, but she didn't mind. It was good to strike instead of being struck.

"What are you doing?" Joe shouted. He leaped forward to wrest the gun from her. She twisted away and her entire body spasmed with agony from her injured ribs. Still, she managed to prevent Joe from taking the gun.

"What's this, Gabrielle?" Major Mulkins asked. "Why attack Ike?"

Panting from exertion and pain, Gabrielle gasped, "He's mixed up in this." She pushed Joe away and swatted Ike on the head for a third time. The gun handle made a satisfying *thunk* as it connected. "You two don't understand. I'll explain."

Before she could tell about being held prisoner in Clantonville, surely at Ike's behest, and Phin's attempted rape — which wasn't Ike's direct fault, but still — Major Mulkins said, "We already know. Ike helped Brautigan take you in Mountain View. We didn't confront him because it would have done no good, and we needed him to guide us here."

Ike managed to rise up to his hands and knees. Gabrielle pulled back the gun to strike again and he flinched. "No more," Ike begged. But his hand scrabbled to grasp a fist-sized rock. Gabrielle didn't notice, but Mulkins did. He stepped forward and pushed the double barrels of the shotgun behind Clanton's ear.

"Hold real still," the Major told him. "Drop the rock, Ike. Joe, that rope we removed from Gabrielle's wrists. Get it, and let's secure this fellow awhile." He looked at

Gabrielle and added, "Beating on Ike is satisfying, I know. But beyond that, nothing's accomplished."

"Something might be," Gabrielle said, and watched as Joe tied Clanton's hands behind him. Having been so recently bound herself, she thought that he should have knotted the rope tighter.

"Whatever Clanton's done, he's done," Joe said. "If ever we see him again, that would be a better time to administer a proper beating. Or will you stay out of Mountain View in the future, Ike?"

"Hell with you and your town," Clanton mumbled. He appeared to have some difficulty focusing his eyes, and Gabrielle was glad. "Never want to go there again."

"Satisfied, Gabrielle?" Joe asked. "Now, for the love of God, let's get you on a horse and heading home. You've had a terrible experience. You need time to recover yourself."

Gabrielle almost told her whole story then, Clantonville and Phin and the rest, but then realized that every moment they wasted here, Cash was being taken farther away by Brautigan.

"Keep holding that shotgun on Ike, Major," she said. "He's going to tell me something." She walked to where Clanton lay sprawled in the dirt, hands tied behind him. Gabrielle tapped Ike's pistol against his teeth. "Ike, I'll hurt you if needed. The Major might blow you to bits with his shotgun. We're all alone here. No one else would ever know." She was amazed by her own words. Apparently, she'd learned tactics from Brautigan. "You'll either tell me what I want to know or you'll die."

"You wouldn't kill me," Clanton spluttered. "You're not the kind."

"Until a few days ago, I wasn't. Now I am."

Clanton peered into Gabrielle's eyes and, finding no comfort there, turned to the Major, who gestured with the shotgun. Clanton swung his face toward Joe.

"Stop this. You were a sheriff once. You can't allow murder."

"Gabrielle," Joe began, and stopped when he saw the expression on Gabrielle's face. He shrugged and said, "Sorry, Ike."

Gabrielle yanked Clanton's head back by the hair and jammed the gun barrel under his chin. "One question only."

Ike yowled with terror. "I'm not to tell anything! He'll kill me if I do!"

"I'll kill you if you don't."

"What, then?"

"Where is Brautigan taking Cash? What's

his immediate destination?"

"Don't know," Ike sniveled. Snot bubbled from his nose. "He never said."

"All right, die," Gabrielle said. Her shin ached. She took a lurching step back and leveled the gun so that it pointed between Ike's eyes.

"No," Clanton pleaded. "I'd tell you if I knew, I swear."

"Then guess." Though Gabrielle's whole body ached, the gun barrel didn't waver.

"I'll help, Ike," the Major said. "I'd figure Brautigan means to take C.M. back to St. Louis, kill him there for his boss. So, where's he riding with him now? How's he planning to get him all the way back East?"

"I don't like that question, Major," Joe said. "Gabrielle, you can't be thinking of attempted rescue. You've been in danger enough. I won't allow any more."

She ignored him. "Where's Brautigan taking him, Ike? You may not know for certain, but you must have an idea."

Ike swallowed. "You try this, he'll kill all three of you. And McLendon. And me, for blabbing."

"Your last chance," said Gabrielle. Her voice was cold.

"Silver City," Ike whispered.

"What? I can't hear you."

333

"Silver City. It's where I met him, where we joined up. He's taking McLendon there. No idea what he's got in mind afterward, though I think he's got some deal in place with the sheriff. My word of honor, that's all I know."

"Silver City's in New Mexico territory, isn't it, Major?" Gabrielle asked. "Stay still, Ike."

"It is, maybe four or five days' ride southeast from here," the Major said. "But it's a terrible, lawless place. Brautigan gets C.M. there, if the sheriff's in his pocket then he's in position to take him on to St. Louis or pretty much anywhere else."

"We need to stop him before Silver City, then," Gabrielle said. "Because that's the way Brautigan and his boss, Mr. Douglass, work. They bribe the lawmen and then do what they please."

Joe said sternly, "That's enough of this foolish talk. Gabrielle, we're going back to Mountain View. Now."

She understood his concern and appreciated it. Sweet Joe, thinking as always of her and nothing else.

"What about rations and water?" she asked the Major. "Four or five days' worth? Fodder for the horses?"

"Gabrielle," Joe said again.

334

"Just a moment, Joe. Major? Have we enough to last four or five days? And, I suppose that much again, getting back to Mountain View?"

The Major shook his head. "Not even close to sufficient. We'd planned on just two days here and the same returning home. We attempt this, victuals will be limited and we'll be drinking seldom and by the sipful. Even then, we'll run out. Maybe the animals will find something to graze on, and maybe they won't. I'm not familiar with the region and don't know if we'll come across water."

"But we can try."

The Major smiled. "I suppose we can."

"I could guide you to Silver City," Clanton offered. "I know the way well."

"And somehow betray us to Brautigan?" the Major said. "Not likely."

"Gabrielle, you cannot do this," Joe insisted. "We're going directly home to Mountain View, no argument."

"You can go, Joe," she said, trying to sound kind and not impatient. "Ride home and be safe. I hope I'll see you back there soon. If not, I'll presume to ask that you see Papa's cared for."

Joe said, "If Brautigan had taken me instead of McLendon, you'd hurry on home."

"No. I'd do this for you too. For anyone dear to me."

"But you're going after Brautigan," Joe pleaded. "He's strong and smart. You can't save McLendon. Brautigan's too much for you, too much for anyone."

"He has been so far," Gabrielle agreed. "But for the entire time, he's always held the advantage. Perhaps he's vulnerable if taken by surprise. I don't think he'll expect us to follow him now. That's my hope."

"I'm not going with you," Joe said.

"All right. Major, you can certainly return to Mountain View with Joe. I feel I must tell you, while I was with Brautigan he threatened to kill you, and Joe, and my father and others, should I disobey him in the slightest way. He'll be quite displeased with anyone joining me in pursuit."

The Major smiled. "I always enjoy visiting New Mexico."

Gabrielle said, "Then I'll welcome the company. We should be going. All right, Joe, why don't you take a canteen and some provisions for your ride home? Whatever you think you might need. The Major and I will manage on what remains."

"You're really doing this," Joe said.

"I am. Rather, we are, the Major and me."

Joe heaved a great sigh. "You're making a

tragic mistake. But I'm going with you too."

Gabrielle was overcome with gratitude. She limped over to Joe and hugged him, ignoring the pain in her ribs.

"I'm doing this for you, not McLendon," Joe said.

"But you're doing it. Thank you."

"We're going to fail."

"But at least we'll try. Shall we ride?"

Ike Clanton, lying on his side in the dirt, hands tied behind his back, hollered, "What about me?"

"Oh, yes," Gabrielle said. "Major, would you untie him? Ike, you may as well ride home. We both know where that is."

"What do you mean, Gabrielle?" Joe asked.

"Just something shared between myself and Ike. And Ike, don't think of following us or trying to ride ahead and warn Brautigan. Because if you do and he doesn't kill you, then we will."

"Cruel words," Clanton said sullenly. "You about knocked my eyeballs crossways. Give me back my gun."

"I believe I'll keep it," Gabrielle said. "As a peaceful, honest man, you should have no need of a weapon. Go on now."

Ike mounted carefully. His head ached, and although there was no blood he still thought that the girl might have split his skull. He rode a little way off and looked back to where the other three were getting up on their horses. "You've not seen the last of Ike Clanton," he bellowed, and the act of shouting made his head hurt even more. Instead of acknowledging his threat, they rode southeast.

"Bastards," Clanton muttered, and then, *"Bitch."* What would Pa say when Ike showed up in Clantonville all battered and without his gun? Though the more Ike thought about it, the surer he became that he was likely to get a hero's welcome instead of a scolding. Thanks to Ike, Pa had made money, a good deal of it. Brautigan was going to kill McLendon, and also the bitch and her two companions if they caught up with him on the way to Silver City. And if that didn't happen, then the three of them would undoubtedly die of thirst or exposure. The country they were attempting to cross was too harsh. So, all witnesses silenced, and profit for the Clantons. Pa might even raise Ike to the deserved position of his second-in-command.

Ike consoled himself with these happy thoughts on his entire three-hour ride back to Clantonville. But when he arrived, his pa gave him a brutal beating for involving the family with Brautigan at all.

PART THREE

PART THREE

21

As Gabrielle rode north across the valley and then up the slope, Brautigan, mounted alongside McLendon, said nothing and allowed him to watch. She was halfway up when two figures rushed down to meet her — Mulkins and Saint, McLendon knew. They led Gabrielle up to the crest, and disappeared behind it.

The moment Gabrielle was out of sight, Brautigan said, "There. You can see she's safe."

"Yes," McLendon said, and added reflexively, "Thank you."

"Look at me," Brautigan ordered, and McLendon did. Up close, his relentless pursuer seemed exactly the same as McLendon remembered, especially his opaque eyes, which were as expressionless as a reptile's. "Here's what you're thinking, or what you're about to think," the giant said. "Your girl is with your friends, she's on her

343

way home, and now you can turn your attention to your own escape. Don't try. If you do, you'll fail, and do you know what will happen then?"

It was broiling hot on the valley floor. Sweat ran down McLendon's face and body. He thought he could feel perspiration pooling in his boots.

"Of course I know," he said, trying to keep his voice from trembling. "You'll kill me on the spot."

"Yes, that, but one more thing besides," Brautigan said. "After I finish you, I'll go back to that town Mountain View or wherever she might be and I'll kill the girl, too, in the worst of ways. I'll take my time. She'll suffer beyond anything you can imagine. You don't want that."

"No," McLendon said, choking on the word.

"This is how it will be. All right, now we'll ride southeast to a certain town. This will take several days, four or five. It's unlikely we'll encounter anyone else. If we do, you'll pretend you're with a friend. You can do it — you're good at pretending. When we get to the town, I'll pick up some papers and we'll make our way back to St. Louis, first by stage and then by train. In each instance, there will be people around us. No one must suspect anything. The slightest wrong gesture and the girl dies as well as you."

"And in St. Louis, Rupert Douglass watches you kill me."

"Yes. But the girl will live." Brautigan looked up at the hill. "Take the mule's halter and hold it snug. The beast carries most of our water and food. You'll ride just a bit in front of me, never more than a few feet between us. Move out now, south for the time being."

"Where exactly are we going?"

"I've no patience with questions, or with idle talk of any kind. Speak only when spoken to, and then briefly."

They rode out of the valley, climbing a southern hill and descending down the other side. Almost immediately, McLendon saw that his new mount was laboring, even though the slopes were not particularly steep.

"Brautigan," he said.

"I specified no conversation."

"It's this horse. I think it may collapse."

"So long as we keep a moderate pace, it should do fine. Now keep quiet and ride."

The land was flat, but not for long. An extended mountain range loomed ahead. After a few hours they were at its northern

345

base. Brautigan told McLendon to stop and dismount.

"Water and piss break," he said, handing McLendon a canteen. "One swallow only. Then do your business."

McLendon did. Afterward, he was surprised when Brautigan walked a few steps away and even turned his back on his prisoner while he relieved himself. Brautigan darted a look at the giant's horse. A Winchester hung in a scabbard from the saddle. Maybe, just maybe . . .

"Don't even think of it," Brautigan said. He buttoned his pants and walked over to McLendon. "My warning about escape wasn't enough, I see. So there must be this." Suddenly, savagely, he punched McLendon in the side. McLendon's breath whooshed out, but that paled in comparison to the absolute agony that flared through his entire body. He dropped to the ground and writhed there, trying simultaneously to drag air into his lungs and not pass out.

Brautigan stood over him. "That's a strike to the liver," the giant said. "Doesn't it hurt considerably? But there can always be more pain." He reached out, grasped McLendon's right wrist, pulled his arm straight out, and stomped with his heavy boot directly on the crook of McLendon's elbow.

There was a muted crunch. McLendon tried to shriek but couldn't. He didn't have sufficient oxygen in his body. He twisted in agony, rolling in the dirt. Brautigan walked a few paces away and watched. Gradually, torturously, McLendon sucked in air.

"All right," Brautigan said after a bit. "Get up. We need to be moving." He walked over, grasped McLendon by his shirt collar, and hauled him to his feet. McLendon managed to stand, but not straight. He was bent at the waist, and his right arm flopped uselessly by his side.

"The body ache will subside in time," Brautigan said. "No organs are ruptured — this time. Don't try me again. As to the arm, nothing's broken there either. But it will hurt to bend and there'll be little strength in it for some time. This will remind you not to be reaching for the rifle. Have you anything to say?"

McLendon wheezed and said, "I don't think I can ride."

"Oh, you can. Now get up on the horse."

It took McLendon several attempts. Brautigan did nothing to help. With only one arm and a body that was still stiff with pain, McLendon tried and failed swinging a leg up and over the saddle. Finally he managed to drag himself halfway up, then reach across his body with his left hand to drag his right leg on the other side of the horse. He felt about with his right boot until he finally found the stirrup.

"With your arm that way, I'll have to lead the mule," Brautigan said. "That was meant to be your job."

Navigating the first part of the mountain range proved difficult. Every step his horse took caused pain to shoot through McLendon's body. It was all he could do not to fall from the saddle. For the first time, Brautigan rode level with him and even sometimes a little ahead. He seemed to be looking for something — McLendon couldn't tell what. Twice he called a short break while he looked ahead to both the right and left, and checked the angle of the sun.

"Here, I think," he finally said, more to himself than McLendon. "South and east now." There were occasional notches between the mountain slopes, and they took one that provided blessed shade. Surreptitiously, praying the giant wouldn't see and hurt him further, McLendon tried flexing the fingers of his right hand. He could, barely. But the arm wouldn't bend at the elbow.

Around dusk they stopped in a small

348

canyon. Brautigan dismounted and watched as McLendon clumsily got down from his horse. "We'll make camp," the big man said. Because of McLendon's injured arm, his captor had to do most of the work. Brautigan unsaddled the horses and took the cask and heavy packs off the mule. He fed the animals oats from a pack and gave them water from his hat. Then he ground-hitched them and spread two blankets on the ground.

"Sit," he ordered McLendon. Brautigan used a knife to open a tin can, which he handed to McLendon. "Cold meals are all we'll have. No fires at night. You can have the contents of that, but no more."

There were peas in the can. The round green vegetables and the juice they were packed in were warm from the sun. McLendon took the can in his left hand and tipped it to his mouth. The peas were mushy and bland. He ate them all, thinking as he did that this was a waste, he was going to die anyway. But if Brautigan thought he was trying to starve himself to avoid execution in front of Rupert Douglass, then he might return to Mountain View and murder Gabrielle too. That couldn't be risked.

When the peas were gone, he dropped the can in the dirt and waited while Brautigan emptied his own can. It was getting dark fast. The stars overhead seemed closer and brighter than they ever had back in St. Louis. McLendon thought it was ironic that he might spend his last days feeling nostalgic for the frontier, since he'd mostly hated the West ever since he'd come there.

"Last piss break," Brautigan said. McLendon tottered a short distance away. His body still ached. He fumbled at his trouser buttons. It was awkward using his left hand for things he always did with his right. Brautigan watched him but didn't seem particularly concerned about attempted escape. "Over here on this blanket," he said when McLendon was done. Obediently, he lay down. Brautigan produced a length of rope and hog-tied McLendon's ankles.

"Since the one arm's not much use to you, this will be the extent of your binding so long as you stay still," Brautigan said. "If I detect the slightest unnecessary movement, you'll have rope snugged around every extremity."

McLendon was uncomfortable. Besides the pain in his body and arm, there were hard lumps under the blanket. Brautigan had spread it without concern for rocks. From the corner of his eye, McLendon saw that Brautigan sat rather than lay down on his own blanket — keeping watch, apparently. McLendon thought, *Does the man never tire?*

Since he couldn't sleep, McLendon thought at first about the most unpleasant of things. After more than two years on the run, he was in Patrick Brautigan's clutches. He'd had nightmares about it, and it had finally come true. There was no sense contemplating escape. The giant was too fast and strong to escape out here in the open, and once they were in a town, on a stage or a train — might it be possible to yell for help, to shout for the assistance of strangers? Brautigan couldn't kill a dozen people at a time. Well, he probably could, but then at least he'd be arrested, brought to trial . . . and then McLendon remembered how Rupert Douglass routinely bribed lawmen and judges. He'd find some way to set Brautigan free and afterward, McLendon knew beyond any doubt, the giant would come for Gabrielle exactly as promised. That couldn't happen, so Cash McLendon was a dead man.

After a while he made himself think about Gabrielle instead. She and Major Mulkins and Joe Saint were probably making their own night camp a day's ride from Mountain View. During the exchange in Devil's Valley,

McLendon saw the ravages of captivity in Gabrielle's appearance and movements. She'd moved as stiffly as he did now — had Brautigan delivered a body beating to her as well? Gabrielle's face was dirty, her hair tangled. The men's clothing she wore was stained with dirt and perspiration. But there was something in her expression, not an absence of fear — anyone would be afraid of Patrick Brautigan — but some additional glint of resolution, even defiance. Whatever he'd done to Gabrielle, Brautigan hadn't broken her spirit. She would recover from the experience, move on with her life. That was worth McLendon's dying for.

Then he imagined how she would move on. Not alone — Joe Saint would see to that. The sheriff turned schoolteacher would delight in McLendon's death. Saint was a clever man. He wouldn't immediately act on new opportunity. He'd take his time, always being there for Gabrielle, comforting and encouraging her to get over McLendon, and then, in six months or a year, he'd again insinuate himself with her romantically, and McLendon had no doubt he'd succeed. The only reason Gabrielle hadn't married Saint before was that McLendon was still alive, still a possibility in her life. With him gone, she'd see Saint as her best remaining alternative. McLendon wanted Gabrielle to be happy — but with Joe Saint? Nothing could be worse.

Except his own death, which would be as drawn out and terrible as Patrick Brautigan could make it. McLendon's bruised liver and damaged elbow were insignificant compared to what awaited in St. Louis. Where would Rupert Douglass want to watch? One of his factories, no doubt, some deep dark place where screams couldn't penetrate thick walls and be heard outside. He'd savor McLendon's agony like fine wine, and afterward stroll home to his mansion, smiling, vengeance achieved at last.

McLendon began speculating how he might ignite Douglass's hair-trigger temper, something he might say or do to goad his former employer into ordering Brautigan to kill McLendon with a single blow. With death a certainty, at least extended agony might be avoided. But as he thought, he was startled to hear a snore. Cautiously raising his head, he saw that Patrick Brautigan had fallen asleep sitting up. The giant's chin rested on his massive chest. His snores weren't loud, but steady, the rumbling of a weary man gaining much-needed rest. This was something new to McLendon, the thought that Patrick Brautigan was in some way human. If he had to sleep, might there be other weaknesses? Perhaps if McLendon stayed constantly alert, he might yet survive. The big man had said they'd be traveling four or five days to get to an unnamed town. Plenty of time for Brautigan to wear down further. Now, how could McLendon bring that about?

He lay still, watching the giant through slitted eyes. There was a little light from the moon. Brautigan snored a while longer, then snorted and abruptly sat upright. He bent over McLendon, who willed himself to lie still, breathing light and evenly. After a few moments Brautigan, satisfied, sat back. Soon, he was snoring again. It was a light sleep — the giant wasn't anywhere near exhaustion. He'd wake instantly at McLendon's slightest movement. But maybe tomorrow night? The next one? Cross-country travel in the West was arduous under the best of circumstances, and McLendon and Brautigan were traversing some of the wildest frontier territory on horseback.

McLendon's arm ached; he stealthily flexed it as best he could. There was little strength or movement in the elbow joint. Not right away, then. He had to give every appearance of submission, had to let Brautigan believe that he'd given up hope. There was very little chance of taking the giant by surprise — his aching arm and body were proof of that — and, even if he did get away, he'd then have to race Brautigan back to Mountain View and Gabrielle. Would she be willing to flee with him? What about her father? Too much to think about. It was enough for now that he had just a glimmer of hope.

Brautigan continued snoring, and McLendon slept.

22

Gabrielle wanted to ride straight across the valley floor and up its southernmost hill in direct pursuit of McLendon and Brautigan, but Major Mulkins convinced her otherwise.

"We can't take Brautigan by surprise if he sees us coming," Mulkins said. "If we cross the valley directly and then are silhouetted on that hilltop, if he looks behind them at all, there we'll be. We need to circle around the base of the hills instead. It'll take longer, but offers considerably more advantage."

So they rode around the hills. Mulkins was alert, Gabrielle was determined, and Joe Saint hoped they'd both soon become discouraged and agree to turn back toward Mountain View. So long as they were following Brautigan and McLendon into unknown territory, Saint believed there was no possible positive result. Their own deaths from starvation or exposure were most likely, especially if they became lost. If they caught up, Brautigan would kill all three of them and McLendon too. The worst alternative was that somehow they'd miraculously save McLendon. Then he and Gabrielle would go off to California together after all. Saint's purpose in joining Gabrielle and Mulkins wasn't to help bring about McLendon's improbable rescue. It was to serve as a constant voice of reason until they were persuaded to give up.

As they circled the hills, he saw his first opportunity. The sun beat down with ferocious power, and Gabrielle was bareheaded.

Saint pulled his horse alongside hers and said, "You'll get heatstroke without a hat. Take mine."

Gabrielle looked flushed and uncomfortable. Sweat streamed down her face. But she said, as Saint knew she would, "I can't take your hat. Then you'd be the one at risk."

"No," Saint said, removing his hat and pushing it toward her. "We've got to get your head covered. If we don't, you'll collapse. Let's pause and think about this."

Major Mulkins heard them and briefly reined in his mount. "Gabrielle, that bandanna around your neck. Use it as a head scarf. That should provide sufficient protection."

Gabrielle smiled. "Of course — how obvious! Thank you, Major." She tied the bandanna in place over her dark, tangled curls and said, "All right. Let's ride on."

It took some time to get around the hills. When they did, a considerable flat expanse stretched out before them, sparsely dotted with rocks and clumps of cacti. Though they stared hard to the south and southeast, they saw no sign of Brautigan and McLendon.

"Perhaps we might look for hoofprints?" Gabrielle suggested.

"There'll likely be none," Mulkins said. "The ground's too hard."

"Gabrielle, we tried, but we lost them," Saint said, trying and mostly succeeding to sound sympathetic. "You've done all that you could do."

"Hardly," she said. "It's only been an hour or so. I'm not stopping now. Major, what do you suggest?"

Mulkins studied the land ahead. "We may not know their exact route, but we still have the general direction. Silver City's somewhere to the southeast. We keep riding that way and chances are we'll sight them sometime. Even if we don't, Brautigan might have to light in Silver City for at least a short while, make his arrangements to bring

C.M. east. Could be we'd catch up to them there."

They rode southeast. Saint thought Gabrielle was experiencing considerable discomfort. She barely winced as she rode, trying not to bounce too much in the saddle, but Saint was well attuned to her expressions and noticed every minuscule grimace. Goddamned Cash McLendon, whose selfishness was the cause of her suffering. When Saint first met McLendon in Glorious, he disliked him for his mistreatment of Gabrielle in the past, and resented her continuing affection for the son of a bitch. After Saint saved McLendon from Brautigan on the night that much of Glorious burned, he sent McLendon on his way and thought he was rid of him for good. When Saint and Gabrielle moved to Mountain View and Saint resumed teaching school, it seemed only a matter of time until he and Gabrielle married. Then a letter arrived for her from McLendon, asking for another chance to win her back. To Saint's horror and disgust, she agreed to let him come and try. Saint knew he had earned Gabrielle's love in a way that McLendon never had. Damn it, he *deserved* her. Because he cared so much for Gabrielle, Saint didn't blame her for inviting McLendon to Mountain View. It was all McLendon's doing. The slimy bastard was a master manipulator. Which meant, once McLendon arrived in Mountain View, that the outcome was never in doubt. Gabrielle chose him over Saint, McLendon's shady past in St. Louis caught up with him once again in the person of Patrick Brautigan, and now here they were, Saint and Gabrielle and Major Mulkins, too, risking their own lives to save someone whose death would leave the world a better place. Saint had come to hate McLendon that much.

These bitter thoughts occupied Saint as they continued riding southeast. They periodically halted so Mulkins could scan the horizon ahead.

"Don't be discouraged that we haven't seen them," he cautioned Gabrielle and Saint. "They're up there somewhere."

In the afternoon they stopped for sips of canteen water. "I'm thinking there'll be creeks or pools of some sort once we gain the mountains," Mulkins said. "It'll be cooler there too. Shade."

"Should we ride through the night, Major?" Gabrielle asked. Saint was offended that she asked Mulkins instead of him. It was as though his opinion didn't count.

"Too dangerous," Saint said quickly. "We

might get all turned around in the dark."

"I think we could navigate decently by the moon and stars," Mulkins said. "But I agree with Joe, for a different reason. Our horses have been going all day. We try to keep them moving all night as well, they'll get worn out. So we'll need to camp, let them crop some grass if they can find any. You need to rest, too, Gabrielle. You've been through hell."

"Brautigan may not stop," Gabrielle protested.

"I think he will. He's from St. Louis. He likely doesn't know his way around here any better than we do."

By dusk they were almost to the mountain range. When they spied a patch of thin grass, Mulkins said they should make camp.

"It's something for the horses, anyway," he said. "They need water too. We've only got the three canteens, but we'd better use part of one for the animals right now." He and Saint poured small amounts of water in their hats and let the horses drink. They sucked in every drop and snuffled at the hats hoping for more. Then Mulkins and Saint ground-tethered them by the grass; the horses cropped at the growth.

"We need to eat too," Mulkins said.

"Perhaps the last of the biscuits might comprise our menu tonight."

"I shouldn't have eaten so many of them earlier," Gabrielle said. "Major, you and Joe divide those remaining between yourselves."

"You need to eat," Saint said. "After all you've been through, you have to build back your strength. I'm fine, I'm not hungry. Major, you and Gabrielle share."

"We all need to eat," Mulkins said. "We've got four biscuits, also a half-dozen cans of food and some jerky. Let's each have one biscuit and save the last one to divvy up for breakfast."

"And coffee," Saint said. "I'll start a fire."

"Don't," Mulkins said. "Out in the open as we still are, the flames will be visible at great distance. If Brautigan's anywhere nearby, he might see. We don't have sufficient water to use any for coffee, anyway. Let's eat our biscuits, wash them down with a sip each from the canteen, and do what we can to get some sleep. We ought to be moving early tomorrow, get into the mountains before the sun's full up."

Both men insisted that Gabrielle have use of their blankets. She lay down on them carefully, trying to find the most comfortable position. Her injuries made it difficult. Saint, watching, could hardly stand it. What must have happened to her?

"I think you need medical attention," he said. "Doc Vance —"

"I'm all right," Gabrielle said sharply. "How many times must I say it?"

"It's something to be discussed," Saint said.

"It's not."

"Let's just sleep," Mulkins suggested. "Joe, I don't think we need to stand a watch. You've got your Winchester handy? I've got my shotgun, and also C.M.'s Peacemaker. Gabrielle, what about Ike Clanton's gun?"

"I tucked it in my waistband during this afternoon's ride, and now I have it on the blanket near to hand."

"We ought to be all right, then," Mulkins said. "One of you hears anything during the night and I don't, be certain to wake me."

"One other thing," Saint said. "I've been thinking. Aren't we going about this the wrong way? We know Brautigan is taking McLendon to Silver City."

"So?" Gabrielle asked.

"Why not return to Mountain View, explain to Sheriff Hove, and have him wire the sheriff in Silver City? Let the lawmen sort this out. Sheriff Hove is a man of discretion. Our names need not come up in it. That decreases the chance of retaliation, should Brautigan somehow walk away free."

"Joe, you're forgetting what a hellhole Silver City is," Mulkins said. "We've all heard how it's got no law to speak of. A telegram from Sheriff Hove would likely be ignored."

"You don't know that would happen," Saint argued.

"Joe, for heaven's sake," Gabrielle said. "If all you're going to do is try and talk us into turning around, then just go back yourself. The Major and I will manage without you."

"I'm only thinking of you," Saint said. "That's my sole concern."

Gabrielle sat up on her blankets. It hurt to do it. "Thank you for that. But I've heard enough about giving up or trying something different. I'll tolerate no further discussion. Stay and help, Joe, or else go."

Saint knew Gabrielle meant it. "If you're staying, so I am," he said.

"All right. Now let's sleep."

Gabrielle was exhausted and dropped off immediately. Soon Mulkins was asleep too. Saint sat with his back propped against a rock and brooded. Gabrielle was so besotted with McLendon that there was no reasoning with her, and Mulkins clearly didn't understand the futility of overtaking

Brautigan and attempting to fight him. What was it about McLendon that blinded others to their own well-being? Saint had never understood his appeal, to Gabrielle or anyone else. He reminded himself, as he had almost every day since McLendon came to Mountain View, that the man was only alive because Joe Saint took pity on him once and saved him from Patrick Brautigan. If Saint only had that night back in Glorious to do over, how different things would be.

He slept and had short, violent dreams.

In the morning, they broke their last biscuit into three parts. After the horses had a little water, they mounted and rode into the mountain range. Some of the going was slow. They had to pick their way through narrow cuts and across rocky canyons. Most of the canyons were shallow, but a few required careful navigation. They dismounted and led the horses.

"At least it's a cool morning," Mulkins said. "We can thank the clouds for that." A thick blanket of light gray clouds blocked the sun.

"Maybe it will rain," Gabrielle said. "Not enough to flood, but something nice and steady. I think getting wet would be refreshing. It would at least wash off some of the dust." All three were coated with grime.

Just as Saint began explaining how it was really too late in the season for rain, the first drops fell. As Gabrielle hoped, the rain came in gentle fashion rather than torrents. Even the horses seemed to relish it, neighing and tossing their manes.

"The best part is, we can replenish canteens," Mulkins said. "That would have been impossible back where it was flat and dusty."

Pools formed in some of the rock formations surrounding them. Mulkins showed Gabrielle and Saint how to place their tin coffee cups so the runoff would drip directly into them. He positioned their one nearly empty canteen to do the same.

"These are tricks I learned back in the war," he said. "When we besieged Richmond, rainwater was our best means of refreshment."

They found enough water pools to allow themselves and their horses several hearty drinks. By the time the rain ended, Gabrielle said she was afraid that she might slosh as she rode.

"I feel so much better," she said. "Don't you, Joe?"

"The water was welcome," Saint said

grudgingly. He'd thought if they became thirsty enough, Gabrielle and Mulkins might yet be persuaded to turn back. One more possibility lost.

Most mountains in the range were separated by narrow valleys. Just past noon, crossing a valley floor relatively thick with vegetation, Mulkins called a halt so that the horses could rest and graze.

"Let's each have a few bites of jerky," he said, producing some strips of dried meat from his saddlebag. "Since we took in considerable liquid during the rainstorm, let's save the canned goods for now."

Saint hated jerky. It always tasted too salty to him; bits stuck between his teeth. He gnawed his strip. Gabrielle took measured bites of hers and seemed to enjoy it. "Will the food really hold out if we have to go all the way to Silver City?" Saint asked Mulkins.

"Water's more crucial," Mulkins said. "Dehydration would lay us low faster than hunger. We're well watered for now. The rain was a blessing. As to the food, we'll just have to be sparing."

"Keep your shotgun handy," Saint said. "Perhaps as we go along we'll roust a jack-rabbit."

"Oh, for now we don't want to be shooting," Mulkins said. "Out here, sound echoes and carries for miles. If Brautigan's anywhere near, he'd hear and be alerted to our presence. We mustn't fire at all."

Saint was annoyed, both with himself for not realizing and with Mulkins for correcting him once again in front of Gabrielle.

"We've not caught sight of them yet," he said. "Ike Clanton could have been wrong. Brautigan might not be aiming for Silver City at all. We could be going in entirely the wrong direction."

"No, it has to be Silver City," Gabrielle said. "Think where Brautigan wanted to make the exchange. He wants to get back to St. Louis, and Silver City is the best way if they have stage or train service there."

"Only stage, I believe," Mulkins said. "But I expect that the stage could get him and C.M. from Silver City to Wichita in Kansas, and from there they've got trains."

They remounted and worked their way past two more mountains, each steep. Saint thought their peaks looked different from the Pinals around Glorious and Mountain View. The Pinals were bloodred and sharp-edged. These were dust-colored and rounded. Still, they took time and effort to negotiate. As the day wore on, Gabrielle was clearly in more pain. Whenever they had to lead their horses, she limped badly.

When they paused for a brief drink in mid-afternoon, Saint said to Gabrielle, "Pull up your pant leg. I want to see your injured shin."

"There's nothing to see," Gabrielle said, but Saint wouldn't be denied. He grasped her left ankle — she gasped in pain — and rolled the pant leg up. Gabrielle's exposed shin was swollen as though a good-sized ball was wedged between the bone and skin. Bruising spread up toward the knee and down to the ankle.

"Jesus," Saint said.

Mulkins, peering over Saint's shoulder, grimaced. "That injury's serious, Gabrielle," he said. "Maybe we shouldn't go on."

Gabrielle yanked her pant leg down. "Nothing's broken. Yes, it hurts. But we're trying to save someone's life."

"You can't walk on that," Saint said.

"Yet I have been. Now we've had our water. We need to move on."

When they came to the next rocky slope where the horses had to be led, Saint said to Gabrielle, "Give me those reins and let me carry you on my back."

She smiled. "I don't need to be carried. But thank you so much for offering." Hav-

369

ing seen the damage done to Gabrielle's shin, Mulkins eased the pace as they walked.

"Slow and steady," he called back over his shoulder to Gabrielle and Saint.

It appeared to Saint that the futility of their pursuit became more obvious with each step. They kept moving southeast, but there was no guarantee they were headed in exactly the right direction to reach Silver City. They might miss it by miles one way or the other, finally fetching up in some remote part of New Mexico with no food or water or much chance of finding any. Gabrielle still looked determined, but it seemed to Saint that Mulkins's expression gradually grew doubtful. If the Major joined him in calling off the chase, surely Gabrielle would have to agree.

The clouds dissipated, the sun broke through, and almost instantly it was so hot that steam rose from the damp rocks around them. It created a foglike effect; fog was rare on the frontier, but Saint remembered it well from his years living back East in Pennsylvania, before his wife and daughter died from a fever and he thought for a long time that his own life was ruined. Then he came West, met Gabrielle, and had hope again. Cash McLendon ruined that. Or perhaps not.

It grew hotter still. The last of the standing water evaporated and the steam was gone. They found themselves on a mountain downslope, facing a cramped valley with another, steeper mountainside to maneuver around on the other side. Saint wiped sweat from his eyes and thought about suggesting they stop for a while, perhaps even for the night. They'd been leading their horses for some time. Gabrielle's limp was more pronounced. It was hard to breathe in the heat. Saint sucked in searing air, preparing to call out to Mulkins a few dozen yards ahead, but Mulkins spoke first: "Quick, look there!"

He pointed across the valley at a spot where the slope of the next mountain curved into what appeared to be a shallow ravine. Gabrielle stared in that direction, and Saint squinted. The lenses of his thick glasses were coated with dust. He took the spectacles off, wiped the lenses on his shirt, and looked again. His heart sank. Perhaps a mile and a half ahead, two men led horses and a mule along the slope toward the ravine. One man was much larger than the other. Without doubt, Brautigan and McLendon.

"What now?" Saint asked Gabrielle. "We see them, we've found them. But what exactly are we going to do?"

"I'm not sure yet," she said. "But we'll do something."

23

Brautigan and McLendon made little progress on their second day. The cuts and ravines intersecting the mountain range were mazelike. They'd follow an apparent route around the base or lower slope of one mountain only to find it rendered impassable by a rockfall or deep, unexpected crevice.

Though his expression never changed, Brautigan seethed. He was angry at the terrain and himself. When he and Ike Clanton had come up from Silver City they'd had to work their way around mountains, and these were surely among them. But they'd never been stymied in their progress. Brautigan had been certain he'd memorized the right route back; clearly, he hadn't. Now that he had McLendon, Brautigan burned to get him back to St. Louis and quickly finish the job. The boss was waiting impatiently, he knew. Why had he sent Mr. Douglass that confident telegram before he set out for Mountain View? Better to have let him wait and wonder until, amazingly, Brautigan appeared with his quarry.

Brautigan rarely indulged in such self-recrimination. He was a man of action, not thought. But in recent days he'd experienced too many frustrations — his dealings with the Clantons, in particular. The more people involved, the better the chance that someone would talk. Newman Clanton could be counted on to keep his word, but his family was cause for concern. Rapacious Phin, loudmouthed Ike. The daughter with the clothespins. Brautigan began wondering whether, after McLendon was finished off back in St. Louis, he ought to return to Arizona Territory and do away with everyone in Clantonville. It would be a considerable task, and there might be as many as thirty to be eliminated. Even for Brautigan, that would be daunting. But he'd discuss it with the boss. If it needed to be done . . .

McLendon interrupted Brautigan's reverie by asking, "Can I have some water?"

"We'll stop in a while," Brautigan said. "After we're past this particular mountain."

"It's been hours since I had a drink," McLendon said. "Could you just pass me a canteen?"

"One short swallow, and then no more talk out of you," Brautigan said. He reined in his horse and unslung a canteen. He handed it to McLendon, noting that his prisoner still had use of only his left arm. He had to rest the canteen on his lap and twist off the cap with that left hand while balancing the cap on his thigh. When McLendon raised the canteen to his lips one-handed, the cap tumbled down to the dirt.

"Pick it up," Brautigan ordered.

"It's hard to dismount with my arm injured like it is," McLendon said. His whiny tone was aggravating. "You could get down and pick it up a lot faster, since you're in such a hurry."

"Get down and pick it up," Brautigan said again. "Or you could lose use of the other arm, and then I'd hog-tie you to the saddle."

McLendon dismounted, nearly falling in the process, and picked up the cap. Some water sloshed out of the canteen.

"Careful, there," Brautigan said.

"There's a whole keg on the mule," McLendon said sulkily. "With as little as you let me drink, that alone would last a month."

"That water's for the animals. You and I have only what's in the canteens. Since you wasted some, you'll not be allowed any more for quite some time. Now hand me the canteen and get back on your horse."

For the rest of the morning and most of the afternoon they did their best to keep heading generally southeast. Much of the time it proved impossible. The mountains wouldn't cooperate. At one point Brautigan decided it would be best to turn back west, ride out of the mountains, and then follow the plains south until, finally, the range ended and they could turn back east below them. But that would add at least another day, maybe two, and back in St. Louis the boss was waiting.

In mid-afternoon, at one point gray clouds gathered overhead and it rained, not hard but steadily. Brautigan didn't know to stop and prop up open canteens to catch the rainwater. He just ordered McLendon to keep riding and the rain dripped from the brims of their hats. The rain and dust mixed into a thin layer of slimy mud, and the horses and mule slipped occasionally as they plodded forward, especially on rocky ground where the footing would have been tricky even in dry weather. At least the rain tempered the heat. Brautigan appreciated that; the back of his neck was blistered with sunburn.

Late in the day they finally struck a shallow ravine that miraculously curled around several mountains and let them make considerable progress. Looking ahead, Brautigan thought he could see trees, a lot of them — could a forest be there? — and a blessed end to the mountains. Once past them, he believed, the rest of the way to Silver City would be easy. Mostly flat land and then, maybe on the final day, an area crisscrossed with sudden, unexpected crevices, but still it would be better than mountains.

It occurred to Brautigan that McLendon had been silent for quite some time. He seemed subdued, resigned to his fate, but with McLendon it was impossible to be certain. If not brave, he was still crafty, always thinking, calculating possibilities. Brautigan did his best to discourage this by giving McLendon an early beating, just as he'd done with the girl. It seemed to have worked. McLendon's right arm still hung limply at his side. After the body beating he'd suffered, the slightest movement must hurt. That ought to be enough to keep him cooperating until they reached Silver City. Brautigan expected McLendon to try something there, encouraged by relatively civilized surroundings, and certain of the fate that awaited him in St. Louis. A second beating might be in order then. Sheriff Wolfe would certainly know a private place where Brautigan could be about that business.

For now, it would be enough to get away from the damned mountains. The rain stopped, the rocks steamed, and Brautigan's entire body dripped with greasy sweat. He'd never concerned himself with physical comfort, but now he longed for a bath and clean clothes and a comfortable chair instead of a saddle. After this job, Brautigan hoped never to return to the frontier, unless of course the boss decided that the Clantons needed to be dealt with.

The end of the long ravine loomed. As Brautigan hoped, it led to the very southernmost tip of the mountain range. A half mile after that, a thick grove of trees beckoned. Brautigan didn't know what kind of trees they were and didn't care. He was about to be out of the damned mountains.

McLendon said, "We haven't stopped to eat. I'm hungry."

"Soon."

"Why not stop now?"

"Another word and you'll be missing teeth. We'll stop in those trees."

They ate jerky and Brautigan had water. Then he watered the animals. There was some grass between the trees and he let them graze and rest. McLendon wanted water, too, but Brautigan wouldn't allow it. There really was no shortage of it — they had three more full canteens. But denying water to McLendon was one more way of reminding him that he was completely at Brautigan's mercy.

"Don't ask again, or there'll be none tonight as well. I don't care if you're thirsty."

After a half hour of rest they moved on. Brautigan felt much better. He cast one glance over his shoulder at the mountains he'd come to hate, then resolutely fixed his gaze on McLendon, who rode just in front of him. Brautigan was concerned about McLendon's horse. He'd originally picked the animal at the Silver City livery because it looked so small and slow — no one riding it could possibly hope to outrun mounted pursuit. Brautigan was no expert on horses, but it now seemed to him that the animal's gait was even slower than before. The rigors of desert and mountain travel were wearing it down.

"We'll get down and walk awhile," Brautigan said to McLendon. "You can lead your horse with your good arm."

McLendon seemed ready to argue. Brautigan fixed him with a steady gaze. McLendon clambered down, making a show of how difficult it was. Brautigan led his horse and the mule. They walked through the trees. A few chirping birds perched on branches. The trees were widely spaced so there was plenty of room to move. Looking through them to the east, Brautigan saw a single towering mountain that seemed familiar. He thought that when he and Ike made their way to Mountain View, this mountain had been on their left. That meant —

"Shit," Brautigan said, loudly enough for McLendon to look back at him and ask, "What?"

"We're too far west," Brautigan said. "We'll turn directly east. See that mountain? We're going to go in that direction."

As soon as they were clear of the trees, Brautigan told McLendon to mount again. His horse grunted. Rest, water, and food hadn't refreshed it much, so Brautigan allowed a slightly slower pace. The mountain ahead of them might be a little more than two days out of Silver City. It was good to finally feel certain he knew the way, that they weren't lost out in the wilderness. Not that much farther to go, then the rest of the way would be stage and train and finally the end of this blasted McLendon business.

They were just below the mountain at

dusk. Though it appeared that way from a distance, the ground wasn't as flat as Brautigan hoped. It undulated in a gentle series of arroyos and low hills, like waves on a slightly restless sea. The colors around them changed, from dull, dusty brown to various shades of tan. There were scattered clumps of vegetation that didn't appear to be cacti. The air seemed fresher. The mountain blocked views to the north, but Brautigan thought he could see fairly well in all other directions.

"We'll stop soon," he told McLendon.

"I think there's something wrong with my horse," McLendon said. "There's a stumble in its gait."

"With a full night's rest, it will be fine."

They came to a saucerlike arroyo, just deep enough to keep them out of any swirling night winds and blowing dust. There was scattered plant matter. Brautigan didn't know if it was something the animals could graze on. If not, they'd fed earlier.

"Here," Brautigan said. "Get down." McLendon slid from his horse. It was hard to tell whether mount or rider looked more the worse for wear. Both stood slumped and apparently spiritless. Brautigan believed the horse but had doubts about McLendon. He seemed almost too submissive.

They gave the animals water and ground-hitched them near some plants. Brautigan did most of the work, all the while keeping a wary eye on McLendon. He told him to get two cans from their saddlebags.

"One of peaches, one of peas," McLendon said. "Which do you want?"

"I don't care."

McLendon chose the peaches and took a long time eating them. He seemed to have difficulty chewing and swallowing. He saw Brautigan watching and said defensively, "I had to walk too far today. So I'm tired and my arm still hurts. I think you broke it."

"I never did. If you're so tired, go to sleep."

Brautigan tied McLendon's legs and, this time, his hands. McLendon moaned when the giant pulled his right arm in front of him and lashed his wrists together.

"See that you pass a quiet night. No more talking," Brautigan said. He decided not to sleep at all himself. McLendon was getting ideas — of course he was. No one would want to die in the terrible way that McLendon faced. Even his love for the girl might be trumped by the instinct to survive at any cost. Not that anything McLendon tried would work. Brautigan was his master in every way. But he didn't want to have to kill

382

McLendon here. The boss wanted the pleasure of watching him die back in St. Louis, and Brautigan did not intend to disappoint him. It occurred to Brautigan that he had turned forty-two. The exact date of his birthday escaped him, but he knew it was sometime during summer. If something went wrong delivering McLendon to justice, if Brautigan failed in even the smallest way, Mr. Douglass might decide that he was getting too old. Brautigan knew all too well how the boss might dispose of an employee who knew too much and had outlived his usefulness. Couldn't chance that. McLendon must not be allowed to make any escape attempt.

All night long, Brautigan watched McLendon. It seemed to him sometimes that the bastard was watching him, too, through half-shut eyes. Let him. If they made better time on the flats instead of the mountains, in two more days they could reach Silver City. After that, Brautigan would be back in his element, and McLendon's end would be blessedly near.

24

The immediate challenge, after sighting Brautigan and McLendon, was to avoid being seen by them. Gabrielle, Mulkins, and Saint dismounted, pulled their horses behind rocks and crouched as they watched the men ahead navigate the mouth of the ravine. They seemed to move cautiously.

"Brautigan's keeping a sharp eye all around, I'll wager," Mulkins said. "Many would rush forward as fast as possible, losing all track of their surroundings in their haste to complete the journey. I have to credit the man. He's too canny for that."

"I wonder about Cash," Gabrielle said. "It's difficult to tell at this distance, but it appears to me that he's somewhat stooped."

"C.M.'s worn out, perhaps, and certainly shaken," Mulkins said. "He's in an awful predicament. Well, look. They're in the ravine now and dropped out of sight. We can move ahead for a bit."

Leading their own horses, the three crept to the ravine's edge. Perhaps thirty feet below and now only about a mile ahead, Brautigan and McLendon moved at a glacial pace. Brautigan looked in every direction but directly behind him. The ravine was perhaps fifty yards wide, and curled southeast. Until it wrapped around the base of the next mountain, Mulkins, Saint, and Gabrielle couldn't enter it without risking being seen. There were no large rocks to use as cover on the ravine floor.

"The man's a master," Mulkins said. "See how Brautigan's deliberately slowed the pace when he's on the flat and mountains rise around him? He knows there could be danger there, people above with good shooting angles. He's giving every inch a thorough looking over."

"Cash's arm is hurt, the right one," Gabrielle said. "It's dangling as he moves. He must be in terrible pain. We've got to get him."

"And how will we do that?" Saint asked. "As the Major said — Brautigan is in complete control of his situation."

"His overconfidence may provide our advantage," Gabrielle said. "There'll surely be an opportunity. Major, how long now to Silver City?"

"I'm not certain," Mulkins admitted. "I'd guess perhaps three days."

"Three days for Brautigan to let down his guard," Saint said. "And if that doesn't happen?"

"Let's not despair," Mulkins said. "We'll watch and follow."

They waited more than an hour before they dared to move forward again. Brautigan and McLendon had disappeared down the ravine. It was very hot, and since the rain had replenished their canteens, the three pursuers allowed themselves a good swallow each.

"Cautiously now," Mulkins said. "Every bend we come to, they might be right on the other side." They led their horses ahead. At one point the ravine straightened again and they didn't immediately see Brautigan and McLendon. Then Gabrielle spotted them, looking much smaller because they had almost doubled their previous lead.

"They're almost to the end of the ravine and the mountains," she said. "Look beyond — aren't those trees?"

"I've heard there were some woods in the vicinity," Mulkins said. "I'd guess when they reach them, they'll stop to rest a bit."

"Maybe we can surprise them there if they

do," Gabrielle said.

Mulkins shook his head. "Better we keep out of sight, see where they get to by dusk."

"But, Cash's arm," Gabrielle said. "If he's hurt —"

"I know it's hard to hold back and observe, but at least he's not hurt so bad that he can't get around," Mulkins said. "We can't just rush in, Gabrielle, at least not yet. If they're getting close to Silver City and there's no other choice, maybe then. For now, it remains watch and follow."

When Brautigan and McLendon reached the trees, the trio lost sight of them again.

"They've probably stopped, as you predicted," Gabrielle said to Mulkins. "I could creep forward and reconnoiter."

"That would be foolish," Mulkins said. "It's easily three hundred yards of clear ground from where you are to the tree line. You can barely walk with that shin of yours. Joe or I could try, but the risk of being spotted is too great. Let's wait and learn where they go from those trees, if we can."

Forty-five minutes later, Brautigan and McLendon emerged. They were back on their horses, but now they rode directly east in the direction of a towering, solitary mountain.

"They might have gotten temporarily off course, or else Brautigan is even wilier than I'd credited," Mulkins said. "Could be, he went farther south than necessary to throw off possible pursuit, making it appear that he aimed for a border town or even Mexico instead of Silver City."

"Do you think he's seen us?" Gabrielle asked.

"I'd say not, because if he meant to lure us in, those trees were a likelier spot than open ground. At least Brautigan knows the way to Silver City, because at this point I surely don't. We'll hold where we are for a bit, let them get a little farther ahead for the present, in case Brautigan's being especially watchful."

Mulkins, Gabrielle, and Saint watched the two riders grow smaller in the distance. Suddenly, they disappeared.

"What's happened?" Gabrielle asked. "They were there, and now they're gone."

"Uneven ground," Mulkins said. "Swales and arroyos. It looks flat from far away, but up close there are all sorts of slopes and hidey-holes. Keep looking. They'll reappear presently."

A few moments later they did, then disappeared again.

"I believe they've got a mile or more on

us now," Mulkins said. "We can follow, but let's be careful to stick to all the low spots ahead and avoid the high ones as best we can." They mounted and moved their horses forward at a walk. Gabrielle rode directly behind Mulkins, following him down arroyos and cautiously up the sides. Saint brought up the rear. At one point Gabrielle glanced back and saw that he had ridden up the crest of a low hill.

"Get off of there, Joe," she called, keeping her voice low because the sound might carry. "Brautigan could see you."

Saint rode down, but a few minutes later Gabrielle saw he was on another hilltop.

"I told you, Joe," she said. "What's wrong with you?"

Saint said, "Sorry, I forgot."

"Well, ride in front until you remember better," Gabrielle said crossly. She was too concerned about McLendon's arm injury to wonder why Joe Saint couldn't keep in mind something so simple.

When night fell, they were still about a mile from the base of the solitary mountain.

"Brautigan and C.M. will be making camp now," Mulkins said. "We creep up to the proper position, we'll likely see their fire." They dismounted and walked their horses, cautiously weaving their way forward through the swales. The quarter-moon provided modest light. Each step had to be carefully taken so there would be no stumbling over rocks or roots. After almost an hour, they still had not spotted a fire.

"Cold camp, then," Mulkins said softly. "More smart thinking from Brautigan. We can't chance stumbling upon them. No telling who'd be hurt in the resulting confusion."

"Should we just stop here?" Saint asked.

"I have a thought," Mulkins said. "Long as we're feeling our way in the dark anyway, why not make for the mountain? Get up the slope a little ways and find sufficient cover. Then in the morning, we'll be able to see Brautigan and C.M. below us and get a sense of where we might try to work our way ahead, take Brautigan by surprise that way. Ambush rather than pursue."

Gabrielle was enthusiastic, but not Saint.

"In this darkness, it's hard enough walking down here. We'll never make it up the side of a mountain."

"If it proves too difficult, we'll think of something else," Gabrielle said. "Time's running out."

"That's so," Saint said. He didn't sound sorry.

Even in near pitch blackness, they had no difficulty finding the mountain. It was as though they could feel it looming. As they approached, there was rustling in several directions: "Night creatures," Mulkins said. The slope was steep but relatively smooth. They hiked almost directly up for a while, then moved around and to their right.

"We want to look a good way east at daylight," Mulkins said. "If a likely place presents itself then, we can try to beat C.M. and Brautigan there."

Gabrielle thought it was well past midnight before the Major said they'd gone far enough. There was no way to be certain of the time. Mulkins wouldn't strike a match to check his pocket watch because, wherever he was down below, Brautigan might notice the tiny, flaring flame.

They chewed jerky and sipped water. "Nearly the last of the food," Saint said. "A few stale biscuits and three or four meat strips are left. What will we do when that's gone?"

"One problem at a time, Joe," Mulkins said. "Right now get some rest." They wrapped themselves in their blankets, but nobody slept. The night dragged.

Finally, a faint pink line colored the eastern horizon. The sky began to lighten in that direction. They were higher on the mountain than Gabrielle would have guessed, at least a quarter of the way up. She was pleased to see that the slope was fairly uncluttered. They could move forward or down quickly and with relative ease.

As the sun rose in the east, they were able to study the land ahead. For a considerable distance, it appeared to be a continuing series of arroyos and swales. Then perhaps twenty miles beyond was another mountain range, its jagged peaks gleaming almost blue in the early morning light. There was also a dark line halfway between their current perch and those mountains.

"River," Mulkins said. "I knew the San Simon flowed down this way, but didn't realize how far. Silver City's maybe twenty-five, thirty miles east of it."

"Do you see anything auspicious for ambush?" Gabrielle asked.

"I'm thinking that next set of mountains. We can hustle down the east slope here, use the mountain itself to screen us from Brautigan. Then as carefully as we can, we push ourselves to get ahead of them. We'll have to risk him spotting us."

"And if he does?" Saint asked.

"We'll hope that doesn't happen," Mulkins said. "We have to try something, Joe."

Next they looked for Brautigan and McLendon. They couldn't locate them immediately. For several long, panic-stricken minutes, Gabrielle thought they might have kept moving throughout the night, and now had too long a lead to be overtaken. But then Mulkins said, "There they are," and pointed a half mile back down and to their right. Brautigan was mounted; the mule's reins were attached to his saddle horn. McLendon led his horse.

"Odd," Mulkins said. "One riding, the other on foot. Has C.M.'s horse pulled up lame? That will slow them some, and work to our advantage."

"Then let's be going," Gabrielle urged. She and Mulkins hastily saddled their horses. Saint moved slower. He gazed back toward the east. The rising sun was in his eyes and he raised a hand to shade them.

"Come on, Joe," Gabrielle said. "We need to hurry."

"Hold on a moment," Saint said. "There's something else moving down there. The sun makes it hard to see."

"Animals. Deer, probably," Mulkins said. "Let's go."

"No, I don't think deer. I can't tell. Come look, Major."

Gabrielle said impatiently, "Joe, if you

don't want to go any farther, that's fine. Just say so, and the Major and I will leave you here."

"Wait, Gabrielle. Major, will you look?"

Mulkins handed his horse's reins to Gabrielle and walked over to Saint, who pointed down south, well beyond McLendon and Brautigan.

"There, maybe a thousand yards. Just past the swale topped by the crooked saguaro."

Mulkins looked. After a few moments, he detected near-infinitesimal movement. Then, a dark head rose briefly above the swale, and an arm motioned forward. A dozen yards behind there was more movement in several places, coppery men stealthily leading ponies.

"Jesus Christ," Mulkins said. "Apache."

25

Goyathlay recognized one of the white men immediately. It was the big one who'd been caught on the San Carlos agency not long ago. Even that first time, Goyathlay wanted badly to kill him. Most victims offered little in the way of enjoyment. They begged for mercy and seemed surprised when they got none. But this one, Goyathlay sensed, had a warrior's spirit. Taken and tortured, he'd scream with anger, not anguish, and take a satisfyingly long time to die. But Clum, the unsmiling San Carlos agent, had been there. All Goyathlay and the other warriors were permitted to do was herd the big man and his chattering white companion off agency land. It was a grand opportunity lost, and now thanks to the gods or simply luck, there was another chance.

It was especially welcome. This current breakout from the agency was so far a dismal failure. Goyathlay had coaxed four younger warriors — Nantee, Datchshaw, Tawhatela, and John Tiapah — into following him on a raid into Mexico. Clum, relatively new to his post, insisted that the Chiricahua stay at San Carlos and leave Mexicans alone, since America and Mexico were at peace. While Cochise lived, this edict was observed by all — Cochise never allowed dissension. But he recently died, and his two surviving sons were weak. Clum and the Americans recognized them as new tribal leaders, but many of the Chiricahua didn't. Traditionally, Chiricahua leaders earned rather than inherited rank. Goyathlay, always ambitious, saw his chance. Many warriors felt stifled at San Carlos. Hunting was bad and the Americans wanted them to become farmers and raise cattle instead. Someone who honored and encouraged the old fighting ways could earn widespread respect and, perhaps, allegiance. Goyathlay thought that if he took a few men raiding into Mexico, after they returned to the agency and bragged about the men they'd killed and the women they'd raped, many others might be persuaded to do the same. Then Goyathlay could break out again, this time at the head of a band sizable enough to ride back to Mexico and establish itself in a camp beyond the reach of Clum and

American soldiers.

This initial foray hadn't gone as he had hoped. The five Chiricahua exited San Carlos in fine style. The agency was sprawling and, observant as Clum was, he couldn't keep track of more than four thousand Apache at once. By the time their absence was noted, they'd be well on the way to Mexico. The four braves recruited by Goyathlay were excited. As they rode, they bragged about their exploits to come. They traveled south without incident, avoiding any contact with whites. This was important. Once in Mexico they planned to fall on small villages and kill indiscriminately. On their return to the agency, Clum would chastise them for escaping and guess what they had been about, but with no proof or witnesses he could do little more. In the greater American scheme of things, a few probable dead Mexicans wasn't worth imprisoning or executing Chiricahua warriors and risking revolt by the entire tribe. White victims would have been different.

But the people of the two villages they'd come across in Mexico declined to co-operate with Goyathlay's plans. They were surprisingly alert to potential attack, and well organized in defending themselves. No Mexicans died or were raped. After five frustrating days they decided to return to the agency. Datchshaw had a flesh wound on one shoulder that needed treatment. Though he and the other three didn't say so, Goyathlay knew that they considered these failures to be his fault because he was the leader. When they were back at San Carlos and the other men asked them how the raid went, they would reply that Goyathlay showed bad judgment in selecting the places to attack. His chance to assume tribal leadership would be gone.

But now this. Nantee had been the first to see them. Riding ahead of the others as a scout — they didn't want to end an already miserable raid being picked up by a patrol of bluecoats — he came rushing back to report.

"Two white men ahead, one riding, one leading a small tired pony. Also a mule. Going very slowly toward the sunrise."

"Finally, some luck," John Tiapah said. "Let's kill them. Then, mule meat tonight."

Killing Americans was far riskier than slaughtering Mexicans. Even the rumor that Goyathlay and the others had attacked whites would result in their immediate arrest by Clum, with a subsequent trial and probably execution. But it seemed to Goyathlay that they were in an isolated place. Besides the two unsuspecting white men ahead of them, there almost surely was no one else to see and tell.

"All right," he said.

As the other men checked their bowstrings for tautness — each had a rifle, but little ammunition remaining after the failed fights in Mexico — Goyathlay said, "First we need to make sure there aren't any others. And how are these men armed? Do they watch out for enemies? You must notice these things, Nantee. I'll go up to look. You others, stay behind. Lead your horses, don't ride." He didn't have to caution them to stay low and use the rolling terrain to stay out of sight. This was instilled in the Apache from childhood.

Goyathlay went forward. The others trailed a bowshot or two behind. Because of his wound, Datchshaw brought up the rear. Should there be a fight, he would participate only if necessary.

Soon Goyathlay saw the white men. That was when he recognized the big one. The other wasn't the man who had been with the big one on the agency. This new white man didn't seem to talk at all. There was no friendship between the two. Goyathlay realized that the small one was the big one's prisoner. The big one had one of the rifles whites called Winchesters hanging from his saddle. Besides that, Goyathlay saw no other weapons, not even a pistol. This was disappointing because guns and ammunition were prized booty. But it was also promising. For Goyathlay to have any remaining hope of being proclaimed leader, the others had to return to the agency with something successful to brag about. Watching the two whites, Goyathlay began imagining what might happen: The small one probably dying fast, there didn't seem to be anything strong about him, and then the big one taking much longer, the music of his screams. Then a feast of mule meat, a few more days' ride and finally enthralled listeners back at the agency, hearing tales of great things accomplished under Goyathlay's direction. What he'd hoped for might still happen.

He reluctantly stopped imagining these fine things to study the area. The lone high mountain to the left, the rolling land, all shallow dips and low hills. Toward the rising sun, the way the white men were moving, there was the river and then mountains beyond that. And after the mountains? Goyathlay struggled to remember. Surely, in the fine old days before Cochise became a woman and surrendered, there had been raids in that direction. All right, now he recalled a narrow split between lower mountains in the range, and beyond the split a valley opening on to flat land where, yes, there was a town. These white men must be going there. For them at their present pace, it would take two days, possibly three. A quick glance up confirmed the presence of gray, mildly threatening clouds. There had been some rain in past days, not a great deal. It was late in the season for storms, but it seemed there might be more. This could slow the white men. Even if not, there was time to draw this out, build even better stories to be shared back at the agency.

John Tiapah crept up behind Goyathlay and whispered, "Let's take them now."

"Not yet. Let them get ahead a little. Then gather the others here with me."

Goyathlay stayed low behind a swale, resting comfortably until the other four joined with him.

"We can play with these men," he said. "A game, some entertainment. There was bad luck in Mexico, no one's fault. But I promised you a good fight and I never lie. This will be even better. We'll follow the white men across the river and into the mountains. On the way we will do things, soon they'll know we are there but they'll never see us. And finally in the mountains or soon after, just when they think they're going to be safe after all, then we finally take them and play our games. After that we return north, tell what we've done. All the other men will envy you. The women will want to please such great warriors. Everything just as I promised."

"They might get away," Tawhatela argued. "We should kill them while we know we can."

Goyathlay shook his head. "Young men like you are too impatient. It's not only that you kill, but how. If we take them now, surprise them, cut their throats and have them dead at our feet right away, what kind of story is that? Are you so unskilled, Tawhatela, that you can't follow foolish white men a while without them seeing you? What do you say, Datchshaw, Nantee, John Tiapah? Are you children who must have your treat immediately? Or are you men who want to savor this pleasure?"

"We're men," John Tiapah said. Goyathlay was pleased by his firm response. The youngster had an array of brothers and cousins who would make fine followers if this one urged them to align themselves with Goyathlay.

"All right, then," Goyathlay said. "Now we'll go after them, keeping some distance

402

for a while. We'll keep walking our ponies, they're going too slowly for us to ride. Datchshaw, you circle a little, make sure these two whites are the only ones around."

"I will," Datchshaw said. He mounted and rode away from the sun and toward the single mountain. But he didn't ride far. His shoulder hurt. As soon as Goyathlay and the others were safely out of sight, he reined in his pony and rested in the shade of a big rock. Before there was this unexpected opportunity to stalk and kill the two white men, Datchshaw hadn't looked forward to returning to the agency. His mother, a stern woman, had warned him not to go. She said that Goyathlay was a fool, an ambitious schemer disdained by Cochise. Any raid led by Goyathlay would fail, she predicted, and all those who rode with him would be punished by Clum. Truthfully, Datchshaw feared the agent far less than his mother, who, even though he was grown, still beat him occasionally with sticks if he got into trouble, which he often did. It seemed to be in Datchshaw's nature to make mistakes, to do things that seemed smart at the time, but foolish soon after. He thought going on the raid with Goyathlay would be a way to restore his reputation, establish him as a man of some substance. But then in Mexico they won no battles and he was wounded besides. What would his mother say? Worse, what would she do to him, probably in front of everyone else? Killing two white men quickly while they could seemed providential to Datchshaw. He believed that once any venture suffered initial bad luck, things never improved. The white men were probably going to get away, and then the presumptive raiders would have to straggle back to the agency as complete failures. His mother would beat him. Everyone would laugh at him. These gloomy thoughts occupied Datchshaw so much that he stayed slumped in the shade of the rock for some time. He didn't bother looking for other whites. Surely there weren't any, this far from their villages. Datchshaw's shoulder throbbed. He put a pebble in his mouth to stimulate saliva — in spite of the clouds, it was still a hot morning — and rode back to report to Goyathlay that he had looked everywhere and seen no one.

The five Apache kept a half-dozen bowshots behind the two whites. They trailed them while spread out in line, with Goyathlay in the center, Datchshaw and Nantee on either side of him, and John Tiapah and Tawhatela on the ends. This ensured that they would not lose their prey amid the hills and arroyos. Goyathlay periodically moved ahead of the others, closing the distance between himself and the white men until he could see them clearly. The small one got up on his pony for a little while, then jumped down again. He said something to the big one and gestured. It was easy to tell he was suggesting that the other man walk for a while. But the big one refused.

When the sun was about halfway across the sky and the river only a little farther ahead, the white men stopped to drink from canteens and eat from cans. They stopped in a very foolish place, near the edge of a deep wash. They did it, Goyathlay knew, to take cover in shade near the rim, but that spot would have made it easy to attack them — the Chiricahua could simply have dropped down and been on them before they knew what was happening. Tawhatela again wanted to attack. He said it was boring to follow them.

"It's going to rain again soon," Tawhatela said, gesturing up toward clouds gradually growing thicker and darker. "If there's a bad storm, we might lose them in it."

"We won't," Goyathlay promised. "The next time they stop it will probably be for the night, and then we'll play our first trick.

There'll be plenty of mule meat for everyone, and tomorrow we'll take them, probably in those mountains ahead. Be patient a little longer."

When the white men were finished eating they tossed the cans on the ground. Then they relieved themselves and resumed their journey, the big man riding and the small one still leading his horse.

"They ought to go ahead and kill that horse," Nantee said. "Anyone can tell it's getting ready to die. The big one's horse could easily carry two. I guess he wants the small one to walk."

The Apache paused to collect the cans discarded so carelessly by the white men. Back at the agency, away from the sight of Clum and his subagents, the cans would be cut into sharp-edged pieces of metal suitable for arrow points. Whites threw away useful things. It was one of the many reasons the Chiricahua felt superior to them.

The rain began just as the white men reached the river. It wasn't a full-fledged storm, but the downpour was steady. The Apache watched as their quarry stopped at the river's edge. Its channel was wide but not very deep, up perhaps to knee-high in a few places but no more than that, even with extra water from the rain. The big man

406

gestured for the small one to lead his horse into the river. The small one argued — it was the first time the Chiricahua had seen him talk that much. They couldn't hear his words and wouldn't have understood them if they had, but the gist was clear. He didn't think his horse would get across. The big man said something, the small man talked back, and the big man hit him on the side of the head. It was an impressive blow, delivered by bending down while still on horseback. The big man struck with such force and swiftness that Goyathlay whispered, "Be careful when we take him tomorrow." Americans seldom required such caution.

The small man, knocked to his knees, rocked back and forth, attempting to regain his senses before standing. When he did, he tugged at his horse's reins, but the horse refused to move. The small man said something to the big one, making sure to stand well out of reach. The big man answered, then pointed at the river. The small one dropped his horse's reins and left the animal standing there. Then he slowly walked down the short, sloping bank and into the river, with the big man riding just behind him. It took them longer than it should have to cross. The small man kept losing his footing and falling completely in. It was very funny and the Chiricahua were hard-pressed not to laugh. They probably could have without danger of being heard. The rain drummed on the ground and they were still several bowshots away. But Goyathlay insisted on silence. It was good practice for when they stalked more alert foes.

When the whites were finally past the river and walking east toward the mountains, the Apache took their turns. As they passed the horse that had been left to die, Tawhatela fired an arrow into its side, then leaped forward to slit the horse's throat as it fell. Usually they would have cut strips of horse-flesh from the dead animal. That kind of food was handy on long journeys. But they looked forward, very soon, to gorging themselves on mule meat, so they left the dead horse for the buzzards.

"I think the white men will stop soon," Goyathlay predicted. "The small one looks worn out. The big one will think they can easily reach the mountains in the morning, then get through them before night, with the white village not far away after that."

He was right. The rain stopped, leaving the ground mucky and the bottoms of the deepest gullies puddled with standing water. The white men splashed forward for a little

while and then paused at an outcrop of
rocks a few hours' ride from the first foot-
hills of the mountains. The rocks were
positioned so that one provided an overhang
and protection from the rain if it started
again. Even before it was fully dark the
white men ground-hitched the mule and
their remaining horse. They gave the animals
grain from a pack while the Apache watched
from a low gully not far away. There were
other gullies and crevices of various depths
nearby; here and on the east side of the
mountains, the ground was abruptly broken
in places, in contrast to the gentle undula-
tions farther west.

After the animals were fed, the white men
had canteen water and food from more cans.

"No fire," Nantee observed. "Maybe they
don't know how to make one."

The whites sheltered under the rock
overhang. The big man appeared to tie up
the small one. The Chiricahua couldn't tell
because it was too dark. Whether or not one
of the men was tied up didn't matter to the
Apache. All they cared about for the moment was the mule. There was really no
sport to stealing it. The animal was tethered
so far from where the big man rested under
the rock that even if he'd heard or seen
them, he could never reach them before

they got away with their prize. Goyathlay gave John Tiapah, as the youngest and also the one related to the most other possible followers, the honor of crawling up, cutting the mule loose, and bringing it back to the waiting Chiricahua. Then they led the mule back toward the river. It was very cooperative and did not bray even once. When they were far enough away from the where the whites were camped, they cut the mule's throat and butchered it. This was done more by touch than sight because it was so dark. They only lit a fire when they were ready to cook. The available sticks and brush were damp from the rain but they patiently struck their flints until finally a spark caught. They soon had a bright blaze. John Tiapah asked if the white men might not see it and the others laughed.

"They're sound asleep," Goyathlay assured him. "They're too lazy to light their own fire and too stupid to look for ours."

The Apache sharpened long sticks, stuck hunks of mule on the ends, and toasted the meat over the fire. They ate ravenously, wiping greasy hands on their deerskin leggings. The resulting grease stains would serve as waterproofing, should there be more rain. When they were done with the meal, they tossed sand on the campfire to extinguish it. Goyathlay told Datchshaw to keep watch while the rest slept.

"I'm tired too," Datchshaw whined. This was such a breach of warrior etiquette — on raids, Apache braves never protested their leader's instructions — that Goyathlay would have been within his rights to order the wounded man to leave them at once. He was tempted, but didn't. A good leader brought everyone home together.

"Do what I tell you," Goyathlay said. "If there's a fight tomorrow, your shoulder is too badly hurt for you to be in it. The rest of us need sleep to be strong. Next time we go out from the agency to fight, you'll be well again and somebody else can stand watch at night."

"But I want to help kill these white men," Datchshaw said.

"And you will. We'll take our time with them tomorrow. Don't let them run away while we sleep."

Excited by what would happen the next day, Datchshaw remained awake the entire night. He took up a position not far from the rock outcrop and watched intently for even the slightest sign that the white men might be on the move. Datchshaw's concentration was such that he was unaware of anything else around him. Only these two

411

doomed white men mattered. After tomorrow, he would have so much to brag about back at the agency that even his mother would be proud.

26

McLendon wasn't surprised when his horse balked at the riverbank. Even when he'd untethered the animal that morning, it showed no interest in moving. Its head drooped and it made wheezing noises. He told Brautigan he thought the animal was finished, but the big man ordered him to mount up anyway. When McLendon did, the horse's legs buckled and he had to get off.

"It can't go farther," he told Brautigan.

"Yes, it can. It's probably stiff from staying still overnight. You can lead it for a while."

McLendon looked ahead of them, at the dark line of the river and the mountain range past it. "Your horse is fine," he said. "Couldn't we ride double?"

"You walk, and lead your horse," Brautigan said. "Get moving."

McLendon made a show of trying to tug

on the horse's reins with his injured right arm, then transferring the reins to his left hand. He detected better flexibility in the elbow bruised by Brautigan's boot but didn't want the giant to know.

Even though their pace was slow, McLendon quickly became winded. The hills and dips weren't steep, but they were constant. He had to keep a constant pull on the reins. Clouds mostly blocked the sun but it remained brutally hot.

"I need to rest awhile," he told Brautigan.

"We've hardly been going an hour. Keep walking."

"I'm not certain I can."

"I could kill you right here," Brautigan said. "You need to remember that. And maybe that horse is better. Get up on it again."

McLendon did. The horse heaved a near-human sigh and stumbled forward. After a few hundred yards, McLendon dismounted and told Brautigan, "It's done for. You might as well shoot it."

"No, it might yet recover. If you can ride it tomorrow, we might make Silver City by sundown."

"You won't let me ride double with you?"

"No."

"Then let me ride a little while you walk,

get my legs rested some."

"No. Walk, McLendon, or face a beating."

The heat intensified, and a new mugginess tainted the wind. McLendon walked east toward the mountains, knowing each step brought him closer to death. Only the place and manner had yet to be determined. Would it be better to stop where he was and goad Brautigan into killing him now, or put the moment off as long as possible, believing every possible moment of life was worth preserving? As long as he still was alive, there was always a chance he might get away from Brautigan. But not much of one. For now, there was nothing to do but walk.

About noon, Brautigan called a halt. He picked a good spot at the edge of a particularly deep wash. There was some additional shade. Brautigan passed McLendon a canteen and said, "I think it will rain soon. Don't think about trying to get away in the storm."

McLendon gulped warm water. "Because then you'd kill me here instead of St. Louis."

"And I'd go back for the girl as well. Don't be forgetting that."

They ate canned peaches. Brautigan gave his horse and the mule water from the cask. Then he looked at McLendon's horse. It stood with its head hanging so low that its nostrils nearly rested in the dirt.

"Show the beast some mercy and shoot it," McLendon said.

"It may be stronger tomorrow," Brautigan said. "If you ride then instead of walk, we'll move faster." He poured more water into his hat and offered it to the suffering animal. The horse snuffled at the water but didn't drink. Brautigan shared the water between his horse and the mule instead.

As they started again the clouds thickened and grew much darker.

"The low areas flood during storms, you know," McLendon called back over his shoulder to Brautigan.

The big man briefly glanced up. "Too much talking. Walk. The river's just ahead."

The first few raindrops splattered on the ground. The temperature dropped remarkably. Even the wind felt cool. But that relief was short-lived as the force of the rain increased. Now the drops pounded with enough force to kick up puffs of dust. Then, as the ground dampened, loose dirt turned to mud. There was hard crust underneath the dirt, so for McLendon the effect was much the same as slogging through thick gravy spilled on a tile floor. Every slippery step threatened his balance.

"Can we stop?" he asked Brautigan.

The giant wiped rainwater from his face. "We're nearly at the river. Keep walking."

The river seemed to be some twenty yards wide. McLendon couldn't gauge its depth. "What now?" he asked.

"Wade across with your horse. Don't try sneaking away. I'll be right behind you."

"It may be too deep to wade."

"Then swim."

McLendon felt overwhelming weariness and despair.

"I can't swim. I've never tried. We need to at least wait until this rain stops, see what the river looks like then. What's your damned hurry? You worried your boss is going to be displeased with you if he has to wait an extra few days to watch me die? What do days matter? Hell, he's already had to wait two more years because you lost me back in Glorious."

Brautigan swung so quickly that McLendon's head seemed to instantly explode. It was a prodigious blow, struck without Brautigan's usual control. McLendon, moaning in pain, dropped to his hands and knees in the mud.

"Up," Brautigan hissed. "Up, you sorry bastard."

McLendon heard the words and tried to

obey, anything to avoid being struck again. But he couldn't stand. His body wouldn't cooperate. Maybe if his mind wasn't spinning so. Still on his hands and knees, he shook his head violently, trying to regain scattered senses. That only worsened the pounding in his skull.

"Up, or I'm killing you here," Brautigan said. "I'll take my time doing it, then find the girl for more of the same."

Not Gabrielle. Slowly, McLendon willed himself to his feet. He swayed as he stood. Something was wrong with his sense of balance.

"The horse," Brautigan said. "Take the horse, lead it across the river."

McLendon swayed unsteadily as he stepped toward the animal. He took its reins in his left hand and tugged. The horse didn't move. He pulled harder; still nothing.

"This horse is done for," he told Brautigan. "You can hit me all you want or kill me, it won't change that."

Brautigan studied the horse and looked at the river. Its surface was pebbled by rain.

"All right. Leave it. Now into the water with you."

"Aren't you going to shoot it, put it out of its misery?"

"I won't waste the bullet. Into the water."

"I'm dizzy."

Brautigan raised his hand. McLendon flinched. "Now," the giant said.

McLendon gingerly eased down the short bank and into the river. Brautigan, mounted and leading the mule, came directly behind him. To McLendon's surprise, the water wasn't deep. It came just over his knees. There was no current either. The problem was the slimy river bottom. Even if his balance hadn't been affected by Brautigan's punch, McLendon would have been hard-pressed to avoid slipping. In his present condition it was inevitable. His left boot skidded and he fell. The water closed briefly over his head. He struggled to stand, slipped, went under a second time. His ass hit bottom and when he sat up his upper body was above the surface up to his shoulders. It was really too shallow to drown in.

"Keep going," Brautigan said.

McLendon did. He fell and went under several times more. When he finally was across, he crawled up the bank and collapsed on the other side, panting like an exhausted animal. Brautigan, holding the mule's reins, sat astride his horse and watched McLendon for a few moments. Then he said, "The mountains aren't far. We'll stop when we reach them. Stand up and walk."

McLendon did his best, slipping frequently, trying to remember to break his falls with his left arm rather than his right. His head hurt terribly, and he lost all sense of time. When the rain abruptly stopped, like someone shut off a pump in the sky, McLendon hardly noticed. He simply plodded forward until Brautigan finally said, "There's a good place up ahead," and pointed at a rock outcrop.

When McLendon reached the rocks, he dropped in his tracks. He didn't think he could move. But Brautigan dismounted and nudged him in the ribs with the steel-toed tip of his boot. "Get the packs and cask off the mule." When McLendon didn't budge, he nudged harder. McLendon grunted and heaved himself up. His legs were rubbery and his ears still rang from the force of Brautigan's earlier blow. He fumbled with the straps holding the packs on the mule's back, then lugged the wooden water cask under the rock overhang.

Brautigan unsaddled his horse and ground-tethered it alongside the mule perhaps twenty yards away from the rocks. "Hand me the pack with the feed in it," he ordered McLendon. After they were fed, the two remaining animals cropped at dripping vegetation. Everything was very wet from the rain.

"Back under the rock now," Brautigan said, and McLendon obeyed. His movements were mechanical; it seemed impossible to concentrate. He'd heard somewhere about concussions. Perhaps he had one. Best, for now, to do as he was told and avoid additional beatings, at least until he regained more of his senses.

Brautigan let his prisoner drink as much as he liked from their last full canteen. "There's enough in the cask to get us and the animals through tomorrow." They ate canned peas. McLendon gagged on some of his. Even swallowing seemed complicated. When he finished eating, Brautigan pointed to a spot under the rock outcrop where the giant had spread blankets.

"Lie down and I'll tie you."

"I won't run," McLendon said. "I'm in no condition."

"I'm tying you anyhow." When McLendon was safely trussed, Brautigan went out to check that the animals were secure. He came back under the rock, rearranged packs and the water cask, and lay down, positioning himself between McLendon and the Winchester. It was rapidly growing dark. The clouds filling the night sky overhead occasionally flashed pink with lightning; thunder rumbled, but there was no more rain.

"We'll be going at first light," Brautigan told McLendon. "No talk until then."

McLendon instantly fell into deep, exhausted sleep. Brautigan meant to stay awake all night, to guard against any last tricks McLendon might try before they reached Silver City. The giant thought about St. Louis, how pleased the boss would be when he arrived there with McLendon. Maybe in Wichita he'd send a telegram ahead, announcing imminent arrival. No, the train to St. Louis might then be delayed, and Mr. Douglass would wonder if Brautigan had failed him again. Better simply to show up with McLendon, provide the boss with the most pleasant of surprises. Brautigan imagined the relief he'd feel himself, finally fulfilling his responsibility to Mr. Douglass, making up for the bungle in Glorious. And with that happy thought, he fell asleep himself.

Brautigan and McLendon woke almost simultaneously just after dawn. McLendon lay where he was, still bound and thinking that his head hurt less; maybe he wasn't concussed after all. Brautigan stood up and walked away from the rock, presumably to piss. He moved out of McLendon's limited sight line. Moments later, he bellowed, "What?" McLendon, curious, tried to sit up but couldn't. All he could do was lie there and wonder. Brautigan seemed to be walking fast in one direction after another. McLendon could hear his heavy boots thudding on the rocks and ground.

"Brautigan," he called. "What is it?"

The giant stalked underneath the rock overhang and hauled McLendon to his feet. "Is this your doing?"

"What's the matter?"

"The goddamned mule is gone."

"I didn't take it. You had me tied up all night so I couldn't move. Maybe it pulled the reins free from where you tied them."

Brautigan shook his head. "I tied them tight. Someone cut them. Part is still tied to the bush."

"But who?"

"Damned if I know. I've looked hard and don't see signs of anyone." He untied McLendon. "Fill the canteen from the cask. We'll take the canteen and one pack with feed and a few cans, leave the rest. We're one day out if we move fast enough."

"My legs are stiff from being tied so long. I need to bend, stretch them a little."

Brautigan began saddling his horse. He told McLendon, "Your legs will get stretched as you walk."

"Can I at least have something to eat?"

"Maybe when we've reached the mountains."

McLendon asked, "Who do you think's out there?"

Brautigan mounted. "I don't know. Probably some miserable drifter saw the animals and a chance to take one."

"Why the mule and not the horse? The horse is more valuable."

"Shut up and walk, McLendon. That way, toward the mountains."

As McLendon started walking, he remembered someone back in Glorious telling him, *Apache are powerfully fond of mule meat.* That was it. It had to be. And if Apache were lurking, they weren't likely to settle for just a mule.

27

During his service as a Union officer in the Civil War, Major Mulkins always endeavored, before battle, to learn how many enemies faced his troops. Now, nearly a decade later and halfway up a mountain in southeast Arizona Territory, the habit reasserted itself and he tried counting Apache. It was difficult. They darted into dips and behind hills, seeming to blend into the land at will. *Three for sure,* Mulkins thought. *No, two more there. Is that another one?*

Behind him, he heard Joe Saint say, "Gabrielle, we have to go back now."

Gabrielle started to reply, but Mulkins said, "Hush, both of you. I need to concentrate." There was more scattered movement down below, Apache or jackrabbits, who knew what. It occurred to Mulkins that it would be easier to count horses. Four, five. All right.

"I think there are five Apache," he said.

"Are they attacking Cash and Brautigan?" Gabrielle asked.

"Preparing to, it seems," Mulkins said. "Five's enough to overcome even Brautigan."

"Then we have to warn them, help them get away," Gabrielle said. "We have a Winchester, Major. Could you shoot some of them from here?"

"The range is too great and my marksmanship too minimal," Mulkins said.

"At least the gunfire would startle the Indians," Gabrielle said. "Perhaps it would frighten them away."

"Apache don't get frightened, and what good would shooting do anyway?" Saint said. "Even if they ran, Brautigan would know someone was up here. Then he might kill your precious McLendon on the spot. We tried. We probably couldn't have saved McLendon anyway, and now with Apache it's impossible."

"We can't give up," Gabrielle said. "There has to be something."

"There isn't," Saint said. "Look down there. The Apache are closing in."

"I don't think so," Mulkins said. "They could have come right up on them if that was their immediate intention. Look at Brautigan and C.M. — they're still going

426

east, same pace, no glances around. They've no idea the Apache are there. They'd be taken easily. I think maybe the Indians want sport. They're going to stalk them a little."

"Which is of no consequence to us," Saint said. "If we intercede, we die, too, and that serves nothing."

"I'm not giving up," Gabrielle said stubbornly.

"We need to do one or the other," Mulkins said. "While we talk, they're moving below."

"A while longer, Joe," Gabrielle pleaded. "We've come so far."

"And what will we do?" Saint demanded. "Tell me something that makes sense."

"I've a thought," Mulkins said. "We do as we initially intended, ride south ourselves using this mountain to screen us for a while. Brautigan's not keeping a sharp eye out, and the Apache are aware of him and C.M., but not us. The river's ahead, then another set of mountains. Maybe somewhere in there we can separate C.M. from Brautigan, get our friend away, and leave Brautigan to the Apache."

"Not much chance," Saint said, sounding scornful.

"Joe, I'll overlook your tone. I know there's not much chance. So does Gabrielle. But we're trying anyway. Like you've been told before — ride back home if you want. Come on, Gabrielle."

Mulkins and Gabrielle got on their horses and began picking their way along the mountainside. Halfway down, displaced pebbles rolled down around the hooves of their mounts. Joe Saint was just behind them.

They rode parallel to Brautigan and McLendon and the pursuing Apache, keeping the mountain in between. Once they passed its eastern base, they had to keep a considerable distance away.

"It probably wouldn't be impossible for the Apache to spot us, so we have to hope they've got their eyes locked on Brautigan and C.M.," Mulkins said. "We'll use these little hills as long as they last. It looks to me like the ground flattens right around the river. Say, Joe, you better take your spectacles off."

"I can't see without them," Saint said.

"But we're riding east and the sun's in our faces," Mulkins said. "A ray reflects off those lenses, the Apache might see the flash. So take them off, put them in your pocket. Long as you can see Gabrielle and me in front of you, you'll be all right."

After a while Gabrielle said, "Major, if we

can't see them right now, how do we know they haven't turned in a different direction?"

"It's a matter of chance, guessing what's most likely. Silver City's almost directly to the east on the other side of the mountains. Brautigan's got to be in a hurry to get C.M. there, then on to St. Louis. I figure he's aiming this way."

"But what if the Apache attack them? Perhaps they already have."

Mulkins wiped sweat from his eyes. "If that happened, we'd hear shots, or whoops, or something. Sound carries out here. Whatever their purpose might be, the Apache are taking their time."

"But they'll . . . do something, certainly."

"They'll know where Silver City is, too, and won't want to get too close. I figure they'll try their luck either at the river or in the mountains. Probably the mountains. Though who really knows how savages think?"

Breakfast had only been canteen water. So when they came upon some scrubby patches of grass shortly before noon, Mulkins insisted that they stop to let the horses rest and graze.

"We'll have a small bite too," he said.

"Animals and humans alike need replenishment."

Mulkins took three strips of jerky out of his saddlebag and handed one each to Gabrielle and Saint. "Tough as they might be, they'll still fill our stomachs some," he said. Saint tried to give his jerky to Gabrielle, who refused.

"You need food as much as I do," she said. "Don't be a fool."

"I can't stand you being hungry."

"I know, Joe," Gabrielle said, her voice softening. "I do know."

They drank some water but didn't give any to the horses.

"They can drink when we reach the river," Mulkins said. "Won't be long now."

Clouds began piling overhead. They were darker than any on previous days.

"Rain again, more of it this time and harder," Mulkins said. "Never saw so much this late in the season. At least you can put your specs back on, Joe."

"Already did," Saint said. "You know, if it rains really hard and long, we'll have to worry about floods."

"I'll confine my concerns to Brautigan and Apache," Mulkins said. "I know this isn't easy for you, Joe. But one way or the other, it'll soon be over."

430

■ ■ ■ ■

Just before they reached the river, the land completely flattened out. Very faintly, more than a mile to their right, moving dots approached the bank.

"We can see them, they can see us," Mulkins said. "Down off the horses, stay still as you can." As they crouched — there were some cacti to duck behind, though avoiding the spines was a challenge — the rain began, hard-pounding drops. They peered through the watery curtain. The ones on the bank were clearly McLendon and Brautigan. They were too far away to be certain what they were doing, beyond that they weren't crossing the river yet.

"Horse problem," Mulkins guessed. "The mount C.M.'s been leading may have folded up altogether."

Then they saw McLendon fall. Gabrielle gasped and put her hand on the butt of Ike Clanton's pistol, which she still had tucked in her waistband.

"Be still, Gabrielle," Mulkins said. "The range is far beyond that gun's capacity." Finally, McLendon stumbled into the river, Brautigan riding behind him, leading the mule.

"Now we should cross, too," Gabrielle said.

"Wait," Mulkins said. "Don't be forgetting the Apache. They're likely right on C.M.'s and Brautigan's tail."

"But Cash and Brautigan are going to get too much ahead of us," Gabrielle protested. "Silver City's not that far beyond the mountains. You said so yourself."

"I know they're going to get up a lead, but I might have an idea about that," Mulkins said. "Tell you in a bit. It all depends on what the Indians do next. We need to sit tight."

They watched McLendon and Brautigan cross the river. Gabrielle moaned as McLendon kept falling in the water. Once as he did, Mulkins happened to glance at Saint. Saint was watching intently, too, and it seemed to Mulkins that every time McLendon briefly disappeared under the water, Saint looked hopeful, then disappointed when his rival reemerged.

The rain stopped abruptly about the same time that McLendon and Brautigan reached the far bank. They kept going east, toward the base of the mountain range. Just after they disappeared over a low hill, the Apache appeared at the river. This was the first time Mulkins had a clean look at them. Five, as he'd suspected. One turned to the horse left behind by the white men and shot it with an arrow, then cut its throat.

"They may stop to dine on horseflesh," Mulkins predicted, but the Apache left the dead horse where it lay and crossed the river themselves, leading their mounts behind them. They reached the opposite bank and continued east in the same direction taken by Brautigan and McLendon.

"All right," Mulkins said. "Let's ease our way over to where they went across."

"Why not go into the river here?" Gabrielle said. "If the Indians attack them now and we're on this side, we'll never get there in time."

"I'm thinking the Apache will still wait awhile," Mulkins said. "If they wanted to kill them now, right there on the riverbank would have been the place. So where they'll do it is in the mountains tomorrow, with plenty of cover. After the mountains, it'd be too close to Silver City, too much risk of being caught in the act."

"You don't know what the Apache are thinking," Saint said crossly.

"No, Joe, I don't. You're the smart man, not me. But I'm guessing as best I can so maybe we can yet save our friend's life. If you have some better way, other than quitting and going home, tell us."

Saint didn't reply. He took off his rain-spattered glasses and tried to dry them on his shirt.

"All right, then," Mulkins said. "Let's move down there along the bank."

They reached the spot where the dead horse lay. Overhead, buzzards swooped.

"The rain kept them off until now," Mulkins said. "Lucky for us."

"Why for us?" Gabrielle asked.

"Because this horse is going to provide our dinner, and they'll have to settle for leftovers," Mulkins said. "Horse meat's not a delicacy, I'm sure, but it's food and we need some."

"Gabrielle can't eat horse," Saint protested.

"No, the Major is right," Gabrielle said. "I suppose we'll eat it raw?"

"The Apache will be keeping all their attention on C.M. and Brautigan, and they're also some distance away now. We can risk a small cooking fire — that is, if we can get one lit. I've got matches, if we can collect any dry kindling after that rain."

"Building a fire will take time," Gabrielle said. "Have we any to spare?"

"We'll eat first, then I'll tell you the rest of what I'm thinking," Mulkins said. "Gabrielle, you find some small sticks, the driest you can. Joe and I will try to get some burnable brush gathered."

Their fire was a poor one, small and sputtering. Mulkins had occasionally butchered deer shot on hunts, but never a horse. He cut through the hide on one hindquarter and hacked out hunks of bloody meat.

"Not pretty, but still edible," he said. They cut and sharpened sticks, then skewered the meat on the sticks and held them over the fire. The meat cooked unevenly. The meager flames were just high and hot enough to sear the outside, but the inside remained raw.

"I want to build a better fire but fear I can't," Mulkins said. "There's just not enough dry wood. We need to eat this meat as it is, and then there's much more to do." He, Gabrielle, and Saint gnawed at the chunks of meat, tearing off the better-cooked bits as best they could. Then they bit tiny pieces of nearly raw flesh, swallowing these without chewing, trying not to think of what was sliding down their throats.

"Now a hearty drink of river water," Mulkins said. "Our bellies won't grumble for a while, and we've still got some somewhat-cooked meat for a future meal. Let's bring up the horses and get them well watered. I know it's full dark, but now comes something difficult."

As the horses drank, Mulkins explained.

"C.M. and Brautigan are no doubt camped somewhere up ahead. Brautigan will figure on getting through the mountains in daylight, and then on to Silver City. He doesn't know the Apache are behind him, or that we are, for that matter. The Indians will wait through the night and pounce sometime in the morning. I've been thinking they'll do so in the mountains and I still believe that's their plan. So I'm figuring this — we'll move straight through the night, try to circle around Indians and C.M. and Brautigan and get to the mountains ahead of them all. Then in the morning we find the best place in there to set up. Maybe we try to take C.M. from Brautigan ourselves, maybe we sneak up if the Indians finally get Brautigan's attention, I don't know. We've got the Winchester and the shotgun and two handguns. None of us are crack shots, but we're well enough armed to put up some sort of scrap. We ought to have the advantage of surprise. That's all I have to offer. I'd welcome your thoughts."

Gabrielle said, "Thank you. That sounds like the best option."

"What if the Apache kill them tonight?"

Saint asked.

"I pray they don't. If they do, if I've guessed wrong, I suppose we'll go on to Silver City ourselves, wire friends in Mountain View to send us money for supplies, and make the long trip home."

"That's reasonable," Saint said. "Now, this keeping on in the night. Isn't that going to be hard?"

"Terribly hard. We'll need to be as quiet as we can. We don't know where the Apache are exactly, or C.M. and Brautigan either. We can't be stumbling right onto them. The night sky's all clouded up, so we can't determine direction by the stars. All right, first thing to do is cross the river. Ready?"

"In a moment," Gabrielle said. She turned away and vomited up undigested shreds of horse.

Crossing the river at night would have been tricky enough, but Gabrielle's injured shin proved an additional complication. Saint and Mulkins put her up on one horse and tried leading all three animals at once, but reins immediately became tangled. The horses themselves were uncooperative. They shied away from getting in the water.

"They might have picked up some scent of the Apache," Mulkins said. "We need to put this river behind us. Gabrielle, you stay mounted and I'll lead your horse across. Then I'll come back and Joe and I will bring the other two."

"I can lead my own horse," Gabrielle said.

"And hurt your leg even more? This is a moment for sense, not foolish courage."

When they were finally across, Mulkins said that they'd move up the bank just a little before striking out for the mountains. It was easy to follow the river. The water gurgled pleasantly. But when they struck out east again in the inky darkness, they instantly lost all sense of time and direction. Saint soon complained that they must be all turned around.

"We're going to end up back at the river," he said.

"If we do, we'll just reverse course and try again," Mulkins said. "But maybe we're all right. Look ahead to the right. Something's flickering. A fire?"

"Cash and Brautigan, or the Apache?" Gabrielle asked.

"Can't tell. You and Joe stay put. I'll try moving a little closer, get a better look."

Mulkins was a middle-aged man accustomed much more to towns than the wild. He did his best to creep softly toward the fire, but kept stumbling over clumps of brush. The dirt was still wet from the rain and when he stepped in especially wet spots that he couldn't see in the dark, his boots made sucking noises. Sighing, he lowered his body to the ground and began crawling. Progress was slow. Finally, perhaps two hundred yards away, he saw four Apache lying by the fire. He'd surely counted five earlier — where was the other one? Hair rose on the back of Mulkins's neck. The Indian might be behind him, ready to strike. Mulkins turned on his belly as best he could and looked around. Nothing but darkness. Well, he'd seen what he could. Now he had to get back to Gabrielle and Joe. Which direction was that? Then lightning flashed above the clouds, momentarily bathing the land in soft pink light. Mulkins couldn't see his friends, of course, but he did briefly glimpse the mountains off to his right. He pivoted left and began crawling again. After what seemed to be hours, he felt far enough away from the Apache campfire to get to his feet. The front of his shirt and trousers were caked with damp dirt.

In the softest voice he could manage, Mulkins hissed, "Where are you?"

"Here," came the reply from somewhere ahead. It was Gabrielle.

Mulkins told them that the Apache had

made camp. "That means Brautigan and C.M. must have stopped short of the mountains too."

"How do you know the Indians haven't already killed them?" Saint asked.

"The Apache seemed to be sleeping," Mulkins said. "Had they taken prisoners, they'd still be wide awake doing bad things to them. No, they're resting up to commit devilry tomorrow. Let's be going, and more careful than ever. I counted four at the fire. There's a fifth someplace. I suspect he's keeping watch on C.M. and Brautigan."

They went on. Once Saint's horse whickered loudly, and they froze in place for long minutes, afraid the Apache had heard and were on the way to investigate. Finally Mulkins said he thought they could go on.

Shortly before dawn they felt rather than saw the mountains rising up in front of them. They swung wide left as they felt the level ground become upslope. "Brautigan and C.M. might be stopped nearby," Mulkins warned. "Soon as it's even somewhat light, we've got to pick our spot to get in here, set up for those we hope will follow."

"How will we decide?" Saint asked, and Mulkins was pleased he'd said *we* instead of *you*. Reluctant as he might be, it seemed Joe still considered himself part of the team.

"Gabrielle, you might be able to tell us," Mulkins said. "When you were with Brautigan, did he show much outdoor sense? Did he act like someone who knew his way around rugged surroundings?"

"Not really," she said. "He was hard and definite with people. But I think he's only really comfortable in the city. He's maybe less certain, in hard country like this, than even we are."

"Then he's going to look for the obvious route, the one that seems shortest between and through these mountains," Mulkins said. "We'll look around and think like him."

Dawn began lightly coloring the sky. When they could see a little, Brautigan's probable route became obvious. The mountain range was wide in length but not depth. Just to the right of Mulkins, Gabrielle, and Saint, a narrow cut bisected two mountains. The one on the right had a sprawling base that extended fully a mile, perhaps two. The mountain on the left had a relatively abbreviated, rolling slope to the north. Going east to Silver City by rounding the slope would be an option, but the cut seemed more convenient.

"We'll ride through it and see what's

441

beyond," Mulkins said, and they did. High rock walls arched on both sides and passage space narrowed in the middle, but after fifty yards the cut opened up into a rocky canyon and then a wide valley. And, though there were more mountains on both sides, the valley itself emptied into flat land to the east. "Silver City straight ahead," Mulkins said. "Brautigan will bring C.M. through the cut and see the rest of his way clear. We can work our way behind some of those rocks ahead, take up position. Brautigan and C.M. come out into the valley, we've got them covered and can see what happens from there."

"I have a thought," Saint said. "We can't fight Brautigan and the Apache too. Let's ride hard for Silver City, tell the sheriff there that Indians are about to fall on white men back here. He could form a posse, maybe arrive before the Apache kill Brautigan and McLendon."

"You know that's foolish, Joe," Gabrielle said. "We heard it from Ike Clanton — Brautigan's already bribed the sheriff."

"True," Mulkins said. "That crooked Silver City lawman and his people get here, they're likely to fight off the Apache and then pitch into us, all to Brautigan's benefit. We can't look for assistance there."

They rode a little farther into the valley and discovered it was crisscrossed with gullies and sudden drop-offs, some shallow, a few precipitous and as much as ten or twenty feet deep.

"Now, this could be treacherous," Mulkins said. "If things get this far and we're among the crevices, watch every step you take. Some of these places offer bad falls."

"We need to pick a spot and get ready," Gabrielle said. "Cash and Brautigan might come through the cut anytime."

"What if Brautigan chooses to go around the mountain on the left?" Saint said. "We'll be here watching the cut, and next thing we know, we'll look around and he's got McLendon through the valley and approaching Silver City."

"If that happens, Joe, I'm going to take my rifle, ride after them, and try my damnedest to save C.M. before they reach town," Mulkins said. "Odds and Brautigan be damned. I've come this far, I'm going to try."

"I'll be with you," Gabrielle said. "And you, Joe?"

Saint shrugged.

"Well, we'll hope it won't come to that," Mulkins said. "Right now I see a promising ridge just ahead. Let's tether the horses, climb up, and prepare."

28

In the morning when he had the horse saddled, Brautigan turned back to McLendon. "Over here. Hands behind you."

"You're going to have me bound as I walk?"

"You don't fool me. This close to the town, you'll have fresh ideas about running."

"Listen, Brautigan. I know this country better than you. No white man stole that mule. It had to be Apache. They're still around and likely to come back at us some more. On horseback, you might get away, but me, on foot and tied up, I'll have no chance. At least let me have my hands free."

For the first time since he'd taken McLendon, Brautigan briefly flashed his shark-toothed smile. "You're a clever one. But it won't work. I don't see any Indians."

"That's because they don't want to be seen. I'm not trying any trick."

"Turn around to be tied."

"My right arm's still hurt from what you did. I don't know if I can bend it that way."

"Hands behind you, or suffer the consequences."

McLendon's head still throbbed from the blow delivered by Brautigan on the previous day. He put his arms behind his back — the movement hurt his right elbow a little; he winced to make it seem more painful than it was — and crossed his wrists. Brautigan secured them with a short length of rope, tying the knot tight.

McLendon said, "At least, promise me this. If there are Apache and they do come for us, kill me before they get me. Anything you might do to me is nothing compared to what they would."

Brautigan took another, longer length of rope from his saddlebag and said, "Stand still." He made a loop on one end of the rope and dropped the loop around McLendon's neck. "For the rest of the way, you're a dog on a leash. Try to run and you'll choke yourself."

"You need to worry about Apache, not me."

"There are no Apache. Shut up about them." Brautigan's inner thighs, already rubbed raw, stung badly as he swung up in the saddle. It felt as though there was gravel under his eyelids. For days he'd been riding through blowing dust. Maybe there were Apache around. Brautigan felt confident he could physically destroy any man or any reasonable number of men. Unless there were a dozen Indians, he'd handle them. This close to Silver City, all he cared about was getting McLendon into town. After that, it should be relatively easy to bring him back to St. Louis and the boss. Best of all, no more riding goddamned horses over mountains and desert.

"Get moving, McLendon," he said. "Straight toward the mountains." His prisoner lurched forward. Brautigan rode a few feet behind him, keeping the rope taut around McLendon's neck. They went directly east for about an hour. Then Brautigan told McLendon to halt.

"This rope's chafing my neck," McLendon complained.

Brautigan didn't respond. He looked ahead at the mountains, which were perhaps two miles away.

"Can I at least have some water?" McLendon asked. "You'll have to hold the canteen to my mouth, unless you want to untie me."

"In a minute." Brautigan studied the mountains intently. Of the two directly ahead, the one on the right was sprawling, the one on the left more conical — it reminded Brautigan of a woman's tit. The left mountain didn't really amount to much. Going around it wouldn't take all that long. But it also seemed to Brautigan that there was what appeared to be a split between the two mountains, something like a narrow passage. Did it go completely through? Because if it did, that would save considerable time. If they got to Silver City early enough, maybe Sheriff Wolfe would lock McLendon in a cell and post a guard. He'd want extra money for doing it. That was all right. Then Brautigan could find a bathhouse where he could soak in a hot tub, get the dirt off himself, and after that buy some liniment to ease the raw flesh of his inner thighs. After that, he would avail himself of a beer or two, and also a hot meal. Personal comfort seldom mattered to Brautigan, but now he found himself craving it. Once he was back in St. Louis, he hoped never to visit the blasted frontier again.

"Some water?" McLendon asked again, interrupting Brautigan's brief reverie.

"Not now. Look in front of us — see that sort of divide between the two mountains?"

McLendon wearily peered ahead. "It's what they call a cut."

"Whatever it's called, you make for it."

"It may not go all the way through."

"Shut up and walk."

"At least keep looking out for Apache. They could be on us anytime."

Brautigan gave the rope leash a savage tug. McLendon emitted a strangled grunt and fell on his back, struggling for air. Brautigan let him writhe in the dirt for a few moments. Then he dismounted and hauled McLendon to his feet. He saw with some satisfaction that the yanked noose had left a raw rope burn around McLendon's neck.

"Not one more word about Indians. I hear such, I'll do things to you beyond any savage's imagination."

McLendon, still gasping air, doubted this was possible but didn't dare say so. "Water," he croaked.

"All right, a quick sip." Brautigan held the canteen to McLendon's lips. "That's enough. Now walk on toward that split, or whatever it's termed."

McLendon was of two minds about how fast to walk. He didn't want to get to Silver City. But he also didn't want to be taken by Apache, and he was certain they were near. The only question left in his life was what horrible form his death would take. All because he'd foolishly thrown Gabrielle over

449

for a crazy rich girl. Now McLendon had trouble remembering what Ellen Douglass looked like.

So he walked at a medium pace. His bound hands tingled, then hurt, then went numb. For a while the sun was a problem. Its heat was blistering, and as the morning progressed it rose above the mountains ahead, its glare directly in his eyes. But when they were about a mile from the mountains, clouds began gathering, threatening and accumulating so rapidly it was as though the sky was clear one minute and dark the next.

"Walk faster," Brautigan growled. "That passage will provide cover."

"We might not make it before the storm starts," McLendon said. His voice was raspy from the rope burn across his throat. "It could flood here fast. We need the closest high ground."

"We're not stopping," Brautigan said.

Suddenly there was wind, strong and from the north. McLendon twisted his head in that direction and saw, to his horror, two Apache on horseback riding hard toward the east.

"Look there!" he shouted to Brautigan, and the giant's head swiveled. "Do you see them?"

"They're not coming in our direction," Brautigan said. "They're aimed for the mountains some distance above us, a half mile away or more. They're just a couple savages seeking shelter. No danger at present. If they come too near, I'll kill them. Keep moving."

"Two Apache could kill us both a dozen times over," McLendon said. "I've fought Indians and I know."

Brautigan's thighs sizzled with pain. If there was a bad storm, it might prevent them reaching Silver City that day, requiring yet another miserable night in the open and then more time on horseback. Brautigan had no patience for McLendon's whining about Apache. When an assignment from the boss was this close to completion, when civilization, even of the roughest sort, was finally at hand, Patrick Brautigan would let nothing delay him further. The savages hadn't even glanced at them as they raced on their ponies. In one swift motion Brautigan jumped down from his horse and clamped McLendon's shoulder in a meaty hand. He shook the smaller man until McLendon's head flopped back and forth.

"Forget the goddamned Apache. Concern yourself with me. Anything else from you, the smallest aggravation, and I will stop

451

wherever we are and I will kill you slowly. I'll start with the small bones and progress to the big ones. You'll hear them breaking. You'll beg me to finish you and I'll make it last even longer. I don't care if the boss is disappointed not to witness it."

McLendon began wheezing some response. Brautigan said, "Shut up," and let go of his shoulder. McLendon dropped to his knees. "Up," Brautigan said, tugging the rope around McLendon's neck. "Get to walking. I think the storm's about to commence."

So it's to be Apache instead of Brautigan, McLendon thought. *At least they'll kill him too.* He stood with some difficulty. It was hard with his hands still tied behind his back. Then he began walking toward the cut in the mountains with the measured step of a resolute condemned man approaching the gallows.

29

Goyathlay was proud of his plan to catch and kill the white men. It offered good sport, and just enough challenge to keep the inexperienced warriors with him happy without expecting too much of them. It was important that he brought all four back to the agency with him, demonstrating that he was an effective war leader who could avoid even minimal casualties. Beyond that, his main concern involved timing — Apache rarely engaged in coordinated attacks. But if it succeeded this, too, would burnish his credentials. Warriors from other camps flocked to Cochise because he enjoyed such a widespread reputation for daring battle strategy. Goyathlay hungered to be known for the same.

"This is what we will do," he told the others. It was just before dawn. "In a little while the white men will start moving again. We'll stay far enough behind so that they won't see us. They're going toward their village on the other side of the mountains, so it will be easy to follow them."

"When do we take them?" Nantee asked.

"This is how it will be: There are two ways through the mountains, one a narrow path between the two directly ahead, the other around one of them — not too hard, but it would take longer. The whites will want to go the short way, probably. Even if they don't, we'll make sure they do."

Tawhatela asked, "But if they get in that narrow place ahead of us and then through, how can we catch them?"

"We're going to be in two places. In a little while, Nantee and I will ride ahead, going around one of the mountains, so we'll be waiting for the white men when they come out the other side of the path in between. And we know they will go that way because you, Tawhatela, and John Tiapah and Datchshaw will drive them there. With you on one end and us on the other, the whites will be trapped in between. Because the path is so small, the big one won't have room to fight. The small one, his prisoner, probably won't fight at all. Once we have them, we'll find a good place and torment them. Then we'll go back to the agency and the people will praise us as great warriors."

From hiding, they watched the white men get up, and chuckled when the big one howled with fury about the missing mule. Tawhatela farted and whispered, "Listen, your mule is braying," and the other Apache laughed so hard Goyathlay was worried the big man might hear them even though he was several bowshots away.

There was more entertainment in the treatment of the small white man by the big one, who tied him with ropes like an animal. Then the whites began moving toward the mountains, the small one walking ahead of the big one, who rode their remaining horse. Their pace was slow enough for Goyathlay to believe they didn't realize any Apache were near. How could they not know? The theft of the mule should have made that clear. It was part of his strategy that the whites should panic and make bad decisions. Any Apache, even a woman or child, would have known better than to take the small trail between the mountains, because, once in it, there was no other way to go. If the white men did the sensible thing, going around the smaller mountain instead, they'd still be captured and killed, of course. That was never in doubt from the time the Apache first saw them. But out in the open, the men they trailed could fight back better.

But the whites obviously had no idea that they were being stalked. All right — Goyathlay would adjust his strategy a little. That was what wise war leaders did.

"Nantee and I are going to ride ahead now," he told the others. "You others stay behind the white men. For now, don't let them see you. We need time to ride around the mountain and get to the other side of that path. After we do, the three of you can let the white men know you're there. Fire some shots, give battle cries. Chase them toward the path between the mountains, but don't catch them. Let them run in. Wait outside there. Nantee and I will meet the white men on the other end. We'll have them caught between us. Then we catch them, but we don't kill them yet. The big one is probably a good fighter. We may have to hurt him a lot before he falls. But even if he dies there, we can still do things with the smaller one. Does everyone understand?"

John Tiapah said, "How will we know when you're ready on the other side?"

Goyathlay had already thought of this. During the day, Apache measured increments of time by the sun's movement across the sky.

"Give us three fingers of sun, then come ahead." By white men's timekeeping, three

456

fingers' movement would total about forty-five minutes. "John Tiapah, you will judge that. I rely on you." The young man beamed — the additional responsibility was an honor.

"Now, you three know what to do?" Goyathlay asked. They nodded. Without another word, he and Nantee wheeled their horses and galloped away.

Nantee was surprised when Goyathlay didn't ride very far north before turning back east toward the mountains. He didn't use the swales and gullies for cover either. Nantee waved at him to stop and said, "Those two white men are going to see us."

"I want them to," Goyathlay said. "They were too stupid to realize we were there last night to take their mule. I want them already afraid when the others ride at them. So you and I will ride just close enough for them to see us now. But we won't be riding at them, we won't even look at them. It will scare them, though, and they'll hurry toward the little path between the mountains. That's what we want."

"If they hurry too much, they could get through before we're waiting on the other side."

Goyathlay sighed. This was why the

Apache on the San Carlos agency so badly needed a new leader. Senses dulled by too much peace, the warriors could no longer see obvious things.

"The smaller white man is bound and walking. He can't go very fast that way. If the big one lets him ride behind on the horse, that will make the horse go slower. Our ponies are fast and well rested. Let's ride, and, remember, when we pass the white men don't even look at them."

They kicked their ponies in the ribs and resumed their gallop. As they did, a great wave of shade swept across the land. Even without looking up, Goyathlay knew that the rains were about to come again, even harder than the storms of previous days. Floods were possible — the terrain around them practically invited them. But to Goyathlay, as to all the Apache, nature was always to be accommodated. If the rain was troublesome for him and his warriors, it would be worse for the foolish white men. He and Nantee kept riding, and soon Goyathlay glimpsed the white men from the corner of his right eye. They were maybe a dozen bowshots away, far enough to be well out of rifle range but still so close that the whites had to see them.

"Ride for the mountain now," he called to

Nantee, and they swung slightly north to begin circumventing its gently rounded slope. The going was slightly slippery from previous rains, but the impending deluge still hadn't begun. Hopefully it wouldn't until they were in place on the other side. There was some cactus on the ground along the slope but not much, easy enough to avoid. A few deer scampered in the distance, looking for high ground before the rain. The instincts of animals were superior to those of man.

They were about two-thirds around the mountain, making good time, when Goyathlay thought about the heavy, near-instant cloud cover, which made it impossible to tell time by the sun. Well, surely any Apache warrior could estimate time in such an instance. Then Goyathlay remembered — he had given timekeeping responsibility to young John Tiapah, barely weaned from his mother's breast. What if the boy didn't wait long enough? The whites might get away after all, and how foolish would Goyathlay seem then? Maybe John Tiapah would get it right. That was what Goyathlay would have to hope.

"Ride faster," he shouted at Nantee, his voice muffled by a sudden strong, howling wind.

■ ■ ■ ■

John Tiapah gave another worried glance at the sky. All these dark clouds — the sun was completely hidden. There was no way to tell, none, how much it was moving. He asked Datchshaw and Tawhatela for their opinions, but neither would give one. Goyathlay was well known for his hot temper. None of them wanted to face his wrath if the attack on the white men was spoiled because of a poor decision. The white men were perhaps six bowshots in front and still, apparently, oblivious to the trio of Apache trailing them. At one point they even stopped so the big one could hit the other one some more.

"Do you think it's been three fingers?" John Tiapah asked again. "It must be, don't you think?"

"Goyathlay told you to decide," Tawhatela said. "All I know is that those two white men are getting close to the path between the mountains."

"If we're going to do something, we should," Datchshaw added. "Unless it's not three fingers yet."

John Tiapah suddenly wished he'd never left the agency, where his mother and sisters

460

took good care of him and his uncles kept him entertained with tales of battle exploits. What would they say if he returned as a failure, one whose mistake brought shame on his whole family? Goyathlay and the others would make certain no one thought it was *their* fault. Better to be too early than too late, John Tiapah decided. Goyathlay and Nantee were good riders. It had been a long time. They were surely around the smallish mountain by now.

"It's time," he told the others, hoping he sounded more decisive than he felt. "Let's get the whites running."

The three Apache whooped, fired shots in the air, and raced their ponies toward the men ahead of them.

30

The gathering storm clouds mirrored Joe Saint's mood. He was unhappy with everything, himself most of all. No matter how much he hated Cash McLendon, it was wrong to wish death on him, as Saint had from the moment he'd learned of Gabrielle's abduction by Brautigan. Saint had hoped, on this long, hard trail from Mountain View to Devil's Valley to here in these godforsaken mountains, that at some point Gabrielle would give up her impossible hope of rescuing McLendon. Normally the most sensible of women, she now couldn't be reasoned with. McLendon had fooled her, seduced her, so much so that she was willing to throw away her own life, and his, and the Major's, in a senseless attempt to save the only man whom Joe Saint had ever come to completely despise. That they were all about to die was obvious. Saint had known it ever since they spotted the Apache.

This attempted ambush would be futile. Brautigan himself could have undoubtedly killed them easily and now there were Indians added to the mix. Saint had done his best to make Gabrielle understand, but she wouldn't be deterred. Now the inevitable end was at hand.

And yet Saint found himself being self-critical. Beyond his raging hatred of McLendon, he was at heart an analytical man, and honest enough to acknowledge responsibility for his own decisions. It had been his choice to stay with Gabrielle and the Major. Further sulking, arguing — what would that accomplish? Now the choice was between dying badly and decently. Saint knew that he was a physical coward. He always had been. But if, as Saint expected, these proved to be his last few minutes of life, he wanted to spend them in a way that made Gabrielle feel proud of him. Should she and Saint somehow come through it alive, well, that was a possibility worth dwelling on. But what if McLendon survived too? Then McLendon and Gabrielle would surely . . . better not think about that. Saint took a deep breath; time to do the right thing, time to change his attitude.

"That ledge looks like a promising place," Saint said, and his tone was so different, so

463

unexpectedly positive, that Mulkins looked startled and Gabrielle smiled. "Here, I'll get the horses tied out of the way while the two of you climb up." He secured the three animals behind some boulders, checking to ensure they wouldn't be immediately visible from the end of the cut that opened into the canyon. Then Saint made his own way to the ledge, which was about fifteen feet up a steep slope and fifty yards to the right of the cut. Some large rocks provided cover. Gabrielle sat with her back against one. Her face was pale.

"My leg is still sore," she explained. "But I'm up here now, and going down will be easier."

"Let's formulate strategy," Saint suggested. "Major, you're the experienced military man. How do you see it?"

"The first thing is, remember that battle plans are only perfect until the fighting starts," Mulkins said. "Something unexpected always happens. What we ought to do is figure how to set up so we can react to whatever transpires. We know we've got C.M. and Brautigan coming through the cut into the canyon. The Apache are going to be behind them. We're figuring the Indians will hold off jumping them until they're in the canyon too. So we take Brautigan, get C.M. away from him, before the Apache get going."

"What if the Apache are right behind them?" Gabrielle asked. "Maybe one of us should watch for that while the other two attend to Brautigan?"

"It becomes a matter of concentrated attack," Mulkins said. "Unless I can drop him with a lucky shot from some distance, it's going to take all three of us to deal with Brautigan. We can't hand-fight him. As long as the Indians hold off until C.M. and Brautigan are through the cut, our best hope is to finish the big man, get C.M. clear, then worry about the Apache. Who, I admit, are considerably worth worrying about. But one scrap at a time is best."

"You say we'll finish Brautigan," Saint said. "You mean kill him."

"If we don't, he'll kill C.M. and, probably, us," Mulkins said. "I know for a peaceable man like you it's hard to think of killing someone."

"We can't be squeamish, Joe," Gabrielle added.

"I'm not. I just want to make sure I understand what we're going to do."

"Well, then," Mulkins said. "Now to divvying available weaponry. First is the Winchester. I'm not the finest shot, but in all

465

likelihood I'm probably the most skilled among the three of us. That would give me the best chance of potting Brautigan when he comes into the canyon. Agreed? Joe, you might hang on to the shotgun. It kicks hard. As to the two pistols, I've got C.M.'s on my belt. Gabrielle, you've hung on to Ike Clanton's. Check to see it's fully loaded."

Gabrielle spun the cylinder and nodded.

"One of the keys will be getting C.M. away and moving as soon as possible," Mulkins said. "Lord willing, he'll be in sufficient condition to fight some himself. What I'd suggest, if we have to close with Brautigan, Joe and I will handle that, perhaps with C.M. pitching in."

"Brautigan sometimes ties his prisoners," Gabrielle said. "Only at night, based on my experience, but there's still that chance."

Mulkins fished in a pocket. "I've got this clasp knife. Here, Gabrielle. Should that be the case, once things commence, make it your job to cut C.M.'s bonds. We'll need him wading in with both fists flying. All right, I guess that's our plan, such as it is." Mulkins pivoted and sighted his Winchester at the cut fifty yards away. He fiddled with the gunsight and held up a finger to gauge the wind. "Who knows? I might just get in a lucky shot, and then we're home free."

"Except for the Apache," Saint said.

"Like I told you, one fight at a time."

They settled in to wait. It was uncomfortable sitting on the ledge. It was all rock, with plenty of sharp edges. They had blankets from their saddlebags but these didn't provide sufficient cushion. Still, it was better than riding or walking. All three of them were physically exhausted. They were hungry too. Saint wondered, if they did kill Brautigan, and if they somehow fought off the Apache, whether the big man might have some canned food or biscuits in his pack. Anything would taste better than undercooked horse; though, if he got any hungrier, horse meat would suit him just fine.

Saint glanced at Gabrielle, who sat slumped against a rock a few feet away. Her eyes were closed and her lips moved slightly. He guessed she was praying. Saint took in her hair springing out in dust-covered curls from under the bandanna wrapped around her head, and the torn man's shirt and tattered trousers that she wore. Poor Gabrielle, who always favored dresses and pretty hair ribbons. Now she was a ragamuffin with a Colt stuffed in her waistband. She still looked beautiful to Joe Saint. What could he have done differently, to keep her from being taken away from him by Cash McLendon? Should he have been more assertive, more commanding? Well, he was who he was, and it was too late to change anything now.

Exhaustion overcame Saint. Despite the dire circumstances in which he found himself, he dozed.

An instant later, at most only a few minutes, he was awakened by several sharp noises, and a long, moaning, *"Noooo,"* from Gabrielle. Even fuddled with sleep, Saint immediately recognized the noises as gunshots, coming from the opposite side of the cut where they waited on the ledge. The Indians hadn't waited until they were into the canyon to attack.

"Goddamned Apache," Mulkins said and snarled.

Gabrielle asked plaintively, "What do we do now?"

"Get out there to C.M. and try to help," Mulkins said. He snatched up the Winchester and slid down the slope. Gabrielle jumped to her feet and her injured leg buckled. Saint took her arm and helped her down. Their progress was slow. Mulkins sprinted toward the cut. More shots rang out on the other side, a cacophony of gunfire.

31

The acoustics in and around the mountains were strange. Some sounds were muffled, others amplified. Goyathlay estimated that he and Nantee were almost around the base of the left mountain. Surely the canyon and valley beyond would come into sight any moment. Then it would be a simple matter of placing themselves at the far end of the narrow pathway, to close it up against the fleeing white men. Goyathlay began imagining how he and his warriors would torture their victims. Perhaps the small one should go first, let the big one watch him suffer and imagine the pain to come. The big one ought to last awhile, maybe the whole rest of the day and into the evening. There was music in the screams of victims.

Then, above the wind, Goyathlay thought he heard brief brisk noises that cut off sharply without lingering reverberation. These sounds could have been any number of things — the snapping of tree branches, for instance, but there were no trees this low on the mountain slope. Heart sinking, Goyathlay guessed he was hearing the faint sound of gunshots. Yes — here were more.

The Apache language contained no specific obscenities. Goyathlay fell back on an epithet he'd often heard used by white soldiers and traders at San Carlos agency: *"Shit!"*

He and Nantee were already riding full out. Goyathlay now hoped that the fight wouldn't be over before he arrived. It was vital that he receive credit for leading it. John Tiapah, Datchshaw, Tawhatela — those three fools were likely to shoot the two white men dead on the spot. There would be hardly any glory in that, and none for Goyathlay himself. Unbearable! Those whites were *his* victims, he had to get to them while they still lived.

32

Brautigan and McLendon were perhaps a hundred yards from the opening of the cut when they heard shots and whoops behind them. Looking back, they saw three Apache racing forward on horseback, brandishing rifles and howling.

Brautigan said, "What?"

"Apache, like I told you. We've got to run."

"Like hell," Brautigan said. He pulled the Winchester out of its scabbard, twisted in the saddle, and took aim. He fired several shots; the Apache momentarily paused, then resumed their charge. Instead of fleeing, Brautigan shifted his weight to get down off his horse. He meant to fight them on the spot.

"Run," McLendon yelled.

"No," Brautigan said. He attempted to dismount while keeping hold of both the rifle and the rope looped around McLendon's neck and momentarily fumbled with both, dropping the rifle. More out of fear of the Apache than any specific thought of escaping Brautigan, McLendon threw his body weight forward and tugged the end of the rope from Brautigan's grasp. Hands still bound behind him, neck rope trailing after him like the long tail of a lizard, he stumbled toward the cut. It was the likeliest way to get away from the Indians.

"Come back," Brautigan snarled. He glanced back at the Apache, remounted, and galloped his horse into the cut after McLendon.

McLendon had no chance to escape him. Brautigan was riding, and McLendon had trouble stumbling straight ahead — having arms bound behind his back threw off his balance. So within moments Brautigan caught up; it seemed, to McLendon, in his panic, that he could feel hot breath whooshing from the horse's nostrils onto the back of his neck. But the passage was so narrow that Brautigan couldn't quite reach down from the saddle and grasp McLendon from behind. He'd have to wait a few more seconds until they either came out the other end of the cut or discovered it was a dead end. Either way, Brautigan knew, he had him. There were still whoops and shots to the rear, but the giant gave little thought to the three Apache behind him. He'd deal with McLendon first, then them.

McLendon, staggering, saw the end of the cut, dark gray sky and charcoal-colored hills beyond, the storm clouds cast their pall over everything and eliminated color. *If I can just get there,* he thought, and then he was through and into the canyon with Brautigan right behind him. The big man leaned forward, reached out, and caught the trailing end of McLendon's neck rope in his huge hand. McLendon was caught up short. Brautigan swept past on his horse. He held on to the rope and McLendon was pulled forward by the noose. It yanked tight, immediately causing him to choke. McLendon was dragged into the canyon, half off his feet and bouncing painfully against rocks. Those collisions hurt, but McLendon's immediate concern was staying upright. If he fell and was dragged, he'd be strangled to death.

At that moment, announced by a clap of thunder, rain began descending in thick, opaque sheets.

33

Major Mulkins ran toward the cut, intending to enter it and hurry to the other side. He was still ten yards away when Cash McLendon staggered out of it and past Mulkins, followed closely by Brautigan on horseback. There was something trailing after C.M., a rope, and Brautigan grabbed it. C.M. staggered off balance and Mulkins raised the Winchester to shoot at Brautigan, this was a real opportunity, the big man was almost too close to miss but moving away, *shoot now*! But as Mulkins raised the rifle it began pouring rain, it was like sledgehammers of water slamming into him, and at the same time a bullet ricocheted off a rock near him and whoops echoed in the cut. The Apache were coming through. Mulkins thought, *Gabrielle and Joe are behind me. They'll have to deal with Brautigan for now. I need to stop the Indians.* He leaned into the mouth of the cut, using the rock wall for cover. The rain pounded down onto the passage but he could see figures moving in it. Mulkins fired a series of quick shots, *one-two-three-four,* and the Apache dropped to the ground or flattened against the sides of the cut. He couldn't tell how many there were. They fired a few shots back, none coming close to him. Mulkins figured that as long as he stayed where he was, with sufficient ammunition and a good shooting angle, he could keep them stoppered up in the cut for a good while. But what was happening behind him? He didn't dare take his eyes off the Apache to look.

Brautigan reined in his horse about fifty yards past the cut. He thought regretfully that he had to kill McLendon quickly and then deal with the Apache. The boss would be pleased McLendon was dead and unhappy that he hadn't witnessed the killing himself. It couldn't be helped.

Brautigan walked toward where McLendon stood stooped and choking, rain beating down on his bowed head. Then he looked past McLendon, back toward the cut they'd just come through, and saw someone standing there shooting. What was this? Visibility was too poor to see exactly where the man was aiming, but it didn't seem to be at Brautigan. That meant McLendon could be attended to first. Several inches of rain were already pooled on the canyon floor. As he walked, Brautigan's steel-toed boots threw off fans of water like the prow of boats cutting through a lake. One sweeping kick at the ankles to knock McLendon off his feet, then a direct strike to the temple. He'd be dead at last.

Gabrielle and Saint were momentarily blinded by the rain. It slashed at them so hard that the bandanna covering Gabrielle's head was practically displaced. Much of her long, abundant hair was uncovered, and some fell in front of her eyes. She brushed it away. Saint shouted, "Look!" and there was Cash McLendon, swaying and looking very much like a sacrificial victim, and Brautigan stalking toward him. Only a few yards separated victim and murderer. They were much farther away, two dozen yards at least, and Gabrielle was so hobbled that they could never get there in time to prevent the killing. She'd been leaning on Saint, using him for support. Now she pushed him away, screamed, "Go ahead, Joe," raised the pistol she'd taken from Ike Clanton and fired a shot that flew wildly in Brautigan's general direction. The giant stopped in his tracks and stared. The thick curtain of rain prevented Gabrielle from seeing his face clearly, but she still recoiled as though some force blazed from Brautigan's eyes to hers. At least he'd stopped going toward Cash. Now his attention seemed to be fixed on Joe, who was not running but at least walking toward Brautigan, shotgun in hand. But why, instead of aiming at the giant, did Joe let the shotgun dangle at his side like that?

Danger of any kind had petrified Joe Saint all his life, and this was a moment of especially raw peril. He'd faced his fear so far, hurrying with Gabrielle toward Brautigan instead of following his instinct to flee in the opposite direction. But when Gabrielle shoved him forward to face the giant on his own, his resolution failed. The man was huge; in the years since Glorious, Saint had forgotten how tall Brautigan was, and how wide. Saint's knees buckled from panic. He was ready to run. He'd turn, grab Gabrielle, and together they would get away somehow — no, her leg was hurt, she couldn't move fast enough. Brautigan would overtake and kill them both. McLendon stood defenseless a few feet away from Brautigan, but Saint paid him no mind. His sole concern was protecting Gabrielle. The giant began walking toward Saint. This was a chance to blast him with the shotgun. But as much as Saint willed himself to, his body didn't obey. His arms and hands trembled so much that he could not raise the shotgun to fire.

Halfway through the cut, crouched down and presenting the smallest targets possible, Datchshaw, Tawhatela, and John Tiapah wondered what was happening. Someone on the canyon end was shooting at them. It had to be the big white man. Where were Goyathlay and Nantee?

The three Apache occasionally returned fire, but they had very few bullets left and whoever was opposing them had good cover. Rain poured into the cut — it was difficult to see.

"We could charge," John Tiapah called. "All three of us wouldn't get shot."

"I can't move fast enough because of my wound," Datchshaw reminded him. "The big white man might get both of you." He flinched as a bullet chipped splinters from the rock wall above his head. Where was the glory in this? If Goyathlay was such a great leader, why was his plan going so wrong?

Footing was treacherous on the canyon

floor. The deluge soaked soft spots into mud, pooled in gullies, and covered flat rock areas with a slick film. Brautigan strode through mud toward Joe Saint. His heavy boots sank a few inches at each step. That gave Saint time to get the shotgun halfway up. Its twin barrels wavered at about knee height — still good enough to stop Brautigan if Saint fired now, but his trembling finger slipped off the double triggers. Just a few more steps and Brautigan would be on him. Saint was virtually paralyzed with fear.

Gabrielle watched, horrified. What was the matter with Joe? She limped a few paces forward and fired her pistol again, pulling the trigger until the hammer clicked on a used cartridge. So far as she could tell, none of the bullets hit Brautigan, but he paused just a little way from Joe to stare at her. He pointed: *You're next.*

McLendon had enough of his breath back to understand some of what was happening. There was shooting. The Apache must have caught up to them in the canyon. But at least for the moment, no one was assaulting McLendon. Only Brautigan seemed under attack, bullets fired in his direction but all apparently missing him. The giant was a few feet away from McLendon, and there was someone standing in front of him. *Joe Saint?* Brautigan paused and pointed at something behind Joe. Then he lowered his arm, and as he did McLendon threw himself forward, trying to knock the giant down from behind and failing completely. There was the sensation of his shoulder slamming into something hard and immovable. McLendon bounced off Brautigan, lost his footing, and splashed down on his face in the muck. Because his hands were still tied behind his back it was hard to roll over. Just before he did he inhaled a quantity of thick muddy water. Coughing, he looked up to see Brautigan standing above him. But the giant's attention was elsewhere — he looked back toward the valley side of the canyon.

Major Mulkins risked a glance over his shoulder. There was Brautigan, and Joe Saint near him, and C.M. on the ground at Brautigan's feet. Joe was standing stock-still, and Mulkins remembered that during every Civil War battle he'd fought in, there were always a handful of soldiers who froze in place, overcome by fear. Joe was out of this fight. Mulkins calculated rain, wind, and distance between himself and Brautigan. Maybe he could shoot the giant from here?

Then there was movement back in the cut and Mulkins fired in that direction instead, the last two shots in the Winchester's magazine. He snatched bullets from his pocket and began frantically attempting to reload.

Goyathlay and Nantee finally rounded the eastern slope of the small mountain and rode hard into the canyon. The sloppy surface made it difficult for their horses to maintain full speed. The animals tried to slow down, but the Apache riders viciously kicked their ribs and kept them on the run. The rain made it hard to see. But now there were clear sounds of shots ahead, there was surely fighting in progress. Then, just barely through the sheets of rain, they saw a hulking figure, the big white man, and there were others around him, not Apache, who were these? Goyathlay and Nantee made for them, but suddenly the ground had splits in it, they had to slow down, it was like this sometimes near mountains, long wide cracks in the ground that could swallow a man. They maneuvered around the worst ones. Then there seemed to be an unbroken path between them and the big white man. They whipped their horses back into a gallop and charged him.

■ ■ ■ ■

Tawhatela was furious. Being pinned down
was no way to earn battle glory. Datchshaw
could whine about his wound, and John
Tiapah couldn't make up his mind whether
to stay, fight, or run. It was time to act in a
way that ensured honor. He threw down his
rifle — he had only two or three bullets left,
anyway — pulled a knife from its hide
sheath, and, screaming defiantly, charged
down the cut. There was a white man at the
end of it, not one of the ones they'd been
following, fumbling with his rifle. Tawhatela
pounced at him, knife raised to strike.

Major Mulkins didn't have time to reload
the Winchester because the Apache was on
him so fast. The Indian swung a knife and
Mulkins blocked the blade with the rifle.
The Apache snarled like an animal and
stabbed at Mulkins again. Mulkins swung
the rifle like a club. The Indian caught hold
of the stock and wrenched it from Mulkins's
grip. He howled triumphantly and brandished the knife. Mulkins drew the Colt
given to him by McLendon, and, as the
Apache lunged for him, aimed instinctively
and fired. The bullet went through the

Indian's eye. He dropped; Mulkins thought he was dead but couldn't take the time to make certain. He fired several pistol shots back down the cut, just in case the other Apache there had ideas about following their tribesman, then reloaded the Winchester as quickly as he could.

John Tiapah and Datchshaw flinched back from the shots. Tawhatela had run to the end of the path and leaped up. After that they couldn't see what happened to him, but since they were again being fired on, his attack must have failed.

"Do we go?" Datchshaw asked. "We might be shot next."

"Not yet," John Tiapah said. "Goyathlay may still do something."

Brautigan was aware of everything going on around him, but not distracted by it. The primary credo of seasoned street fighters still prevailed: deal with the most immediate threat first. There was shooting from the mouth of the cut, but for the moment none of it was directed at him. McLendon, still tied up, thrashed in the mud. No threat there. Someone — it was the girl! — had fired at him with a pistol, but she now watched helplessly, apparently out of bullets. Just in front of Brautigan was a scrawny, bespectacled man holding a shotgun down along his side, familiar from somewhere. The giant decided to eliminate this one first, easy enough, he'd never get the shotgun up in time, but as Brautigan began to step toward the man he caught a flash of movement from the corner of his eye, something coming up into the canyon directly at him. He swiveled his head and saw Indians, two of them, up on horseback and riding at him. But they weren't coming as fast as might be expected; their mounts seemed to dance around, and this gave Brautigan time to set his feet in the thick mud.

Goyathlay rode ahead of Nantee. If the rain hadn't been so blinding he would have pulled an arrow from his quiver and skewered the big white man. Experienced Apache warriors could do this accurately from the saddle, even when their horses were at a gallop. But the rain and wind were too wild. Even at close range an arrow would be blown off course. So Goyathlay simply used his horse as a battering ram instead, intending to crash the mount full tilt into the big man and knock him sprawling. After that, down and dazed, he'd be easy prey.

But the horse's last few strides were over rain-slicked rock and its unshod hooves slipped just enough to throw the animal off balance. It still ran into its target, but the contact was glancing rather than solid. The big white man staggered slightly but kept his feet. The horse, with Goyathlay astride, careened within a few yards of one of the crevices that crossed the canyon; this one was wide and deep to the measure of one tall man standing on another's shoulders. The bottom was unforgiving rock. Goyathlay hauled back on the hackamore in his horse's mouth. The animal slid, struggling to keep its balance, and skidded along the ground, forelegs crumpling underneath its body. Goyathlay had the brief sensation of tumbling in space, and then he was down hard, though the horse took the brunt of the tumble. Badly injured, both forelegs snapped, it whinnied piteously. Goyathlay's breath was knocked from him. He struggled to drag air back in his lungs; he could sense more than hear nearby struggling. Nantee must be fighting the big man, and Goyathlay needed to help him.

Nantee saw Goyathlay and his horse slam into the big man. With the rain it was hard to see what happened after that. Nantee blinked a little rain out of his eyes and after he blinked Goyathlay and the horse were gone, just disappeared. How was that possible? Then he saw horse and rider not far away, both down but moving. Nantee now had to choose between aiding Goyathlay and fighting the big white man, and that was an easy decision. He'd come on this raiding trip for glory, and killing the white man in single combat would earn it. Nantee yanked his horse to a stop, leaped down, drew his knife, and attacked.

The collision with the horse staggered Brautigan but didn't really hurt him. A bruise or two, perhaps. Nothing to hinder effective movement. The first Indian and his mount were down somewhere to the right. That Apache might be back, but for now there was another who dismounted and charged Brautigan with a knife. The footing beneath Brautigan's boots was gummy but that was no critical impediment. Hands would do nicely for this one. The Indian tried to close, he probably was used to being the quickest one in a tussle, but Patrick Brautigan had never met the man who could move faster than he did in a fight and that remained true now. He caught the Apache's knife arm and twisted. The savage yelped with pain.

Up close, his dirt-smeared face registered shock.

As soon as the second Indian dismounted and ran at Brautigan, Gabrielle saw her chance. She stuffed the empty Colt into her waistband and moved forward. She couldn't run, her leg was too painful for that, but she ignored the agony as best she could and stumbled ahead. As she passed Joe Saint she cried, "*Move,* Joe," and thought he blinked but it was hard to tell, so much rain dripped from the lenses of his spectacles. Then Gabrielle stumbled a few more steps and knelt at McLendon's side where he lay in the mud. She opened the Major's clasp knife and said, "Turn so I can free your arms." McLendon stared at her, hardly able to believe she was there, and Gabrielle snapped, "Roll over and let me cut the ropes." He did, and she saw the rope burns on his neck from being dragged by the noose; they were open and a mixture of blood and rain dripped from them. She hacked away at the ropes, they wouldn't cut, was the knife blade too dull? And then a body flew past.

Brautigan disposed of Nantee quickly. He got one hand on the Apache's head, another on his neck, and twisted. There was a snap as loud as a gunshot, and Nantee went limp. To preserve as much fighting space as possible, Brautigan threw the dead man away, flinging him almost directly over Gabrielle where she crouched by McLendon. *All right, now the girl,* Brautigan thought, because the skinny one in glasses still stood frozen with fear. Then from the corner of his eye Brautigan detected more motion, the first Indian, the one who ran his horse into him, was up again. He turned to kill this one.

Goyathlay charged Brautigan with the intent of attacking, but changed his mind in mid-stride after he saw Nantee die and be tossed aside. Up close, this big white man exuded evil, he was surely possessed by some bad spirit — faced with such supernatural power, even Cochise would have retreated. Goyathlay's horse was too crippled to ride, but Nantee's stood nearby and Goyathlay spun, nearly slipping, and leaped on its back. He dug his heels into the animal's ribs and it ran hard toward the cut, the horse had its own instinct for the best getaway.

Major Mulkins's attention was still focused down the cut. The Apache remained there, he was sure, and might charge any moment.

Then there was something coming up behind, hoof beats in a rhythm different from the pounding of the storm, and then even before Mulkins could completely turn, a horse was on him and then past into the cut, there was an Apache riding it, where had he come from? It happened too quickly for Mulkins to react — before he could shoot, the Apache on horseback was well past. Now the Indians on the other end of the cut were reinforced. More things were happening behind Mulkins; he briefly tore his eyes from the cut to look. But the storm was so powerful that the raindrops seemed to comprise one solid, constant block of water hammering down. Mulkins couldn't see what was going on in the canyon. Run back there to his friends and leave the cut unguarded against the Indians? He wasn't sure. But Mulkins had learned through combat experience that indecision inevitably led to disaster. One or the other. Well, he'd come all this way to save C.M. from Brautigan, and C.M. and the big man were back in the canyon. Mulkins turned and ran in that direction.

Goyathlay nearly bowled over John Tiapah and Datchshaw. He didn't bother dismounting. "Get on your horses, we're leaving," he

489

told them. "Where's Tawhatela?"

"He ran down the path toward someone shooting at us and didn't come back," Datchshaw said. "Did you see him there on the other side?"

"No, Nantee and I were fighting a bad spirit," Goyathlay said. "It lives in the big white man. It's angry now and might be coming after us. We need to get away."

"What about Nantee and Tawhatela?" John Tiapah asked.

"The bad spirit has them. Now let's ride." Goyathlay began galloping north. John Tiapah and Datchshaw mounted and rode after him. There would be no great stories to tell back at the agency.

With one Apache dead and the other gone, Brautigan didn't know or care where, the giant turned his attention back to the girl and McLendon. In two quick steps he towered over them.

Gabrielle frantically hacked at the rope around McLendon's wrists with the clasp knife and finally cut through it; his arms were free. Just then she was grabbed by the hair and yanked in the air. It hurt so much, strands and curls were ripping out at the roots, but most of her hair held firm and

490

she dangled on tiptoe at the end of Brautigan's arm.

"I warned you," he said.

Gabrielle ineffectively slashed at him with the clasp knife. Brautigan swatted it out of her hand, then drew back his fist.

Joe Saint had seen everything happen, the one Indian running to Brautigan with his horse to no apparent effect, the second Indian being killed so easily. He'd heard the shots fired from the direction of the cut between the mountains. He'd felt the pounding of the rain. All of Saint's faculties were fully functional except his ability to move. It was very odd. He wanted to but couldn't. Then Brautigan had his hands on Gabrielle, he was suspending her in the air by her hair, and now back went his fist, *he was going to kill her,* and because Joe Saint couldn't let that happen, he finally moved. He grasped the shotgun by the barrels and, reaching up, swung the heavy stock against Brautigan's side. The force of the blow would have knocked almost anyone down. Brautigan blinked, dropped Gabrielle, and grabbed Saint by the front of his shirt. The handful of saturated fabric tore free. Saint staggered back a step. Brautigan snorted; without looking, he kicked at Gabrielle

491

where she lay on the ground. The side of his boot struck the top of her skull, not a killing blow but enough to render her dizzy. Then in a single graceful motion he whirled and kicked Saint hard, driving the steel boot tip deep into his left armpit. It seemed to Saint that something ruptured inside; molten agony surged through every inch of his body. Brautigan reached for Saint again. Saint tried to shift the grip his right hand still held on the shotgun. He got his finger through the trigger guard and feebly attempted to aim and fire, but Brautigan was too close and quick. He got both massive hands around Saint's neck and began squeezing, because this skinny one had struck him hard enough to hurt and choking seemed the right way to kill him.

Major Mulkins, running through the rain, slipping sometimes, saw Saint in Brautigan's grasp. He stopped and aimed his Winchester, but his friend and the giant were locked so close together that he was as likely to hit Saint as his intended target. Mulkins dropped his rifle and threw himself on Brautigan. Without releasing his two-handed grip on Saint, the giant drove an elbow into Mulkins's face, breaking his nose and knocking him out. Brautigan resumed squeezing Saint's throat. Saint's eyes bulged. The shotgun dangled helplessly from his fingers.

With his arms finally free, Cash McLendon was able to build some momentum as he charged Brautigan from behind. This time he plowed into the back of the giant's knees. They bent only a little. Brautigan took his left hand from Saint's throat — his right was sufficient to hold Saint in place, though not to completely throttle him. With his left hand, Brautigan caught McLendon by the shoulder and pulled him close. Their faces were pressed together. Brautigan's teeth were bared, his breath erupted hard and hot from his nostrils. McLendon's fingers scrabbled for the shotgun. Saint, wheezing badly, tried to raise it again. Brautigan let go of Saint's throat and wrapped his long arms around him and McLendon, clamping them both in a double bear hug. McLendon felt certain that his ribs were snapping. His left arm was trapped at his side, but the right one was free. Both of Saint's arms were pinned. He almost dropped the shotgun but McLendon got it, he had his hand around the trigger guard and tried to get his finger on the trigger. Brautigan sensed the danger and then saw it, McLendon with the shotgun in his right hand, and he stepped back, carrying both men with him, shaking them back and forth, trying to loosen McLendon's grip on the weapon. McLendon gritted his teeth against all the pain he felt — Brautigan's lethal embrace was tightening, it was hard to draw breath — and tried to pull the gun up, forcing it between his body, Saint's, and Brautigan's. Saint seemed almost unconscious. Brautigan tottered just a little, the rock beneath his boots was slick, and that provided McLendon with the most fleeting of opportunities. He tried to jam the shotgun barrels against whatever lower part of Brautigan's body it could reach, but his right elbow was still weak and gave a little as Brautigan squeezed hard again, and McLendon's finger twitched reflexively on the trigger. There was fire from both barrels, and at such close range the buckshot tore the toes off Joe Saint's left foot. Saint screeched, a keening, high-pitched wail. Brautigan flung him away, tore the shotgun from McLendon's hand, and threw McLendon down in the mud.

Brautigan paused a moment and looked around as best he could in the deluge. There was little movement anywhere in the canyon. Major Mulkins lay unconscious, Gabrielle was down and trying to gather herself, Joe Saint sprawled nearby with blood pumping from of what remained of his foot. All three would be easy to finish. First would come another killing, a satisfying death delayed too long. Brautigan didn't think of the boss now, didn't take into consideration Rupert Douglass's obvious preference to witness this execution. Professional pride was involved. This was the right moment. Only Cash McLendon had ever escaped Patrick Brautigan. His perfect record would now be restored.

Brautigan walked to where McLendon lay and nudged him in the ribs with a steel-toed boot. "Your time's up."

McLendon groaned. His whole body hurt. He tried to think of some way out but couldn't. Gabrielle was down, the Major, too, and Joe Saint was shot, no one was left between him and the giant.

Brautigan kicked McLendon in the ribs, first lightly and then harder. All McLendon could do was roll away. Brautigan let him roll a little, then, as McLendon tried to stand, kicked his feet out from under him. McLendon fell hard, skidding on wet rock. As Brautigan stepped toward him McLendon tried to roll away again, but stopped short when his left arm flopped into space. He was on the edge of a crevice with an abrupt drop-off. He looked down, saw it was seven feet deep, maybe eight, some water in the bottom and a gentler slope on the other side. If he rolled in, it would momentarily put him beyond range of Brautigan's kicks. Even staying alive a few more seconds seemed worth whatever pain resulted from the fall. But the giant stepped over him, placing a foot between McLendon and the edge.

"You can't get away from me. You never could. Good-bye, McLendon," Brautigan said, and raised a boot high above McLendon's head.

For years, McLendon had involuntarily imagined this moment, when Brautigan had him and there was no escape. *What will Killer Boots do to me?* he'd wondered. Now he knew. In this final moment, he thought not of himself or Gabrielle, but of how little bits of mud stuck to the sole of the boot that was about to come down and crush his skull. He raised a hand to try and block the boot, a gesture as futile as standing on a track trying to stop a speeding train, and took a long, last breath.

Gabrielle threw her empty pistol at Brautigan. She was on her knees and couldn't throw very hard, but it glanced off his shoulder and surprised him. He instinctively twisted to look back at her as McLendon's hand caught his raised foot. The boot Brautigan had planted on the ground lost traction on the wet rock. It slipped out from under him. McLendon was able to push up just hard enough on the other boot for Brautigan to lose his balance completely. The big man toppled and disappeared. McLendon wondered, *What happened to him?,* then realized Brautigan had fallen into the crevice. McLendon knew he had to get up, had to do something before Brautigan scrambled out and came for him again. He staggered to his feet and looked for something to hit the giant with, saw only the empty pistol glistening in the mud. Back in Mountain View, he'd watched Sheriff Jack Hove buffalo a miscreant by grasping the barrel of a Colt and using the butt as a hammer. It probably wouldn't work on Brautigan, but if nothing else it would be a way to die fighting, which McLendon found that he wanted to do. He grasped the pistol by the barrel and braced himself for the big man to come roaring up from the crevice, but Brautigan didn't. For a moment McLendon was aware of the smacking noise the rain made striking the rocks, and Joe Saint keening where he lay in a mixed pool of water and blood. Then there was Gabrielle's voice: "Go down and kill him."

McLendon's glance darted about. Brautigan had to be coming.

"Go kill him," Gabrielle called again. She was back on her feet and pointing toward the crevice. "He fell down there."

McLendon gingerly walked to the edge and looked down. Brautigan lay on his back, not moving. His right leg was bent at a hideous angle. Even through the curtains of rain, McLendon could see that a thick, jagged end of bone had torn through the flesh of the giant's thigh.

"He's hurt," McLendon shouted to Gabrielle. "His leg is broken."

"So kill him," Gabrielle said for the third time. "I've got to see to Joe." She limped over to where Saint lay bleeding and moaning. Gabrielle pulled the sodden bandanna from her neck and fashioned a tourniquet on his ankle, above the missing toes and arch of his foot. She leaned over and whispered in Saint's ear.

McLendon looked down again at Brautigan. It seemed impossible that the big man was really helpless. He might spring up even on one leg. McLendon didn't want to go near him. He went over to Mulkins instead. The Major was sitting up and holding his head in his hands, spreading his fingers so they wouldn't press against his smashed nose.

"Where's Brautigan?" Mulkins asked.

"He took a fall and his leg's broken. I think we're safe from him for the moment. How are you? Can you let me see your face?"

Mulkins moved his hands and McLendon gasped. The Major's nose was completely flattened, spread out along his cheekbones. Blood and snot seeped from both nostrils, but the rain washed a lot of it away. The area around Mulkins's eyes was puffed, and they were completely shut.

"I can't see, but it's just from swelling," Mulkins said. "That'll go down soon enough. Is everyone else all right?"

"Gabrielle is. Joe was shot, some of his foot's gone."

"Attend to Joe, then. I can sit here all right while you do."

McLendon went over to Gabrielle and Saint. She had inserted a stick under the bandanna tourniquet and twisted it tight.

"We've got to get Joe to a doctor soon, or he'll bleed to death," Gabrielle told McLendon. "Did you finish off Brautigan?"

"No, I —"

"Why not?"

499

"I wasn't sure how. All I had was the empty gun you threw at him."

Gabrielle gestured. "Go over there and pick up the shotgun. Use that."

"That's what shot Joe. It's empty too."

"There are more shells. I think Joe has them." She said softly to Saint, "I have to get something. I'll try not to hurt you as I do." Saint groaned as she reached in his pocket. McLendon noticed that Saint's glasses had fallen off. They lay beside him, jumping a little as they were struck by the rain.

"Here," Gabrielle said, thrusting two cartridges into McLendon's hand. "Load and go shoot him."

McLendon didn't move. "Let's just get Joe and the Major and get out of here. I don't think Brautigan can move. If we leave him, he's as good as dead."

Gabrielle glared. "We've got to get Joe out of here. You're afraid to go near Brautigan, aren't you? All right, you hold Joe's tourniquet in place and give me the shotgun. I'll do it."

"You don't want to kill someone."

She held out her hand for the shotgun. "Brautigan has to die, and we have to know it for certain. If we don't, all of us will be afraid for the rest of our lives."

McLendon thought, *Gabrielle's right. This is my fault, and it's on me to finish.* "I'll go." He cracked the shotgun, ejected the used shells and inserted two new ones. "Back soon."

He cautiously made his way back to the crevice, expecting Brautigan to appear at any moment. But the giant still lay apparently senseless at the bottom. McLendon walked around — the crevice narrowed enough to step over a few dozen yards away — and slid down the more gradual slope on the other side. The dirt there had been churned to sludge by the rain; the bottom of the crevice was solid rock under six inches of water. The water rose as the rain continued. McLendon wondered for a moment if he couldn't just clamber back out of the crevice and leave Brautigan lying there unconscious. If it kept raining and the water rose high enough, the giant would drown instead of McLendon having to shoot him. But Joe Saint was badly hurt and there was no time to be lost.

McLendon moved within a few yards of Brautigan and stopped. He raised the shotgun, aiming at the big man's head. But what if he missed? The body was a bigger target. McLendon shifted his aim, but still was uncertain. If he only wounded Brautigan and left assuming the giant was dead, what if he somehow survived and came back again for McLendon, or, worse, Gabrielle? She was right. McLendon had to make certain, and to do that he had to get closer.

He forced one foot after the other in increments of inches. McLendon could hear Brautigan's ragged breathing now. What if he blasted him with both barrels and Brautigan still got up? He'd always thought about Brautigan killing him and not the other way around.

A little closer. Brautigan was still on his back, eyes shut, raindrops bouncing off his body. Two steps away, McLendon raised the shotgun again, squinted down the barrel, sighting on the giant's face. His finger tightened on the twin triggers. Almost, almost . . .

Brautigan's eyes opened. Still flat on his back, he swiveled his head and looked directly at McLendon, who nearly dropped the shotgun.

"I — You —" McLendon stammered. He was very afraid.

Brautigan didn't speak. His eyes shifted in one direction, then another, analyzing, measuring, and then returned to McLendon.

"You can't get up," McLendon said,

speaking more to reassure himself than inform the big man. "Your leg's hurt too bad."

Brautigan still didn't say anything. He grunted with effort and rolled over on his stomach. The protruding thighbone scraped against the rock. Brautigan began crawling toward McLendon, who retreated and mumbled, "Stay back."

Brautigan kept advancing, long arms extended in front. McLendon, mesmerized, watched the giant's hands, the huge splayed fingers, each looking almost as thick as a normal man's wrist.

"Get away from me," McLendon said.

"Kill you," the big man muttered, and McLendon's gut spasmed. He tasted bile at the back of his throat.

"Get away," he repeated, his voice trembling.

Brautigan continued crawling on his belly, left foot pushing forward, right leg dragging. He was almost close enough to grasp McLendon by the ankle. "Kill the girl too," he said.

McLendon swallowed. "No, you won't." He aimed the shotgun, pulled the double trigger, and blew Patrick Brautigan's head completely off.

It took time to climb up the mud-slick slope. Back on even ground he saw Major Mulkins on his feet, waving his hands in all directions like a man swatting at dozens of flies and missing. "I'm over here, Major," he called. "Stand still and I'll come to you." He took the Major's arm and began leading him to where Gabrielle still knelt beside Saint.

"The shotgun blast," Mulkins said. "What happened?"

"Wait until Gabrielle and Joe can hear." He guided Mulkins over. Gabrielle took the Major's hand and helped him sit. "Brautigan's dead," McLendon said.

Gabrielle said, "You're sure?"

"I am. His head is gone."

"Good," Gabrielle said, sounding savage. Then she said crisply, "We need to be going. Joe, we're taking you somewhere there's help. All right, how many horses do we have? The three we rode here must still be tethered, and isn't that another over there?"

"Brautigan's horse," McLendon said.

"Then we'll all have mounts, if someone will fetch them."

Because Mulkins couldn't see and Gabrielle had to keep Saint's tourniquet in place, that task fell to McLendon. First, he used the shotgun to kill Goyathlay's crippled horse. As he gathered the other horses he kept thinking, *Brautigan's dead, he's really dead, and I'm alive.* It didn't seem possible.

When he brought the horses, Gabrielle continued taking charge.

"We'll have to lift Joe up very carefully. Cash, will you find a blanket in one of the saddlebags — yes, that one will do — and let's cut some strips, bind up Joe's foot tightly. There's still some bleeding but not as much."

Once Saint was on a horse, though slumped in the saddle, Gabrielle said, "I'll ride beside Joe and hold him steady. Cash, you'll have to lead the Major's horse."

"I'll stay with Joe and bolster him," McLendon said. "I'm bigger than you, it will tax me less. You guide the Major."

"I'll ride beside Joe," Gabrielle said in a tone that brooked no denial. "You see to the Major."

It was only when everyone was mounted that they realized they weren't certain where to go.

"Mountain View's perhaps five days' ride northwest, maybe even six what with the mud and probably flooding," McLendon said.

"Not possible," Mulkins said. He tipped his head back and pushed his chin forward, as though he might see with it while his eyes were swollen shut. "Those Apache are likely waiting for us on that side of the mountains."

"They've scattered, Major."

"I doubt it, C.M. What they are, is wily. They'll lurk out of sight for a while, then rush in to catch us unaware. And even if there weren't Indians between us and Mountain View, it would still take too long to reach. Maybe you've got a full belly, but the rest of us are in a bad way regarding food. We're too hungry to last long on the trail without a meal. We must ride east. I estimate Silver City's not far in that direction."

"There's a few cans and some biscuits in Brautigan's saddlebag," McLendon said. "That might tide you over a while. Silver City's a dangerous place. The authorities there are in league with Brautigan."

"*Were* in league," Gabrielle corrected. "He's gone now, his deals are off. We can't ride for Mountain View in any event because Joe needs a doctor as soon as possible. So it must be Silver City."

They rode out of the canyon and down into the valley, going very slowly. Saint swayed so much in the saddle that Gabrielle had to ride on one side of him and McLendon on the other, both helping to keep him in the saddle. McLendon had to use one hand for that and lead Mulkins's horse with the other. He was a poor horseman at best and almost fell off a few times himself. Soon Saint began mumbling incoherently. They had nothing to give him for the pain. Twice his horse stumbled and he screamed. Gabrielle talked constantly to him, a low stream of positive words about how she wouldn't allow anything else to happen to him, everything was going to be all right, and she promised that he would be fine.

After a few hours, the rain slackened and finally stopped altogether. They rode through mud and circumvented crevices and gullies filled with standing water. Mulkins had estimated that Silver City was perhaps thirty miles away, but they only made about ten miles before dark.

When they camped, Gabrielle used all their blankets to make a soft, dry bed for Saint, and to cover him snugly. He refused food. The others split two cans of peaches, saving the half-dozen biscuits for morning. When McLendon and Mulkins were about to stretch out on the still-damp ground and rest as best they could, Gabrielle sat next to Saint and held his hand.

"You need to sleep yourself," McLendon said.

"Not with Joe in this precarious condition," Gabrielle said. "I'd never forgive myself if he needed me and I was asleep." They'd been able to kindle a small fire with matches and brush. By the light of its few flames, McLendon saw that Gabrielle had lost whole patches of her beloved hair. Numerous bare spots, some the size of silver dollars, stood out in stark contrast to the remaining long, dark locks on the top of her head. There was an indescribable weariness in her eyes.

"How's your shin?" he asked, mostly for something to say.

"I'm fine," Gabrielle said, as though she answered a general rather than specific question. It was obvious that she wasn't. He touched her hand and she smiled faintly, then turned back to Saint, who was groaning.

McLendon sighed and lay down next to Mulkins. The Major said, "What's wrong, C.M.?"

"You can't see me because your eyes are swollen shut. How do you know something's wrong?"

"Don't need to see you; I heard you just now. What is it?"

"Hard to say. I'm alive and that's a surprise. But there seems no joy in it."

Mulkins sat up. Swollen flesh covered his face from brow to cheekbone. His flattened nose pressed in between. He looked barely human, and his voice wheezed.

"It's likely to take some time for you and for all of us," Mulkins said. "We've experienced terrible things and it's natural to feel unsettled. Let's get Joe to a doctor in Silver City, and worry about everything else after that."

It took McLendon a while to even doze. The rope burns on his neck stung badly, but when he considered the injuries suffered by Saint and Mulkins, his own hurts seemed trivial. Even though it had in no way been his intention, technically he and not Brautigan had shot and crippled Saint — McLendon felt some guilt from that. Would Saint hold a grudge because of it? More important, would Gabrielle? He tried comforting himself with the thought that Brautigan was dead, and he was finally safe. But what next?

Finally, McLendon slept a little. He woke in the middle of the night from indistinct, troubling dreams, and looked around.

Mulkins snored beside him, loud blatting noises from his mouth rather than his smashed nose. The fire was almost out, but in the glow of its remaining embers he saw that Gabrielle was still awake and seated beside Joe Saint, holding his hand and staring into the darkness.

34

They stayed in Silver City for five days. As soon as they arrived, they inquired after doctors. There were two in town. One was drunk and sleeping it off. The other was on a hot streak in a poker game and didn't want to be interrupted. His name was Hutcheson. When McLendon insisted that he step away from the card table because a terribly injured man needed immediate treatment, Doc Hutcheson said he'd do it for a hundred dollars cash, or twice the amount of the pending pot. When McLendon reported this to the others, Major Mulkins produced the wad of greenbacks McLendon had given him before surrendering himself to Brautigan.

"We've got a degree of financial comfort, C.M.," he said. "Tell that doc to tend to Joe at once."

Doc Hutcheson cauterized what remained of Saint's foot to prevent infection. Beyond that, he said, there was nothing to do but wait until the wound healed and then "buy the poor bastard a stump. It'll be pricey because it'll have to be special-fitted, 'less you want me to trim it all off back to the ankle. Then you could buy a plain wood foot and strap it on, which'll set you back considerably less." They said they'd wait and see.

Hutcheson also treated the Major's broken nose. He said there were always lots of these in Silver City. He twisted the cartilage this way and that while Mulkins tried not to scream. When he was done, the Major's nose was shaped almost normally. Hutcheson said the bridge would always be somewhat crooked. Mulkins's facial swelling subsided quickly, and he could see again.

The doctor judged Gabrielle's shin badly bruised but not broken. He raised his eyebrows at the rope burns on McLendon's neck but made no further comment. Hutcheson prescribed a salve that stung worse than the untreated wounds had. McLendon used it once, then discarded it.

Saint couldn't travel until his foot scabbed over sufficiently. They took two rooms at a shabby place called the Estes Hotel, which, despite its cobwebby corners and oilcloth curtains in lieu of windows, was still one of the better places in town. McLendon shared with Mulkins. Gabrielle insisted on staying with Saint. The crippled schoolteacher spoke very little, except to indicate he was in constant pain. Even then he usually ignored the other two and talked only to Gabrielle, keeping his voice low so as not to be overheard. Mulkins and McLendon took their meals in Silver City cafés, then brought food back to the hotel for Saint and Gabrielle. Saint moaned that he was too weak to go out, and she wouldn't leave him.

After two days, Gabrielle was finally persuaded to go shopping for a little while. She needed a dress to replace the ragged men's clothing she wore, and also a kerchief or bonnet to cover the bald spots on her scalp. She insisted that both Mulkins and McLendon stay at Saint's side while she was away; one of them should run and fetch her if Joe took a bad turn in her absence.

Mulkins had speculated to McLendon that Saint's moodiness could probably be attributed to embarrassment: "He's brooding on how he froze up during the fight, I believe." So while Gabrielle was gone, they sat on either side of Saint's bed and took turns reassuring him that there was no cause for shame. Mulkins told of how many brave Union soldiers suffered temporary paralysis before rushing into battle and distinguishing themselves, "just like you did, Joe. I'm told that you threw yourself right into Brautigan when he went for Gabrielle." McLendon described his own hesitation as Brautigan crawled toward him at the bottom of the crevice. Saint lay impassively on his bed, giving no sign that he heard. When Gabrielle returned, he held out his hand to her. She dropped her bundles and rushed to his side.

"You can leave now," she told McLendon and Mulkins. "Joe's upset that I left him."

That evening after Saint was asleep, McLendon insisted that Gabrielle come down to the hotel lobby with him. There was one dusty couch to sit on and McLendon led her there.

"What is it? I can't leave Joe for long," Gabrielle said.

"That's just it. You hover over him constantly. We haven't talked at all."

Gabrielle self-consciously adjusted the kerchief around her head. She thought, hoped, that all the hair would grow back, but as yet there was no sign that it was. "We will. For now, I've got to get Joe safely home."

"And after that?"

"Don't do this to me. I need time to

think." With that, she left, saying that Saint's dressing needed to be changed.

Later, Mulkins and McLendon were walking back to the Estes Hotel after a tasteless chili supper when they were stopped in the street by a short man wearing a gun on each hip.

"I'm Wolfe, the sheriff," he said, gesturing to a badge on his vest. "People tell me you and a couple others came into town in poor condition, with someone shot up pretty bad. What occurred?"

"We ran into Apache," Mulkins said.

"I'd heard some were off the San Carlos agency. Kill any?"

"I got one," Mulkins said.

"Good for you. I wish ever' last damned one of them was dead. Maybe someday." The sheriff looked thoughtful, then said, "Which direction did you arrive from? Possibly the north?"

"We came in from the west, though the mountains," McLendon said.

"From Tucson?"

"That direction, yes. Why do you ask?"

Sheriff Wolfe hooked his thumbs in his gunbelt. "I've been expecting someone coming from the north for some time. Big man, deputy lawman out of St. Louis. Probably have a prisoner with him. You happen to encounter any such?"

McLendon said, "I believe we'd remember if we had."

"Well, I hope he shows soon," Wolfe said. "The bastard owes me money."

After one more day, and for another fifty dollars, Doc Hutcheson pronounced Saint fit to travel. They wired Rebecca Moore in Mountain View that they were on the way, and purchased stage tickets. It was a difficult trip. They traveled from Silver City to Tucson, from Tucson to Florence, and from Florence finally to Mountain View. Because Saint needed to ride with his wounded leg extended, they had to purchase five seats instead of four. The constant rocking of the stage seemed to cause him considerable discomfort. Gabrielle dabbed his brow with a dampened bandanna and urged him to be brave just a little longer. McLendon's heart sank. It was obvious to him what was happening. If Gabrielle had a blind spot in her heart for McLendon, a willingness to overlook his faults and believe in him beyond the limits of credulity, she had one for Joe Saint too.

As soon as they arrived in Mountain View, Gabrielle put Saint to bed in his house and then rushed to the White Horse Hotel to see her father. Mulkins and McLendon walked to Garth Gould's livery, and informed him that the three horses they'd rented were now in Silver City. They gave him money to pay for the animals' return, and said that there was a fourth horse in Silver City with them. Gould could have that one too. Then they went back to the White Horse. Mulkins immediately met with staff there, checking on what happened while he was gone. McLendon went upstairs to the room he shared with the Major. He took off his boots and lay down on the bed. Thinking was too upsetting and sleep seemed impossible. After an hour he got up and walked to the Ritz. It was early evening. He took a table toward the back and ordered whiskey. He drank that, then another, and as he was finishing the second Sheriff Jack Hove came over.

"I just saw Major Mulkins at the White Horse, and his face was somewhat battered," Hove said. "I asked what transpired, and he said it wasn't worth discussing. Perhaps you could enlighten me?"

"I've nothing to add," McLendon said. They'd agreed not to discuss with Hove anything that had happened. If the sheriff traced Brautigan back to Rupert Douglass, that would only cause more problems.

"I'm glad Miss Tirrito is back safe," Hove said. "I'd like to know more about how she vanished in the first place."

McLendon stared into his tumbler and swirled the last drops of whiskey with a forefinger.

"There's a rumor Joe Saint's resting at his house with his whole leg shot off," Hove continued. "Think he or Gabrielle might be more forthcoming?"

"Sheriff, I'm asking you to let this thing be," McLendon said. "Don't talk to Gabrielle or Joe about it. Can you please take my word that, whatever happened, justice eventually was done? No one's going to say any more."

Hove regarded McLendon, taking in his exhausted posture and sad eyes.

"All right, at least for now," he said. "So long as I've got your word that whatever trouble it was, hasn't followed you back to my town."

"No," McLendon said. "There's no chance of that."

"Will you and Gabrielle be going on to California as planned?"

McLendon waved for a third whiskey and said, "At least I will, anyway."

■ ■ ■ ■

Gabrielle put McLendon off when he tried to speak privately with her. She always claimed that she was too busy. She'd resumed her old desk job at the White Horse, she had her father to care for, and now Joe Saint too. Doc Vance did some surgery on Saint's foot, removing bone splinters, stitching up open wounds, measuring for a wooden partial foot to be ordered at considerable expense from a special place on the East Coast. Orville Hancock said he'd pay for it, because Joe Saint was a good man who contributed to the town's well-being. The wooden foot might take six months to arrive, but once it did and Joe got used to it, Doc Vance predicted, Joe would walk nearly normally again. Doc thought that right now the schoolteacher could get around on crutches and resume his job, too, but Saint claimed he was still in too much pain. The schoolhouse remained vacant and the town children ran around the streets instead of being in class. Out of respect for Saint, their parents chose to wait until he could return to duty rather than hire another instructor. Everyone agreed he was a fine schoolteacher, better than anyone else they could get.

Because he was broke again, McLendon looked for work. Mayor Camp's feed store and bowling alley were still shut. Orville Hancock said he'd take on McLendon in some administrative position at his mining operation, but that was more of a commitment than McLendon would make. He was hired by Tim Flanagan to help out at his livery. McLendon mostly handled horse rentals. As had been the case at Camp's bowling alley, people liked doing business with the hero of Adobe Walls.

At night, Gabrielle was always with Saint, cooking him dinner, helping him to bed, reading to him to help him fall asleep. McLendon went to the Ritz saloon, sitting with Major Mulkins and listlessly drinking beer. Sometimes they were joined by Rebecca Moore, but never by Marie Silva, who had unexpectedly left town. They talked of various things — the weather, the opening of a new Chinese laundry, the latest alleged assassination by the Witch of the West as reported by Mac Fielding in *The Mountain View Herald.* But it was understood that Gabrielle was not to be discussed.

Finally, after nearly three weeks, McLendon intercepted Gabrielle one evening on her way to Saint's house.

"It's time to talk," he said. "I've been patient. But I need you to tell me what you want to do."

"You're presuming that I know myself," Gabrielle said, fussing with her kerchief. Her hair was growing back, but slowly.

"I understand what you went through, at least some of it. I can imagine the rest. It was because of me. I'll spend the rest of my life making up for it."

Gabrielle looked down the sidewalk. People were lined up outside the new Chinese laundry, which advertised a special opening-for-business rate of five cents a shirt.

"Some things can't be made up for," she said. "Like Joe's foot."

"I'm sorry for Joe, but now I'm speaking of us. Has that changed?"

"Everything's changed. For now I want to deal with one day at a time, and not think about anything more than that. At some point I will, again."

"I sympathize. All you've been through, of course you have much to consider. But what should I do in the meantime?"

"It's for you to decide. Though you've not said so, I know what's really bothering you is the time I'm spending with Joe. What happened to him was because he loves me. He didn't deserve being crippled. My hair is coming back, the Major's nose is healed, and you're fine to go on as you please. We've got bad memories, but that's all they are. His disfigurement is permanent. He needs encouragement to go on. It's really the rest of Joe's life that's in the balance."

"The rest of Joe's life," McLendon repeated.

"Exactly. And now he's expecting me. It's difficult for him to change the dressings on his foot by himself." For six more weeks, McLendon waited. When he saw Gabrielle she was friendly but never anything more. Saint recovered to the point that he could sit in front of his house in the evenings. Gabrielle was often with him, getting him cups of water and resettling his maimed foot on a stool. Major Mulkins advised further patience, but McLendon finally couldn't wait any longer. He went to the stage office, where he still had credit for two passages from Mountain View to San Francisco, and told the manager there that at least one would be used in three days. It was Tuesday, so he would leave on Friday morning. McLendon needed the time in between to tend to things in Mountain View. He quit his job at Flanagan's Livery and used a little of the money he'd saved for new shirts, trousers, and an inexpensive valise in which to pack them. At McLendon's request, Orville Hancock wrote him a glowing letter of recommendation to the Smead Company in San Francisco.

"They'll set you up right," he promised.

Wednesday evening, McLendon found Gabrielle again. He told her that he was leaving for California on Friday morning. He loved her and still wanted her to come with him.

"You're pressing me," she said. "I've never liked that."

"I know."

Gabrielle reached under her kerchief and scratched her head. The hair sprouting there itched. "And now will you deliver me a fine speech full of promises about the wonderful life we'd have in San Francisco?"

McLendon shook his head. "No more speeches. I can't guarantee our lives there would be wonderful at all. Unexpected things happen. Who knows? But I'd try my best. That, I can promise."

She looked stricken. "If you'd give me more time . . . There's my father, and you know I have to think of Joe."

"Yes, so you've said. It's the rest of Joe's life."

"Please understand," Gabrielle said, and

rushed away.

On Thursday, McLendon waited. He sat in the White Horse lobby for a while, ate a lingering breakfast at Erin's House, and strolled along the wooden sidewalks of Mountain View. He wanted to be easy for Gabrielle to find without being too obvious about it. But she stayed behind her desk at the hotel. At noon he glimpsed her hurrying to Saint's house. Most days she brought him lunch.

Many people greeted him as he walked. Word was around town that he was leaving the next day, and everyone said they were sorry he was going and wished him well. There was some consolation in this. It was the first time in years that he wasn't leaving somewhere on the run.

He also had a conversation with Mac Fielding, editor of *The Mountain View Herald.* Fielding came up to him and asked, "Will you grant a farewell interview?"

"To what purpose? If it's to announce I'm leaving, from the farewells I'm receiving, it appears your readers already know."

Fielding produced a pencil and notebook from his pocket. "It's also well known that you disappeared for a while with Major Mulkins, Joe Saint, and Gabrielle Tirrito.

Now you're all back, and Joe is a cripple. It's a story that needs to be told."

"No, it doesn't," McLendon said. "I'd take it badly, should you place one in print."

"You're leaving anyway," Fielding said. "And if you won't talk to me, it's the privilege of the press to speculate."

Cash McLendon had fought and survived at Adobe Walls, and fought and defeated Patrick Brautigan, if only by luck. These experiences had provided him a certain resolution, which now made itself evident in his voice and gaze.

"Don't do it," he said, and Fielding retreated a step.

"People have the right to know," he said plaintively.

"Not in this case," McLendon said. "You won't write about it, now or ever. Do we understand each other?"

Fielding stuffed the notepad and pencil back in his pocket and said huffily, "Men like you will be the death of a free press."

McLendon said, "Or men like you will be. Good-bye, Mr. Fielding."

After dinner on Thursday night, McLendon went back to the room he shared with Major Mulkins at the White Horse. He sat on the corner of the bed, resting his chin on his hands and trying very hard not to wonder where Gabrielle was, and whether she would knock on his door.

She never did.

The stage left Mountain View for Florence and points west at ten on Friday morning. Just after nine-thirty, McLendon and Major Mulkins began walking from the hotel to the station. It was several blocks. The Major insisted on carrying McLendon's valise.

"Are you sure you don't want to see Gabrielle and at least bid her farewell?" he asked. "You know that she's upstairs in her room." Earlier, Gabrielle had sent the Major a note, informing him that she was indisposed and unable to come down to work that day.

"It would be too hard for both of us," McLendon said.

"Will you at least send word to me of how to reach you, once you're in California and situated? I believe that it's possible, even likely, Gabrielle will reconsider at some point and want to send you word."

"I doubt it, but I do want you to know where I am. It's pleasant to think that I can stay in touch with old friends again."

Mulkins smiled. "Then you believe we'll have future meetings?"

"Certainly, if you find yourself in California. I doubt I'll return to Arizona Territory — there are too many memories here."

They reached the depot. A team was hitched to the Florence stage. Mulkins handed the valise to McLendon, who passed it along to the driver to be placed in the storage compartment at the rear of the stage.

"There's also this," Mulkins said. He unbuckled the gunbelt around his waist and handed it to McLendon. "I've had the loan of your Colt long enough."

McLendon handed it back. "Keep it, Major. I'm done with guns."

They waited for the station manager to call passengers aboard the stage. Besides McLendon, there seemed to be only two others, itinerant salesmen by the look of their cheap suits and bowler hats. It was a three-bench, nine-passenger stage. McLendon thought that he'd have plenty of leg room, at least until they reached Florence late that afternoon.

At ten o'clock precisely, the station manager bellowed, "Stage departing, Mountain View to Florence." Mulkins extended his hand, and McLendon warmly shook it.

"I hold our friendship dear," he said. "I'll never forget all you've done for me."

"Likewise," Mulkins said. "Travel safe." He stood and waved as the stage pulled out.

The route to Florence passed all the way along Main Street in Mountain View. McLendon pulled back the cloth curtain and stared out one of the paneless window openings in the passenger cab, looking at Erin's House and the Ritz, and reflecting that it was impossible to escape the past. Poor decisions had more lasting effect than good ones. It was up to him now to salvage his life out in California.

The White Horse loomed ahead, and after that it was the end of town and out into the country. McLendon was about to pull the window curtain closed when the driver shouted, "What? Whoa," to his horses and brought the stage to a stop. There was muffled conversation, the driver leaning down to speak to someone.

Gabrielle opened the passenger door and climbed in. She wore no bonnet or kerchief. Her hair had mostly grown back, and she once again adorned it with ribbons. She sat down on the bench next to McLendon and the stage lurched forward.

"As soon as we're settled, we must send for my father," Gabrielle said briskly. "I would think in a month, if not sooner. Rebecca Moore can't care for him indefinitely.

If Mr. Hancock wrote a letter to his parent company as promised, that should gain you immediate employment. Even if not, I can find work. It would be agreeable if you could close your mouth."

McLendon's jaw had dropped.

"What are you doing?" he asked.

"I neglected to pack and have only the clothes I stand in. As soon as our stage makes some civilized stop, I'll need to get some things."

McLendon had to say it. "But what about Joe?"

Gabrielle said defensively, "Well, it's the rest of my life, too."

NOTES

In fiction based at least partially on history, it's always important for readers to know what's true and what's altered for storytelling purposes. In almost every way, I've tried to make *Silver City* an accurate representation of 1874 in Arizona Territory. The details — from fashion to guns to Mayor Camp's bowling alley — are accurate. Mountain View itself is based on real-life Globe. The Clantons did set up Clantonville, but their efforts to establish it as a town failed and they moved southeast, where Ike and Billy Clanton eventually participated in momentous events in Tombstone. During the time in which this novel is set, future Tombstone mayor John Clum was the agent at San Carlos, and Goyathlay (Geronimo) was there.

I took liberties with some geography. In general the descriptions of the land between Silver City and (mythical) Mountain View are correct, but I moved a mountain range or two and manipulated the boundaries of the San Carlos agency.

I want to apologize to everyone who has lived, lives, or ever will live in Silver City, New Mexico. The Silver City in this book shares only its name and general location with the actual place. Everything else springs directly from my imagination. I'm sure real-life Silver City was and remains a fine place. I just love the name, and couldn't resist using it.

If you've enjoyed this novel and want to know more about the history of the region, I strongly suggest reading *The "Unwashed Crowd": Stockmen and Ranches of the San Simon and Sulphur Spring Valleys, Arizona Territory, 1878–1900* by Lynn R. Bailey (Westernlore Press, 2014). I relied on it for many of the facts and geographic descriptions presented in *Silver City*.

ACKNOWLEDGMENTS

As usual, and above all, thanks to Ivan Held for suggesting that I write a fiction series based in the so-called Old West. I will always be grateful to all of my friends at Putnam, past and present. Maybe someday soon we can meet for a reunion lunch at The Ear. I'm buying.

It was a privilege to work with Christine Pepe, a dedicated, caring editor.

Jim Donovan, my agent, never lets me down.

James Ward Lee and Carlton Stowers always read along as I write. Their comments and constructive criticisms make my books better. Doug Swanson helped with this one too.

I'm grateful to Anne Collier, Chuck Smith, and Kevin ("Cap") Mulkins for invaluable research assistance.

Special thanks to the inspiration for Cash McLendon's first name.

Everything I write is always for Nora, Adam, Grant, and Harrison.